USA TODAY BESTSELLING AUTHOR
DALE MAYER

Lovely Lethal Gardens
03-04

Corpse in the Carnations
Dagger in the Dahlias

LOVELY LETHAL GARDENS, BOOKS 3-4
Beverly Dale Mayer
Valley Publishing Ltd.

ISBN-13: 978-1-773364-03-2
Print Edition

Books in This Series

About This Boxed Set

Corpse in the Carnations

A new cozy mystery series from USA Today best-selling author Dale Mayer. Follow gardener and amateur sleuth Doreen Montgomery—and her amusing and mostly lovable cat, dog, and parrot—as they catch murderers and solve crimes in lovely Kelowna, British Columbia.

Riches to rags. … Chaos calms. … Crime quiets. … But does it really?

After getting involved in two murder cases in the short time she's lived in picturesque Kelowna, divorcee and gardener Doreen Montgomery has developed a reputation almost as notorious as her Nan's. The only way to stop people from speculating, is to live a life of unrelieved boredom until the media and the neighbors forget about her. And Doreen aims to do just that with a tour of Kelowna's famed Carnation Gardens. Plants, more plants, and nothing whatsoever that anyone could object to.

But when she sees a fight between a beautiful young woman and her boyfriend, she can't help but be concerned. Concerned enough that she follows the couple out of the parking lot and through town. And when gunshots interrupt the placid afternoon, it's too late to worry about how her nemesis, Corporal Mack Moreau, will feel about her getting involved in yet another of his cases.

With bodies turning up in the carnations, and a connection to a cold case of a missing child from long ago, Doreen has her hands full, not least with trying to keep her involvement in the investigations a secret from her Nan, Mack Moreau, and especially the media. But someone's keeping up with Doreen's doings... and that someone can't afford for her to find the answers to the questions she's asking.

Daggers in the Dahlias

Riches to rags. ... Chaos quiets. ... Crime is circling. ... And cold cases never cease ...

After almost a month in picturesque Kelowna, Doreen Montgomery still can't keep her notoriety to a minimum or her nose out of other people's business. Now those suffering from the loss of a loved one seek her out, wanting her help. While the last thing Doreen wants is to have the media discover she's involved in another cold case, she is already hooked on the details ...

But even more is going on. News has gotten out that Nan's old house is brimming over with valuable antiques, antiques Nan collected and left for Doreen, and the seedier elements of their lovely town are circling like vultures. With her animals in full assistant mode, Doreen must investigate the cold case, right the wrongs of the past, and keep her home safe, all while evading the media—and Corporal Mack Moreau.

USA TODAY BESTSELLING AUTHOR
DALE MAYER

Corpse in the Carnations

Lovely Lethal Gardens 3

Chapter 1

In the Mission, Kelowna, BC
Wednesday, One Day Later... from her last case

D OREEN SAT CURLED on the couch. All she had wanted
was three days. Three days of peace and quiet. Was
that in the cards? She doubted it. As much as she desperately
wanted to be out of the limelight and rejoice in the peace
and quiet of living in her Nan's house, she had a bad feeling
in her gut.

Her brood was sedate—even Goliath, asleep on the other end of the couch with Mugs—all her furry or feathered
babies obviously understanding how Doreen really needed
that from them at this time. Thaddeus rubbed his beak along
her cheek, then closed his eyes, happy to just sit on her
shoulder.

Unfortunately she found no peace or quiet outside her
home, not yet today—but it was early morning—and not for
the last two days for sure. The reporters were still at her
door, even at this hour. The newspaper journalists were still
writing articles about how Doreen had helped solve the
decades-old cold case of Betty Miles's death, and Nan and
her cronies were still enjoying being the center of attention

by giving numerous interviews, supposedly on Doreen's behalf. Doreen had told Nan how that was totally fine, just happy that Nan had found something, other than her illegal betting activities, to bring excitement to her life.

Indeed, Nan glowed with it.

But, as for Doreen, she wanted to be left alone. At that thought, her phone chimed. She glanced at her cell and groaned. But she hit the Talk button anyway. "You better have a good reason for bothering me, Mack." She slid farther down on the couch until her head rested on the armrest. Thaddeus shifted his position but refused to give up his spot on her shoulder.

"I figured for sure that, by now, you'd be all pepped up, raring to go," he said.

She could detect the worry in his voice and had to smile. "I am, and yet I'm not. Have you any idea how deep the lineup of reporters is outside my front door? I know this is a small town, but it seems like the news hit the wires all the way across the country."

"You're a celebrity," he said, laughing. His voice softened. "But, no, that's not an easy position to be in."

"I didn't murder anybody," she exclaimed, sitting up straight to peek through the curtains. "Why are they haunting me?"

Thaddeus squawked, shot her a disgusted look when she disturbed his nap on her shoulder, hopped up to the back of the couch, then he wandered over a few steps and proceeded to close his eyes again.

"It's like everybody thinks I'm the one who's done something wrong," she said reaching out to pet Mugs, then stroke her fingers across Goliath's back.

"Remember the last time?" he asked. "This too will blow

over."

"Sure, but every time I find a new body," she said in exasperation, "they look at me as if I had something to do with it."

"Not that you had something to do with the *making* of the dead bodies," he corrected, his light humor sliding through his voice, "but that your arrival precipitated all this. Or maybe you have some sort of psychic ability. You don't, do you?" His voice held a curious note to it.

She chuckled at his tone. "I think, by now, both you and I would know if I did."

"Well, you need something to cheer you up."

"What have you got for me?" She stood, walking over to peer through the round window on the front door. Instantly camera flashes went off. She stepped back and walked toward the kitchen. "Have you got a nice puzzle for me to work on?"

"You mean, like another case?"

"It would get me out of the dumps." Her tone turned crafty. "You know how I like a good puzzle."

"You could pick up some jigsaw puzzles," he exclaimed. "That's a much safer hobby."

"Murderous puzzles are much more fun." She chuckled, knowing he'd hate her answer.

"And much more dangerous," he snapped. "You could have been killed last time."

She shrugged. "You live and you die. At least I'd be doing something I wanted to do."

"Solving cold cases?"

She grinned, hearing the hesitation in his voice. "You have another cold case you're looking into, don't you?"

Silence.

For the first time since she had awakened before dawn

5

today, her boredom and sense of a dark cloud hanging over her almost lifted. "It's not my fault this town is a den of iniquity," she stated. "Just think of all the nastiness hidden here for so long." She could feel that same sense of excitement surging through her when delving into Mack's cold cases. "Are you going to tell me the details?"

"No," he said, no hesitation in his voice this time.

"And why not?" She waited. If he wanted to play a waiting game, that was no problem. She could play that game too.

Finally he said, "It's not really a priority."

"Maybe not to you," she said. "Cold cases *are* a priority to the families."

"I didn't say a death was involved."

"That would be even better," she said. "Then I wouldn't trip over any more bodies, at least not right away."

"I'd be totally okay if you wouldn't trip over any more *anytime*," he said.

"Suits me," she said. "I'm okay to not find dead bodies ever again."

"Besides, it's not a cold case I wanted to talk to you about. I'll think about that first."

"Damn." She let out a heavy sigh. "So what is it then?"

"I was talking to the city council. They want to redo the big sign with the garden as you enter the city limits. You know the Welcome to Kelowna sign surrounded by flower beds?"

"Yeah, mostly begonias I think," she said. "At least one of the rings around the sign are begonias."

"*Ugh*," he said. "I'd be happy not to see any more of those anytime soon."

She nodded. "They're nice to look after, and they don't

grow too crazy outside, so they don't need a ton of maintenance. They're easy for large gardens and make great borders or plots." At the word *plot* she winced.

He chuckled. "I can see that having you around will be a constant reminder of dead things and everything associated with them."

"Maybe. And what about the city council? What were you talking to them about?" Her mind zinged to her ever-dwindling pile of money, and she was deeply concerned about it. "Hope it's important. And, if it involves money for me, the answer is yes."

He chuckled. "You don't even know what it could entail."

"Doesn't matter," she said. "I'm about out of the money I found in Nan's pockets before donating and trying to resell some of her unwanted clothes. Which means I'll be diving into that little bit of savings I have."

"And the gardening you did at my mom's place? That'll be a regular thing, if you're okay with that."

"I am absolutely okay with that," she said. "What you pay me will put food on my table."

"Speaking of food," he said. "Did you turn on the new stove?"

She pivoted and walked out of the kitchen. "What stove?"

He sighed. "The stove you paid one hundred dollars to replace. A lot of people went to a lot of trouble to make sure you had something safe to cook on."

"There's the trick," she said, "the word *cook*."

"I'll tell you what. How about this Sunday I bring over the fixings for something simple for breakfast or lunch, and I'll show you how to cook it."

7

"Simple would be, like, eggs," she said, "and I highly doubt you want eggs for lunch, do you?"

"Not an issue for me. I love eggs anytime," he said. "Don't you know how to cook eggs?"

She pulled the cell from her ear so she could glare at the blank screen.

"Okay, okay, okay," he said. "Stop glaring at me."

She gasped. "How did you know I was glaring at you?"

"I could hear it in the heavy silence of the phone's speaker," he said drily. "And eggs are easy. How about we do omelets? They are a little more substantial than plain eggs."

Her mind filled with the soft fluffy omelets her chef used to make for her. "With spinach and caviar and gruyere?"

Mack replied with that heavy silence again.

"Oh. Okay, so what do your omelets normally contain?" she asked.

"Well, spinach is one possible ingredient," he said, "but anything I have on hand. Like bacon, ham, leftover meat. You can put veggies in it if you want." His tone said he really didn't see the point. "Meat and eggs are a perfect combo. ... Plus cheese."

"Well, ham and cheese omelets are good too," she said. "Can we add mushrooms?"

"Sure," he said. "We can sauté a few mushrooms. So are you up for a cooking lesson?"

"Yes," she said slowly. But she needed to ask him something, and it was kind of embarrassing.

"Speak up," he said in that long-drawn-out sighing way of his.

As if he knew she was making a big deal out of nothing but needed to get it out first. "Am I paying you for it?" she asked in a rush.

He laughed. "No, you're not paying me for a cooking lesson. Not with money, not with gardening work, not with bartering or any other method."

She beamed. "In that case, I'm looking forward to cooking lesson number one coming up. Omelets it is."

"I'll bring the ingredients. You'll write down everything I do, okay?"

"Okay."

"And, on Tuesday, you'll repeat the menu, on your own," he said. "You'll take a picture and send the final results to me, so I can see how you did."

She chuckled. "Probably better if you come back and watch me make it the second time, and then you can taste the results."

"Done," he said.

She frowned suspiciously, wondering if he hadn't planned on that in the first place. "So you need to bring ingredients for two meals," she said swiftly.

He howled with laughter. "You know what? You might not know how to cook, but you sure know how to negotiate a deal." And, on that note, he hung up.

She grinned to herself, until she realized he hadn't told her all about the city's Welcome garden—or about the cold case. She called him back, but he didn't answer. Then she sent him a text. **What about the city?**

He sent her a map and a handout with his return text. **They're looking for suggestions about what to put in these two beds.**

She walked to her laptop, turned it on, and transferred the image and the PDF on her phone to her computer. There was the sign, Welcome to Kelowna. She could see the mature plantings around it. And the indicated beds were on each side of the sign. **Suggestions for what?**

Types of flowers, why those flowers, money, as in a guesstimate for the cost.

I haven't a clue on the money, she typed. **And, even if I do tell them what I would do, what's that got to do with anything?**

They're looking for bids. The winning bid gets to do the job and to make the money.

She perked up when she heard that. Then she opened the PDF and read the one-page document. **Okay, but it says to submit this by midnight tomorrow night.**

Yeah, he replied. **That's why I called you earlier this morning. So get at it.**

Chapter 2

GETTING AT IT was complicated. Doreen was in the third local greenhouse, checking out the prices of perennials, Mugs walking patiently at her side. She had all kinds of ideas from lipstick plants to carnations. She thought carnations would be gorgeous. But, to get the color she wanted at a wholesale price, that would be the trick.

So far nobody she had talked to was interested in giving her a bulk-buy deal. She knew somewhere in the Okanagan region she could set up something like that, but she hadn't done very well tracking that down. She wondered if she could put in a bid for doing the work and have the city pay for the cost of the flowers on their own. Surely the city gardeners had access to plants she couldn't even comprehend *and* at bulk pricing.

It made sense to her, but she didn't know if that was the proper procedure or, if not, if the city would go for it. Still, she could try. But, at the moment, she was running out of ideas of where and what she could put together. She loved the idea of roses, but they took work. Carnations, not the long-stemmed ones though, she could do in layers. Longer in the center and then shorter as they went out to the edge.

That might look pretty cool.

With ideas buzzing in her head, she wandered through the greenhouse, writing down notes. When somebody called out her name, she turned without thinking, and a camera flash went off in her face. She growled. "Stop doing that."

"You're a celebrity in town." The man chuckled as he turned and walked away.

She sighed and slipped out the side entrance back to her vehicle, Mugs at her side. There she sat in her car for a long moment.

Somehow she hadn't associated getting out of the house as also being her first step into the public eye after the latest news had broken on Betty Miles. Doreen had been so focused on escaping the house that she had forgotten what she'd be escaping into. But her exit had worked out better than she had thought. She'd forced the media crowd to part to let her drive away, and she wouldn't return until she was darn good and ready.

As she sat in her car, she watched an old couple arguing nearby, standing at another parked vehicle. They looked so comfortable, as if the calm complaints had been told many times over. When they finally got into a vehicle and drove away, she wanted to laugh and to cry.

A loud engine had her turning to watch as a young woman drove up in a fancy scarlet Mini Cooper. Although what was *mini* about the new model, she didn't get. It looked bigger than her Honda. She watched as the woman got out, perfectly coiffed top to bottom. Doreen recognized all the work that went into that look; yet she had absolutely no interest in looking like that again.

She studied her currently close-cropped fingernails. They were clean, but her hands showed the ravages of gardening—

no weekly manicures or special fingernail soaks to keep her hands perfect anymore. Just healthy outdoor work in Mother Nature's glory. But still, Doreen needed to pick up some good hand cream. As she glanced back at the gardening shop, she wondered if they'd have a working hand cream—like, for professional gardeners. She was well-past using fancy hand lotions for her skin now. But the gardeners at her former home had small green pots of stuff they used daily. A drugstore might be a better option for that—and cheaper.

Then she thought about making yet another stop and decided she'd check here anyway. She hopped back out of the car, held Mugs' leash, and beelined to the far corner containing the walls of shelves for everything associated with gardening. Sure enough, the hand creams were on a triangle-shaped display.

As she studied the different choices, she could hear somebody speaking in the background.

A man said, "After what you've done, you'll now do as I tell you to." His tone was ugly.

Doreen stiffened. Mugs shifted at her heel, tugging at his leash to sniff the flowers an aisle away. She looked around cautiously to her left but didn't see anyone. She peered to her right, around the stand of hand cream, and saw two people around another corner. The man was large—six feet, maybe six two—glaring down at the stunning blonde Doreen had seen getting out of her car earlier. But, instead of being daunted, the blonde had shoved her face into his, and, in a hard voice, she said, "Well, with me or without me backing your decision, you'll end up planted in the daisies. *Not* me." The blonde turned in a huff and strode away.

Doreen tried to get out of her way, but the blonde delib-erately knocked Doreen sideways. The air rushed out of

Doreen's chest with an *oomph*. Mugs barked loudly, edging closer to the blonde.

The blonde turned, looked at Doreen, and said roughly, "Mind your own damn business. And keep that chubby pooch away from me."

"I didn't say a word," Doreen replied. Then, unable to help herself, she snapped, "And he's not chubby."

Just then the man came around the corner, towered over Doreen, and sniggered. "No, he's fat. And you won't say a word, will you?"

She glared up at him. "You can go murder and plant all the people you want. Just keep me out of it. And stop insulting my dog."

He laughed. "Wow. You've got a hell of an imagination, don't you?"

But she could see the worry in his eyes. He walked away but not before she grabbed her phone and took a picture of his profile as he turned a corner. It was probably a shitty photo, but maybe somebody could figure out who he was, if need be.

With her cream in her hand, she headed to the long line at the front counter. She watched the blonde ahead of her step out of the line, as if she couldn't be bothered to wait, and, in a hurried stride, headed for the front doors.

Doreen put down the hand cream on the counter, raced outside, and, with her phone, took a picture of the woman. As she walked to her car, Doreen snapped another picture of the Mini. She was getting damn good at using her cell phone at her hip to take images on the sly. She was pretty sure Mack wouldn't be happy with her doing this. Neither would the people she'd taken pictures of. But it seemed like everybody else snapped cameras in her face. So what the hell?

She wondered if it was safe for her to follow the woman. But that was an idiotic move. She had witnessed a minor tiff between two people who'd uttered empty threats. Nothing to do with Doreen. And hardly a life-threatening situation. She should just mind her own business ...

Until she watched the big bully hop into a huge black truck and drive off aggressively behind the Mini.

Doreen chewed on her bottom lip indecisively, not liking the menacing growl of the truck's engine. Those humongous trucks always seemed to be driven by asshats.

At that term she grinned. Swearing wasn't something she was terribly comfortable with, but the words slipped out more and more. And unfortunately Thaddeus heard—and repeated—most of them. She wanted to utilize forms she could say comfortably that would give the same meaning without lowering her standards. The internet was full of alternate swear words, but she didn't want anything that just everybody used. Of course, *asshats* was a popular one. Still, she kind of liked it.

She hopped into her car and drove out, following the truck and the Mini Cooper. She didn't know why exactly. Was she that bored? It'd been three days since she'd solved the cold case of poor Betty Miles who'd been dismembered thirty years ago by her best friend, Hannah Theroux. Three days, that was it. What was she, some kind of a dead-body junkie?

Still, the argument between the two people had seemed like a viable threat, now that she thought about it some more, in light of the demanding man now following the woman. Not that the woman had seemed threatened by the man's words. She'd given as good as she got.

While following those two, Doreen realized she was

heading in the direction of the Welcome to Kelowna sign. She perked up at having a viable excuse to give Mack for going in this direction. She really did want to take a look at the two beds the city was considering updating. Doreen should have done that in the first place because, without knowing the size of each, she would have no idea how to budget for her time or for the number of plants needed.

It took another five minutes to reach that area. Both vehicles continued ahead of her. She frowned as they turned off and went around the corner and past the sign. She pulled in a small strip mall close by so she could park and walk to the sign the rest of the way up the road.

As she hopped out, she studied the direction the other vehicles had taken. It looked like a dead-end street. Maybe, when she was done here, she'd take a look there. In the meantime, she grabbed her notepad, and, with Mugs at her side, she strolled over to look at the big garden, about fifty feet across, with the Welcome to Kelowna sign in the middle.

She took several photos of the two smaller garden beds the city was looking for options on. The heart-shaped beds were pretty and could use something extremely unique. Her creative artistry piqued, she had almost too many choices to consider. As she wrote down more notes, she checked out the dryness of the soil, the type of mulch used, and saw how the city's gardeners had used a cutting tool to create a shallow trench at the garden's edge to keep the grass from encroaching. Which was smart because public-area maintenance requirements in a city this size were massive and expensive. Even though the city likely employed an army of gardeners, there was always too much to do and not enough man-hours to do it.

Mugs lay down in the grass, happy to be on a field trip. He rolled over and snuffled along the ground, enjoying himself. She chuckled. "I should have brought the others with us. They'd love it here."

Of course, the cat and the bird were much harder to control. She returned her attention to the gardens. Her mind buzzed with various plant options. She wondered if they could keep rubber plants here because they were huge statements that could be in the center of each of those heart-shaped beds. Not just one rubber plant but maybe four or five of them. She'd seen many big planters on the city's sidewalks and in the malls using the same idea. It would tie together the inner-city landscaping with the outer-city designs.

"Come on, Mugs. Let's go."

After letting Mugs into the car, she hopped back into her vehicle. Rather than going home, she proceeded where the two vehicles had gone. Just a quick trip to make sure everything was okay. She went around the corner to find the truck parked a few houses down on the left. With her phone, she took a picture of it, getting the license plate number. The truck appeared out of place compared to the run-down house it was parked at, which in her mind looked like a crack house. One of the typical druggie houses seen in a big city that others avoided. They were usually pretty easy to avoid because they were generally clustered with more houses of the same in a particular neighborhood. Yet the houses on either side here looked more upscale. This particular derelict house was hardly a place she expected the blonde to go.

Doreen was in the Rutland area of Kelowna, and Nan lived in the Mission area. Rutland was a poorer area, not low-class by any means, and the city was certainly doing a lot to revitalize the area. It had the lowest-priced real estate in town too. Great for enticing developers.

As she drove slowly past the truck, she could see the bright red Mini Cooper parked beside it. That looked really incongruous with the decrepit house. *Maybe those two were developers? Maybe they had bought the house and planned to level it and rebuild?* She shrugged, wondering what their deal was, but knowing it wasn't her business.

She drove ahead to a cul-de-sac at the end of the road. She pulled around in the circle and slowly drove past the house again. She had absolutely no excuse for doing what she did next—nothing that would pass muster with Mack. But she didn't even think twice about it.

She pulled up to a nearby house and parked. In a pretense of taking Mugs for a walk, she got out on the sidewalk and headed away from the house, crossed the road, and strolled on the sidewalk opposite the house in question. She was being nosy, and she knew it. But she and Mugs were just taking an innocent walk. Not like she was on private property with No Trespassing signs posted.

No harm done.

Spit. Spit.

She froze, wondering where to look, wondering if she could have mistaken that sound, but it came again. *Spit, spit.* Followed by a cry.

That all came from *the* house. "Mugs, let's go." She raced to her car, hopped in, and drove back to the garden store, where she called Mack from the safety of her car in the parking lot.

"What?"

"I think I heard gunshots," she said without preamble.

"What the hell? Where?"

She winced as she told him about the couple's argument and taking pictures of them and their vehicles and then following them.

"You did what?" he roared.

"Okay, okay. I know I shouldn't have followed them," she said, "but it doesn't change the fact I think I heard gunshots."

"It's also quite possible you heard something *other* than gunshots," he said. "Like a car backfiring."

"Yes, maybe," she said. "Maybe, maybe, maybe. But *maybe* not."

He groaned. "Fine. What's the address?"

"I don't know the house number," she said. "But it's on Hawthorne Street, the third house in from the corner—on the left side if you're coming from the Kelowna sign."

"Oh, that's what you were doing there."

"I had to see how big the beds were. How else could I give a decent bid?" She hoped he would believe that was her main reason for going there in the first place.

"I'll take a look," he said. "But you go home. Will you do that?"

"I will."

"Did you bring any of the animals with you?"

"Just Mugs." She reached over to pet the basset hound's head. Mugs let out a corresponding *woof* into the interior of her car.

"At least you've got him, although I don't know that he'll be much protection against an attack."

"As you well know," she snapped, "he's great protection—when needed."

"Maybe," he said. "But maybe not. I think you guys are a comedy of errors."

"Okay, that's possible," she said defiantly, a trifle hurt. "But it works. We're all family." And on that note she hung up. She reached over and gave Mugs a big cuddle. "Let's go home. Back to the rest of the family."

Was there ever a better word? Nope. And she couldn't think of a better place she wanted to be right now.

Chapter 3

THE REPORTERS STILL lolled around her driveway. They all stood at attention and snapped pictures, their flashes lighting up her front yard as she drove in. A couple were determined to stand their ground, but she continued to drive forward steadily. They would either get out of the way in time or get mowed down. She was hardly in the mood to discuss this with them.

As she drove into her driveway, she pulled in front of the garage and parked. Too bad she hadn't had a chance to empty the garage so it was useable. It would give her a chance to get away from prying eyes. While Doreen had been sorting through some of Nan's stuff in the house, the garage was a whole different story.

With Mugs in tow, she walked toward the front door. What she should have done when she was out was grab some food. She was damn near out of crackers and cheese and peanut butter and everything prepackaged. Since Mack had told her that ramen noodles were supposed to be cooked, she'd begun microwaving them with water. A constant source of poor nutrition. She had to chuckle at it all.

From the front stoop, she could see Thaddeus, the great

big goof, looking out the window. She had closed the curtains before she'd left because of the reporters. In fact, the curtains had been closed for days now. But the parrot had worked his head between the folds so he could look outside.

Pulling his head back from the curtains, he was blocked from her sight. She knew he'd be perched on the sofa cushions waiting for her to enter. She could hear him inside, squawking, "She's home. She's home." Doreen opened the door and cried out, "Yes, Thaddeus. I'm home."

Mugs gave a *woof* as he went in and jumped onto the couch—almost on top of the cat—as if to tell off Goliath, the monster cat sprawled on the center cushion, for being there. Goliath's hiss and one swipe of his claws were followed by one last bark, and Goliath ran off. Then Mugs lay down on the couch with a disinterested glare and closed his eyes.

Doreen groaned, closed the front door with a shake of her head, and walked into the kitchen to put on the teakettle. She dropped her notepad on the counter and said out loud, hoping Mack's ears were burning, "You're welcome, Mack. Somebody might have just died. But that's all right. Don't be worried about me or them."

She wasn't being fair, of course, because Mack was worried about her safety when following the couple. Maybe they'd had a lovers' tiff, but, regardless of the nature of their argument, it was none of Doreen's business. The fact of the matter was, she was bored. They'd caught her eye, and she hadn't been able to let them go.

On that note she sat down at her laptop and continued her research, looking for pictures of large beds of carnations in Kelowna. She didn't want to make a mistake and pick the wrong plants. Although she loved carnations, what did they look like when they were en masse? Google Images brought up several nice pictures of local gardens. Thinking maybe she could drive around and take a closer look at these, she made herself a cup of tea and put it into her travel mug.

Besides, she was restless, and Mack telling her to go home wasn't sitting so well. Technically she did go home. She just planned on leaving once more. If she could do something constructive, then she should. Right?

She put the leash on Mugs again and ushered Thaddeus and Goliath into the car too. This trip would be a family outing. Thaddeus rode in the back passenger seat, Mugs on the other side, with Goliath riding shotgun because, ... well, because he would never let anybody else sit here. Life was just that easy for Goliath. But then, when you were a thirty-pound Maine coon with claws and teeth, life was pretty easy.

Doreen slowly backed down the driveway, once again inching past the reporters, ignoring the flashes of their cameras going off in her face. She wondered if she should tell the media camped out in her front yard about the gunshots she had heard earlier. They'd all pack it up and head to the new crime scene, right? But that was hardly fair to the police. The media could disturb their initial investigation. When she was clear of the pesky reporters, she headed back into town.

She drove toward the first of three carnation sites she wanted to see firsthand, starting with the one farthest away. Once there, she let the animals out to walk with her. This was a huge public garden set beside the entrance to one of the many big vineyards privately owned by the Pollock family. The garden bed was absolutely gorgeous. She could see from where she stood how the tall carnations drooped sideways somewhat, probably because of the last rain they had had here—like a month ago? Kelowna didn't receive a lot of rain, but, when it came, sometimes it poured heavily and would knock the flowers flat.

As she studied these, she found they were recovering but would likely never stand straight again. So maybe these carnations weren't the best choice.

Now Dianthus carnations were a different story. Bright, colorful, cheerful, almost always in bloom, particularly when mature plants. Those might be a better answer. Still, Doreen had two more existing carnation gardens she should look at.

The next garden was much smaller. The carnations were planted in circles and surrounded by what looked to be heather. Interesting choice as the heather would be striking with its purple blooms in spring. She'd always loved heather. It was hard to argue with anything that shouted out with joy that the new year had arrived, that spring had finally sprung, and that basically told everybody to get off their butts and to get out of their houses because it was a new world out there. She smiled at her own quirkiness and got busy taking pictures.

At the third garden, the carnations were planted in stripes. A dwarf type apparently was used as the flowers were about two-thirds the heights of the others she'd seen, yet the size worked lovely as a centerpiece. She studied the garden from the front and then walked all the way around to see the whole effect.

She froze, her breath coming out in short choppy gasps. Forcing herself to move, her gaze still locked on the bed, she called Mack. His line was busy. She tried a second time, then a third. When she still couldn't get through, she switched to Camera mode, but, before she could take a picture, her phone rang.

"Nothing is there at the house on Hawthorne Street," Mack said. "No vehicles, nobody outside. The doors to the house were unlocked, but the house itself appears empty when we peered in the windows." Fatigue colored his tone of voice. "So it's a false alarm."

"No, it's not," she said. "I need you to come here. Like *now*."

"Doreen, are you okay?" His voice was sharp.

"No," she snapped. "I'm not okay. Come here, right now," she said.

"What are you talking about?"

She cried out, "I'll show you. Hold on. I'm sending a picture." She hung up, switched back to Camera mode, and took a picture of the absolutely stunning carnation garden and the dead body lying in the middle of it.

Chapter 4

AFTER SHE SENT the photo, Doreen didn't have long to wait before Mack called. "You didn't just find her, did you?"

"Yes, I did. She's the one I saw and followed earlier," Doreen said. "She's the woman who'd been in the fight with the man."

He swore softly into the phone. "Why didn't you call me?"

"I did, three times," she exclaimed. "You didn't answer." She hung up on him, gathered her animals, headed back to her car, and sat inside, wondering at her delayed reaction. She should be shaking by now, shouldn't she? It wasn't that she was getting numb to seeing dead bodies, but she had just seen this woman very much alive and very assertive in the face of a belligerent man. And that should be enough to shatter anybody's world. It was slow to come, but, after her initial disbelief, then grief slipped into Doreen's heart and soul. That poor woman. She'd been so vibrantly alive just hours ago. Doreen had admired her spunk.

Doreen wrapped her arms around her chest and rocked gently back and forth in the seat. Thaddeus crossed over to her shoulder and gently rubbed his cheek against hers. "Body in the garden. Body in the garden."

"We really need to add to your vocabulary," she said softly to the bird. She reached up and stroked his feathers, loving how very affectionate he was. He rubbed up and down her cheek, catching the wet tear streaking from the corner of her eye.

Goliath hopped across the seat and landed in her lap, as if expecting her to have nothing to do but pet him. She picked him up in her arms and squeezed him tight. And he let her. That was the surprising part. He didn't even growl at the strength of her hug. He must have sensed that her crying meant he should allow it for now. She buried her face in his soft fur and whispered how much she had missed knowing him in his early years. He was such a blessing in her life.

She had no sooner finished saying that when Mugs barked from the back seat. She chuckled. "Yes, Mugs. I love you too, buddy."

What she really needed was for Mack to get here before anybody else arrived. She did not want to be found alone with the body. But she felt she had to stay, to be protective, to watch over the poor woman.

As if anyone could do anything else to hurt her now. … She was already dead. So sad. … People could be a nasty lot sometimes, and she didn't want some heartless kids to come and take pictures to post on the internet.

When a hard knock came on her window, she let out a shriek. Mugs barked furiously. Goliath reached up with his big paw, putting it against the window, his claws out. She hit the button, lowering the window, hearing Mack shouting at her.

"You and that menagerie," he said, his face grim as he

took in the occupants of her car.

"Hey, I only took Mugs last time," she said. "Maybe I knew I would need the solace of bringing them all this time."

"You should be home, where I told you to go," he said, "safe and sound, not out here again. What are you even doing here?"

"I came to see what a large clump of carnations would look like. I was thinking of the Kelowna garden bed design. It's hard to visualize carnations en masse. On Google, I found three large beds nearby. This is the third one. And that's the woman I saw at the gardening center earlier this morning."

"The one you said had the fight with the driver of the black truck?"

She nodded. "Yes. And then I followed her to that house where I found her red car parked. When I went home and did some research on the city bid, then came out here, I didn't expect to see her at any of these three gardens. You can't blame me for this," she stated, raising both hands in frustration.

Goliath, in a disgruntled temper because she'd stopped petting him, hopped over to the passenger's seat and curled up in a ball. She pushed open her car door, smacking into Mack's knee.

"Ouch." He stepped back, glaring at her as she hopped out, Thaddeus on her shoulder. "I didn't do anything," she said again.

"I get that." He pulled his hands through his hair, but his expression seemed intent on just pulling his hair.

She snickered. "It's not my fault you live in such a murderous town."

"Remember how you live here now too." His gaze narrowed as he lifted a finger to point at her.

"Point that thing at me again, and I'll bite it off," she said defiantly. "And how come you came alone?"

"Because I had to make sure I wasn't pulling the team together for nothing. *Again.*"

"Hey, you had a team together already at Hawthorne. They just didn't look hard enough there." She stared up at him. "And are you really telling me that I don't know what a dead body looks like?"

He crossed his arms over his chest, his fingers thrumming on his arm as he said, "Well, you haven't seen very many when they still have flesh on them, have you?"

She tilted her head to the side, then nodded. "Good point." She closed the car door behind her, leaving Mugs inside. When he barked, she groaned, opened up the back door, and let him out. "Come on. Come on," she said to Mack. "Let me show you."

"How about you just stay here," he said, "and I'll go look?"

She leaned against the car door and crossed her arms over her chest in imitation of his previous pose.

He shook his head and headed toward the carnations. "You're impossible."

"Go all the way around to the other side," she said.

He reached up a hand in acknowledgment.

How silly to even give him instructions. If he couldn't see the body from here, it had to be on the other side. She studied the art piece in the center of the garden, a statue of maybe a husband and wife, with their arms wrapped around each other in a hug. The garden decorated the entrance to a large building, the Family Planning Center. She wasn't sure what You, Me, and Us meant on the sign. Maybe marriage counseling? But the media would spin this in an ugly way to say that this relationship had ended in murder. Not the type of publicity anyone wanted.

Speaking of publicity, she did not want to be here when the media found out about this. She watched as Mack stared down at the poor woman, his hands on his hips. She walked toward him. "See?" she said. "I don't make up this stuff, you know."

"I wish you were though," he said. "Just once. Her name is Celeste. Celeste Bingham. Her long-time boyfriend is Josh Huberts."

"Oh my. You knew her," she murmured. "I'm so sorry. That makes it much worse. But at least you know where to start your questioning."

He nodded. "A lot of people knew her," he said. "She's an up-and-coming businesswoman. She won the award for top businesswoman entrepreneur last year."

Celeste's body was rolled on her side, her legs crossed, her hands splayed out, one on either side, so her hip twisted over.

"It doesn't look like she's been posed," Doreen said.

"Not sure about that," he said. "That's kind of a common pose, symbolizing joining hands around the world."

"No clue what that means," she said. "I'm presuming the shots I heard earlier were for her."

"How many did you hear?"

"I thought two at first and two more. But I don't know that I heard them all."

"Well, she's obviously been shot. It'll take the coroner to figure out if that was the cause of death and to confirm how many bullets he finds in her body."

She shoved her hands into her pockets. "Any chance I

can go home and get out of this upcoming crime scene with the cops and the media?"

He snorted. "Apparently this is your penance for wanting to have more excitement in your life. And for not leaving your house as I asked."

"Hey, you told me to go home, and I did. You didn't tell me to stay there. And I would love to be hiding out in my house again," she said. "At least until the media crap dies down. They don't need to know I'm involved in this one, right? But that won't happen unless you let me leave now."

"Go on. Go home," he said. "I'll come by later and get a statement."

She could hear vehicles coming toward them. She rushed to her car. "Come on, Mugs. Let's go before they get here."

But she wasn't fast enough. Three cruisers pulled up just as she got into the front seat. Two officers waved at her; one frowned, then looked over at Mack.

Mack just whistled to get their attention and said, "Forget her. The body is over here."

The men headed toward Mack.

She backed up and turned her car toward home. She knew this scene would get uglier before it got any better. And, right now, the last thing she wanted to do was get caught at the scene of another crime. She hoped no one had seen her here, but she had been here during regular business hours on a weekday, so anybody from the Family Planning Center surely could have seen her from the offices. Although she hadn't seen anybody going in or leaving the center. She frowned. She saw no cars. The building didn't seem to have any lights on.

She shook her head. If she had a dead body in her front yard, she sure as hell would have called for help. And, of course, being her, she'd have been outside, figuring out what was going on.

She drove home extra slow, making sure nobody would have any cause to look at her sideways. She didn't want to draw even more attention to herself.

Since she had all the animals, she decided to stop in to see Nan instead of going straight home. Besides, she could do with a hug. She pulled up outside the retirement home, where her grandmother lived, and parked. Taking the animals with her, she grabbed the leash, clipped it to Mugs' collar, and walked down to the corner where Nan lived. She couldn't take the animals through the building, and the gardener here seemed to think Doreen was a constant threat to his perfect blades of grass. Nan was lobbying to get stepping stones put in so Doreen could make her way into Nan's apartment without disturbing either rule. But, so far, neither side was bending. So, as a consequence, Doreen had to continuously sneak into Nan's garden patio area. Since she hadn't warned Nan that they were coming, Doreen wouldn't barge in. Nan was a character. As such, there were just some things Doreen didn't want to know.

She hopped onto the patio and called out, "Nan, you there?"

When no answer came, she pulled out her phone, sitting at the small bistro table to call her grandmother. It rang and rang. Finally, on the tenth ring, as Doreen was about to hang up, Nan answered.

"Oh, dear, how are you?"

"I'm fine," Doreen said humorously. "Where are you?"

"We're in the communal area." Nan's voice turned crafty. "I just picked up my share of the winnings."

Doreen groaned. "Are you getting into trouble again?"

"No, no, no. I'm not in trouble at all. It was just a harmless bet."

"Sure it was. As long as Mack doesn't find out about it. *Again.* I thought maybe I'd come for a cup of tea, if that's convenient."

"Of course it is. Of course it is."

"Good," she said. "Because I'm on your patio."

Nan gave a gasp and said, "Oh," and the phone shut off.

The next thing Doreen knew, Nan barreled out the glass doors, her arms open wide. Doreen chuckled, reached down, and gave her grandmother a hug. "I wasn't sure if you were busy," she said with a wink.

Nan beamed. "Sometimes I am busy, but right now I'm not, so this is perfect."

Doreen shook her head and sat down again. "The animals are missing you," she lied.

"That's nice of you to say," Nan said. "But the truth of the matter is, I think they're very happy with you. You've added a ton of excitement to their lives."

"Maybe," Doreen said, "but that doesn't mean they don't miss all the cuddles and love you give them."

"Maybe," she said. "Let me put on the tea. I also have a wonderful carrot cake, if you'd like a piece."

"I'd love a piece," Doreen said happily. "I missed lunch somehow."

She thought of all the places she'd been today, figuring out if it was worth it for her to put in a bid for the city landscaping job. She didn't know what to do about it for certain and, at this particular moment, felt like it was all a waste of time. With her fledgling gardening business, she probably needed more experience and more time to deal with bidding on a city project.

Nan returned with a plate of cake and half a sandwich on another plate. With a disapproving sniff, she put both down in front of Doreen. "You better eat this then. What am I going to do with you?"

"I was just busy, Nan, that's all."

"You haven't been buying any groceries, have you?"

Doreen smiled. "I have been. A lot of them. But I still haven't figured out how to make that stove work."

"Your mother never did teach you anything worthwhile, did she?"

"How to get a man apparently worked," Doreen said snidely. "She was right. Everything else fell into place. The trouble is, she didn't give me any long-term advice on how to keep that man." Her voice became dry.

"Do you miss it—being married or your former life? Do you miss him?"

Doreen shook her head. "Absolutely not, and I'm not used to having a ton of food. Remember how he always said eating would make me fat? So I was never served a proper portion. Maybe it was perfect training for right now."

"No luck on a full-time job, dear?"

"Not yet. But I am taking over Mack's mom's gardens on a weekly basis. That won't pay much, but every little bit helps."

"That's good news," Nan said in delight. "And, of course, it'll throw you together with your handsome detective more and more too."

Doreen knew she should probably tell Nan about the omelet-making lesson but didn't want to get her hopes even higher that Doreen would attract such a handsome and decent and hardworking boyfriend. She did not want her grandmother to be matchmaking any more than she already was. And Nan didn't seem to get that things had to happen in their own time—if anything was there to begin with. But her grandmother meant well, and she'd been a huge help these last few weeks. Things had been so chaotic since Doreen's arrival that she hadn't had much chance to find her new normalcy.

"What you need is a new case," Nan said. "Something to catch your attention."

And again Doreen had to hold back the words ready to blurt out. No way she could tell Nan about what Doreen had just found.

"A day job would do the same thing," Doreen said with a smile.

"Did you ever check with Wendy at the consignment store regarding any sales?"

"I've been avoiding hearing from her either way," Doreen admitted. "If I did get money out of some of your things," she said, "I figured it would be better to hold off collecting it until I needed it. This way, I keep really tight control of the little bit of money I do have."

"Too tightly controlled," Nan said.

"Hey, when there's no money, there's no money," Doreen said with a smile. "But maybe I'll stop on my way home from here, or, since I have all the animals with me, I could just call Wendy."

Nan nudged the plate with the sandwich toward her granddaughter. "Eat up."

"I'm not eating your dinner," she said.

"You better," Nan said. "It's salmon. So, if you don't eat it, I'll throw it in the garbage, and that'll make Midge very upset with me."

Doreen knew how much Nan hated salmon. Doreen

picked up the sandwich, and, sure enough, it was salmon with onions. She took a bite and gave a happy sigh. "Well, your loss is my gain. This is excellent."

"It's also huge," Nan said. "What do I want with a sandwich that big? And one made with salmon?"

Doreen looked down and realized her half was, indeed, quite big. She ate happily while they waited for the tea to steep, and, when it was ready, Nan poured it and served her a cup.

Doreen smiled and thanked her. "I can't keep coming here for food," she said.

"You will adjust in time," Nan said reassuringly. "And I will always share the food I have."

At that Thaddeus walked over to rub her cheek, but his gaze was on the carrot cake. Nan chuckled, picked up a piece off the corner, and put it down in front of him. Immediately he pecked away at it.

Doreen grinned. "He doesn't require much to keep him going," she said. "That's a good thing because—between the dog food, the cat food, and the birdseed—these guys cost more to feed than me."

"Nonsense," Nan said. "They should not cost more than you. You should be eating much better than you are."

"I will do better," she promised. "Let's see what Wendy has to say today. I'll be getting a little money weekly from Millicent's garden, so that'll make a difference too."

"Did you contact the garden center for seasonal work?"

She nodded. "I did, but something came up about the last cold case I was on." She winced. "I guess the Theroux family wasn't too impressed when I exposed Hannah for who she really was. I think the garden center has a family connection to the Therouxs."

Nan looked at her with a frown; then her face cleared. "Oh my, Oliver is part of that Lansdowne family. Being related to poor Betty, he might have had a say in that."

"Oh." Doreen thought about that for a moment, then shrugged. "I was hoping for a job there, but, if they're holding that Betty Miles case against me, well ..."

"It'll blow over," Nan said comfortably, settling back in her chair. "Did the detective give you a new case to look at?"

"I don't think Mack considers me on his team or that he should give me any cases." Doreen picked up a chunk of carrot cake, took a bite, and moaned. "Oh my. This is good."

"Do you like it?"

Doreen nodded. "It's excellent." She looked at it and then at Nan suspiciously. "Doesn't have any marijuana in it, does it?"

Nan went off in peals of laughter. "No, it doesn't. I prefer the one that does though, you know."

Doreen sighed. Ever since marijuana became legal in the state, Nan didn't seem to enjoy her pastime as much as she used to when it was a hidden secret. Something about doing what you weren't allowed to do seemed to appeal to her. "Who made this?"

"Midge," she said. "She brought it over with the salmon sandwich."

"Nice neighbors," Doreen commented.

Nan nodded. "I've got another piece of cake you can take home for dessert, plus the other half of the sandwich can be your dinner. At least that way I know you're getting some more food in your stomach today."

Doreen chuckled. "I'm eating, honest."

"What you need is to start cooking."

"On Monday I'm learning to make an omelet."

Nan's gaze lit with interest. "Omelets? Interesting choice."

"I miss eggs," Doreen confessed. "And I haven't bought any because I don't know how to cook them. I tried them in the microwave, and that was a nightmare."

"How did you cook it?" Nan's face was suspiciously bland.

"I put it in and cooked it for eight minutes," she said. "I was pretty sure that's what the recipe said that I read on the internet."

"So you just set it on the tray for eight minutes?" Nan looked at her in surprise. And then she giggled. "Don't tell me. It exploded, right?"

Nonplussed, Doreen looked at her. "How did you know?"

At that, Nan howled. "That would have been quite a mess."

"It was terrible," Doreen said. "Egg was everywhere." She grinned herself. "I'm glad I'm providing you with lots of entertainment these days."

When she could stop laughing, Nan reached across and patted her granddaughter's hand. "I'm so happy you're close by. I haven't had this much fun in decades."

Even though the laughter was directed at her, Doreen was happy to see her grandmother so bright and cheerful. "You can laugh at me all you want, as long as you keep feeding me." She popped another bite of the carrot cake in her mouth. "This really is divine."

Without a word, Nan went back into the kitchen, and, when she stepped back out again, she had a piece all wrapped up that was twice the size of what Doreen had eaten and the other half of the sandwich. "You take this home with you.

You'll enjoy it more than I will."

Doreen moved it off to the side. "I won't say no." They finished their tea in companionable silence, and then she said, "I should leave and call the consignment store. Time to face the music and see if we've gotten anywhere with some sales." She hesitated. "Somebody—and, no, I don't remember who suggested it—said maybe you had antiques in your house."

"Yes, there are ..." Nan nodded. "When you get time, you should have someone appraise them."

"If you don't mind, maybe I will. Maybe something very valuable is there."

"Be positive," Nan said. Her phone rang inside her apartment. She got up and said, "I'll be right back."

While Doreen watched her grandmother go into her bedroom, she finished her tea. She didn't know how long she had before the most recent gossip filtered through the old folks' home, but she wanted to be gone before anybody heard about Doreen finding another dead body. Just then her phone rang. It was Mack.

"I'm about to come over," he said. "Are you at home?"

"Not yet," she said, standing up. "I'll be there in a few minutes. I stopped off at Nan's to have a cup of tea."

"You didn't tell her, did you?"

"No, and I was just thinking how I need to leave quickly," she said, "before they know anything here." She picked up Mugs' leash and scooped Thaddeus onto her shoulder, calling Goliath to join them. "I do have to say good-bye to her though."

"If she's not there beside you, you can bet she's getting the latest gossip," he said in an ominous voice. "You can't tell them anything."

"I wasn't telling her anything," Doreen said. "You must

learn to trust me." And she hung up. As she turned, she saw Nan was back, her eyes bright with interest. Doreen groaned. "I have to run, Nan. Thanks so much for the cake and tea and the sandwich. I'll call you later." She kissed her grandmother on the cheek and ran across the grass before Nan had a chance to ask anything. In the background Doreen heard a man speaking.

"Did you ask her if she knows anything about the body?"

"No, no, no. I didn't get a chance to ask. I think Mack called her and told her to be quiet."

Doreen got into the car, gathering her pets inside, and, with a wave to Nan, reversed out of the parking lot. Soon afterward she pulled into her driveway, ignoring all the reporters, their cameras flashing while calling out questions. She rushed inside, shooing the animals ahead of her. Once safely in her home, she let the animals all go their own way. "Holy crap, you guys. We are about to have more chaos again."

Thaddeus perked up. "Chaos is good. Chaos is good."

She turned to glare at him. "Chaos is *not* good. Chaos is *not* good," she emphasized. Her phone rang just then. She looked down to see it was Nan. She sighed and answered it. "Nan, I just got home. What's the matter?"

"Well, since you ran off so quickly, dear, I didn't get a chance to ask you about the body."

"What body, Nan?" she asked.

"The one you must have found that Mack was giving you trouble over," she said. "Dear, we really do need details."

"What details and why?" she asked, her suspicions growing.

Nan chuckled. "For the bets of course. Call me back when you can." And she hung up.

Chapter 5

DOREEN TOSSED HER cell phone on the countertop and screamed at the empty kitchen in sheer frustration. After a moment she felt better. Only Mugs had decided he should accompany her in this ritual and was still howling. As he slowly stopped, she could hear Thaddeus kicking up a fuss, marching across the table, crowing and cawing, like he was singing some kind of a crazy-ass tempo. That was probably what she had sounded like to him.

She tossed her purse and jacket beside her phone and walked over to the coffeepot. "It is definitely time for a cup of coffee," she muttered to herself, deliberately not counting the cost of her increased coffee habit.

She also knew that Mack would arrive soon, asking her questions. He always drank her out of coffee. But still, he also made a mean pot. Even though she'd tried everything she could, and it was good coffee that she now made, he had that magic touch. It occurred to her that maybe what made it better was how she didn't have to do it herself. That was a consideration, since she still had fond memories of all the coffee she used to have in her former life, none of which had ever been prepared by her hand. Living in a multimillion-dollar house with a rich lifestyle had a lot of perks. And delightful coffee every day whenever she wanted it was one of them.

She ground the beans, filled the carafe in the back of the coffeemaker, and pushed the button for it to start. Then she walked over to the fridge and opened it up. If nothing else, she should put away the carrot cake and sandwich. She really wanted to eat the cake because it was so damn good. But half of that was because she was so stressed.

Finally, when the coffee was done, she grabbed a cup, pushed open the back door, and stepped onto the veranda. It was old and creaky, but the place was hers, and right now she needed that solace.

With the animals following along in her wake, she wandered down the garden. It was only here in her backyard, finding private space where nobody else could interfere, that she managed to destress. Almost on automatic pilot, her feet took her to the creek. She perched on the log close to her property but just ever-so-slightly on public access. There she sat, watching the water trickle down the creek bed. It was so soothing.

Mugs walked into the creek until his big thick feet were covered in water and drooped his head down so he could take a drink. Of course his ears drooped down with him, so they sank into the water too. She sighed. "Mugs, could you at least lift them out of the way, so they don't get wet every time?" He just gave her a sad basset-eyed look and kept doing what he was doing. She said, "I guess I should be happy you're not going for a complete swim."

With his typical disdain of everything that Mugs did, Goliath sat perched on a rock, his tail wrapped around him in a perfect formation. The cat stared down at the water in fascination but with an equal amount of revulsion. She couldn't imagine him ever fishing. He was just too dainty, even though there was nothing dainty about him. But he hated water. And, at the same time, it seemed like he couldn't leave it alone. She wondered how he ever reconciled his relationship with that stuff.

Thaddeus, on the other hand, walked up and down the log she was on, calling to Mugs, "Drink the water. Drink the water."

She chuckled at him.

He cocked his head, looked at her, preening in the fresh air. He really was a lovely addition to her family. She'd never considered having a bird as a pet before. She had to clean up after him, as well as after the cat and the dog, but she enjoyed the bit of housecleaning she now did. The vacuum was pretty old, but luckily it still worked, and that was all she cared about. Knowing that this was her place made a huge difference too.

Hard to believe she'd been here for a couple of weeks now. The house felt like home. It still smelled like Nan, yet musty, mixed with old dust. Doreen was slowly getting it into better shape, which was a miracle, considering she had no money for that. It boiled down to good old hard work.

Doreen had brought up the antiques with Nan but had forgotten to ask her if she knew the history of any of the pieces. Doreen also needed to find an antiques specialist. Hopefully to advise her if some of these pieces were valuable.

Speaking of which, … Doreen walked back to the house and stepped inside to retrieve her phone from the countertop and dialed Wendy's number at the consignment store as Doreen headed back to the log at the creek. "Hi, Wendy. This is Doreen."

"Hi, Doreen," Wendy said gaily.

She was always so happy. Doreen was kind of jealous of her in a way.

"What can I do for you?" Wendy asked. "Or do you have more clothes to bring in?"

"Actually I don't," she said, "although there might be a bit more. I still have the master bedroom to go through."

"Oh, my goodness. Was all that stuff you brought before from the spare bedroom?"

"Yes," Doreen said with a half laugh. "It was."

"Goodness. You should sort through the rest and bring it to me," she said. "I've sold several of the pieces and one of the fur coats. Now remember. I don't pay anything to you for a while. I pay ninety days out, in case people return items."

"No, no, I understand that," Doreen said quickly because she hadn't in the least understood that at all. Wendy had probably explained it to her, but, as Doreen's former husband would say, she just didn't *get* money. She wasn't stupid; she just didn't realize how these cycles worked. "So you're saying that, after ninety days, you'll call me and tell me how much money there is for me?"

"Yes, and then I pay on the fifteenth of the next month after the ninety days. It's a lot of accounting, particularly when my customers are allowed that ninety days to bring something back."

Doreen trusted Wendy. Whether that was the right thing to do or not, Doreen didn't have a whole lot of choice. "What did you sell the fur coat for, by the way?" she asked curiously. "We didn't really discuss prices on any of the items I brought in."

"Nope, but I think I've sold about one-hundred-dollars'

worth of stuff for you already," she said, "and that's without the fur coat. I sold it for one forty-five." Her voice turned distracted as she said, "I can look it up for you, if you like."

"No, no," Doreen said in delight. "I'm just glad to hear you're selling some of these items. Very encouraging,"

"And," Wendy said, "hopefully we'll double or triple that amount before the ninety days are up. Especially if you bring in more stuff, maybe we can get you a bit every quarter."

"That's a good idea." Doreen brightened. "Now I'm looking for an antiques dealer in town."

"I don't know about a dealer," she said, "but Fen Gunderson owned his own antiques shop. He's retired now, but he has an excellent eye. If you're looking for some advice, you should talk to him."

"And where would I find him?" she asked.

"He lives in Upper Mission."

She'd been in Kelowna long enough now to understand where she was living was *the Mission* and to the south of her house was *Upper Mission*. It made no sense to her geographically. But, hey, she didn't determine the boundaries of the area. "I will look him up and see if he'll talk to me."

"He's easy to find. He volunteers at the Mission Bible Thrift Store. You can always find him in the back testing toasters and any other godforsaken appliances people bring in." Wendy went off on a happy laugh. "He's a sweetheart though. I'm sure he'd love to come to Nan's old house and see what she's got. He could definitely tell you which pieces are valuable."

"That would be ideal," Doreen exclaimed. "I have no way of knowing what's valuable and what isn't."

"Exactly," Wendy said. "I do have people at the store

waiting for me now. So, when you get a chance, go through some more clothes and come over, even if you just want to visit—you're always welcome."

She hung up, leaving Doreen sitting beside the river. She looked back at the old house that needed a new roof and at the veranda that listed sideways. Yet, she smiled. It was hers. It was a roof over her head. With a little bit of work and a whole lot of goodwill and elbow grease, she would do just fine.

When she heard her name called out, she shouted back, realizing she shouldn't have done that. It could be anybody. And *anybody* tended to be reporters.

Immediately she heard a disgusted sound from behind the fence of her neighbor. "What are you doing hiding out back there?" he/she asked.

Doreen frowned. She had yet to figure out the sex of that speaker based on that unisex voice. She'd met the man of the house, and, as far as she understood, a wife lived there. But Doreen had yet to meet her. And this disembodied voice from the backyard talking to her had never identified itself, so Doreen didn't know if it was the husband or the wife.

"I'm not hiding out at all," Doreen said in exasperation. "I'm out here enjoying the creek."

"Dirty thing," the voice said. "And stop yelling. You're disturbing my nap."

Doreen raised both hands and shook her head. Even here apparently, minding her own business in her own backyard, she was a problem. But, as she looked toward the house, she saw Mack step onto her veranda. She smiled and waved, then stood. Thaddeus raced toward her. She bent down and let him climb onto her hand and lifted him to her shoulder. Mugs barked joyfully at their visitor.

Goliath looked at them all with that disdainful and haughty lord-of-the-manor look that seemed to say, *You don't expect me to greet everyone, do you? Just because you do …*

Mugs, on the other hand, already raced madly toward Mack. Mugs apparently thought Mack was just fine. As a watchdog, he sucked, usually barking *after* she heard a knock on her door. However, he'd had his uses these last few days, so it was all good. Besides, she loved that adorable mutt. He was family. He'd been there for her through thick and thin, and she loved his jowls, every wrinkle of them.

As she walked toward Mack, she held up her cup. "There's a fresh pot of coffee."

His face lit up. He turned and disappeared into her kitchen.

She chuckled. "Who'd have thought my one and only friend in this town would end up being a police detective?"

She was still smiling until her gaze landed on the brown dirt patches across her garden.

Mac stepped outside. "Now what's bothering you?"

"The mess your men left," she snapped. She strode up the veranda steps and glared at him as she entered her kitchen. "They should fix it."

"We've discussed this already," he said in exasperation, "many times over. They're not fixing anything."

"They're the ones who ripped apart all of my backyard." She put down her cup and filled it. He'd taken the largest mug in the house, so there was barely enough for her to have another cup. With her coffee in hand, she walked to the kitchen table and sat down.

"They didn't dig it up. They removed a dead body hidden on your property."

"But I didn't hide it," she said with logic. "So that's got

nothing to do with me."

"Forget it," he said with a shake of his head, joining her at the table. "You're not getting free *gardening* work done for you by the RCMP."

She sighed and propped her chin on her palm. "So what did you find out about the case?"

"There is no case." He pulled out a notepad, put it on the kitchen table, and scooted his coffee cup back. "So let's get your statement."

"Right," she said.

She repeated what she'd done from the time she'd seen the couple in the garden shop, right through to when she found the body. When she finally ran dry, she realized she'd drunk the rest of her coffee. She stared longingly at the empty pot.

He glanced at her and then at the pot. "Go put on another one."

She shrugged and sat where she was.

"Are you trying to get *me* to put on a pot?"

She gave him a wide-eyed innocent look. "Of course not. Why would I do that?"

But he didn't seem to believe her. He stared at her, then said, "You make a great pot these days. What difference does it make who prepares it?"

She crossed her arms over her chest, settled back in the chair. "I just don't want any more."

He finished his cup, looked at it, and said, "If you don't want any more, do you mind if I put on another pot?"

She leaned forward eagerly. "No, no. You go ahead."

He glared at her. "You're being foolish. Your coffee is every bit as good as mine is."

"Do you think so?" she asked. She watched as he took

exactly the same steps as she had done to brew coffee.

When the coffee dripped happily, he sat back down again. "Yes, your coffee is every bit as good as mine is."

Thaddeus, at that point, disappeared into the living room. When he got bored, he returned and hopped up onto her knee, climbed up her arm onto the table. He walked to her cup and pecked at it. She shooed him away and moved the cup. "He just started doing that. I don't understand why."

"Has he got lots of food?"

She stood, walked over to make sure herself. "After forgetting a few days ago," she said, "I felt so bad that I'm probably overfeeding them now."

In the front hall, she found the bag of birdseed, grabbed a handful, and set it on the kitchen table. Thaddeus went at it. She groaned. "At the rate he's eating, I'll have to buy another bag soon."

"Have you bought any yet?"

She shook her head. "No. So far all the supplies Nan left are holding me in good stead."

"Good," he said. "Your money will go a little further then."

She nodded. "Not very far but far enough. Now tell me what I need to know."

He looked at her in surprise.

"What caliber were the bullets that killed her? How many times was she shot? What was the cause of death? I'm presuming it was the bullets," she said, "because I saw her just a short time earlier. However, her neck looked a little bruised, and I don't remember seeing that earlier."

"You noticed that, did you?" he said. "I noticed it too." He tapped his notepad with his pencil. "The thing is, until the coroner has a chance to check her over, we won't know the details."

She nodded. "How the hell did the old folks' home know right away?"

He groaned. "No clue. The Family Planning Center was still shut down since that unpleasantness last week."

"What unpleasantness?"

He shot her a look. "Didn't you hear about it?"

"I didn't even know that building existed until today," she said. "So tell me."

"It's a Family Planning Center, and they're pro-choice," he said. "A big kerfuffle occurred last week as a couple of men went in and hassled some of the women in the waiting room. It was bad enough they had to shut down the center while they reconsider security options."

"Were the men ever charged?"

He shrugged. "I haven't heard."

"Do you work active cases or just cold cases?"

He let out a gust of air. "As you know, I do both."

"So what was the cold case you were going to tell me about before?"

He shook his head. "Oh, no you don't. I want to know more about this couple. Did you hear any of their conversation?"

"I told you that part already," she said. "So is your cold case a murder, drugs, theft?"

"None of that," he said.

"Missing kids?" she guessed.

He shot her a look.

She crowed. "I'm right, aren't I?" She clapped her hands like a child.

He shook his head. "I'm not telling you if you're right or

wrong. The bottom line is, we're not going there right now."

She nodded. "Okay, because really we have an active case we need to be working on. You gave me the name of the deceased and said she's a businesswoman, but what business does she own?"

He sighed. "She's the one who handled the funding for the Family Planning Center," he said. "She runs a service that connects financiers to businesses."

Doreen stared at him for a long moment as the implications set in. "So her body was dumped in front of a building she helped to start?"

He nodded.

She sat back, her hand covering her mouth. "Wow," she said. "That's interesting."

He shrugged.

"Of course it could be worse," she said. "She could have created a candy shop. Maybe she would have been dumped in a vat of fudge or something."

He stared at her.

She chuckled. "Okay, okay. You know me. I'm just sorting through all the negatives, then finding something bright and cheerful to balance it out somehow."

"Finding a body in a vat of chocolate fudge," he said, "is not cheerful."

She shrugged, grabbed her coffee cup, and walked over to the pot. "Maybe not but there is fresh coffee, so I'm having a cup." She poured some and sat back down, waving her hand over the top, wafting away the steam. "It's a missing kid, huh? Interesting case."

He ignored her and tapped his notepad. "Are you sure you didn't see anything else?"

She frowned. "I thought the Family Planning Center

building was empty, but I had this creepy feeling that somebody was watching me, you know? But then, when I turned around, I didn't see anybody in the windows."

"No. Like I said, it's been closed."

"Unless somebody was working, getting caught up, taking care of business while they didn't have to deal with the public," she said calmly. "We know a lot of people would do that. What about janitors?"

He nodded. "No one answered the officers who knocked. Just because you have an odd feeling isn't some reason for me to jump to conclusions that somebody in there was watching you."

"But not a reason not to say so either," she said with a chuckle, picking up her cup and taking a sip. As soon as she tasted it, she smiled.

"What's that smile for?" His voice was suspicious but edged with humor.

Her smile fell away, and she stared at him innocently.

He sighed. "Is it better?"

"To my sadness," she said, "it is."

At that, he laughed. "You're crazy. You know that, right?" he said affectionately.

She shrugged. "But you like me anyway, so it's all good. How many kids went missing?"

"Three, but they weren't all connected." He stopped and said, "Goddammit."

She laughed. "All boys?"

His brows came together. "What makes you think they were boys?"

"I don't know. I had good odds of being right, and I'm pretty good at playing the odds."

"Like grandmother, like granddaughter," he said with a

head tilt and raised eyebrows. "In that case, you should buy a lottery ticket. It would solve your money problems."

"*Hmm.* That's true. The problem with that is, you have to have money in the first place."

He grinned. "True. I'll leave you now." He stood, grabbing his notebook. "Make sure you don't talk to anybody about the case, please. I'll probably come back with some more questions later. But I'll call you before."

"Good enough," she said. "Are we still having our cooking lesson on Monday?"

"No reason not to." He turned and walked out.

Chapter 6

Wednesday afternoon...

REMEMBERING WENDY'S COMMENTS to bring her more resale clothing, Doreen took the remaining piece of carrot cake and a cup of tea and walked up to the master bedroom. She'd moved her clothes in but hadn't moved Nan's out. A huge double closet ran along one wall. In truth, she'd been saving this chore for a rainy day. But, right now, the distraction would be good, and seeing Thaddeus's food dwindling down daily was another constant reminder that she needed more money. Since Nan had this habit of hiding or losing track of money in a lot of her clothing, it had been a huge source of extra cash for Doreen the last time she went through Nan's clothing. So much so that Doreen was still using that found money for groceries.

She started at one end of the closet, pulling out about a half-dozen hangers, all with evening clothes on them. She held up a couple dresses and whistled. "Wow, Nan. When would you have ever worn these?" One was sparkly, looked like a 1920s' dress from the Gatsby era. But it was seriously stunning and silver. She laid down all the dresses on the bed and hung up that silver one on the back of the door and checked its condition. It was really gorgeous, also in great shape. And, from the size of it, would fit Doreen.

She frowned. "I'll never have anyplace to wear something like this." Yet she was loathe to let it go.

She kept it on the back of the door while she checked out the other things she'd pulled out. Each was a dress in a very different style, very unique. They weren't necessarily Doreen's style. However, she would never have said they were Nan's either. But it revealed Nan's fashion sense and personality at a much younger age. And, man, she must have been a party animal.

Still, these dresses were of excellent quality and that meant a lot in terms of selling them.

She set aside two more she was interested in for herself, and three she hung on the curtain rod on the small window to decide on later. And then she went to check through all the pockets but found nothing. She pulled out two more dresses, disappointed because no cash was found in the pockets.

She found something in the next dress with padded bra cups—a fifty-dollar bill tucked into one bra cup. Stunned, she pulled it out. But then thought about all the times she'd gone out for an evening. If she didn't want to take a purse with her, but needed to have some pocket money, this would be a perfect hiding place. That made her go back and check every one of the other dresses. That was the only dress she found more money in, but she did make sure she checked them all out very thoroughly, including the waistbands.

She worked steadily for another hour, going through another good portion of the closet. Some of the items were not today's style, yet were classical styles Doreen could wear anytime. At least she hoped so.

When her phone rang, she answered it absentmindedly.

"Bitch," came the stranger's voice at the other end.

"Pardon me?"

Click.

She snorted. "Well, it's not like I haven't been called that before."

She put down the phone and returned to the dresses she'd pulled out on the bed. One was a hippie-style muumuu. She laughed. It might be fun if she ever gained a couple hundred pounds, but she couldn't imagine wearing it now. It was made with such a gorgeous material though. If only she could sew; she could do so much with it. She placed it in the pile to be taken to the consignment store.

The next one she thought was a knit *dress* but instead was almost a floor-length cardigan. It was gorgeous. The material was soft, smooth, and silky. She checked the pockets and crowed in delight as she pulled out a change purse. It was beaded in some kind of gold lamé, which would have gone with one of the dressier frocks, not necessarily the cardigan.

She opened up the coin purse to find it crammed with coins and bills. Carefully she emptied it on the bed. There were a lot of coins, maybe ten dollars' worth, along with several twenties. As she peeled open the twenties, she found a fifty inside. She stared in amazement. "Nan, how could you possibly have misplaced all this money? I'd have gone nuts if I was missing fifty dollars."

When the phone rang a second time, she didn't think anything of it. "Hello?"

"Bitch, you'll die too."

Snick.

"Once, okay, whatever. *Twice,* now you're being a pain

in the ass," she said.

She waited to see if the caller would ring her a third time. But nobody called back. Checking for the telephone number, she just found Unknown Caller. She wrote down the time of both calls and waited to see if another one would come.

She turned and studied the coin purse. It was such a cute thing that she didn't want to get rid of it. She wasn't sure she wanted to sell the long cardigan sweater either. She took it off the hanger and put it on in front of the full-length mirror. It stopped just about midcalf and was a thick sage green with big rolled-up cuffs at the wrists.

She wrapped it around herself and smiled. "I'm keeping you," she announced. And then the phone rang for a third time. She saw the same Unknown Caller designation on her cell phone screen and answered it. "Hello."

"You'll get yours, bitch."

"You are getting boring," she said. This time she hung up the phone first.

And grinned.

Chapter 7

Thursday morning...

WHEN SHE WOKE up the next day, it was hard to believe it was morning. She'd had a restless night. Even though she'd had the last laugh on her unknown caller, and he hadn't called back again, the incident had still worked its way into her nightmares. She wasn't sure what the man's problem was.

"Or for that matter," she muttered aloud to the empty room, "if it's connected to *any* of the dead bodies I found. He's obviously a bully, trying to scare me by threatening me. Like Mack would say, just because my caller mentioned me dying too doesn't necessarily mean he's connected with Celeste's murder."

She rotated her neck slowly as she sat on the side of the bed. A heavy head landed in her lap as Mugs rolled over and stretched out. She bent down and scratched his long belly, ending up with a cuddle of his ears. She loved those big floppy ears of his. They were so silky. "You can stay here, Mugs, but I need a shower."

As she hopped up, she saw Thaddeus on her bedroom windowsill, looking at the backyard. She frowned. "What are you doing over there, Thaddeus?"

He turned a gimlet eye in her direction and gave a head tilt toward the window, like saying, *Get over here, idiot, and look. About time you finally woke up.*

She walked toward him and looked out the window. Nothing appeared to be different. She frowned. "I don't know what's bothering you, little one, but I don't see anything to be worried about."

He gave a half a squawk and ruffled his feathers, almost as if insulted she hadn't seen what he'd seen.

She studied the backyard again, but it didn't appear to be any different. But then a lot had been going on in her backyard, so she wasn't sure she could write off Thaddeus's observations that fast. It had taken her a while, but she'd come to realize that the animals really did have some sort of intuitive knowledge of what was going on around them.

Turning away, she headed for a shower. When she came out with the towel wrapped around her, Thaddeus still stood lookout at the window. What really bothered her was his focus. He wasn't a predator by nature, though she supposed in the wild he would have been. Something out there he was keeping watch over.

She stood beside him, yet again studying the same direction he was so focused on. He stayed fixed on the back right corner. It almost looked like where the fence ended and the creek wrapped around the neighbor's fence.

She crouched behind him, so she could get a bead on his line of sight. "I know you're smarter than I am, buddy. But I sure can't see what you're seeing." He never moved. "We could go downstairs and go outside, see what it is," she said, almost as a peace offering.

He squawked and hopped onto her shoulder.

She chuckled and said, "Okay. I'll take that as a yes. But let me get dressed first."

And that he didn't want to do. She struggled into her clothes, finally forcibly removing him from her shoulder, putting him on the headboard. Once dressed, she put him back on her shoulder and walked downstairs, Mugs at her side.

As she walked down the last set of stairs, she saw Goliath sprawled on the bottom step. She groaned. "Why would you choose to lie there?"

The only acknowledgment she got from him was a flick of his tail. She snorted. "You're trying to trip me, aren't you? And then what will you do?" she snapped. "I'll be laid up with a broken leg, and nobody'll get you food."

He rolled over onto his back and stretched. Reminiscent of Mugs' earlier move, she chuckled, stepped over the huge feline, squatted down, and gave Goliath a couple gentle strokes. She straightened and said, "I'm loving all this animal time, but I'll turn into an animal myself if I don't get coffee."

She walked into the kitchen and put on the coffeepot. All the while, she looked out in the backyard, wondering what had bothered Thaddeus so much. As soon as the coffee was brewed enough that she could grab a cup, she snagged an old worn-out, chipped mug she'd decided had more character than the brand-new flashy ones and opened the back door. Mugs raced through the kitchen and dashed out. He barked and wouldn't stop.

She frowned at him. "Mugs! What's the matter?"

Just as quickly, a streak of orange caught her eye as Goliath bolted outside after Mugs. On her shoulder, Thaddeus squawked loud and hard.

"Okay, okay, okay," she cried out. "I'm going. I'm going." She walked down the rear veranda steps and onto the pathway that led through the garden. As she did, she marveled at how much better it looked without the broken-down fence that cut off her view of the creek. It really opened up the backyard. She couldn't wait to get into her own backyard gardening project. But she wanted to get a workable plan down on paper first.

Her ideas were pretty rough so far, and she didn't want to do a half-assed job. She took pride in her work, and it was quite possible her own gardens would be portrayed in a portfolio of what she could do for other people's homes. So Doreen didn't want to mess it up.

She strolled down the path, quickening her pace. Mugs sat down, his butt firmly planted on the ground, and Goliath sat beside him. Curious, she joined them for a look. "Hey, what's going on?" she asked. "*Nothing* is here."

But they both looked at her in disgust. She groaned, feeling like the animals all thought she was half-baked. Whereas the general population thought animals weren't as smart as they really were.

She stared down at the area, wandering a couple feet forward, but she still couldn't see anything amiss. She stepped out farther, wondering if her animals were looking at the creek, which had become the source of all things curious and wonderful and, in some cases, deadly.

As she wandered up and down the edge of the creek, she turned to look at her three animals. Thaddeus had joined the two on the ground, and now all three just sat there, staring at her, as if to say, *Come on. Get it, will you?*

The trouble was, she didn't know what they were talking about. She crouched beside the creek but figured, if it were something in the water, they would be at the water's edge.

Instead they all stood back about six feet, looking almost toward her feet.

She studied the distance between her and her animals. Just then her phone rang. Seeing it was Mack, she answered the call.

He said, "I might have some more questions for you today."

"Sure," she said in a distracted tone.

"What are you up to?" When she didn't answer right away, his voice sharpened. "Doreen, talk to me. What trouble are you in now?"

She glared into the phone. "Hey, be nice. I didn't have to answer the call, you know."

"Why wouldn't you answer the call?"

"I had three threatening phone calls last night," she said calmly. "But I got the last laugh."

"What the hell are you talking about?" he roared. "Why didn't you tell me?"

She snickered. "The messages were short. Just *bitch, bitch, you'll get yours.* That kind of stuff," she said. "But, on the third call, I told him he was getting really boring, and I hung up on him first. I haven't heard back from him since."

There was silence, then he said, "Did you taunt some stranger who was threatening you?"

Still squatting at the edge of the creek, staring at the ground, she sat back and frowned. "I don't know that I would call it *taunting* exactly …"

"I would. Did you consider the fact somebody out there just murdered a woman and may very well have seen you following them?"

"I highly doubt they would think I was any kind of threat," she said. "I mean, let's get real."

"Yes," he said, his voice turning hard, cold. "Let's get real. You hear an argument. You follow a couple. You hear gunshots. You find a dead body. Then you get threatening phone calls. All in the same frigging day. Is that real enough?"

She winced. "Okay, so I didn't mean it that way."

"I did," he snapped. And then he groaned. "You have such a strange sense of right and wrong."

"Maybe. But at least it's my sense." And she disconnected the call.

As she sat here, she muttered, "Damn, damn, damn." Of course he was right. She was still a little out of control after being so fettered under her soon-to-be ex-husband's thumb. She made all her own decisions now, but was she making good ones? Not necessarily. Mack was pissed she'd followed that couple, and, the trouble was, she didn't even really have a reason for it. Well, except for her gut feeling and that the truck had followed the Mini.

But maybe they were attending the same meeting? It wasn't like Doreen thought the woman was in any real danger, which would have been a whole different story. But yet, the woman *could* have been in danger. Doreen just thought the way the couple acted was curious. Doreen would like to say she was psychic, but that would make her a pretty shitty psychic, since she didn't save the woman's life by warning her. So, while Doreen wasn't exactly sure what the hell was going on with her unknown caller, in the end, she decided that Mack had a good reason to be disgruntled with her, what with her not being an accurate psychic and all.

She also hadn't really considered that the caller last night was serious. His tone had been too mocking. As if he was pulling a child's prank.

She straightened up, threw out her arms at the animals, and said, "You guys need to pinpoint what you want me to see because, from this position, I can't see it."

The look on Goliath's face was enough to make her glare at him. "Stop being so arrogant and just show me."

And the damn cat got up, did a forward stretch like one of those silly yoga poses with his butt in the air waggling, and his claws came down on something in front of them.

She heard a metallic *clink* as his claws met something hard.

She dove forward. "Why didn't you say so?" A small corner of something stuck just barely out of the ground. She'd never have noticed it because it was all rusty and covered in mud. "No clue what this is," she said.

She tried to pinch the corner and tug it loose, but it wouldn't move. She needed a shovel.

"We have to go back. I need some tools. This looks like it could be a bigger job." She wiggled the rusted muddy piece again but still got no movement. "And I'd prefer gloves." She looked down at her fingers.

Appropriately Thaddeus squawked at her.

She glared. "Don't tell me that you saw this last night and have kept an eye on it all night? It's hardly big enough to see from where I'm standing, forget about from the second story of the house." But, as she looked up toward her house, she realized it was in a direct line with her bedroom window. She groaned. "Okay, so you guys just might be the weirdest animals on the planet."

Mugs barked.

She grinned at him. "That's all right. I love you anyway."

She grabbed her coffee cup, and her phone rang. It was

Mack again. She clicked Talk and said, "I'm not answering this." And she hung up. And then she realized what she'd done.

She threw her head back, her gaze up at the sky, and groaned. "Well, that'll make his morning. If he tells his coworkers, they will all think I'm crazy."

Then again they probably already did. She'd seen the looks on the guys' faces when they arrived at the carnation garden yesterday. They had to wonder at anybody who could find bodies on a regular basis like she did. What no one seemed to understand was that she didn't go looking for them.

Okay, so yesterday she was looking, but she wasn't expecting a body. She was searching for carnation beds to see what they would look like en masse. Surely it wasn't her fault somebody had decided to drop the body in the carnations. Besides, she certainly wasn't seeking any family planning. The last thing she had in her future was the prospect of children.

That caused her a pang of regret because that possibility had always been out there, just never at the right time. But somehow plans changed. Anyway, she needed gloves and a shovel. She marched toward the house and put her phone on the kitchen countertop. "Mister Smarty-Pants Mack, if you call again, I truly won't answer. I'm leaving my phone right here."

She refilled her coffee, grabbed her gloves and shovel, and headed back toward the creek. Maybe, with any luck, this would be something fun for a change. And not something that would lead to more murdered people. She was decidedly not in the mood for murder—unless she was the one who got to help with the investigating of the murdering.

Chapter 8

B ACK OUTSIDE IN the garden Doreen placed her cup of coffee off to the side. "Mugs, don't dump that."

He gave her a sad look. She chuckled.

She shooed the animals away so she had a little more space to work in. They were still sitting as they were before, in front of the buried mystery. With her gloves on, she tried again to pull the exposed corner.

It was thin, and it was metal. It looked as if it had been here for a while.

With the shovel, she scooped away some of the dirt and rocks around it, hoping for a way to loosen it up. Slowly, bit by bit, it worked. It resembled a license plate. And that made no sense. How would a license plate get washed down the creek? Unless it had come through the debris flow during the high water runoffs in spring.

As she'd learned, all kinds of things came down in that spring runoff. And not necessarily anything she wanted to see. It was kind of sad in a way, but that was the routine of Mother Nature.

Finally, with lots of back-and-forth action, she loosened the item enough to pull it out. She lifted it and stared at the banged-up piece of metal. "So now we have a license plate." She looked around at the three animals staring at it, like it was a viper. "What are we supposed to do with this?"

"You could give it to me for a change," Mack said from behind her, reaching out one palm.

She looked up at him, begrudgingly handing over her find. "Who invited you?"

"I invited myself," he said darkly. "What the hell do you mean, *I'm not answering this call* and then hanging up on me?"

"I didn't think it through," she admitted. "I just answered you and hung up."

He chuckled and shook his head. "You realize I was standing in the middle of the office, howling at your response. So I was forced to tell the guys what you'd done."

She glared at him as she straightened, brushing the dirt off her knees with one hand. "You *would* tell them," she snapped. "Probably just to make fun of me and to cement my reputation as an idiot."

"Oh, you have a reputation all right," he said with a nod of his head. "But hardly as an idiot."

"As what then?" she asked curiously.

"Maybe as somebody who has more than enough bad luck to get caught up into trouble time and time again."

She snorted at him. "Well, they can just get over it. If they did their jobs, I wouldn't need whatever magical ability I have to attract bad luck." She pointed at the license plate he now held. "I know it's not a normal question, but have you ever seen that before?"

He rolled his eyes. "Close to fifty thousand people live in this town. Do you really expect me to remember all their license plates?"

"I figured, since this license plate was buried close to my property, and, considering the recent Betty Miles case, I wondered if it was related."

Frowning, he shook his head. "It's a truck license plate."

She studied the letters and numbers. "Whatever. Why don't you run it through your database and see if it comes up with anything?"

"And why would I do that?"

She raised her hands in exasperation. "Maybe the rest of the truck is buried around here too. And potentially," she added, "it might have something to do with another case."

"Wow, you're really desperate and bored."

"Not anymore," she said. "Apparently we have another murder case to solve." She beamed up at him.

He shook his head. "No, no, no, no, no. *I* have a new case to solve. *You* don't."

"It's not my fault somebody killed her while I was out there."

"What do you mean, they killed her while you were out there?"

"While I was at the run-down house, I heard the gunshots. As I told you."

"We only have your word for that." His gaze narrowed at her in warning.

"Are you telling me that you haven't gone inside the house to check?"

"We have officers there now," he said. "We had no reason to go inside the first time."

"Good," she said. "I was afraid, just because I was the one who told you about it, that you might get stubborn and not check it out. But, if that's the actual crime scene, well, all your forensic evidence will be there."

"Thank you very much for your Detective 101 insights," he said sarcastically.

She punched her hands onto her hips. "If you're in a bad mood, you can leave."

"I want one of my IT guys to look at your phone, see if we can trace your threatening caller."

She ignored him but knew he would win out in the end.

It was his turn to raise his hands in surrender. "What is it about you," he asked, "that sends me around the bend?"

"I'm irresistible," she said. "If nothing else, you get to solve cold cases. Maybe they'll give you a medal for the Betty Miles case."

"It should be you who gets the medal," he muttered.

"Okay, does it come with a cash reward?" She shot him a cheeky grin.

At that, he snorted. "No, you're supposed to do your duty as a good citizen."

"Yeah," she said. "The trouble is, this citizen is broke."

"Did you check with Wendy?"

Doreen nodded. "I did. But I didn't understand that ninety-day accounting stuff."

His face turned sympathetic. "It makes sense she would do it that way."

"I guess," Doreen said. "But I have to wait a long time for that money." Then she brightened. "On the other hand, I did start going through Nan's stuff in the master bedroom. I found a whole pile of clothes that I'll keep," she said. "And I found a couple hundred bucks in cash already." She beamed. "I don't know how she got through life losing that kind of money all the time. But I'm grateful for it."

"Did you ever consider she might have salted the clothing?"

"Salted?" She couldn't make the connection between adding salt to clothing and why Nan would do that.

His face broke into a wide grin. "Meaning, she might have planted that money in the pockets for you to find."

She stared at him blankly. "Do you think Nan would do that?" Doreen hoped not. Made her feel like a pity case.

"No idea," he said. "But, if you think about it, she knew you were in a tough spot. This is a great way for you to find extra money."

She frowned. "Well, I can kind of see her doing it. But Nan should keep her money. It takes some of the fun out of it."

"So forget about it," he said. "Just because it could be a salted gold mine, doesn't mean it is." When his phone rang, he answered it as he turned away from her. "Okay, fine," he said. "I'll be there right away." He turned back to her. "I've got to leave. Try to stay out of trouble."

"What are you talking about?" she asked. And then she spied the expression on his face and knew. She asked eagerly, "They found something at the Hawthorne house, didn't they?"

He shrugged and walked toward his car.

She ran up behind him, Mugs running ahead, Goliath weaving between their feet. Almost tripping over him, she swore, "Goliath, damn it. Get out of the way."

Mack laughed. "See? Even your animals are trying to keep you in line."

"Good luck with that," she scoffed. "I'm right though, aren't I? Aren't I?"

He glared at her.

"Yes, I am," she said. "Woohoo! Now what you really should do is thank me for that because I just made your job much easier."

At the corner of her house he spun around. "And how do you think this phone call had anything to do with you?"

"I told you where the shooting took place," she said. "I found you one body. So do I also have to find her killer?" she added with a note of asperity in her voice.

"Just because you saw two people arguing at a public store," he said, "doesn't mean he shot her."

"No, of course not," she said, trying for a bland face. "But, then again, it's a good place to start."

"No," he said with a meaningful smile on his face. "We'll start with the body at the crime scene." And then he was gone.

It took her a minute to think through his last statement. She ran out to the front yard. "You mean, there's a second body?" she cried out.

She came to a dead stop as reporters stood, eager to hear her words. *I walked right into this media nightmare, didn't I?* She shook her head as Mack drove away, a big grin on his face. She turned around and hastily ran to her backyard. For the first time in a long time, she closed the gate with a firm *click* behind her. Maybe that would keep out the predators. She couldn't guarantee it, but she could hope.

In the backyard, she walked onto the veranda and sat down with her cell to see if there was any news on Celeste's body. Sometimes the local stations did a pretty decent job in keeping up. Indeed, already a report on a body had been made because of the unexplained police presence at the Family Planning Center.

Thaddeus hopped up onto the veranda table, checking to see if any birdseed was here. She looked at him and said, "You know what? Because you're eating enough for two, I'd wonder if you were pregnant."

He gave her his most shocked look. She burst out laughing. As she did, her phone rang. She looked down to see it was Nan. "Hi, Nan," Doreen said gaily as she got up and refilled her cup with the now-cold coffee from the pot. It had shut off while she was outside with Mack.

"How are you, dear?"

"I'm fine," she said. "What's up?"

"I just worry about the effect on your mental health when you keep finding all these dead bodies."

"I didn't say anything about finding any dead body," she said. "What are you getting at, Nan?"

"Well, a dead body was found," she said, "and I'm pretty darn sure you're the one who found it."

"What makes you say that?" she asked warily.

"Because you're finding all the dead bodies so far. You really should allow other people to find them."

Doreen stared aghast at her phone. "Nan, you make it sound like I'm being greedy."

"Well, you are, in a way."

"Do *you* want to find dead bodies?" she asked her grandmother.

"No, no, of course not. But, if you find them all, what are the police supposed to do?" she said in her most reasonable tone.

Along with most of the other conversations with Nan, this one had turned bizarre. "Are you just fishing for information for the betting pools?"

"Of course not," she said. "I'm really worried about your health. Your mental health."

"My health is just fine. I'm worried about my bank account," she said bluntly.

"Did you contact Wendy?" Nan asked curiously. "She should have some money for you by now."

"Why does everybody ask me that?" Doreen asked, laughing. "Yes, I did. And, yes, a few things have sold, but I won't be paid any money for at least three months."

"Oh my," Nan said. "That doesn't sound fair."

"I don't know if it's fair or not, but it's the way Wendy does business," Doreen said. "It doesn't really leave me a lot of options."

"What about the antiques?"

"Wendy did give me the name of somebody to contact. A German guy who works at the Mission Bible Thrift Store on a volunteer basis to fix small appliances or something."

"Fen Gunderson?" Nan asked, her voice rising.

"Yes that's the man."

"He had an antique shop," she said, "but I'm not sure he isn't a bit of a thief."

Doreen shook her head at that. "Why would you say that?"

"Because Gloria bought a toaster from that place which he supposedly fixed. She took it home, and the first time she used it, there was a puff of black smoke, and the darn thing never worked again."

Doreen could hardly hold back her smile. "How much did she pay for it?" she asked gently.

"A whole two dollars," Nan said. "She was really upset."

"Did she take it back?"

"Of course not," she said. "The store has a no-refunds policy. But she did talk to him about it when she went there the next time. They were not helpful. As a matter of fact, I think they thought she should have been delighted to have found one at all, and its working condition was not guaranteed."

Doreen could just imagine. She stood here, grinning like a fool, as she thought about how much coming to Kelowna and living close to Nan had enriched her life. Nan and her friends at that old folks' home were such characters. "Maybe she should buy another one," Doreen suggested.

"Why waste another two dollars?" Nan asked.

Thinking of Mack's words earlier, Doreen asked, "Nan, did you leave money in your clothing in the upstairs bedroom?"

"What's that, dear?" Nan's voice sounded distracted. "I probably did. You already found some in the spare bedroom. So why wouldn't I have left some in the master bedroom?"

"I have no idea," she said. "It's all right that you did. I just wouldn't want you to have done it on purpose."

"Why would I do something like that on purpose?" Nan asked, curiosity in their voice. "That would be foolish."

"Are you sure you're okay for money?" Doreen worried her bottom lip. "You can have all the money I find. You know that, right?"

"We've already discussed this before, dear. Yes, I'm fine," Nan said. "You know I have lots of money. All the money and the contents of that house are yours to keep."

"Are you sure?" Doreen asked. "I do worry you don't have enough money."

"Oh, my dear, I'm so grateful that you're close by. You do warm my heart."

As her words replicated what Doreen's thoughts had been earlier, she had to smile. "I love you too, Nan."

And, with that, Nan hung up.

Chapter 9

Thursday late afternoon...

DOREEN STILL HAD a little of the afternoon ahead of her. As she sat here at her kitchen table, she wondered about the common sense of doing something with that proposal to bid on landscaping the city's beds. It had to be submitted by tonight.

Bringing up the website link Mack had given her, she wrote up something, keeping her almost ex-husband's constant business lessons in mind. *Give them lots of details that say nothing. Make it detailed enough that they get an idea. Keep it vague enough that you don't promise anything.*

She sighed. "I hate to think I've learned anything useful from you, you big rat," she snapped. She left the laptop open with the draft onscreen, then saved it to make sure she didn't have to redo it all. She only had another four or five hours left to submit her bid. She was still undecided if she should or not.

She took a look around for food, realizing she had little more than the last of the carrot cake and half sandwich. She scoffed the sandwich only to realize it wasn't enough to keep her going. She'd need to round out her meal with ramen noodles again.

She studied the stove for a long moment, knowing she still had days to go until the omelet lesson. Just the thought of an omelet was enough to make her taste buds drool. She looked forward to learning how to cook anything. The internet was full of all kinds of tips, and the food created always looked absolutely *fantabulous*. Then she looked at all the foodie shows online, but nobody there really dealt with the beginner stuff.

She grabbed a package of ramen noodles, stuck them in a bowl, covered it in water, and put it in the microwave. She knew that true foodies would be horrified by what she did, but, hey, it was food. She brought out the carrot cake, set it on a plate on the table, and went in search of protein. But she didn't have a whole lot left. Then she remembered the rest of the rotisserie chicken.

She pulled out the one-fourth left, and, with a grin at her odd pairing of ramen noodles, carrot cake, and one-quarter of a roasted chicken, she sat down to a meal. Her tummy was almost full when she was done, and, with a cup of tea and the carrot cake she had yet to eat, she moved upstairs to the bedroom.

There was just something about treasure hunting, about going through Nan's clothes and finding money. Just like the last time, Doreen brought a bowl to collect everything she found. That included the change purse, two fifty-dollar bills and several smaller bills and lots of little stuff.

As far as she was concerned, this closet was a gold mine. She kept hoping she could find more in other areas of the house but figured she needed to finish this room first. She hadn't forgotten about the garage sale idea, but she hadn't done anything about it yet. Meanwhile, she had to sort more clothes to take to Wendy. That was what she would do now.

With that thought in mind, she delved back into the master bedroom closet. It was a much slower process in this bedroom because Doreen found a lot of clothes she didn't want to give away. A lot of them would sell easily at the consignment store because they were so unique. But, at the same time, Doreen didn't want to let go of anything that she could use herself because shopping for new clothes was horrifically expensive.

Nan had traveled a lot in her younger years, and it looked like she'd bought a lot of clothes from her various holiday destinations. And thankfully she hadn't bought touristy things. No T-shirts with the names of Hawaii and various cities on them were found, but several really nice, long flowing skirts she set off to one side after checking to make sure they had no pockets.

Then she found a cropped jacket that had a small pocket in it. And she crowed with delight when she pulled out a five-dollar bill from the pocket. Nan's closet was such a life-saver in so many ways. It kept Doreen busy when she was bored. It gave her enough pocket change to definitely keep Doreen alive right now while she figured out how to get on her feet. Then the consignment store sales would bring in more money later.

Doreen had no problem with getting a job she could do, but she hoped not to go into a fast-food industry or waitress-ing. Although the thought of getting a meal as part of her hours was not something to scoff at.

She'd definitely lost weight since she'd moved into Nan's house. Ramen noodles didn't provide a ton of nutritional benefits, but she was doing her best with what she got. She was proud of how far she'd come.

Honestly, she was damn proud of helping solve these cold cases. If the police department would even say thanks by way of food, she'd be happy.

The little jacket in her hand was also gorgeous. She had to put it on. It stopped just at her ribs and looked awesome. It was an emerald green, but it wasn't flashy. Knowing she couldn't let it go, she put it off to the side with the other things she was keeping for herself and reached for another item hanging in the closet.

The next piece was a strapless gown. She had to wonder how long these clothes had been around. *Long enough that they were now back in fashion?* She knew this dress wasn't her color, and she'd never wear it, so she searched through the folds to make sure no money was tucked in the bra cups, like she'd found before. Finding nothing, she then put this one in the consignment store pile.

As soon as she gained more room in the closet, she could get her own stuff better sorted. Not that she had much, but she still had a suitcase she had yet to open. Determined to make a bigger dent in the closet than she had so far, she grabbed ten more hangers and brought them out, laying them on the bed. And one by one she went through them. She found another pocketful of change and a twenty-dollar bill tucked inside one of the dresses.

Nan obviously didn't want to go out without money, and she wore designer clothes that absolutely wouldn't allow for purses or sweaters or jackets without detracting from the overall look. So she had tucked money inside.

With Doreen very carefully going through each piece of apparel, she ended up with a small fortune in Nan's pin money. It was a lovely system of using safety pins to keep money in her clothing. Of those last ten items alone, Doreen ended up putting all but one into the consignment store pile.

Afraid she'd missed something in them, she would go through each piece again before she tucked them into the bag going to Wendy. This was kind of like a sport.

With those hangers done, she grabbed another ten. As she brought them out of the closet and lay them on the bed, she realized the closet rod was still too full to accept any of Doreen's own pieces. Nan had jammed in years and years, if not decades upon decades, of clothing in there. Doreen would spend days sorting through this.

She pulled up the first piece on top of the newest pile, a pantsuit with pockets that held money. She decided this was the best closet-sorting process she'd been through yet. The jacket had money in the inside pocket, which looked like a twenty-dollar bill when she pulled it out. But she was delighted to find a fifty tucked inside it too. She checked all the other pockets, then went through the pants. Sure enough, tucked inside with a safety pin was another ten. It was also an excellent suit, made of wool.

Frowning, she set it off to the side that she'd keep for herself. She'd try on all these in that pile to see if they would look good on her before making her final decision to keep any. She was a bit of a clotheshorse, and some of these items were quality made, as in a serious quality.

She went through the next few dresses, more of a shirt-waist style. But only one of them had a pocket yielding a five-dollar bill tucked inside. She put three dresses in the consignment store pile and then found another silk dress to add to Wendy's pile.

Doreen gasped when she held up the gold lamé. "Wow, Nan. This is incredible."

And again, tucked inside the bra cup, she found a ten-dollar bill. This one was hard to see. It had a slice in the material and just a bill folded up inside. Very smart of Nan. Again this made Doreen worry she'd missed something in all the others.

She squeezed the dress slightly to make sure nothing more was tucked inside but didn't find anything. Another stack on the bed had been done. Staring at the growing pile of bills in her bowl, she realized Nan had lost some serious money here.

She rephrased that because Nan hadn't lost it. She had deliberately pinned money inside so that, if she was out for an evening, she didn't have to take a purse. It was an interesting concept. It had also meant Nan had a lot more disposable cash than Doreen had supposed.

By the time she went through three more stacks of ten hangers, she had created a slight bit of relief in the over-crowded closet. She could now shuffle the hangers back and forth a little with at least an inch or two of room.

Her consignment store collection was massive too. She grinned at that. But the bowl on the bed with the multitudinous bills and coins made her really smile. Although the stacked clothes she meant to keep were also pretty damn fine. Nothing in that pile would really work for around the house, or for her nonexistent job, but at least it gave her clothes to wear to go out, should she ever get that opportunity. Deciding she'd take one more big stack from the closet, she grabbed what looked like at least fifteen hangers this time. She could almost hear the closet groan with relief, and the rod seemed to spring back up as she took more weight off it.

"Sorry, old house. You've really been abused, haven't you? Unintentionally of course."

She laid the hangers on the bed, once again marveling at the diversity of clothing, everything from pants to jackets to sweaters to dresses to skirts. There was just everything. In the middle of the pile appeared to be two bathrobes too. She held them up, looking at them critically. No money was in either of them, but she didn't have a decent bathrobe as she'd forgotten her silk one in one of the places she'd stayed. These were quite nice, kind of like those found in the five-star hotels. She set them off to the side and made her way through the rest of the clothing.

When she came to four pairs of pants, she pulled them out one by one, checked the pockets, found money in every one of them and several pieces of paper. She dumped all the contents, checked the pants over thoroughly, and held them up to her waist, finding they were all too short for her. When she thought about that and considered the capri styles of today, she couldn't just throw them out. They were good quality, and she might have a need for them. She put them in her pile to keep and found she was running about fifty-fifty on the pile sizes.

For a long moment she felt guilty about that because, if she could sell something, she needed the money more than the clothes. And then she realized it didn't matter, since this was just her first round. She would end up trying on twenty or thirty of them, keeping only one in ten hopefully. She just needed to keep doing what she was doing.

The trouble was, she was getting tired, and it was dark out. Tomorrow would be a whole new day. She sat down on the bed. When her phone rang, she picked it up and looked at the Unknown Caller designation. She snorted and answered it. "What do you want?"

She heard a startled gasp on the other end.

Getting angry, she added. "Stop stalking me."

"Me?" the person asked. "Who are you talking to?"

"Well, you called me," she said. "What do you want?"

"I was talking to Wendy at the consignment store," the man nearly yelled.

Immediately she realized what she'd done. "Oh, my goodness. Is this Fen Gunderson?"

"Yes," he said. "Who did you think you were speaking to?"

"Somebody made three nasty phone calls to me last night," she said in a rush of shock. "I'm so sorry. I assumed it was him when I saw it was an Unknown Caller."

He sounded mollified at that. "Wendy said you're looking for some assistance with antiques."

She bounced off the bed. "Yes! Nan's house is full of them, but I don't know what might be worth anything and what's really better off at a garage sale."

"I could come by and take a look, if you'd like," he said. "But apparently you've got an awful lot going on. Maybe you don't want me interfering."

"I'd love your help," she said. "Honestly, … if you wouldn't mind, I would absolutely so appreciate your assistance."

"When?" he asked. "I don't have too much free time."

"I understand," she said. "Anytime that works for you would be great."

"Maybe tomorrow?" he asked. "Tomorrow is Friday."

"Tomorrow is perfect. What time?"

"I start at the Mission Bible Thrift Store at noon," he said. "How about I come by, … let's say, at ten o'clock?"

"Perfect," she agreed. "And again I'm so sorry."

"If you have a phone stalker, I can understand your reaction. You stay safe now." And he hung up.

"Oh, my goodness. I'm so bad at this. I didn't even give the poor man a chance to speak," she told the animals.

Goliath looked completely uninterested, as if he expected that from her.

Mugs was stretched out on the bed with his eyes closed. She'd covered him up with half the clothing as it was.

She would never get to bed if she didn't at least sort through the mess she had piled there. So she grabbed one of the large bags she'd found in the bottom of Nan's closet, confirming it was empty first, and then went through every piece once more before giving it to the consignment store. She found another ten-dollar bill, but that was it.

With all the clothes bagged up for consignment, she made a heap on the nearby chair of all the clothes she contemplated keeping. Then she quickly undressed, got ready for bed, and curled up under the blankets.

Thankfully no more threatening calls came that night.

Chapter 10

Friday morning…

SHE WOKE UP the next morning, bouncy and full of energy. She would finally get some answers about all the antiques on the property. And then she'd talk to Nan about it because no way would Doreen sell specific pieces of value without Nan's permission. Regardless of its worth, maybe Nan had an emotional or sentimental attachment to some of them.

Breakfast first, then a little bit of gardening in her own backyard, and she found herself waiting impatiently for Fen Gunderson to arrive. When she finally saw a vehicle drive up and park in her driveway, she rushed out the front door. The older man who walked up had a cane and appeared to be one step away from death. But then he smiled at her, and she realized he was probably only about in his mid-seventies.

She walked down the front porch steps to meet him. "Thank you so much for coming," she said with a bright smile. "Let me apologize again for the poor reception you got from me on the phone last night."

He waved away her words. "No apology necessary. Particularly when you live alone. One can't be too careful."

She agreed. So far, she hadn't been too concerned for herself or the house, but, if valuable antiques were here ... She led the way up the front steps, then turned to him. "Did you know my grandmother?"

He stopped and frowned. "Did she pass on?"

"Oh, my goodness, no," she said. "She used to live here, that's all. That's why the past tense. She's at Rosemoor Manor."

A look of relief settled on his face. "Oh, that's good," he said. "I've known Nan for a long time. She's quite a character."

Doreen wasn't sure from his tone whether he meant that in a good way or a bad way. She imagined Nan had created both her share of enemies and friends.

Doreen led him inside to the living room. "She left me everything in this house," she said. "As you can see, it's incredibly overstuffed. And I would like to sort through what is of value and what isn't."

He stopped in his tracks and looked around the room. "Wow. She has packed it full, hasn't she?"

Doreen chuckled. Mugs, who'd been on the front porch steps with her, kept sniffing around the old man's trousers. She reached down and pulled him back. "Now you stay out of the way, Mugs."

At that moment, Thaddeus, snoozing atop his living room roost, opened his eyes and squawked at the disturbance. Doreen walked over and chuckled. "Sorry, Thaddeus. We didn't mean to disturb your sleep."

Fen smiled. "Isn't that a treat? I've met this guy a time or two."

Thaddeus crowed, "A time or two. A time or two."

And they both chuckled.

She motioned at the living room as a whole. "Maybe we should start here."

He agreed. He leaned his cane against one of the chairs and walked toward the nearest piece of furniture, a large rich mahogany hutch pushed up against the staircase. She figured it was about six feet tall and took up a good four-foot-wide space. A nice piece but she'd do a lot to be rid of it. It really slowed progress down the hallway. Plus it was in the way, and it made the room look so much smaller.

Fen nodded, then looked at it again. "Can you pull it out slightly?"

She joined him at that side of the hutch, reached down, and pulled it forward slightly, thankful it shifted relatively easily on the hardwood floor. She didn't want to scrape the floor and damage it or the piece.

He muttered as he looked over the back of the hutch, then returned to the front, and continued to murmur.

She wasn't exactly sure if the muttering was good or bad or if he was not quite all here. She walked into the kitchen, grabbed a notepad, took a picture of the piece they were discussing, and put a numeral one on top of the notepad page.

When he finally turned to her, he said, "It's a nice piece, not very rare, but it's a good maker. Hannover always was known for the pride of their product. But their stuff before 1960 was better. This is a 1960s piece," he said. "I can't find any proof of that of course, but I would wager this is some of their lesser quality work."

She frowned at that. "So this is a less valuable piece because of that?"

He nodded sagely. "Yes, my dear. It'll still fetch you a nice price. You know, maybe eleven to twelve hundred dollars."

She stared at him. "How much?"

"Eleven to twelve hundred dollars. Now if we could prove some kind of a history to it, we'd likely get more, and provenance would help to age it properly. If it is before 1960, it would be worth twice that."

She made notes as fast as she could as he continued on and on about the color and the stain job and the corners. Something about how the corners had been done was extra special. So it made him question the 1960 date of the piece. He'd gone back to muttering as he opened every drawer, every door, checking the joints inside and out.

Finally he turned and said, "Ask your grandmother if you would find any receipts for it."

She nodded. "I will."

With his help, she moved the piece back up against the wall. "Well, that's obviously worth a more favorable amount of money than I had expected," she admitted.

He turned and pointed to the small corner table in the back. "Now that is worth a small fortune." He looked at her. "Do you mind if I take a closer look?"

She shook her head. "Please, be my guest."

She took a picture of the item as he muttered over it. It was just a small corner table. But he had it upside down, tapping the base.

"Take a picture of this," he said, "because that's your maker's mark. And that's what makes this worth at least seven, maybe eight thousand dollars."

She froze, almost dropped her notebook and pencil. "For *that* piece?" Her voice rose in a squeak.

He nodded. "Absolutely." He looked at it again. "It's a lovely piece." He stroked the top in admiration, almost as if it was a loved one or a beloved pet. He sighed happily. "That is so worth making the trip for."

"I'm so glad you're here," she said. She didn't want to admit to him that she had been ready to put it outside at the curb and stick a Free sign on it to see if anybody wanted to come by and cart it off for her.

"When you're ready to sell some of these pieces," he said, "let me know, and I'll put you in touch with an auction house."

"Is that a good idea?" she asked anxiously. "Isn't an antiques dealer better to deal with?"

"You could, but then you'll lose money on their commission, which usually runs thirty percent," he said. "Special antique auctions are held where you'll get top dollar. Still have to pay a commission, but the auctions usually command a much higher selling price."

"Wow," she muttered as she continued to write.

After that he studied piece after piece after piece. And one that she particularly liked was all done in knotty pine. He looked at it, shook his head, and said, "This is one of those Swedish put-together-from-a-box things. I think they call it prebox." He never checked for a maker's mark.

She stared at it. "I really like it."

He shot her a look of disgust. "You're surrounded by beautiful pieces, and you chose the cheapest in the entire place." He shook his head and moved on to the next item.

She groaned. "I think it was the color of the wood I liked," she offered. She didn't want him to look at her lack of taste and take it as her disdain of the work he did.

"That's what all wood looks like," he said, "before it's treated. Most of these pieces are stained. That one barely has any finish on it." He stroked the side of it and said, "You feel that roughness to it?"

She reached out and nodded.

"That's because they didn't do a full sanding, another coat, then another sanding, followed by another coat. All they did was a basic sealant. Cheap," he said. "Keep it if you must, if you like it. But, since you're looking to sell some of these pieces, then sell the ones you don't care about. Because a lot of money is here in this living room."

By the time they had gone through just this room, she was stunned. So many of these pieces were real antiques. Her soon-to-be ex-husband would be over the moon. Nan had never, in any way, made a comment about the value of the pieces she'd left behind. It was just too much for Doreen.

She sat down on the couch beside Fen. "May I get you a cup of tea?"

He looked at her gratefully. "If you wouldn't mind," he said, "a glass of water would be preferred."

She nodded and rushed into the kitchen, where she poured him a glass of water and put on the teakettle for her.

When she returned, he was studying the couch under the window. It had faded and showed its age. But it had big wooden arms sticking out from the big puffy cushions. And all along the back was more wood. Ornate scrolls covered the entire thing. It was comfortable, but it was very outdated. She wasn't a fan.

Goliath, on the other hand, lying atop the back of the couch, appeared to love it. He stared at the stranger in the house, and the stranger stared back.

She was about to hand Fen his glass of water when he said, "You do realize that cat is lying on a ten thousand dollar piece of furniture?"

She almost dropped the glass of water as she gave it to

him. "How much?" she asked in a faint voice.

He smiled. "You had no idea, did you?"

She moved her head from side to side. "No. But it is definitely music to my ears."

"If you're not an antiques person," he said, "you're sitting on a gold mine."

She pointed to the couch and questioned, "Literally?"

He patted the side. "We need to see the underside. Although I already know what this is. It's a Queen Anne couch. Circa 1818," he said. "You can tell from the designs on the footings here."

She was seriously gobsmacked. She sank down into a chair. "I had no clue." She hated to envision that all her money worries were over because, so far, these were just figures. Not a sale in hand nor any money in her fist.

He pointed at the chair she was in. "That is a matching chair you're sitting in."

She bounced up. "Is it worth something too?"

"Because you have this partial set," he said, "the two pieces, it'll add another easy five thousand dollars, possibly ten thousand dollars to the total price. It was part of a large bedroom set originally. I doubt you'd have the other pieces, but I'm happy to see this much of one."

She wanted to break out in a song and dance, but, at the same time, she could feel the tremors rocking through her. "I need to talk to Nan," she said. "I wonder if she had any idea."

"Oh, she knows," he said. "I talked to her about this couch a long time ago." He looked around and frowned. "Do you know where the other chair is?"

She looked at him blankly.

He pointed at the chair. "Nan used to have two of

them."

Doreen said, "Just a minute." She ran upstairs. Sure enough, in the master bedroom, underneath the heap of clothing she had taken off her bed last night, was the matching chair. Carefully she removed the clothing and picked up the chair, carrying it to the living room.

His face lit up when he saw it. "Turn it upside down for me, will you?" She flipped it over, and he crowed with delight. "See here? That's the maker's mark you want, and it confirms it's part of the same set." He sighed happily. "Please tell me that you'll sell these."

"Oh, I'm selling them," she said. "I can't afford not to."

"You see? That's where you're different from Nan. She could afford not to. She loved them, and she used them well. In your case, if you don't love them and could use the money, you're probably better off selling them." He shot a look at the cat again, who was now stretched out over the couch cushion. "The more damage, the less value."

She wanted to snatch up Goliath. But he was likely to dig in his claws even deeper.

He eyed the coffee table. "That may be part of the original set as well, if you find a maker's mark underneath. I'll leave that to you. Plus we really need those provenance papers."

She nodded. "How could this set possibly not sell?"

"The animals could deteriorate the value very quickly." He chuckled. "When I get home, I'll make a few calls. I might get an appraiser to connect with you. Better to get one who can deal with buyers too."

"Yes, please," she said. "Selling these pieces would help a lot to open up this living room."

He nodded. "And, while you're at it, you may want to

offer up the Turkish rug you're standing on."

She jumped back onto the hardwood floor.

He nodded. "It's very old. I've talked to Nan several times about selling it."

"It's for sale," Doreen said, hating the busy pattern, making it hard to see anything else in the room. "But it does need a major cleaning."

"Don't touch it," he said. "You'll ruin it."

"Why is that?"

"Because it's wool with silk threads through it. It must be commercially cleaned by a specialist."

She swallowed hard and nodded. She hated to even think about the number of times she might have spilled tea on it. "I know I sound terribly money-minded, but what would something like that fetch?"

He shrugged. "The appraiser will do a much better job at estimating its current worth. But I would say at least six, maybe seven thousand dollars. It could easily be twice that, depending on the condition of the rug after a proper cleaning." He leaned over and separated the threads.

She could see the deep rich cream color underneath. "Is it supposed to be that color?"

He smiled. "The damage doesn't appear to be all the way through. It's just surface dirt, so it should wash well."

She wanted to sit down but didn't have a clue where she could possibly sit. And then she looked over at the hearth of the fireplace, which she had yet to light, and sat down on the slate. "The sooner you can put me in touch with somebody, the better," she said quietly.

"What about Nan?"

She nodded and held up her notebook. "I'll visit her this afternoon."

"Good." He straightened up. "Maybe I could come back in a few days, after you talk to the appraiser." He looked around the room. "Honestly, the sooner you sort out these pieces, the better, so you can see what else is here. It takes time to go through so many pieces."

She nodded. "Absolutely. Thanks for offering. First though is the appraiser. You will send me the contact information, won't you?"

"I don't plan to die on the way home, so you'll be sure to get it when I get there."

She flushed. "I'm so sorry." She blustered her way through an apology. "I don't know what's gotten into me."

"You see a sudden source of income here, and I imagine you've had a pretty rough time of it lately," he said. "But I'm happy the antiques will reenter the world to some collector who will love them. Nan has loved them, but her time here has gone. And they're not your thing, are they?"

She winced. "Not really."

He looked scathingly over at the light-colored pine hutch. "Anybody who loves this should part with the antiques." He made his way out the door.

"That doesn't mean I don't want to see these items go to somebody who will love them," she said quickly.

He waved at her. "I'll call you when I get home."

And she had to be satisfied with that.

Chapter 11

Friday early afternoon...

S HE WENT INSIDE, made herself a cup of tea, and sat at the kitchen table in a daze. The numbers on her page were adding up to an incredible amount. So much so that she had to stop looking at that figure because, like Fen had said, he wasn't an appraiser. It had been his business, but he was out of that. She needed an appraiser, and she needed somebody who would buy this furniture from her. Its estimated value was absolutely unbelievable.

It was already almost one o'clock. And now she felt even worse for her lack of manners. She should have offered him tea earlier and something to eat. But what? She had nothing to eat herself. Still, her lack of manners, something that would never have happened when she was still living with her husband, horrified her.

She sat, drinking her tea and munching on crackers. She checked the time, wondering if it was a good time to visit Nan. It was a balance between Nan's meals, her social life, and naps.

Finally she couldn't wait any longer. She picked up the phone and called her grandmother. "Hey, Nan, are you up for a visit?"

"Always. Did you have any specific reason?" she asked.

"I just spoke with Fen."

"Absolutely," she said, "come on down then. I'll put on the teakettle."

Hanging up the phone, Doreen finished the last of her cup of tea and called the animals to her. She put the leash on Mugs and looked over at Goliath. "Do you want to come too?"

His tail switched, as if saying, *Do cats meow?*

Thaddeus walked up Doreen's arm and perched himself on her shoulder. He was strangely still. She wasn't sure if that was a yawn or just a sleepy-eyed look at her. But he kept opening his beak, as if taking gulps of air.

She walked out the door of the kitchen and then raced back to lock the door. She'd always been incredibly cavalier about locking up the place. But now that she knew so much money was tied up in the furniture, she was almost giddy with excitement, and yet, petrified with worry. What if somebody stole the things now that she'd had the estimator in here? And how could she stop anybody from finding out? That would be the problem with telling Nan.

Doreen frowned as she considered the issue, walking toward Nan's apartment. When they got there, she looked around. Dennis, the gardener for Rosemoor, was at the other end and quite busy. With Mugs in hand, she raced across the grass. She just made it onto the patio when Dennis, as if knowing she was here, turned and lifted the shovel, shaking it at her. She just smiled and motioned at Nan, seated at her bistro table.

Nan chuckled. "You two do have fun fighting, don't you?"

Doreen pulled out a chair. "Not really." She glanced at her grandmother to catch the sparkle in her eyes. "You look like you've been having a fun morning."

Nan went off in a bout of chuckles. "We set up a whole pile of betting pools," she said. "It's great stuff." She reached over and patted Doreen's hand. "I think you have done so much for this town."

"Thanks, Nan," she said drily. "You know I intended on making a good impression," she said. "Not making a fool out of myself and becoming notorious."

Nan waved away her granddaughter's objections. "*Pshaw*," she said. "I'm too old to care, and you're too young to let it bother you. Forget about the others."

Easy for Nan to say. Because, in a way, she *was* too old to care. Nan had been doing her thing for a long time. In Doreen's case, she was just figuring out what her thing was. She waited until the tea was poured and then asked, "Nan, you said I could have everything in the house. Is that correct?"

Nan nodded. "Did you find more pocketsful of money?" she asked with a twinkle. "I used to leave money attached inside my dresses. We had the cutest little safety pins, and the money would slide in the clothes wherever, and you'd never know. Then I didn't have to take a purse. Purses were such a drag, especially when dancing. Any time I took a purse, I forgot it, lost it, dropped it at least half a dozen times. They're really no fun to look after."

Doreen nodded. "But back then you had coat checks, didn't you?"

"Of course, but a purse was an accessory. It's not like you would hand that over, would you?"

"I guess not."

"Certainly not. Like you wouldn't hand over a necklace or a bracelet," Nan added.

As Doreen thought about how much purses were an accessory for a woman, she realized how accurate Nan's comment was. "True."

"Exactly," she said. "And, yes, I did say that you can have everything in the house."

Doreen was still figuring out if purses went into coat checks or not and had to bring her mind back to the real topic of their conversation. She smiled. "Apparently you have a lot of valuable antiques in your house."

"*Your* house," Nan said comfortably. "I do love those antiques," she said. "But, after a while, they wear on you."

"Sorry?" Doreen asked in confusion. Sometimes she wondered if Nan deliberately changed conversations on her to confuse her. "Regardless. I understand that you've had them for a long time." She spoke cautiously. "So I wondered if you would have a problem if I got rid of a few of them."

"Don't worry about those pieces. I figured you'd want to redecorate," Nan said. "An old woman's old house full of old furnishings is hardly appropriate for a young vibrant woman, like you."

"But they are worth a lot of money," Doreen argued. She didn't want there to be any misunderstandings. "And that is your money. Those are your antiques, and I don't want to take that money away from you."

Nan looked at her. "They won't be worth *that* much money." She settled back comfortably.

"They are worth *a lot* of money," Doreen corrected. "Why didn't you sell them?"

"Oh, because they brought me good memories. And, when you get to be my age, and you don't need the money, memories that make you smile are worth everything."

Doreen could see that, but, for her, it was an astronomical amount of money. She still worried that Nan didn't realize just how much money was involved. "Did Fen ever tell you how much all that stuff was worth?"

"Well, I paid a pretty penny for some of it," Nan admitted. "And it's probably aged nicely with time."

"He wanted me to ask you if you have some kind of written history—receipts—on the pieces. He said it would increase their value."

Nan tapped her fingers on the bistro table. "I had a large folder with all that stuff. Or maybe several folders." She pursed her lips. "I can't remember where that went. Give me time to think about it, and I might remember."

"And …" Doreen said. "I'm still really worried that, if I sell some of those pieces, you'll be upset afterward."

Nan looked at her in surprise and chuckled. "I get that you're really worried about me, sweetie, and I appreciate that. There's nothing more valuable in my old age than to know you care about what happens to me."

"But, Nan, some of those pieces are worth *big* money," she said.

Nan leaned forward and asked, "How much?"

"Ten, twenty, thirty, forty thousand *dollars*," Doreen whispered in a very low voice. "It could add up to a ton of money."

Nan looked at her for a long moment and then said, "So, if you put all that money in the bank, you could earn interest off it—enough so you could live off it, couldn't you?"

Doreen stared at Nan, tears slowly filling her eyes.

Nan reached over, covered her hand, and said, "We have

a shared goal, my dear. And that's to make sure you're well taken care of. If those old pieces of mine can bring you a pretty penny, then you do your utmost to get the most for them that you can. Do you hear me?" She waved her teaspoon. "Don't you let anybody steal that stuff from you."

"Fen Gunderson went over the pieces in the living room this morning," Doreen said. "He's supposed to get me in contact with an appraiser."

Nan chuckled. "Wait until he sees the basement then."

Doreen's heart almost stopped. She leaned forward and whispered hoarsely, "Are you saying more antiques are down there?"

Nan looked at her and then laughed. "Oh my, you haven't been down there yet, have you?"

Doreen stared at her. "Honestly, I didn't remember there was a basement."

"Yeah, the door is behind all the furniture in the living room," she said. "That's why you haven't found it." She chuckled. "You know something? You might get enough money out of that old house of mine to set up a nice little trust fund, and you won't need a full-time day job. You could do what you want to do. Set yourself up a little garden design business. Or sit in the backyard and have a cup of tea and do nothing."

"I'd rather be an amateur sleuth," Doreen said with a wicked grin at her grandmother.

At that, Nan went off again in laughter. When she finally calmed down, she leaned forward. "What body did you find this time?"

Knowing she had to give her something after the conversation they'd just had, Doreen said, "You can't tell anybody and no betting pools. Promise?"

Nan frowned, warring with that. Finally she nodded. "But only because you insist. I promise."

Doreen told her about the woman she had found in front of the Family Planning Center. "Her name, according to Mack, is Celeste Bingham. I met her earlier that day too, making finding her that much worse."

Nan gasped, her hand going to her chest. "Seriously?"

Doreen nodded. "I was looking at beds of carnations, thinking about the city asking for bids, and found three in town to look at. That center was the last one I went to." She frowned and thought about it. "I think I was supposed to submit that last night." She reached up and rubbed her lip. "Darn. I missed the deadline." She looked at Nan. "I was on the fence about whether to submit a bid. I don't do this on purpose, you know?"

Nan smiled this time, and compassion was in her voice. "I'm sorry, sweetie. Finding her would have really hurt, especially if you'd just seen her earlier. Not to mention throwing you off the rest of your day."

Doreen nodded absentmindedly.

Nan leaned forward. "Where exactly did you meet her?"

And she realized that she hadn't told Nan about seeing Celeste at the garden center. "I never really met her," she quickly backtracked. "Sorry I didn't realize what you were asking." She glanced at her watch. "I've got to go back now."

Nan hopped up. "Just a minute." She walked into the kitchen and came back out with another half sandwich and piece of carrot cake. "I had saved this last night for my dinner, but I was more tired than hungry," she said. "You have it for your dinner tonight. I'll feel bad if it goes to waste."

And how sad that just the sight of that sandwich set her

stomach growling. She smiled at Nan, bent to kiss her cheek gently. "You take care tonight."

"You take care every night," Nan said. "Get an appraiser in, and then we'll talk. I might know a few tricks to get the best price." Grateful for that much, Doreen smiled and gave a finger wave. Nan gave Mugs a big cuddle and then Goliath, who was sprawled out on the floor. Thaddeus had been suspiciously quiet the whole time. Nan walked over. "What's the matter with Thaddeus?"

"I'm not sure," Doreen said. "He found something by the creek," she said. "In fact, all of them were curious about this thing in the backyard. So I dug it out of the lawn because he wouldn't leave it alone. It was a license plate. And ever since then, he's been like this. Just really tired, not eating. Although he was eating earlier but not a ton." She studied him. "He's looking better now though."

"He gets like this when he's depressed," Nan said. "A license plate?" She frowned, shaking her head. "That creek picks up and drags down the most incredible things."

"I was thinking the same thing," she said. "I gave it to Mack when he stopped by."

"When was this?"

"Yesterday. Time to go." She scooped up Thaddeus. She stopped at the edge of the patio and peered around the corner to see if the gardener was near, then, calling Goliath to her—who wandered at a slowed pace, enough to drive anybody crazy—she raced across the grass until she was safely on the other side with Mugs.

Goliath, on the other hand, took a few steps and lay down in the middle of the grass.

Dennis came running toward Goliath.

Nan looked over and said, "Go on, Goliath. Go on."

But Goliath lay in the grass, watching the gardener come toward him, his tail twitching ever-so-slightly, like he was either pissed or waiting for somebody to attack.

"Goliath! Goliath!" Doreen said, crouching on the ground.

Even Mugs started to bark.

Dennis raised his shovel like a baseball bat, as if to swing at the cat, but Nan's voice rang out, "If you touch one hair on that animal," she roared, "I will make sure you never have a job in this town again."

He froze then turned and glared at her. "No walking on the grass."

"It's a cat," Nan said, her hands on her hips—the first full outrage Doreen had ever seen from her grandmother.

Of course that side of her grandmother would appear when defending an animal or a child. That was Nan through and through.

Dennis backed off.

Goliath stared at him disdainfully. When the gardener was far enough away, Goliath got up and sauntered away ever-so-slowly, as if to say, *Ha, ha, ha,* as he crossed the grass to join Doreen and Mugs. When Goliath neared the basset hound, the cat smacked Mugs across the face, then ran as fast as he could, heading home.

Nan laughed. "Oh, my goodness," she said. "You and Mugs have enlivened things so very much," she called out with a wave. "Thank you for coming for a visit."

Doreen nodded, shot the gardener a fulminating look, turned her back on him, and stalked away. In her own way she was just as infuriatingly arrogant as the cat. At least she hoped so. But, to be honest, Goliath pulled it off ten times better than she did.

They walked beside the creek back home. Doreen carried the sandwich and carrot cake. She was mindful of all the things that could happen between now and getting those antique pieces sold. At the moment she wanted every expensive piece in the house gone. And that was pretty ridiculous, considering that she used to live in a houseful of incredibly expensive furniture too. At the time though, she hadn't realized, A, how much it was worth, and, B, how that money could have been better spent on other things.

But to know that kind of money was in Nan's house now terrified Doreen. What if the furniture went missing or was seriously damaged, like by a flood or rainwater coming through the roof?

As soon as she got home, she took pictures of everything, documenting the contents. She hadn't even insured the home and its contents. Maybe Nan already took care of that. That was something she needed to check on right now. Hopefully a policy was already in place. Otherwise ... how was Doreen supposed to pay for it?

She took photos all throughout the place, covering all the different antique pieces she'd heard about this morning.

Out of the eleven pieces in the living room, seven were extremely valuable, two more so. And she was totally okay to have the light-pine hutch be her only piece of furniture. Particularly if everything else would add up to an amount of money that would give her a monthly stipend.

She couldn't think of a better dream for herself right now. The payout didn't have to be very much, just enough to cover her monthly bills and so she had money to buy food with. If so, she would be ecstatic.

Finally she finished the picture-taking downstairs and then thought she'd photograph the upstairs too. She walked into the spare room, took pictures of the bed and the dresser. Then she headed over to the master bedroom.

She'd been sleeping in a massive four-poster bed without a thought. It was the same ornate pattern the couch was. Frowning, she took several photos of it and then of the small matching night tables. It had a makeup mirror and a low counter with drawers up and down both sides. It was kind of cute but not her style.

With those pictures taken, she couldn't forget Nan's comment about the basement. But, if she couldn't get into the basement, nobody else could either.

In the kitchen she took more photos but didn't think anything here could possibly be of value. But the dining room was a different story with its large table and eight big matching chairs. It was a nice set, and she highly suspected it was worth a lot of money. Also the matching double hutches.

With all those pictures on her phone, she transferred them to her laptop. As she did so, she thought about Fen Gunderson and, using Google, searched his name. According to the articles she scanned, he was well known in the antiques world, so apparently had a lot of connections. He'd been busy with his antiques store until a terrible tragedy had stuck his family.

As she read farther, her heart started to pound. "Maybe this is the cold case that Mack won't tell me about." One of Fen's grandkids had gone missing, decades ago. The little boy was coming home from school but never made it.

She sat back and wondered. Then decided there was only one way to find out. She picked up the phone and called Mack. When his growling voice answered, she asked, "Does the cold case you're talking about concern Fen Gunderson's grandson?" A shock of surprise could be heard on the other end.

"Who told you about that?"

"He was here today," she said. "I asked him about some of the furniture in Nan's house."

"About time you got rid of some of that junk," he said cheerfully. "It's really overwhelmingly stuffed in there."

"Yeah, and now I'm wondering about hiring a security guard," she said. "Apparently some of these pieces are worth money. Like serious money."

"Really?" His voice rose at the end. "Oh, shit. Nobody had better find out. You don't even have a decent lock on the door."

"I know," she said. "Fen's supposed to call me this afternoon—actually he was supposed to phone earlier," she said. "But I went to Nan's to talk to her about selling the antiques."

"Of course you did," he said affectionately. "And I'm sure she was more than happy for you to do that."

"How did you know she wouldn't want the money herself?"

"I didn't know about that particularly," he said. "But, if she gave you the house, and she included the contents of the house, plus she left you to care for Thaddeus and Goliath, I presumed she was more than happy to see you get some money out of the furniture."

"Besides the furniture is pretty ugly," Doreen said.

"Glad you said that," he said. "Antiques are definitely not my style."

"Anyway, Fen Gunderson is supposed to put me in touch with an appraiser and potentially an auction house that could handle the sales."

"Wow," he said. "That's terrific!"

"I know," she said. "I admit I'm feeling pretty anxious about the whole thing."

"I can see why. If you're afraid of somebody breaking in, you can always prop a chair under the front and back doors."

"She said something else that kind of blew me away."

"What?"

She said, "A lot more antiques are in the basement."

After another moment of silence he laughed. "That is one sly Nan," he said. "You better get that appraiser in there fast."

"Not only an appraiser," she said, "but I have to find a way to move this furniture out of here to an auction house, if that's what I end up doing."

"True enough," he said. "True enough."

"So you didn't answer my question," she said. "Is the cold case you mentioned about Fen Gunderson's grandson?"

"Maybe."

"No *maybe* about it. Why won't you tell me?"

"You'll probably dredge it out of the archives anyway," he said. "So, yes, Fen Gunderson's grandson disappeared on the way home from school. He was the third young boy to go missing within a period of eight months, but he didn't fit the same profile as the other two. They were part of the foster care system, and both were quite a bit older."

"And nobody ever saw him again?"

"He was supposedly seen getting into the truck of a local handyman, Henry Huberts."

She remembered another case with a murdered handy-man and groaned. "And nobody tracked him down? Nobody could find him?"

"We did get the license plate number, but we never found either of them again." Only with this bit, his voice deepened and a long silence stretched out between them ... but with a sense of expectation on his part.

Her heart sank as her mind connected the pieces. "Uh-oh."

"Yep," he said. "*Uh-oh* is right. So you know I have another question for you."

"You mean, I have one for you," she said. "It's the same license plate I just pulled out of the creek, isn't it?"

"It is," he said. "Now you answer my question. What the hell do you know about this case?"

Chapter 12

Friday mid-afternoon...

AFTER GIVING MACK some answers, not really having anything much to offer, she hung up the phone. She'd finally convinced him that she knew absolutely nothing about the case, but she would look into it.

"Don't bother," he'd warned her. "Enough is going on in your life. You focus on those antiques."

"I'd love to," she said, "but it'll hardly be a fast answer."

"Maybe it is," he'd said. "If Fen Gunderson didn't contact you yet, and he said he would, then you should contact him."

"I'll have to check," she said. "He might have left me a message."

"Find out," he said. "And by the way my work schedule has been changed. I have Sunday and Monday off next week. We're short staffed this week so I offered to work tomorrow. So I can't help you on Saturday."

"Okay. When do you want me to work at your mom's house?" She couldn't understand where the week had gone.

"If Sunday works for you," he said, "then I can pay you on Monday when I come over for your first cooking lesson."

"Oh, that sounds even better," she said brightly. "I'll be sure to stop by Sunday."

He hung up the phone.

Sitting in place for a long moment, she then couldn't resist. She grabbed her laptop to research the case of Fen Gunderson's missing grandson. The information was sparse, though many of the newspapers tried to blow it up, making a tiny bit of information into something more newsworthy.

She went through as many articles as she could find, wondering if she should try the library archives again. It was about the only way to go back that far to see if anything helpful could be found in the old articles. Mack wouldn't give her a copy of the case file, and that was too damn bad. She didn't want to ask Fen, hurting the old man by bringing up bad memories. It may have been a long time ago, but some pain just never went away.

She checked the time, realizing it was eight o'clock. "It seems like it was just eight o'clock in the morning," she muttered.

She had an hour before the library closed, according to the internet. Each day of the week seemed to have a different closing time. Why couldn't it be the same every day? She grabbed her keys and drove away, noticing the news reporters were finally gone from her yard. She laughed out loud. "They don't even know I'm the one who found Celeste's body."

Still chuckling to herself, she went around the few corners to get to the library. She parked and walked inside.

The librarian, Linda Linket, raised her head and frowned. "What are you here for?"

Doreen's heart sank. "Hey, don't I even get a smile and hello?" she said with a light sense of humor.

Linda pulled her glasses down on her nose so she could peer over the top of them. "It depends what you're here for."

"Books?" she snapped. She walked past Linda and headed to the popular fiction section. Just for show, she picked up two that looked interesting, looked at the back cover blurbs, and put one back, keeping one. Then she headed to the microfiche machine.

She moved back in time to twenty years ago. She should have asked Mack for an exact date, but he hadn't been happy to give her anything. She flicked through as many of the articles as she could, but it was frustrating because she couldn't find anything with the Gunderson name. But then maybe the grandson's last name wasn't Gunderson.

"What are you looking for?" Linda asked from behind her.

"Information on Fen Gunderson's missing grandson," she said.

Linda's eyebrows slowly rose toward her hairline, and she shrugged.

"Fen's doing me a favor. I just wondered if I could do something to ease the pain of his loss."

Linda looked even more surprised, shrugging again.

Still feeling like she had to explain herself, Doreen said, "I'm trying to figure out something I can do. I know that's a huge loss in his life, and maybe I can do something to memorialize his grandson's life or to give Fen closure. That might make him happier or give him some peace," she said lamely.

It was a good idea. She didn't know if other people had done it or not. She imagined his friends and family had, way back when it originally happened. But, of course, she had not been part of his life then. He wouldn't even know she had heard about the case.

"You're not far enough back," Linda said, motioning at the microfiche. "It was closer to thirty years ago now. You're also looking for Gunderson's last name. But his daughter married Martin Shore. His little boy was Paul Shore."

"Ah." Doreen wrote it down on her notepad and thanked the woman. She went back to the microfiche, hoping Linda would leave. But she stood here, watching as Doreen searched through twenty-nine-year-old newspapers. Finally she found an article entitled "Missing Boy from Kelowna." She read it through. "It's so sad," she whispered.

"It was devastating for all of us at the time. He was the second or third to go missing that year," Linda said. "I knew Paul too. I was his piano teacher."

She turned to face Linda, seeing the person she was inside for once and not just the guardian of the information Doreen was hunting down. "I'm sorry," she said sincerely. "I can't imagine."

Linda nodded stiffly. "Whatever you do, be sensitive. It's a sore spot for many of us." She turned on her heels and walked away.

Relieved the woman wasn't looking over her shoulder anymore, Doreen quickly read through the article once more, writing down a few bits of information, but there was almost nothing said.

People reported seeing the boy get into a large beat-up white truck, belonging to the handyman, Henry Huberts, who disappeared at the same time. Foul play was suspected. The little boy never showed up again.

She just couldn't imagine the heartache the parents and the whole family had gone through. Knowing that your little boy came home at a specific time every day, you looked outside, expecting him to arrive, or you worried.

She researched a little more, getting as much as she could, but there just didn't appear to be anything more. It was like any normal day, except the little boy headed home from school and never made it. He just dropped off the face of the Earth. The end.

She shook her head. "No way to find closure with that," she muttered. She stood with her notebook, looked at the piece of popular fiction she'd picked up, walked to the front, and checked it out.

Linda handed it back to Doreen and said, "I don't know how, with all the stuff you seem to do as your hobbies, you have time to read these mystery books too."

"They intrigue me," she said honestly. "I love the puzzle part of them." With that, she returned to her car.

Back home, she decided it was time to turn in for the night. So much was going on, and her mind was buzzing. She thought maybe the book in her hand might be the answer to getting a good night's sleep. But, as soon as she got into bed, her mind buzzed harder. She groaned, got out bed, crept downstairs, not sure why she was creeping when it was her own house. Just to make her feel better, she stomped all the way back up.

As she got to the top, she swore she heard a door shut. She froze. Mugs came off the bed and barked like a madman at her feet. He raced downstairs.

Horrified, she followed him. "What's the matter, Mugs?"

She walked to the fireplace and picked up the poker. She almost chuckled. It was just such a bad-movie response that it was hard to resist.

Mugs barked as he circled the living room, going into

the kitchen and the dining room. Then he headed back toward the front door.

"Do you know anything at all?" she asked him. "Or are you seriously just barking for the sake of barking?"

He went to the large hutch and continued to bark.

The hutch had two large doors. She did not want to open either and find an intruder. But she didn't have a whole lot of choice. With the poker in hand, she opened one side of the hutch. Mugs went up to it and sniffed.

Only shelving was inside. "See? It's nothing," she said. "Absolutely nothing."

But, just to be sure, she checked that the front and back doors of the house were locked. Taking Mack's advice, she grabbed a chair and propped it under the front door, then repeated with another chair at the back door. She didn't know if it would make any difference, but she felt better.

She marched back upstairs, determined not to let the old house spook her. Of course, now that she knew about the antiques, just leaving her house was hard enough. And to think about somebody getting in and knowing about the antiques terrified her. She wondered if she should contact a security company. But that would be an added expense. Yet, it would be foolhardy not to spend a few bucks a month on a service that protected thousands of dollars' worth of expensive antiques. She'd look into that more later.

Meanwhile, would Fen Gunderson have told anyone? He might have seemed like a nice old man, but old guys loved to talk. Maybe he said something to somebody who said something to somebody else, and now, all of a sudden, her house had been targeted.

Chapter 13

Saturday morning...

SLEEPING IN FITS and starts, she woke up the next morning at six thirty and groaned because, as far as her body was concerned, it was time to get up, whether she'd gotten enough sleep or not. Who woke at these hours? Especially on a Saturday? Her mind was foggy, and everything was hazy. Still, she got up, dressed, and went downstairs to put on some coffee. She looked out at the backyard. So many plants and bushes were thriving out there, even with the past neglect, that she didn't know what to do. Because right now everything felt a bit too much.

She didn't know where her normal love of life and excitement had gone. But she figured it went with the hours of sleep she was supposed to have but didn't get.

She opened the back door and stepped onto the porch and stopped. She stepped back inside, picked up her phone, and called Mack.

"Now what?" he asked. "Can't a guy get any sleep?"

She winced as she realized what time it was. "I'm sorry," she said hurriedly. "I propped up kitchen chairs at the two doors, like you told me to." She took a hard gasping sob.

"Hey, easy, easy. What's going on?" he asked in concern.

"Well, I just opened the back door and stepped out ..."

"And ..." he snapped when she hesitated.

"The chair I had propped up at the kitchen door was gone. Somebody had moved it. Somebody was inside my house when I put those damn things against the doors, and then they moved one away from the kitchen door to get out."

"Stay right there. I'll be there in ten."

She stood with her hands trembling, holding the phone against her chest. The dog wandered around, completely unfazed by anything, or so it seemed. She wasn't even sure what the heck she was supposed to do now. The coffee was about twenty feet away, and it seemed too damn far. But she badly needed a cup.

Her head spun. She had touched the doorknob, which was probably a stupid thing to do. Her breaths came hard and fast, and her panic alternated from rising to falling as she waited for Mack. She knew it would be at least ten minutes because he didn't sound like he was out of bed yet.

But, true to his word, ten minutes later he rolled up the driveway. He hopped out and came through the front door. Or he would have, except she hadn't unlocked it. He pounded on the door.

She cried out, "I'm here. I'm here. Give me a moment." She moved the chair from under the handle and let him in.

He sighed. "Come here." He opened his arms.

She fell into them and burrowed deep as his arms closed around her. She knew he could feel the trembling up and down her spine, but she had no way to hide it. It had been a truly scary moment to realize somebody had been in her house. And she had no idea who or for how long or even what they did while here.

"So let's start at the beginning." He led her to the kitchen, where he could see the rear kitchen door on his right and the front door on his left. "So you propped up a chair," he pointed to the one near the front door, "and you did the same to the back door, correct?"

She pointed to the chair closest to the table. "I put that one under this door. And then I went to bed."

"What made you do that?"

"I was in bed," she said, "and I thought about getting my laptop. I came sneaking down, though I didn't know why I was sneaking. I was really angry because I felt like I had to sneak. So I stomped my way back up the stairs. But, at the top, I thought I heard a noise, like a door shutting down here. And Mugs heard it too. He set up, caterwauling. So I came back down, grabbed the fire poker, and searched the house. We couldn't find anything, but," she said, frowning, walking over to the big hutch, "Mugs stood in front of this hutch and barked at it until I opened one of the doors to show him it was empty."

"This one?" Mack asked. He stepped forward and threw open the double doors. Inside was just shelving on one side and hanging closet space on the other.

"Exactly," she said. "That's what I saw last night. Of course, I only opened half of it." She stared at the other half that was for hangers. "I suppose he could have been hiding in there, but Mugs wasn't barking then."

"What did Mugs do then?"

"He watched as I put the chairs under the doors, then I went upstairs again," she said. "I didn't sleep well because I kept waking up. And I kept having, you know, horrible nightmares. I finally came down, put on coffee. I opened the back door and stepped out, and that's when I realized a chair should have been there for me to move first."

He nodded. "Okay, so you had a midnight visitor. You don't know when they arrived. Were you home all last evening?"

She gave him a shamefaced look and shook her head. "You know? I was thinking, as soon as I left, that I shouldn't have left, because what if Fen Gunderson had said something about the antiques in the house? What if this guy was coming in to check it out himself?"

"Considering the size of this furniture," he said, looking around the living room, "there's a good chance he was doing exactly that. Which means your house is now a major issue."

"But he couldn't have taken anything with him without some help and without waking me up," she said. "I really didn't sleep well."

"Unless it was small," he said.

She gasped and ran into the living room. She stopped in the middle with her hand against her chest. "Oh, thank God."

"What?"

She pointed at the antique table in the corner. "That thing is supposed to be extremely valuable," she said. "I don't remember how much. So many figures are rolling around in my head, but I think Fen said it was like seven or eight thousand dollars."

"What?"

She nodded. "I'm scared to even touch it. For all I know, a fingerprint decreases the value by two thousand dollars."

At that, he chuckled. "Hardly. Nan has abused that little table for years. Plus fingerprints can be buffed away."

"I know," she said, "but now I'm really scared."

"You took pictures yesterday, didn't you?"

Relieved, she nodded and pulled up her phone. "I photographed a lot of stuff, some of the smaller things and all the bigger pieces too."

"So let's walk around and make sure the pictures still match everything."

It took them an hour to check that everything was still here.

When Mack was satisfied, she put away her phone. "I should have thought to do that myself."

"Two heads are better than one on something like this," he said. "Besides, at least now you know he didn't leave with anything. Probably because you heard him. So what that means is, we now must ensure everything is secured."

"I need to get the appraisals done."

"You won't get that done quickly," Mack said. "It'll probably be a couple days. I don't know that anybody is local."

"Fen mentioned an auction house, a big one. But I don't remember now. It sounded like a woman's name." She frowned. "But that can't be right."

"It's Christie's," he said. "That's a big one. And, if they're interested in all this, you should do well by them."

"That's what I'm hoping," she said. "But I don't know how much commission they take."

"What you take away is still more than you had with all this just sitting here. At least they'll bring in the right buyers."

"Okay, that makes sense," she said. "But what do we do to get them in now?" Just then her phone rang. "It's Fen Gunderson," she whispered. She answered it. "Good morning."

"Good morning," he said. "I contacted the appraiser. He wants to call you this morning."

"Okay, thank you," she said. "By the way, did you mention to anybody that I had these antiques?"

"No," he said. "You don't stay in my business for long when you open your mouth. I didn't mention it to anyone but the appraiser."

"Not even in passing that you were coming to look at Nan's antiques?"

"No, why?" His voice was loud.

"I had an intruder last night," she said. "And I wondered if it was related to the antiques."

He gasped. "Oh, my dear. Are you okay?"

She nodded. "I'm fine. But now I'm really worried about the antiques. If word gets around a lot of money is tied up in these pieces, then I'm in trouble."

"Yes. Yes, you are. You should contact a security company," he said.

"I did think about that earlier. Okay. I can check that out while I wait for the appraiser to contact me. What was the name of the auction house you were talking about?"

"Christie's. The appraiser will help put you in contact with them. They'll need to have photographs. Then they'll probably send somebody out to verify the pictures. Also to see if any provenance can be found on any of these pieces."

"Right, provenance," she said. "That's what you told me about yesterday. How, if I can prove the history of any of the furniture, then it's worth a lot more."

"Exactly, my dear. So talk to Nan."

After he hung up, she turned to look at Mack. "He says he didn't speak to anyone. The appraiser is supposed to call me this morning."

"Okay," he said. "I'm not sure what to do about keeping you safe though. If Fen's correct, and that much money is tied up in here ..." He shook his head as he looked around the room. "This room is absolutely stuffed."

"I know," she said, "but the thing is, we didn't really take note of this stuff when Nan lived here, like any little old lady's house. But now that I'm here, and I'm looking at it all, and it doesn't suit me, so it seems like it's just *old* stuff."

"And you're cleaning out already," he said. "You've already done one bedroom, didn't you?"

She nodded. "And I'm working on the second one now."

"I might know a couple guys who would be willing to do drive-bys past the place," he said. "I don't think I can get any budget money to have the cops do it."

"The trouble is, the more people you mention it to, the quicker the news gets around. According to Nan, everybody already knows everything before the media does."

He nodded. "That's very true. We'll see what we can do though. In the meantime, I have a murder to solve."

"Yes, you do," she said. "Did you ever find the boyfriend, Josh Huberts?"

He shot her a sideways look.

She nodded. "Of course you did."

"But not the way you think," he said gently.

She frowned at him. "What do you mean?"

"He was the DB at the scene."

It took her a moment to figure out what *DB* meant *Dead Body*. "Oh, my God! You mean, he's dead?"

He nodded. "Looks like a self-inflicted wound."

"So he kills his girlfriend, dumps her in front of the Family Planning Center, goes home, and shoots himself?" It *almost* made sense.

As Mack rolled his shoulders in a big shrug, she realized it was probably something he'd seen many times.

"I don't know," she said. "That seems like a lot of effort to then turn around and take your own life."

"It depends," he said. "You know people in a rage often do things they regret. These two were known to have had a very volatile relationship."

"But it's very cold and calculating to dump her body on the grounds of the Family Planning Center," she said, "and then to return to the house where he shot her just to shoot himself. That takes it from passionate rage to very clear thinking. Wouldn't he talk himself out of suicide at that point? Plus that wouldn't work according to the gunshots I heard. Two and then two, right in succession. So, unless you found more bullets, ... I don't think that theory will hold."

"Forensics is on it," he said. "But that is what it looks like. We have to wait for the coroner to get back to us with his ruling as well of course."

She was happy for him if it was solved so quickly. "It would be nice if it was an open-and-shut case. What about the vehicles, did you find those?"

He nodded. "They were parked in the back. It would be nice to have a quick close to this, so don't go making trouble where there isn't any," he warned.

She gave him an innocent look. "Don't know what you're talking about."

"The other thing you could do potentially," he said, "is rent a storage locker and put all this stuff in it."

"Sure. And how will I pay for the storage unit and who'll look after the storage locker?" she asked.

"Good questions," he said with the laugh. "But at least those units are behind locked entry gates, and you would have a lock on the storage container itself."

She frowned, not sure how she felt about it. "Maybe. I'll think about it."

"You do that. In the meantime, I'll send somebody around to see if we can grab some fingerprints."

She brightened at that idea. "That's a good thing. Check the chair and the doorknob and the hutch. I don't know what else. Obviously mine and Fen Gunderson's are all over the place."

He nodded. "Okay. I'll see you in a little bit then." At that, he took off, not giving her a chance to ask why she'd see him again.

In the meantime she would get some food and that coffee she had forgotten about. Because, as soon as that local appraiser called her, she would need all kinds of information from him.

Chapter 14

Saturday mid-morning...

SHE LOOKED AT the local appraiser, stunned. "Those numbers ... They're just flabbergasting," she said.

He chuckled. "They are, indeed. You've got quite a windfall here. I talked to Nan many years ago about selling this living room set." He looked at the couch and chairs. "That you've got both chairs is amazing."

"You mean, the two side chairs and the couch?" she asked.

He nodded. "They were originally part of a large bedroom set. But to find even three—four, counting the coffee table—pieces together is pretty special. There should be a little end table and a large bed with night tables and more. If you had the entire thing, I think you'd be looking upward of fifty thousand dollars. Possibly a lot more."

She sank into the closest chair.

He smiled. "Only if the set was complete."

She swallowed hard. "Do you want to come and take a look at the bed I've been sleeping in?"

"Are you serious?"

She shrugged. "It has the same kind of scrollwork on the

posts as the couch does."

His face lit with excitement. "Where is it?"

She pulled herself to her feet and letting Mugs race ahead so he didn't trip her as they went up the stairs. As they got to the top, she saw Thaddeus sleeping on one corner bed post and Goliath stretched out across her bed.

The appraiser came into the room and exclaimed, "Oh, my God! Oh, my God! It is! Oh, my goodness." He just stood with his hands over his mouth in absolute delight.

"So I guess I'll be looking for a new bed then?"

"Do you want to sell this?" He turned to her. "I do have private buyers, and I can put you in touch with the auction house."

She nodded and pointed at the night tables. "I think they're the same, aren't they?"

He removed the lamp from one and carefully picked it up, rotating it to check the back. He sighed happily. "Not only is it one of them, but it's absolutely the same mark as the couch and the chairs downstairs. We must do a further exam to ensure they're all the exact same set of pieces. But it looks like you have almost a complete set."

"I would like to sell it," she said. "I'd like to sell as much of it as possible. I won't sleep well or at all, knowing so many valuables are in the house, and I don't have a security system."

He looked absolutely horrified at the idea. "Give me half an hour to get this process started. Do you have a table where I can sit down and work?"

She led him back downstairs to the kitchen table, where he made phone calls as he opened his laptop. "Do you have photographs?"

"I have what I took yesterday." She brought up her laptop and showed him what she had.

"Okay, it'll take me a few hours to photograph the maker's marks, and we do need to see if you have any provenance for these pieces. But the fact is, the furniture bears the marks, and that'll give it a certain amount of value. If they're legally obtained, or if you have some bright and colorful history you can document, that'll add more value to it." The excitement never left his countenance.

She nodded. "How quickly can we make any of this happen?"

"Not that quickly," he said. "I get that you're worried and want to move it. But it'll still probably be at least a week."

She sighed. "Okay, then I need to make sure this place stays safe."

"You certainly do." He focused on her. "And I know the bed is one you've been sleeping in, but ..." He let his words dwindle away.

She nodded. "Maybe I shouldn't sleep in it anymore?"

"I don't even want to say that to you," he said, "because obviously it's been in good use all these years, and that's what it was intended for." He spoke apologetically.

She nodded. "Still, I'm not sure I need to sleep in that particular bed."

"But we're jumping ahead of ourselves here. Let's get the photos done. Then you can get back to me after we've heard from Christie's. *Maybe.* I don't know which is better. I think for this set, probably Christie's," he said, "but I will contact them. And they will want to see the photos, so that'll be first. I do have a camera with me. I'm quite used to taking photographs, if that is okay with you."

"Yes. And ..." She hesitated.

He looked up at her. "What is it, my dear?"

"I already had an intruder last night," she said. "After Fen Gunderson was here. I'm just a little worried that, once you take the photographs and leave, there'll be, you know, other people finding out about this."

"It certainly won't be from me," he said, "because I'll get a finder's fee. So it's in my best interests to help you make this auction happen with Christie's. If anybody steals anything, it's not because of me."

"Of course," she said. "I don't mean to imply you would steal anything. I'm just really nervous."

"With good reason," he explained. "Let's get the photographs done and take care of that part."

It was a methodical and slow process. They upended every chair and took pictures from every angle. As they went through the entire living room and then the master bedroom, he taught her how to check for the marks and what particular mark was left on each of the sets.

By the time they were done with the bed, both night tables, and the living room furniture—including the coffee table—she understood what he was excited about. "So you're saying, all seven of these pieces—the coffee table, two chairs and the couch, the two night tables and the bed—all had that same maker's mark, plus the same little ... I don't know what you call it ... but the number of the set."

He nodded. "Exactly. Not only do you have most of a ten-piece set, but they are also part of one set made at the same time. Now a few pieces are missing, which is a shame, but it's certainly understandable after all these years that they aren't all here."

She walked around the first floor. "I know a basement door is here somewhere, and Nan did say she had more pieces down there, but I haven't found the access door, and I'm sure we can't deal with all that at the moment anyway."

He nodded. "If we do find it as we go forward, it'll just add to the excitement. At the moment, what you have is already pretty incredible."

She gave a happy sigh and sat back.

"Now I must ask you," he said. "Do you have the right to sell these?"

She nodded. "Nan gave me the house and its contents. We have legal documents to that effect, and I spoke to her yesterday about the antiques in particular. She said they're mine to sell as I want."

"That's very generous of her," he said. "Does she understand the value of all these pieces?"

"I gave her a lot of the values as I understood them yesterday from Fen, but of course, I didn't know about the set being that much more. I can certainly ask her again, but I'm pretty sure she'll give the same response, telling me it's mine."

"That would be lovely." He almost rubbed his hands together in glee. "I'll send off these photos to Christie's. I have an agent there I deal with. I should hear back by tomorrow afternoon at the latest."

She smiled. "But you said it would take at least a week."

"Yes, for the overall sales and delivery process, it could be quite a bit longer," he said. "But I should speak to someone from Christie's by phone by tomorrow. So just keep it to yourself, don't tell anybody, and live your life."

She smiled.

He looked at her, reached out to shake her hand, and said, "Remember all these pieces have been here for years. So don't panic, don't worry about damaging them, just live your life."

She walked him out the front door and smiled. He turned and put his card in her hand.

She went back in and tucked the card into her purse so she wouldn't lose it. She sat down in the living room, thinking of the words he had just said about living her life, yet, she was absolutely petrified to sit on the couch. It was too freaking much money. As long as she could keep these valuable antiques from being gossiped about, then maybe she would be fine. Then she could focus on finding out more about Fen Gunderson's grandson.

And something was seriously wrong about Celeste's body being found on the Family Planning Center property and her boyfriend's at the Hawthorne house. She knew the police wouldn't find out all the answers, especially if they had decided this was a murder-suicide case. She knew the questions from the authorities would just stop. They wouldn't even be looking for answers.

Then she remembered what she'd said to the appraiser.

She picked up the phone. "Good morning, Nan," she said when her grandmother answered the phone.

"Good morning. How did you sleep last night?"

"Okay," she said. "I think we had an intruder in the house."

Nan's gasp of shock filled the phone.

"I'm okay though," Doreen said.

"I'm so sorry, dear. We never did put any kind of security in there. It seems like, all the years I lived in the house, it was a very different town. But nowadays we have a lot of homeless people. Maybe he was just looking for a place to rest."

"Nan?" Doreen hesitated, not knowing how she would

broach the subject.

"Yes, dear?"

"Did you tell anybody about the antiques?"

"No, of course not," she said. "But lots of people already know about them. I've been collecting them for years, decades even. I've had various people over to appraise them. Have to, for insurance purposes."

"So the house and the contents are currently insured?" Doreen asked, holding her breath.

"Of course, dear."

Doreen waited for more, but her grandmother said nothing else. "Where did you get the bedroom set and the couch set from?"

"Well, that was my grandmother's. I didn't buy that. When you ·sleep at night, my dear, you're sleeping like royalty." She chuckled. "That entire set came from her. But I'm not exactly sure where she got it. I think it's been in the family for well over one hundred years."

Doreen stared at the phone. "From your grandmother?"

"Yes, my dear. I was born too, you know."

She said it with such a sense of humor that Doreen laughed. "Of course you were. And a sweetheart you are now. I imagine you were an absolutely adorable baby. What about your mother? Didn't she want the set?"

"She hated antiques, so my grandmother gave it all to me. And she had had it for all of her married life. That was close to fifty years, if not sixty," Nan said thoughtfully. "I've had it since, jeez, since she passed away, so it's been at least eighty years, if not one hundred years, in our family. I was born late in my mother's life, and Mother was born late in Nan's life."

"You have no idea where your grandmother got it?"

"No. It's in the paperwork in a folder somewhere."

"Right. I haven't had a chance to look for that yet." Doreen spun around in the kitchen, wondering where the folder could possibly be.

"What about the body at the Family Planning Center?" Nan asked. "Did you hear any more about that?"

"Yeah. The boyfriend, Josh Huberts, was found dead at the house where I heard the gunshots," she muttered. Her gaze studied the cupboards in front of her. She opened them, looking for the paperwork.

"Interesting," Nan said. "Because, once you realize who it was, I figure it has to be related to Fen Gunderson."

Doreen froze. "Nan, what are you talking about?"

"The boyfriend was the grandson of the handyman accused of kidnapping Fen Gunderson's grandson."

"Seriously?"

"Yes," Nan said. "It was a terrible time back then. And I don't know that the handyman really had any evil reason for picking up the boy. Maybe he was just giving him a ride home."

"What time of year did it happen?" Doreen asked, trying to confirm the details from the newspaper articles." It was summertime, right?" She thought it was May or June.

"Oh, my goodness. Must have been late spring or early summer. We had high floods that year," Nan said. "And I know that really hampered the search efforts. They had assumed originally he had drowned because lots of the streets were flooded, and we had flash floods all the time. But that theory was tossed out the window once somebody came forth and said they saw Paul get into Hubert's truck."

"Oh," Doreen said. A lot of thoughts were piling in on her. "Nan, if you hear any more about that, or if you have any thoughts about where that provenance folder is, can you let me know? I'll be staying home mostly for the next few days, just so I can keep track of what might be... To make sure nobody tries to steal my antiques."

"Not a problem," Nan said. "I wouldn't mind coming over. Maybe today or tomorrow. A lot of history is in that old house. Now, as I recall, one or two of the pieces had hidden drawers." Her voice faded away.

Doreen's ears perked up. "Seriously?"

"Yes, absolutely. But I don't remember which ones. And I'm not sure how to get into them anymore. I remember playing with them at my Nan's house and always finding little candies and toys hidden away."

"That sounds absolutely lovely," Doreen said warmly. "Anyway, Nan, I'll talk to you later. Whenever you want to come over, just let me know. I can either come and pick you up in the car, or I can walk there, and we can walk home together."

"Ha. I'm walking just fine. When you least expect it, I'll show up."

After she hung up, Doreen grabbed her notebook and wrote down what Nan had said. Then she opened up a file on her laptop, labeling it Paul Shore.

As soon as she had a file started, she wrote down the details as she remembered them. Because all she could think of was that lost little boy and how his grandfather had been so very helpful to Doreen. It was the least she could do.

As soon as she finished that, she searched through every one of the kitchen cupboards, looking for Nan's folder. If that had any kind of provenance for these pieces, then she needed it. And she needed it soon. She didn't have a clue how much money all this stuff would bring in the end. It wouldn't be enough to set her up for life, she guessed, but, if it gave her some kind of a monthly income until she was a little better established, she would be more than happy with that.

An hour later she was beyond frustrated. She found no folders in the hall closet, in the front closet, in the living room closet, or in any of the kitchen cupboards. She groaned, made herself a cup of tea, and walked out to the living room to sit down again. This time she sat on the floor. Then she remembered what Fen had said about the carpet. And she bounced back to her feet. She walked into the kitchen, grabbed a kitchen chair, and brought that to the living room to sit on.

"This is ridiculous," she said, realizing she was being foolish. She'd already spilled coffee and tea on the furniture and the rug. She put her tea on the coffee table with a coaster, grabbed her laptop, and sat on the couch. She loved that Nan's grandmother used to hide treats in hidden drawers in some of these old pieces. That was an absolutely special memory. And she was grateful she had the relationship she did with Nan now.

"Life is too short," she said.

As she researched Fen Gunderson's grandson, she checked the weather reports way back then. It would take a lot of research to get into the weather patterns from that time, just when they were starting to keep records and way before digital records were made. She wondered if the weather stations could help her.

She picked up the phone and called the local station to ask for the weatherman. When she couldn't get through, she got his email address and sent him a query. About an hour later her phone rang.

"Hey, this is Charlie from the weather station. That's a really interesting question you've got there. What are you into?" he asked curiously.

"I was checking the weather for twenty-nine years ago in the months of May and June," she said, not giving away too much information.

"Are you hot on another case?"

She groaned, realizing he already knew who she was. "Not really," she said. "Just looking at the weather patterns for help in redoing Nan's garden." It was only half a lie because she certainly did want to know the weather patterns here.

"We do have something digital here, but it's not easily accessible. Let me go back twenty-nine years ago, since 1990 ..." His voice trailed off as he clicked away on his keyboard. "Oh, wow. That was a really crazy summer with tons of flooding. The worst in one hundred years, I believe."

"Right. I heard something about that. Something about how the river rose to crazy heights."

"Yeah, absolutely. It was so strong that year that we had cars in the river."

"Were they ever pulled out?"

"You'd like to think so," he said, "but the river back then was very deep, and it flowed right into the lake, so it's hard to say."

"How long did the flooding last?"

"We had flash floods off and on for about three or four days because of the mountain's snowmelt. Everything on top melted, came down, and we had a lot of heavy rainstorms at the same time too. Kind of like a perfect storm of various elements. We ended up with this massive flood that just didn't quit. Is that what you're looking for?"

"Yeah, do you have anything you can pop into the email for me to refer back to?"

"Sure," he said. "If it brings up anything interesting, let me know, will you?"

She chuckled. "Not sure what you're talking about but will do." She hung up.

Now she had a pretty damn good idea what happened. And yet, she had to believe that the authorities and even the family members were checking on the weather way back then too at the time of the boys' disappearances.

She sorted through the years of weather, then realized she needed to ask Charlie one more question. She hit Redial.

When he answered, he said, "Wow. Found something already?"

"No," she said. "I was wondering, considering that was a year with heavy flooding, have we had a year since then where it's been incredibly dry? You know? Like, where the lake would be at its lowest point in one hundred years?"

"This year," he said. "It's been one of the driest years ever. Our rainfall is way down. The mountains had almost zero snow last year. Remember how the ski mountains were in trouble?"

She didn't tell him anything about not having been local back then because she didn't want to remind him how she had just arrived and was causing the current chaos. "So what does that mean in terms of the lake levels?"

"It means, by the time we hit August, September, October," he said, "it should be pretty darn low."

"Oh, interesting. Of course you don't have any underwater radar or anything like that, do you?"

"No," he said. "But a bunch of stuff was done when people came looking for Ogopogo. A research company wanted to find critters in the lake, and I know they did all kinds of stuff, but I don't think any of that is publicly accessible."

"Do you know what company it was?"

"No," he said, "but it shouldn't be too hard to find. They were in the news quite a bit because, of course, everybody was taking bets on whether they would find the Loch Ness Monster of Okanagan Lake."

"Interesting. So you're expecting this summer we should have the lake at its lowest level?"

"This whole year was pretty bad. We had a lot of heavy snowfall, which means heavy flooding to come," he said, "so the city opened the locks and let out water from the lake in preparation for the spring runoff levels. Then, when the heavy flooding didn't materialize, the lake itself didn't rise as much as was expected."

He explained it very well, but, for her, it was hard to process all the information. She nodded though, as if she understood. "Again, any chance of you putting that down on paper? Because that was a lot of information."

He laughed. "Sure. Sounds like I'm giving a history lesson to somebody from out of town."

"Well, I am partially," she said. "I've been around Nan lots. But that doesn't mean I remember all this stuff."

"Good enough," he said with a smile in his voice.

She hung up again, and, going off in yet another tangent, which was very unlike her, she searched for drought areas in town, realizing the entire Lower Mission area was a floodplain. So it was flooded with high waters whenever the water from the rivers and the lake went high, but then it became a drought area whenever water levels dropped even lower than normal. It made a lot of sense.

But so did something else.

She researched companies that had done any kind of deep water imaging of the lake. But she wasn't getting any true hits for what she needed to find out. Then she remembered how Charlie had said something about *bets* and called Nan. "Have you ever placed a bet on whether they would find a Loch Ness Monster in Okanagan Lake?"

Nan laughed. "Oh my," she said, catching her breath. "I made so much money on that bet."

"Why would anybody bet on that?"

"Because somebody here suggested they had seen a Loch Ness Monster and that it would be found with the new technology, so a lot of people were determined to agree because they really wanted to see it. Whereas, I was of the opinion that it didn't matter how good the technology was, some things we were never meant to know."

Doreen happened to agree with Nan on that one. "Okay, so you bet against it. Why would you have made so much money?"

"While I was sitting in a coffee shop," she said, her voice lowered so nobody around could hear, "I heard a couple folks from the research crew discussing their project. They were running out of money, and they had until midnight the next night. So, as soon as I heard that, I knew exactly when to set my time for when the research company would call it quits. Midnight obviously. And I was right on, which paid with a heavy bonus." She laughed. "Best bet I ever placed."

"Do you remember the name of the company that did the imaging?"

"A science lab research thing ..." she said, her voice thoughtful. "Oh, I remember, Oceanic. They came in with a minisub and some fancy radar machine."

"Okay," Doreen said. "That's something I might be able to look up."

"Wait, wait, wait," Nan said. "Don't hang up yet."

"That's all I needed to know. Thanks, Nan." And she hung up before Nan could ask any more questions.

Then she deliberately turned off her phone so her grandmother couldn't call her back. She didn't want anybody asking questions she wasn't ready to answer, and then she researched the corresponding articles.

By the time she was done, she was exhausted. And as she looked at the phone, she realized it was already dinnertime on a Saturday evening. Yet she hadn't even had lunch yet. She groaned. "If Mack knew that, he'd be all over me."

She turned her phone back on to see several messages. She sighed, checked them out, and, sure enough, two were from Nan, but one was from Mack. She called him back. "Hey," she said. "I had the phone turned off. Things got a little crazy here."

"How did it go with the appraiser?"

"It went very well," she said. "Then I talked to Nan a bit more, and apparently the big set—couch, chairs, coffee table, my bed, night tables—were all part of a bedroom ensemble from way back when. So all the pieces are going to the auction house, if and when they want them. So we had to take photos, note the maker's marks, any damage to the pieces, ... you know, all that good stuff."

"Wow," he said. "That sounds hugely positive."

She laughed. "It really does. I'm super excited. I know it won't be enough to replace what I lost from a proper divorce settlement, but Nan was the one who suggested I might be able to invest some of it, so I get a little bit of a monthly income, at least enough to live on."

"That sounds like something you should seriously think about," he said with surprise. "Nan sounds like she's very astute when it comes to money."

"Maybe," she said. "And she didn't buy those particular antiques that make up that one big set. They were handed down to her by her grandmother."

"Well, there's some of your provenance," he said.

"Some," she said. "She's trying to remember years and dates, and that's a whole different problem."

"Sure, but if you get your great-great-grandmother's name, you could do some research on that too."

She hadn't even thought of that. She crowed in delight. "This will keep me busy for a few weeks."

"Of course it will," he said.

"Except for one thing. Did you know that the guy who supposedly committed suicide, Josh Huberts, was the grandson of the handyman accused of taking the missing boy, Paul Shore? That Josh Huberts is the grandson of Henry Huberts?"

Dead silence came from Mack's end of the conversation.

Chapter 15

"WHERE DID YOU hear that?" Mack asked.

"Nan," Doreen said. "Once she heard the Huberts name, she was all over it. ... And Linda, the librarian."

"I didn't even think of that." He groaned.

He muttered away in the background, and she could hear the keys on his laptop clicking. "It doesn't mean it has anything to do with the other though," she said quietly.

"No," he said, "but the fact that we have a dead family member—and the license plate of course—always makes me very suspicious."

"Of course it does," she said. "But it doesn't have to be related. Just keep that in mind."

He chuckled. "Isn't that my line for you? You're the one always trying to make big bad things happen out of nothing."

"Maybe," she said. "But I have a lot to focus on right now."

"Speaking of which," he said, "a couple buddies of mine were talking about the problem with your house. Two of them are on patrol tonight, and they'll take a couple drive-bys once an hour while you're asleep. I think you need to take extra care for the next few days, until we get this straightened out. But they will continue to keep an eye on your place. And there'll be no charge. Just concerned citizens giving you a hand."

She smiled. "Thank you," she said with heartfelt sincerity. "I really appreciate that."

"So you should," he said with a chuckle. "And now you owe me one." He hung up.

Into the empty room she said, "Ha, you're the one getting the credit for closing all these cases, so you owe *me* one. And, if my current theory runs true, you'll be able to close yet another one."

But it was too early to crow about that. She still had a little work to do first. As such, she sat down and continued to read the articles on Oceanic. The company was out of Washington. She frowned, realizing it was already past business hours, and she couldn't contact them tonight. But she sent an email, asking if they had done the study on Okanagan Lake within the last few years. She'd forgotten to ask Nan for the year this was done, and weatherman hadn't mentioned it either.

She rewrote the email so it didn't mention a year. Just any of their research with imaging on the lake itself.

Once she sent that off, she was done for the moment. She had so much stuff in progress that her head was spinning.

At that moment, Goliath jumped onto her lap and insisted on a cuddle. She groaned, gratefully sank back into the couch, pushing away from her laptop, and just held him for a moment. But he wouldn't have any of that. He kept butting his head against her chin.

"Did I forget to feed you again?" she whispered. She could hear little meows in her ear. "Well, it wasn't just you I forgot to feed. I didn't get any lunch either."

She got up and went to check the animals' food supplies, and, sure enough, all of them were out of food. As soon as Mugs heard her grab the dog food bag, he came running. She served him a generous portion, realizing the bag itself was getting a little low.

"Mugs, we need money," she said.

Mugs barked, as if agreeing.

She fed Thaddeus and gave Goliath a can of soft food. "If nothing else, guys, we'll get paid if we work for Mack tomorrow. Thanks to Mack. That should help us a lot."

It wouldn't be much but enough for her to get a few more groceries or alternatively get food for the animals. Depending on her own food supply as to which one would come first.

Then she remembered the money she had in the bowl upstairs. When she had removed the pile of clothing to bring the chair down to show to Fen Gunderson, she'd put the clothing on top of the bowl, so it would be hidden when the appraiser was here.

She wanted to just have a bath and chill for the evening. But she wasn't at all sure about sleeping tonight. She needed it—she was really exhausted. She also needed some food. She went through her cupboards again and found it would be either cheese and crackers, which sounded deplorable because she was tired of the same foods, or a hot bowl of ramen. That won hands down.

With yet another bowl of ramen while the darkness settled outside, she propped chairs up against the inside of the front and back doors, leaving a light on downstairs so others would think she was still up. She closed the curtains to project just a glimmer of light outside and headed upstairs. She kept her bedroom light on low as she looked at the big bed, wondering at the centuries—well, at least the decades—of use it had had.

"Nan, you did a hell of a job taking care of this for your grandmother. You knew where it came from. And you wanted it to go to me, even if I sold it. That's huge for me. It is so huge."

On that thought she wondered if the provenance folder was somewhere in this room. She looked under the bed, dismissed the night tables which weren't even big enough for a folder, then she opened the closet doors and groaned. As soon as she did that, everything came cascading forward. She still had yet to get through even ten percent of the closet's contents. Stacks of clothing remained everywhere.

"This is a major job," she said to the animals. "But, hey, we're up for it. The payout is incredible."

She prepped herself for bed and hopped in. As she lay here thinking about the years and years that people had slept on this very spot, it made her smile. Something was so very comforting about that.

The thought that she was sleeping on thousands of dollars was less than comforting. She'd become cavalier about money when she had lived with her husband. Since she didn't *get* money—or so he said—he took care of the finances. She resided among so much opulence, but she had no idea of the costs or the brand names or where it all came from—a brand-new piece from a store or a family heirloom handed down? None of that had really occurred to her.

Realizing that the bed she was now on probably was worth more money than her marital bed just astounded her.

Her husband had been all about how much money he had spent on their furnishings, impressing himself more than Doreen. She would cheerfully have traded it in for a regular bed and used the money to help somebody in need.

She hadn't realized how many people were in need until she became one of them.

Chapter 16

S O MUCH WAS going on in her head that it was hard to calm down. She was excited over the potential sale of the antiques, panicked with worry that something would happen before she could cash in on them, and feeling guilty as hell because these pieces had been in her family for a century. How did that make her feel? They all had enough money that they could hang on to these pieces and enjoy them. The devil inside whispered to her, *You don't like the furniture anyway, so what the hell? Just get rid of it.*

But it was definitely a toss-up as to what she should ultimately do.

Shaking her head, she also pondered the cold case she'd been working on. But she couldn't get any more information to confirm or deny her hypothesis. She knew the townspeople would have gone looking for anybody missing in the floods. That was an obvious thing to have done. But where could the little boy and the handyman have gone? Apparently there had been no signs of them ever since.

And that was strange too. Henry Huberts had family in Kelowna; he also had family in the nearby towns of Vernon and Penticton. So you'd think somebody there would have heard from him. But, if he'd done something absolutely horrible, then he probably would have walked away from everything he had known and never returned. She couldn't imagine doing something like that.

Then she stopped and drew herself up short. "Okay, so I've done something like that," she said, "but I didn't walk away from Nan—just my old life with my ex. Not that I had much choice. Besides, Nan was my cornerstone in this crazy new world."

Then she had to consider the intruder last night. Was he coming back? She was tempted to grab a blanket and sleep on the couch. At least then he would wake her up. Up here she might miss him.

The more she thought about it, the more she felt that was a good choice. She grabbed her comforter and called the animals. "You guys might as well come downstairs with me," she said. "You'll be my alarm system."

She made a bed on the couch. It seemed odd to be sleeping on something worth so much money. But she figured that more than one person had slept on it over the years. She laid a sheet down to preserve it, which also felt stupid. But it didn't matter. She would do what she had to do.

She stretched out, shutting off the light, leaving her upstairs light on. She pulled the comforter over her and felt measurably better. Nobody would sneak in here now without her knowing it.

But they might try.

She frowned and thought about that. Then she left her warm covers and grabbed the poker from the fireplace. With that at her side, she curled up in a ball, Goliath laying on her hip, Mugs at my feet, and Thaddeus resting on the back of the couch. And she snoozed away.

A low warning growl from Mugs at her side woke her up. As she shifted, Goliath dug his claws into her hip, and it was all she could do to hold back her yelp. She looked up to see Thaddeus's eyes gleaming in the darkness as he stared toward the kitchen. The kitchen was out of sight, but the doorway that led to it was where something had grabbed all their attention. She listened, hearing the doorknob rattle. If it was the same person who had come last night, she figured he should know a chair was there. So it wouldn't work to get back in again. She carefully moved Goliath and snuck out of the covers with Mugs at her side, placed a hand on the back of his neck, and whispered, "*Shh.*"

Goliath rose and stretched, arching his back high into this weird witch's cat look. And Thaddeus, not to be left out, jumped onto her shoulder, digging in his claws in his panic to not be left alone.

She crept forward, and, with the lights out, she could see a shadow outside at her kitchen door. The poker was firmly in her hand as she got closer to find out who the hell was here. She should have checked out the front to see if a vehicle was parked anywhere. Not that an intruder would be stupid enough to pull up into her driveway. But, if he had, then Mugs would have definitely heard that.

But the intruder had full access to her backyard now. Something she hadn't considered when she had pulled down the dilapidated rear fence. Not that she'd been considering assholes breaking and entering her property either. She'd been all about cleaning up the rat's nest of three different mixed fencings and opening up her view to the creek. But it also meant it was easier for people to creep into her yard.

She frowned, seeing the same shadow, wondering how she could open the door suddenly and smack him one.

The doorknob turned again. This time somebody had a tool scraping on the other side. *He's trying to pick the lock.* She frowned deeper and crept along the kitchen to see if she could see from the kitchen window by the table, but he was behind the framework of the door, so she couldn't see him. She knew he couldn't come in this door because of the chair propped underneath.

She crept back to the front door, taking a quick look for any suspicious or unknown vehicles. At the bottom of the cul-de-sac was an old flatbed pickup. She stared, wanting to go outside to take a picture of the license plate but was afraid to.

She pulled out her phone and sent a text to Mack. **Intruder at back door. Trying to pick lock.** Then she turned off the volume on her phone, leaving it in her hand so she could feel the vibrating buzz instead. She crept back into the kitchen to see who wanted in.

He appeared to have given up on the lock and stomped his feet on the veranda. She was surprised he let his frustration get the better of him because, if she'd been upstairs, she would have heard that.

Then she heard him swear. With an ear cocked against the door, she still didn't recognize the voice.

A buzz in her hand alerted her. She backed out of the kitchen, hoping the intruder hadn't heard her. What she wanted to do, if he disappeared to the front door, was to go and see who it was.

There was one simple line from Mack. **On my way.**

But she knew he'd be at least ten minutes. Could the animals attack the intruder enough to detain him? And, if so, should it be at the front door or at the back door? If she unlocked the front door, and he came in ... That was the last thing she wanted, having her intruder inside to see those antiques. Nan had had her door open for anyone and everyone all those years she had lived in this house, and these antique pieces were still sitting here. But the minute word got out that the pieces were worth big money, Doreen knew everybody would view things differently.

And they had, as witnessed by her two intruders to date. Or one guy coming back a second time.

She vacillated between her choices, when her intruder gave the doorknob one last hard shake, then he stomped down the veranda steps. He was a large man, wearing a black hoodie, with a baseball cap under the hoodie. She watched as he disappeared, at a run toward the front yard.

She raced to the front door, not worried about being quiet. He tried the front door. She watched as the knob turned in his hand. The simple little closure defeating him. He brought out his tools again.

She held up her phone in Camera mode, ready to take a picture, but the curtains on the big front windows were closed. It was too dark for a flash because it would bounce back, reflecting off the window. That wouldn't work for her either. No way in heck would Mack get here fast enough. As soon as he did arrive, this guy would run. The best thing she could do was sneak out the back and come around to the front and see if she could trip up her intruder.

With that thought in mind, she went to remove the chair at the kitchen door, propped it open for the animals, and then slipped around to the side of the house. She could see headlights turning down toward the cul-de-sac as she came around to the front. But her intruder still worked on entering the front door.

He saw the lights coming and crouched below the railing. The light came up, going over his head and coming down and around the corner. Sure enough it was Mack. She wanted to cheer.

When her intruder realized the vehicle was coming toward him, the guy bolted down the front porch steps and tried to run away. But he came first into contact with Goliath, who snuck between his legs, tripping him. As he fell flat to the ground, Mugs barked in his ear.

With the fireplace poker in hand, she stomped her foot on his back and held the poker tip against the center of his neck. "Don't move," she said in a deep, dark voice.

He squawked and lay still. As he squawked, so did Thaddeus, crying out, "Body in the garden. Body in the garden. Body in the garden. Body in the garden." He wouldn't shut up.

Mack ran over. "Thaddeus, are you okay?"

The bird stopped speaking and preened. "Thaddeus is fine. Thaddeus is fine."

Mack had a flashlight and shone it at the man underneath her foot but caught sight of the poker and followed her arm up to Doreen's face. "Are you really out here confronting your intruder?" he asked.

She glared at him. "You know how I feel about the contents of that house."

He raised both hands in utter frustration. "This guy could have killed you."

"And I could have killed him." She poked the point of the poker into the guy's neck for emphasis.

"Yeah," the guy called out. "What the hell is going on?"

"You were trying to break into this person's house." Mack squatted in front of him.

"Get that dog off me."

Mugs was on the guy's back, his mouth full of the guy's shirt.

"Nah. I'm not doing that. I'm not exactly sure what technique he's using, but he's usually a pretty good watchdog."

"It's my house," the guy blustered. "I forgot my key."

At that, Doreen poked him harder in the neck. "That's my house," she snapped. "How dare you?"

"Oh, no you don't. That was Nan's house, and she lost it to me in a poker game."

"Oh, yeah? And when was that?" Mack asked in a drawn voice.

"Two nights ago," he snapped.

"Well, that's nice," Doreen said. "It wasn't her house to bet in a poker game. It's in my name. Legally. Like, two weeks ago. And I don't believe you. She would never have put up the house in a poker game."

"She said I could have anything I wanted."

"That's nice, but it's not hers to give away," Mack said.

The man glared at him. "She said it was hers."

"Well, it's not," Doreen said. "It's mine."

The guy tried to roll over and look up at her.

"I'm Doreen, Nan's granddaughter," Doreen said, "and you're nothing but a dirty rotten liar."

"Dirty rotten liar. Dirty rotten liar," Thaddeus squawked, his wings wide as he flashed his brand-new words at everyone loud and clear.

Mack leaned back on his haunches and chuckled. "I thought you were teaching that bird to say nice things."

"I forgot," she said. "Who knew he'd pick up that phrase?"

"Dirty little liar. Dirty little liar."

The man groaned. "I'm not lying."

"Yes, you are," Doreen said. "Because you were trying to pick the locks to get in."

"Of course I was," he said. "How else am I supposed to get into my new home?"

"In the middle of the night?" Mack asked. "I don't think so."

He reached around Doreen, grabbed the guy's arms, and hooked him up with handcuffs. He turned to Mugs, who didn't appear to want to let go of his quarry. "Sorry, big guy, but I have to take this perp down to the station and arrest him for breaking and entering. And attempted assault and attempted theft."

"I didn't steal anything," he roared. "And you're the ones who assaulted me."

"You're trying to break into my house," Doreen said. "I'm allowed to defend my home."

"I didn't steal anything," he snapped.

"How do I know that?" she asked. "You were in my house last night. Weren't you? I'm still trying to figure out just what you might have stolen. And then you came back this time, so you were obviously back for more."

"You don't know anything," he spat out. "I was just looking around the place. I wasn't hurting anything."

"No, you were casing my place." She glared at him. "Looking for what you could steal. Admit it …"

"Hey, I wasn't hurting anything," he blustered, but Mack had heard enough.

He hauled him to his feet, dumping Mugs unceremoniously to the ground.

But Mugs wasn't to be deterred. He grabbed a hold of the guy's pant leg and tugged it. With Mack pulling in one direction and Mugs in the other direction, the guy was being torn in two. Doreen figured it was better to walk Mugs toward Mack's car so at least the basset hound was going the right way and was a help, not a hindrance.

At his car, Mack put the guy in the back seat and turned to look at Doreen. "Are you all right?"

She sighed, staring at her intruder. "I am. But, I'm not real fond of him."

The intruder glared at her from the back of the vehicle.

She looked over at Mack. "Do you know who he is?"

"Not yet," Mack said, "but I will find out. Go on. Get some sleep. The excitement is over for tonight." He hopped in the vehicle and drove away.

Chapter 17

Sunday morning…

T HE NEXT MORNING she woke up, still sleeping on the couch but feeling a whole lot better. She stretched, groaned slightly at the way her back didn't appreciate the new sleeping position, and realized it could have something to do with the weight of Goliath, lying on the small of her back.

She moaned. "Goliath, you need to go on a diet."

A huge furry arm stretched over her shoulder, the paw coming to rest on the inside of her forearm with the claws out to squeeze ever-so-gently.

"Okay," she said, "maybe not a diet. Still, you are one heavy cat."

He stood and shoved his face into hers. Very gently, and hanging on to his body, she twisted underneath him so the cat was now stretched out on her belly. She looked around to see Thaddeus perched on top of the couch, sleeping. Mugs, aware that she was awake, now shoved his jowls into her face, probably out of jealousy of Goliath.

She chuckled. "Good morning, guys. We had an eventful night again, didn't we?"

She checked the clock and saw it was already eight. Good thing she didn't really have anything to do today. She would go to Mack's mom's garden, but now Doreen hated to leave her house. She also had more research she wanted to do. And that would take a bit of time.

Since it was eight, maybe she had some email responses. As she stood, she groaned. "Coffee. We'll put it on first. Then we'll have a shower."

And that was what she did.

When she came back downstairs forty minutes later, dressed and her hair no longer dripping, she felt marginally better. When she checked her emails and saw a response, she felt a hell of a lot better.

Instead of jumping into the message from Oceanic, she grabbed a cup of coffee first, then sat down at the table with a piece of toast. She slowly read through the email and crowed in delight. They had completed a project in the lake. They had been looking for the large mammal that everybody had spoken about but hadn't found anything. And was she looking for something in particular?

She wrote back and gave them the location she had been worried about, thanking them for any information they had.

With that sent off, she finished her toast and coffee, considered contacting Mack to see if he'd gotten any more information out of her intruder. But maybe Mack had gone to bed really late after questioning her intruder. She didn't know how that worked with him. She sent him a quick text. **It's morning! Did you get any information out of my intruder last night?**

Instead of texting her back, he phoned. "He's still saying it's his house, and he wasn't trying to break in."

"Well, it's not his house," she said heatedly.

"No," he said, "but he's figuring, by saying that, he'll get off without having any charges pressed."

"What does he do for a living?" she asked suspiciously. "And what's his name?"

"What are you gonna do with that information?"

"See if he has any connection to Nan. I'm afraid somebody overheard a conversation about the antiques here."

"That could be possible," he said. "His name is Brandon Byers. I believe he's a janitor at the elementary school."

"Huh," she said. "I wonder if he does part-time work over at Nan's retirement home too."

"I can find out," he said. "Anyway, relax, have a good morning, and, if you get a chance to go to Mom's garden, go for it."

"I'm just really hesitant to leave this place alone," she said.

"With good reason," he said cheerfully. "But you can't be a prisoner. You need to do other things."

"I know that," she said. "Even when I am at home, apparently things get me into trouble."

"Exactly," he said. "So don't worry about it." And he hung up.

She thought about it and knew he was right. She had a key, so she could lock the doors. She could leave the chair propped up against the front door. The garage was full of junk, and its doors were inoperable. If she could get that garage cleaned out, she could park her Honda inside and lock that door too. It was just such a mess in there.

Nan hadn't gotten rid of anything in this house for the last forty or so years. At least from the looks of it. Because Doreen would reap the reward for that, she could hardly complain. She would look up who this asshole was who thought he could walk into her place first.

She called Nan, her source of all information. "Do you know a Brandon Byers?"

"Oh, the new janitor," Nan said. "Yes, I absolutely do. He works here part-time. Why?"

"He tried to break into my house last night. I think your retirement home needs to hire somebody different. I suspect he overheard our conversation about the antiques and decided to come look for himself."

Nan was horrified. "Oh, my dear, that's terrible. Do you think he's the same one who was there the previous night?"

"Yes, it was him both times," Doreen said, not wanting to think about the alternative. "If two different men were involved, that would be awful. I don't want to think about two intruders."

"That would be too much of a coincidence," Nan said comfortingly. "I will be sure to tell the management here."

"Yes, because, if he's overhearing those kinds of conversations, he could be going into apartments and stealing things at Rosemoor Manor," Doreen said. "You can't trust him."

"Now that you mention it, there have been some complaints about a few pieces going missing. Vernon said somebody took twenty dollars off his dresser. I wonder if Brandon was around then."

"Somebody needs to investigate that," Doreen said heatedly, "because Brandon was certainly here last night. Mack took him down to the police station for questioning. I don't know if they'll charge him or what, but I sure as heck don't want him left on the streets."

"That was really foolish of Brandon," Nan said. "He'll lose both jobs because of this."

"It sounds like he *should* be losing both jobs," Doreen said. "Think about it. The guy is a thief. Oh, by the way, he also said he won the house in a poker game with you."

At that, Nan's outrage turned into sheer anger. "I would never bet the house on a game. Not even in any of our betting pools. Not when it was mine. And certainly not when it was yours."

"I knew that," Doreen said. "I told him that too."

"I'm glad you did," she said. "How dare he spread such horrible rumors about me. And why?" she cried out. "What could he possibly expect to get out of that?"

"Access to the antiques," Doreen said.

"Wow," she said. "So did you ever figure out who was your caller?"

"Interesting," Doreen said. "I wonder if that was him too. I'll mention it to Mack. I'd love to have that locked down too."

"I figured it had more to do with the recent murders, what with the guy threatening you would be dead next."

"Could be," Doreen said in a noncommittal voice. "I don't know for sure though." With that she signed off with her grandmother. But she felt better now. The retirement home could do something about Brandon.

Doreen still couldn't shake off the feeling that maybe he'd nicked something from her place the first night. After all, he was actually inside that time. The trouble was, so many knickknacks were here that she couldn't begin to pinpoint what he might have taken. And her antiquities appraisal had been based on the larger furniture pieces. She'd taken multiple pictures herself, but so much stuff was here that she couldn't be sure ...

In order to push along the sale of these expensive antiques—and to get them out of her home—Doreen needed that provenance folder of Nan's. In the back of her mind, Doreen thought it would be either in the master bedroom closet upstairs or in the basement. She now remembered the basement from her childhood—where Nan had kept her canning supplies for her preserves. Doreen remembered a musty smell on the furniture at the time. And how she hated going down there because of the poor lighting and the spider population.

Now any antiques down there could be ruined if Nan hadn't properly protected them from the musty damp environment.

But that wasn't today's priority. She did have to get to Millicent's garden. She was probably better off doing that right now. With that thought in mind, she packed up, grabbed a pair of gloves, a water bottle, an apple, and the animals in tow, she walked the creek way around to the garden. Millicent didn't have access to the creek from the back of her yard.

Doreen walked around to the front of the block. As she walked up to the front porch, she saw no sign of Millicent in the window. Doreen carried on through to the back, hoping at least Mack had told his mom that Doreen would be coming today. As she stopped at the backyard gardens, she smiled to see how much work they'd done. The begonias had been transplanted. The daisies had been transplanted. The irrigation was being installed, with some of the digging in progress. Lots of weeding was also in progress, and the shrubs still needed some pruning.

She got to work. She was sticking to two hours every week and just keeping up with what was absolutely necessary. And then, as more was required, Mack would give her a hand to cut back on some of the heavier physical work. It wasn't that she cared about that. She was more than happy to have the hours and to do the work. But some of it was too heavy for her to do alone.

She lost herself in her work, only coming up for air when her watch told her that two hours was up. She was happy with the amount of weeding she'd accomplished, but still so much was left to do. She should, by rights, be working four hours a week here. But she knew money was tight for them to pay somebody too.

She collected her animals, who had done nothing but sniff and wander around the garden, enjoying themselves, and started back to her place. She went along the creek again, absolutely loving the pathway, focusing on that, easily ignoring things swept downriver that she'd found. That was good because the last thing she wanted to do was find more ugly things in the water. It would just spoil the creek for her.

Having found a dismembered arm had been a huge shock. But she was quite happy in that she and Mack had found the rest of that body too, and the poor woman could be put to rest, all the pieces of her in the same place.

Leaving the creek at the pathway to the cul-de-sac, Doreen sauntered back home. As she walked past Ella's empty house, the neighbor who had accused Doreen of interfering in all kinds of stuff. But with Ella now facing a trial for murdering her brother, Doreen figured Ella's house would be for sale soon.

As she walked closer to her place, the old neighbor on the other side of her stepped out to grab the newspaper. He looked at her and frowned. She looked at him and smiled. "Good morning."

"What's good about it?" he asked.

"Well, the cul-de-sac isn't clogged with reporters," she said cheerfully. "That's something good."

He glared at her. "They wouldn't have been here in the first place if you hadn't moved into the neighborhood." He turned to walk back inside.

"Have a nice day," she called out as his door slammed. She chuckled. "Life is too short to get mad about something like that," she said to the animals.

She turned to make sure Goliath, ever the straggler, was still with her. But he appeared to be wandering through the garden bed. She wondered about getting a harness for him too but figured that would lead to nothing but a huge fight. "But it might be entertaining. Come on, Goliath. If you don't come now, I'll start researching harnesses for cats. And then you and Mugs can walk together."

As if he understood, Goliath screeched past her and raced across the lawn to the front porch, where he hopped onto the railing and stared out with a sense of disdain.

She just grinned. "Perfect timing and a perfect place to come home to," she announced as they walked up. "It's lunchtime. Now, do we have anything left to eat in the house?" She answered her own question. "Of course not. Why would there be food today when there hasn't been some on any other day?"

She walked into the house and headed straight for the kitchen. And froze. She slowly took five steps backward so she could look at the living room and damned if one chair wasn't upside down.

She gasped and cried out, "Somebody was in here again."

She ran around the room and the lower floor, checking to make sure nothing was missing. She returned to the upended chair that went with the couch and the bedroom set.

The maker's mark had been exposed for all to see.

Chapter 18

SHE CALLED MACK. "I was only gone for a couple hours to work in your mom's garden," she cried out. "Now what am I supposed to do?"

"I guess the answer to that is, stay home," he said quietly. "But I'm not sure that's a great answer, depending on who is doing this."

"Do you still have my intruder locked up?"

"No," he said heavily. "He was released on bail this morning."

She froze. "Why didn't you forewarn me?"

"I didn't know until just a few moments ago."

"So you guys let go the one guy we caught breaking into my house?" she yelled. "Why?"

"I didn't, but, yes, the prosecutor said to release him," he said. "Of course, if we can prove he was the one at your house this morning or two nights ago," Mack said, "no way would he get out of jail again."

"The legal system is so broken." She sat down on the couch. "This is really sad."

"It is. You need to make sure nothing is missing."

Once again she gave a half-hysterical laugh. "Remember

what this place looks like?"

"I know," he said. "Look. I'll see if we can get you a basic security system set up temporarily. I know you can't afford to get a proper system, but this is getting serious. Let me talk to my boss, and I'll get back to you."

She still shook with outrage, not fear, which she thought was amazing, but also felt such anguish that somebody would try to take what could be a life preserver from her.

She headed into the kitchen and put on a pot of coffee. She didn't need a caffeine high by any means, but it would be a soothing comfort drink. As she'd worked hard all morning, she also needed food.

The coffee finished dripping, and she poured herself a cup. With a peanut butter sandwich, she sat down at the kitchen table and tried to eat slowly. But she was too hungry. When the sandwich disappeared in a few bites, she got up and made herself a second one. She could understand why people were addicted to them. Although, if it was all she had to eat, she'd get sick of them eventually.

When the phone rang, she was grateful to see it was Mack.

"I'll be over later this afternoon," he said, "with some security equipment. We'll set it up at the front and the back doors and will ensure every camera is directed toward the antiques. I'll bring a team to canvass your neighbors, seeing as your latest intruder was there in broad daylight, but also to gather and to process fingerprints found on the chair, the doorknobs, the hutch."

"Thank you. And thank your boss for me."

He chuckled. "I'll explain how to use the security system when I get there."

With that she had to be satisfied. At this point, she was

bound and determined to document everything else on this floor. She figured the basement door was behind that massive hutch in the living room. But the basement was a project for another day; she had more than enough to keep her busy for a long time yet. After taking more photos of hopefully every little thing in the living room, she felt it was time for a cup of tea. But then Mack drove up. She opened the front door and beamed at him. "Thank you very much for helping out."

"I think the boss figured maybe we should since you've helped us so much."

She was delighted with that answer, ushering in the men.

Apparently Mack, with his big grin, thought it was a good one too. He pointed to a tall skinny man beside him. "This is David. He'll help me install this." Mack pointed to the other two guys, dispersing in her living room. "Those are some of my forensic guys, who will gather fingerprints."

"Perfect," she said, reaching out to shake David's hand. "Thank you all very much," she said, including the two fingerprint guys already at work.

David just gave her a sideways grin. "No problem, ma'am."

She backed away. "I'll put on some coffee for you." She went into the kitchen, almost skipping.

With the coffee on, she stood in the kitchen–living room doorway and watched as two men dusted for prints while Mack and David set up cameras and her temporary alarm system. "Is this something I will control or you guys?" They didn't answer.

When they started swearing, she realized something was not working out. She tiptoed back into the kitchen, whispering to Mugs, "We should leave them alone."

Thaddeus had different ideas. He continued pacing the floor around the men, generally getting in the way.

Exasperated, Mack turned to Doreen. "Get Thaddeus out of here, will you?"

"Thaddeus, come on. Come over here and leave the men alone."

But Thaddeus just cocked his head and shot a gimlet look her way.

She sighed and walked into the living room. "These men are having some trouble. Just leave them be." She squatted and picked him up just as David swore.

"Goddammit," he said.

Instantly Thaddeus repeated, "Goddammit. Goddammit. Goddammit." And he preened as if perfectly delighted to have a new phrase.

She groaned. "David, if you don't mind …"

He looked up, horrified at the bird waiting for him to open his mouth and to potentially give him another choice of words. "I had no idea he would do something like that," David said.

"Nobody does," Mack said. "He is the damnedest bird."

"Damnedest bird. Damnedest bird," Thaddeus said. And then, as if realizing how irritating he was, he cackled with a roaring laughter.

Everybody stopped and stared at him. She shook her head. "He's demented. Nothing I can do about it," she said.

"Except you could take him away," Mack said drily.

That sounded like an order. With Thaddeus on her arm, she backed into the kitchen and sat down with her laptop. Because David and two more policemen were here with Mack, she wouldn't pester him with questions about the other cases they were working on. But she had a lot of notes and questions herself that she needed to work on. And the biggest one was, who was Josh Huberts, the grandson of the handyman Henry Huberts?

He and Celeste had been arguing at the gardening store, but that didn't mean he was a murderer. Now that he was dead, Doreen wanted to know who had killed him, or had he really killed himself? She wondered about why somebody would take their own life. If you had just killed the woman you loved—in a fit of rage or a bout of temporary insanity—and immediately afterward realized you would spend the rest of your life in prison for that one fatal second of action, then maybe it made sense. But only if his suicide was just as motivated and just as reactive, as in the seconds following Celeste's murder.

Not that Doreen would ever do something like that, but she had thought that killing some people at various times in her life might be a nice—and permanent—answer to some problems. She just wasn't the kind to go through with it.

She researched the grandson's past, hoping that maybe, just maybe, something would pop up. But not very much was out there on him. He had kept a fairly low profile. She wondered and worried, and then thought about the Family Planning Center. Maybe the choice to place Celeste's body there wasn't directed against the center itself; maybe it was more against the people running it.

As she researched that angle, she realized that the owner of the center, Cecily Bingham, was the sister of the dead woman, Celeste Bingham. Doreen just loved small towns. Everybody was related to everybody else.

Surely Mack already knew about that familial tie, right? He wouldn't dismiss this connection so casually, unless the higher-ups were tying his hands. She shook her head at the legal system that could leap at a murder-suicide solution so quickly just to supposedly solve a crime.

Delighted with that tidbit, she brought forward her notes and added these to her collection. Maybe Huberts had a problem with Cecily. Then Doreen searched online for information on Josh and Celeste. But nothing came up, just hints and innuendos from social media about their relationship problems and the occasional online article regarding abortion. Seems Josh was against abortions, whereas both sisters were advocates. The older sister, Celeste, was mentioned in many articles as she rose to prominence as a businesswoman. Cecily was often mentioned as an activist.

"Now what are you working on?" Mack asked as he walked toward her with a mess of electronics in his hands. He pointed to the kitchen door. "We'll set up another one here."

She beamed in delight. "I guess I should mention the garage door. It's not locked, but it doesn't open either. The door is jammed shut and probably has been for years."

He looked at her. "I keep forgetting about the garage."

She nodded. "I do too. For one, you can't even get in there, it's so damn full. And, for another, the garage door into the house has been behind boxes of crap, so I don't think anybody could get in or out that way."

He walked over to the far side of the dining room, which met up with the storage area off the kitchen where the washer and dryer were. By wiggling through the stacks of boxes there, he tried to open that door. It wouldn't budge. He shrugged. "Well, I presume they're not coming in from there."

"I can't even get any of the garage doors open," she said. "I asked Nan about it, but I never did get an answer. She kind of brushed it off."

He stared at her.

She nodded grimly. "I know. Do you ever think a deep dark secret could be in there?"

David chuckled. "Nan has been collecting crap since forever. I'm not sure I'd call her a hoarder. As you look around this place, there's lots of room to sit. It's clean, although it's crowded."

"Yeah, you haven't seen the inside of that garage though," Mack said. "There is another door on the other side of the garage. I looked in the window one time, but stuff was piled so high that I could barely even see past the window itself."

"Maybe we should check if it's still that way," she said.

He looked at her in surprise. "Have you seriously never been in there?"

She shook her head. "No, because, like you, I couldn't get in, and I couldn't see in. I've got enough to deal with on the inside of the house. I'm still working my way through her closet, for crying out loud. I'm only about ten percent, maybe fifteen percent, through it."

"At least she enjoyed her life," David said.

"At least she *is* enjoying her life," Doreen corrected. "My grandmother is happy and healthy, living at Rosemoor Manor."

He nodded. "I've seen her there. My grandmother is in there too. She says Nan keeps things lively."

"Oh, I can imagine," Doreen said. "She's a constant source of entertainment for everyone." She didn't want to discuss the garage at the moment. She motioned at the kitchen door. "Are you doing the install now, or do you want coffee first?"

She wanted to distract them because she *had* looked in that side door. The fact of the matter was, it looked like junk upon junk upon junk had been amassed in the garage. Cleaning that out would take more effort than she had at the moment. That it was also possibly jam-packed with antiques filled her with excitement, but she had more than enough trouble dealing with the antiques she had already had appraised.

She poured coffee for the two men—the other men gone already—and handed them cups while they discussed how to set up the second set of alarms.

As she listened to them, her phone rang. It was the appraiser.

"I've got the photos forwarded to Christie's," he said. "They should be in touch with me over the next day or so. I just wanted to give you that update."

She grinned when she got off the phone. Mack cocked his head in question. She shrugged. "The appraiser just gave me an update, that's all," she said smoothly. She gave David a half glance.

"David works with me at the station," Mack said. "We're hardly here to steal your stuff."

"You could probably steal a ton of stuff that would make me quite happy," she said. "And save me paying for dump runs."

David nodded. "We had lots of dump runs at my grandmother's house too. But nothing was valuable in all her junk. She was one of those who liked to collect things. Dolls, garden gnomes, those little traveling spoons. I think, by the time we were done, we found over ninety-four garden gnomes."

"Oh, those would have been adorable to add to gardens," Doreen cried out. "What did you end up doing with them?"

Mack sighed. "What he did was, he asked everybody if they wanted one or two, and they came to his grandmother's house and were allowed to pick up two each."

"I love that," she said. "Spreading the joy around."

"I was thinking more about spreading the junk around and not having to dispose of them myself," David said, laughing. "But I think people enjoyed their gnomes."

"Absolutely," she said, "What's your grandmother's name?"

"Sheila. Sheila Monterey."

"I've seen some stuck in the corners here and there. I guess Nan intended them for the gardens, once they were cleaned up. I'll have to remember to ask Nan whether any of the gnomes she has here came from Sheila's place."

"I doubt it. At the time I think Nan was collecting a few more of them, and my grandmother was very much of the opinion that Nan already had enough."

"It's almost like people thought she did have a hoarding problem," Doreen said. "When I came into the house, it never occurred to me. And honestly, it still doesn't seem like anything close to a hoarder's house. Although the basement and garage *are* probably full of junk ..."

"It looks that way," Mack said. "Let's deal with the inside of the house. Then we'll deal with the rest."

"Good plan." She glanced around the kitchen. "How much longer do you think you'll be?"

"Why? Trying to get rid of me already?" Mack asked.

As the ding of the arrival of an email sounded, she chuckled and walked over to her laptop to check her inbox. It was from Oceanic with the Okanagan Lake surveys. She raised her eyebrows as she read. "Oh, good."

"*Oh, good* what?" Mack asked suspiciously.

She shrugged. "Nothing. Just a little hobby of mine."

"Your hobbies tend to get me in trouble," Mack said.

"Actually they tend to get you accolades." She clicked on the email and looked at all the attachments. She had specifically laid out the area she was interested in. "We're in a dry season currently, right? And the water is likely to get much lower when we hit summertime, correct?"

"I'm not sure what water you're talking about," David said, "but, if you're talking about Okanagan Lake, then, yes. It's likely to drop another couple of feet, if not more. Unfortunately the city made a mistake earlier this year and let out too much water from the dikes, so the water levels will be low, and we'll be conserving water soon."

"It's already happening," Mack said. "People are only allowed to water their gardens two days a week, and that'll stop too if the water supply drops any lower. We haven't had any rain in thirty days, so we're definitely heading into a drought."

"I guess all kinds of things must come up when the lake drops."

"To a certain extent, yes." Mack turned to study her curiously. "Where are you going with that idea?"

She shrugged. "Maybe nowhere. Any new leads on the poor woman in the carnations?"

He shrugged. "Read the newspapers. That'll tell you."

"Ha," she said. "The reporters are always trying to get the story out of *me*."

"Are they still bothering you?" he turned and asked.

She shook her head. "No. They don't know I'm the one who found her, so that's all good."

"You do have the darnedest luck tripping over bodies, don't you?" David asked with a smile.

The men stepped back from their handiwork.

It didn't take very long to do the back door. She was surprised at how efficient they were on the second door.

Mack showed her how to work the remote for turning it on. He then opened the back door, a horrible shriek going off. He shut it off immediately, but Thaddeus still squawked in pain, and Goliath was nowhere around. Mugs barked like crazy.

She crouched to hug Mugs. "Hey, buddy. I'm sorry about that."

"Yeah, that'll wake up all of you," David said.

"It's kind of a rough system. It's not for long-term," Mack said. "It would be better to get a proper system in here and to arm the windows as well."

She hadn't even thought of the windows. She looked at the big window in the living room, then glanced at Mack.

He shook his head. "I highly doubt they'll come in that way. There's no way to do it quietly."

She nodded. "This should hopefully do what I need done for the next few days anyway."

He turned as he looked at his watch. "On that note, we have to leave."

The two men packed up their tools, and, before she had a chance to say, *Thank you*, they were gone. She stood on the front porch and watched as they drove away. They presumably had other police work to do, and this was just a timeout in their day. Since they'd been here for well over an hour, they were probably well past being late for other work.

She hadn't had a chance to ask Mack any case-related questions. She groaned and headed back to her laptop.

She studied the map the company had sent her of the entrance to Mission Creek, then all the accompanying images. She didn't have a program that would let her look at them close enough, leaving her wondering if anybody did.

It was fascinating to consider. She studied where the mouth of the creek became more of a river, where it widened and changed color, darkening as it deepened. She had only been down there once, maybe twice. The path along the creek did go all the way to the end though. Maybe she should take a long walk and sort it out.

How far was it? And then she realized it was less than a mile. Determinedly she picked up her coffee mug, filled it, and called Mugs to her. Goliath looked at her. "Do you want to come too?" She looked twice at the alarm panel and talked herself out of setting it. After all, they were only going one mile away. One mile there. One mile back. How long could that take? Plus with Mack's presence here again, surely the intruder wouldn't come again today in broad daylight.

Would he?

With Thaddeus on her shoulder, she headed out into the backyard, Goliath walking beside them. He sauntered with a nonchalance that made her smile. Mugs, on the other hand, sniffed everything, overjoyed to be outside. Thaddeus even seemed to enjoy the outing as he ruffled his feathers and chirped on her shoulder.

"Now you sound like a normal bird," she said, chuckling.

He leaned over and brushed her cheek with his beak. She loved it when he did that. She hadn't considered birds to be affectionate, but this one definitely was.

It was a beautiful walk. They passed the cul-de-sac in the path they normally took to get to Nan's. Goliath and Mugs both thought they were heading that way, but she kept going. The creek widened and became a lazy rolling stream of water. It was beautiful.

The spring water runoff had definitely come and gone. Now the river level was much lower. She understood it would get lower yet. But she didn't know how low, considering the lake was already down from its normal level.

She kept walking, enjoying being outside, loving the birds and the trees blowing gently in the wind. She had a good six-foot-wide walkway to lead her. At this point, it was a public walking path. Houses on one side were fenced for privacy.

Then she reached a crossroad with a bridge. The path went underneath. She stayed on the path, and, of course, private property was on one side, but, on the other side, she walked alongside the water.

Eventually she came to where the river dumped into the lake. She smiled. Mugs was having the time of his life. Goliath, on the other hand, was still walking as if this was too much bother.

She stopped, realizing just how very empty the area was. She really enjoyed being in a small town again. Kelowna was a step back in time. She knew both sides of the river were slated for big developments, but they planned to leave a boardwalk in place for the foot traffic.

She proceeded to the point, then realized she was trespassing because it was now private property. She frowned and walked into the river bed. She didn't like people trespassing on her place, so she didn't intend to here. It was just hard to know where one property started and another stopped. The corner was definitely the prime place, but a huge sandbar was down here too. She stood on it, amazed.

How big did this sandbar actually get in times of extreme drought?

An old man at the corner looked at her. She walked over and said, "Sorry. Am I trespassing here too?"

He shook his head. "My property ends along the water line. That sandbar has been around for a long time, but, with the low water levels, it's huge this year," he admitted.

"Was it here all the time, like thirty years ago? It looks like it would stop anything coming down the river from getting past here," she said. "I can't imagine the amount of debris that's built up on the river side of this sandbar."

"Oh, that's because the river has filled in so much," he said. "Thirty years ago we used to have sailboats and motor boats up and down this river all the time. But the rocks came down from the mountaintops and slowly filled in this river. It used to be a huge wide basin here. Couldn't touch bottom. We'd be boating all year-round. Now with the whole thing filled in with rocks, boats can't be used here."

"Oh," she said in a crestfallen voice. "Well, that shoots that theory."

"Why? What are you talking about?"

"I was just wondering if a vehicle could have been washed away in the heavy spring runoff water or a flash flood some twenty-nine years ago," she said. "If it could have been washed down here, would it now be buried?"

"During that ugly flood we had twenty-nine years ago, a truck or a car could certainly have been washed down here, and chances are we would never have seen it. It would have sunk another couple hundred yards out. When the fast-moving water hits the wall of nonmoving lake water, it slows down quickly and drops any debris it carried downriver just offshore where the lake bottom drops off. The sand follows the same pattern," he said. "So, a hundred yards past, that's where it would be."

"Does anybody ever come here to look for missing vehicles?" she asked.

He frowned at her. "You know? I'm not so sure they have. Not in the thirty years I've been here. But, if they didn't look right away, I imagine it would sink deep enough and fast enough that nobody would ever know."

"And how would someone go down there and look?"

He frowned at her. "Do you have a particular reason for asking?"

She made a wry face. "I'm working on a theory that a man and a boy in a truck that went missing twenty-nine years ago might very well have been caught up in the floods and are lying at the bottom of the lake here."

His eyebrows shot up. "You're talking about Gunderson's grandson Paul, aren't you?"

She shrugged. "The story intrigued me. It's very unusual for a boy and a man, as well as the truck, to never pop up again."

"There are chop shops that could have easily changed the color of the truck, cut it up into parts, and sold them on the black market. And you could disappear if you just drive halfway across the country or even across the border."

"But it was also the year of the heavy flooding. What if that handyman wasn't a killer or a pedophile? He didn't have a criminal history, so what if he just helped the boy get home, and he made the decision to cross a bridge when it went out, or when the floods came over it, and they got washed down here?"

The man stopped for a moment; then he said, "You know what? I've never thought of that. Apparently it was pretty rough there for a while. The flooding went on for days."

"My point exactly," she said. "I gather the river gets the highest at about two o'clock in the morning, but it doesn't make sense that the little boy would have been out at that hour."

"Sure. But logjams are a fact of life on a river. We clean up a lot of the fallen debris during the year, but we can't get it all, and the logs can collect, then break free at any time, and come down in a massive torrent of debris," he said. "If that truck got caught up in something like that, it'll be out there." He pointed to the lake beyond. "The question is, how far beyond, and how could we possibly know?"

She nodded, looking to where he pointed.

"Well, now that you got me thinking about it," the man said, "I'm a scuba diver myself, but I've got bad lungs now too. But I do belong to a club. I could mention it to them and see if anybody's interested in going down for a practice run or maybe just a fun diving outing."

"Not much fun though," she said with a sad smile.

"No, but it's a mystery, and I love those." He grinned at her. "And I guess that means you must be Doreen."

She wrinkled her face up at him. "How did you know that?"

He chuckled. "You've found enough dead people already to make a name for yourself." He motioned at the wide expanse of lake in front of them. "If you think the truck might be out there, then I think we should consider looking for it." He stopped and looked at her. "Have you talked to the police about it?"

She shook her head. "Not really. I know it's a cold case because Mack mentioned it to me. But honestly, the reason I thought of it is because the license plate from that truck the little boy was said to be in when he went missing just unearthed in the back of my garden, or Nan's garden, and it borders the creek. So, if the truck got caught up at my end, and the license plate ended up torn off with such force, then I imagine that truck would have gone for a header down here and didn't have any hope of being stopped."

"Wow. That would make so much sense because we had that massive logjam come down. ... In all these years everybody thought he took off with that little boy and now ..." He shook his head and stared back out at the lake. "I never once considered that maybe he got caught up in that logjam. But it makes sense."

"What kind of person was Henry?"

"He was a good guy," the neighbor said. "I would have sworn by him back then, but everybody had so much bad to say, once the little boy was known to have been picked up in his truck. I guess I got caught up in public opinion, and I never did know what to think about it."

"I think that's the worst," she said sadly. "Everybody has an opinion when things go wrong, but often they don't know the truth."

"True, but once everybody knew he'd picked up the little boy, all the negative gossip started."

"Exactly, and all without proof," she said. "And how sad is that? This is just my running theory. I did contact the company that did some imaging of this area, to see if they had pictures that would show a truck or something down there. But I can't see the images close enough on my monitor."

He looked at her with respect. "Wow. That's a really smart thing to do. What you need is a tech company with that kind of capability."

"I don't know anyone in that field," she said. "I'm new in town, so I really don't know the local companies."

He snapped his fingers several times and said, "But you know something? I do. My son works for an IT company. And my nephew works in the video-gaming industry, and graphics are definitely something they do."

"But this would require looking through photographs, maybe getting satellite images, even something more intense to see what is down there. I understand it's very deep, and, like you said, filled with mountain rocks. I don't know of anything that would show us exactly what's down there."

"No, you're probably right," he said. "The best thing would be to search ourselves. And, if that one truck is there, how do we know there aren't half a dozen more down there?"

"I figured, because the water was so low this year and getting lower, that maybe now would be the best time to see what exactly is down there."

"I like it," he announced. "And I like you. You're an out-of-the-box thinker. And that's a good thing."

She laughed. "The only reason I thought of it is because Thaddeus here"—she pointed to the bird on her shoulder— "found the license plate in my backyard."

The man looked with interest at Thaddeus, who had been quiet up until now. Thaddeus rose up on his feet, flapped his wings, and said, "Thaddeus here. Good day."

The old man chuckled, reached out, and gently rubbed a finger down the bird's breast. "Nathan here. Nice to meet you, Thaddeus." He looked down at the menagerie at her feet. "I understand these guys go with you everywhere."

"They've become family," she said with a smile. "This is

Mugs." She rattled his leash, and Mugs sat down and raised a paw.

Enchanted, the neighbor dropped down, picked up the paw. "Nice to meet you, Mr. Mugs."

She didn't correct him on the name. Goliath, not to be left out, sauntered between Mugs and Nathan to get a pat too.

When Nathan finally straightened, he was enthralled with the critters. "I think you're a heck of a good addition to the town."

"I'm glad you think so," Doreen said, "because I'm not sure anybody else does. It's been kind of crazy getting used to being in town, and then with so many issues popping up right away ..."

"Nope. That's a good thing. Those poor people needed to be found. And, if it took somebody like you from out of town to do it, well then, so be it." He turned to face the lake. "Now I'm really intrigued. Do you have any contact information? I'll make some phone calls and see what I might find out." He pulled a pair of glasses from his shirt pocket and a little piece of paper.

In her purse she found a pen. She wrote down her name and phone number and handed it to him.

"I'm Nathan Trusswell," he said with a smile.

She nodded. "If you find out anything, let me know." At that, she turned to walk home, but pivoted and said, "Nice meeting you."

He was already walking with purpose toward his house. He reached up a hand and waved at her in good-bye.

She sauntered back home, feeling a warm glow around her heart. It was a nice one-on-one, even if only one neighbor appreciated the fact that Doreen had brought a new perspective to town. Because, the more she thought about it, the more she really warmed to the idea that poor Henry Huberts hadn't kidnapped the little boy at all.

He'd been doing a neighborly thing to help Paul, and instead they both had died in a terrible accident. And, as even Nathan had said, there'd been a huge log pileup in the river above her place. And one bridge had collapsed during that flood season. If the truck had been caught up in either event it would have had a terrible outcome. Back then the bridges were small wooden constructions. They had to be replaced over the years. Even the one closest to her was new, as in three years old. And the wooden one before that was an improvement on the one that had been there thirty years ago. So, in a way, her theory made a sad, grievous type of sense.

Chapter 19

Monday morning...

F OR THE FIRST night in a long time, she slept beautifully. When she got up the next morning, she carefully followed Mack's instructions on how to disarm the alarm system. It worked. She stepped outside to smile at the sun dappling across her backyard. Today was a good day. She propped open the back door, then walked inside to put on coffee. The phone rang as she pushed the button to grind beans. Mack, ... calling to see if everything was okay.

"I would have called you," she said, "but I got the alarm system off on my own."

"Are you still on for omelets?" he asked.

"Can't wait until you get here," she said. "I'm starving."

He chuckled. "I'm loading all the ingredients into a box. I'll be there in about twenty minutes. We can make breakfast instead of waiting for lunchtime."

Smiling happily and delighted to have a chance to eat a real meal and to learn something new, she walked around outside in the garden while the coffee dripped. Thinking about the garage, she went to the window in its back door entryway and tried to see in, but the glass was so dirty and so dusty, it was hard to see through it. She checked the door-knob, finding it was definitely secure, and it looked like the wood of the door was jammed, same as the interior door. She wondered if that was an ominous sign or just a typical Nan thing.

She went to the front yard, tried to lift the rolling garage door, but it wouldn't move either. As long as it was secure, she was good.

As she walked away from the garage door, Mack pulled up and parked in her driveway.

"What are you doing now?"

She motioned at the garage door. "Just thinking that, if I can't get in, likely nobody else can either."

He nodded. "Good point. Come on. Let's get some food."

She held open the front door for him as he came in with a box. He lowered it onto the kitchen table and brought out bacon, onions, garlic, fresh spinach, cheese, and eggs. Plus the mushrooms she had particularly asked for. She watched in delight, carefully taking notes, then shot a video as he worked.

He groaned. "Why the video?"

"Because I'll forget everything I see," she said. "And I'm determined not to fail at this."

He glanced at her, a gentle smile on his face. "You know, it's okay to fail."

She looked at him in surprise, then shrugged. "It's never been okay to fail before, and, by now, I've felt like a failure in many, many ways. I would just as soon skip that this time." She watched as he cut the bacon into small pieces and pan-fried it with chopped onions and garlic. She sniffed the air with joy. "Oh, that smells absolutely divine."

Mugs barked at her heels, running around in circles.

She reached down and petted him. "I know, buddy. It's food. We haven't smelled such an aroma in many months."

With Mack laughing and telling her exactly what he was doing and how he was doing it, he slowly built an omelet, adding mushrooms and spinach leaves to the skillet. Then he cracked the eggs into a bowl, beat them until smooth. Removing the cooked veggies to another bowl, he then poured the eggs into the hot pan. When they were mostly cooked, he layered the veggies over the egg and topped it all with grated cheese. As she watched, he folded one half over on top of the other, covering up the freshly laid cheese, and then he put a lid on the skillet.

"I only do this so the cheese melts faster."

When he took off the lid, the omelet looked absolutely divine. With an easy maneuver, he draped it onto a cutting board and cut the big omelet in half.

She was still filming when he plated each half and moved them over to the table. She stopped the video, grabbed the toast she'd put on, snagged the butter, and brought both to the table. "This looks fabulous."

"Now you know how to do it," he said.

She nodded and looked at the stove. "I just have to get up the nerve to try."

"No," he said. "Tomorrow you're doing it. No nerve required. You'll just start, and you'll make something exactly like this."

"It seems like a far-off dream," she admitted. She cut her first bite, took it into her mouth, and sagged in joy. "This is wonderful."

"And it's easy to make," he said. "You'll see very quickly how you can make all kinds of gorgeous things."

"I hope so," she said. "I was eating all kinds of gorgeous foods before."

"Speaking of which, have you had any contact with your husband lately?"

She shook her head. "Why would I?"

"When is the divorce proceeding supposed to be completed?"

"I don't think we can start until one year after the separation." She didn't want to talk about her almost ex-husband. He was the last thing on her mind.

"I spoke to my brother again."

She stopped and looked at him, confused for a moment as to who and what his brother was. "Oh? Why?"

"Remember my brother is a lawyer," he said, "and he says you can stop the property award process, even though you've signed the paperwork. And he also said something else I'm not sure you'll be happy about. He wants to file a complaint against your lawyer."

Her jaw dropped. "Can he do that?"

Mack chuckled. "Absolutely. Particularly if you're a lawyer filing a complaint against another lawyer. What she did was gross misconduct. And it shouldn't be allowed, nor should her work be allowed to stand."

"But I'm the one who signed all the paperwork," she said. "Wasn't that onus on me?"

"Not if you followed your lawyer's advice," he said. "Which you did."

She thought about it for a moment. "We're back to that I-can't-pay-him-yet thing though."

"Nick is willing to see what he can do for free," he said. "If it becomes something more complicated, then we'll take another look at what might require funding. It's possible nothing will."

She looked at Mack, trying to hide her innate suspicion of attorneys. "You know I trust you. But I don't know your brother. And he *is* a lawyer," she said quietly. "I'm not making bad guys out of all them but ..."

"*But,* in your experience, that's what you've found so far." He nodded. "I get that, but I trust my brother. He's a good guy. If he says he can do a lot without requiring money, then I suggest we let him do everything he can possibly do without requiring you to pay for his time. You don't know, but maybe your lawyer will have a change of heart when she realizes he's putting in a formal complaint, and she could possibly end up barred from practicing law."

"Can he do that?"

"If he can prove she's dishonest, is a liar and a cheat, as in your case, then who knows what can happen?"

"When did you hear about this?"

"Last night," he said. "My brother contacted me to say your situation wouldn't leave him alone, and he wanted to help. If he could do something that wouldn't take too much time, he was more than ready to do so. Particularly, he wanted to see the documents you signed, and he wanted the contact information for the lawyer who represented you."

She snorted. "You know what? I'm kind of down with him making trouble for her," she said, "but I really don't want it to come back on my ex-husband because then he'll turn around and make my life miserable. When he doesn't get what he wants, he gets really ugly."

"And he wants her?"

She shrugged. "I'm pretty sure he's had her many times over," she said in a dry tone. "The thing is, he doesn't want to share his money."

"But you're entitled to a large share of it," he said.

"Not according to my lawyer."

"And that's what my brother is saying. Your husband built that business while you were there. Nick needs some details so he can take a closer look at it. But, even if you don't want as much as you're entitled to, you shouldn't be without anything. And that's the problem. Look at you. You're living on the money you found in your grandmother's pockets for Christ's sake."

She glared at him. "You're ruining a beautiful omelet."

He stopped and then nodded. "Good point." He chuckled and took another bite. "So you'll repeat this for me tomorrow?"

She shrugged. "Well, I'll repeat something. Obviously it won't taste quite like this though."

"You might be surprised," he said. "There are many meals you can make without too much effort."

"Maybe." But the conversation was hard to come back from. Even though he meant it to help her, she felt depressed. Any mention of her ex-husband and their nasty separation sent her mood plummeting. "Why don't we talk about something better?"

"Like?"

"The guy who broke into my place," she said. "He's a janitor who also works at the retirement home where Nan lives. And they've had a bunch of thefts. I'm wondering if anybody will look into that." She gave him a pointed look.

He frowned at her in surprise. "Nobody mentioned a theft issue."

"I imagine it's kind of a common problem," she said. "They don't want the bad publicity. But, according to Nan, there have definitely been theft issues."

"And you think it's him?"

"It's pretty obvious he's got a problem," she said. "And he works there and at the elementary school too. So who knows? I'm pretty sure he's the one who made the threatening phone calls to me too. I don't know why, unless he just wanted me to get out of town for a few days to clean out my place …"

"That's possible. As for Nan's comments, there's nothing we can formally do until we get a written complaint …"

"If you were to actually question the suspect," she snapped, "he might confess to it. To all of it, if we're lucky."

"And yet, he's been released on those other charges," he said with a raised eyebrow. "And I need a formal complaint to proceed on the Rosemoor thefts. Until then, I can't."

"I know. That doesn't mean he won't be back here for some other infraction," she said with a snort. "Characters like that tend to stay true to form."

"Yes, they do," he said. "And we're back to that formal complaint part, so I could talk to him about that." He pulled out his notepad and jotted down a couple things.

"You know a lot of people living there at Rosemoor. Why don't you talk to them? Doesn't have to be a big police matter. But surely the retirement home would like to see a problem like this go away. Maybe it's happening at the school too? Employee theft is a massive problem, no matter what company you work for," she said with some authority. "My ex used to complain about it all the time."

"That's because he was probably doing it himself," Mack said with a chuckle.

"Can't argue there. I should have seen it happening, you know?" she said quietly.

He settled back and put down his fork on his empty

plate. "Should have seen what happening?"

She figured there was probably a rule about not talking about your ex with single men, but he'd brought up the issue himself. "I should have seen that he was involved with somebody else."

"I think the spouse is often the last person to know. And then it's little things that make you suspicious. But, if they're any good at what they're doing, they don't let on easily."

"I was suspicious," she said, "but I had no clue it was my lawyer."

"Was she a friend of the family?"

She shook her head. "No. She worked for him on some projects. I don't know why I thought it was a good idea to hire an attorney he already knew."

"Who suggested it?"

Doreen looked at Mack in surprise. "She did. I guess that should have been my second indication. But she was all girl talk, how this was so tough, and she was so sorry for me, and she'd do her best for me, and ..." Doreen shook her head. "The truth is, I'm a gullible fool. I just didn't see all that betrayal going on right under my nose."

"Most don't because they are honest people who expect people to be equally honest with them," he said easily. "That's why it happens so often. And why the lying people get away with it."

She nodded and then stared down at the last couple bites of her omelet. She cut it up, put one piece in her mouth, and sighed happily. "You are probably the best omelet-maker I've ever met."

"And have you met many?" he asked drily.

"*Chefs*," she said with a wicked grin. "I've met lots of chefs."

"Did you have one in your house?"

"Of course we did. No way my husband would have anything less than the best for his dinners," she said in a mocking tone. "And he still used to complain all the time."

"In what way?" Mack asked.

"Not enough seasoning, too sweet, too salty, too hot, too cold, presentation wasn't up to snuff." She shrugged. "He needed to work behind a counter himself to understand what it was like to be part of the working-class people."

"And yet, you didn't have the same attitude?"

"No. I tried to get him to be nice. He used to mock me in front of them. They felt sorry for me. And I bet they weren't surprised when he replaced me."

"You are the usual age for that."

She looked at him, then nodded sagely. "That's what one of my friends told me. Along with *I should have done something in advance to prepare, and why the hell had I been so blind?* A woman I knew walked away from her marriage— one in which she and her husband looked really happy—and hooked up with an older, richer man. When I asked her about it, she said, of course, she didn't love him. But she would get replaced sooner or later, and she wanted to make sure she was the one doing the replacing, and she got a *step up* in the meantime. Since then her husband died, and she's very wealthy. I never could be that calculating. I never looked at my future and saw dollar signs."

"No," he said. "But neither did you look at your future and pick an old geyser who'd hopefully die soon and leave you all his money."

"Nope. Apparently I had no plan at all. The good thing about that is, I had Nan. And she apparently made all the plans for me." Her voice softened. "She could see the writing on the wall, even when I couldn't."

"For that, you should be grateful."

"I am," she said. "I have learned more about love and family since leaving my husband than I ever did up until then."

"What about your mother?"

"My mother had a string of men. She'll only go out with one if expensive gifts are involved. She's not a prostitute." She smiled. "But, when you're supposedly high-class, gifts are important. She would say they're very important for women her age. She has a collection. She has them appraised every once in a while. When she needs money, she'll sell them off. She was never angrier than with one of the men she had thought was a great mark. He had given her gifts, but, when she got them appraised, they were cut glass, not diamonds." Doreen chuckled at the memory. "It's not fair that I laugh, but she was so outraged at the deception, and I thought she deserved it."

"It doesn't bear thinking about," he said.

"It's a whole different world," she said. "But my mother was in a different kind of a class. She saw her old age coming and was grasping, trying to preserve her young looks for as long as she could. Whereas this friend of mine just jumped ship early on before her looks went, so she wasn't caught in that position."

"I almost want to say that was a good business tactic," he said, "but, as a man, I'm fairly outraged."

"Get over it," she said with a grin. "I don't think the old guy particularly minded. He died in bed, having a jolly old time probably." She gave a bigger grin. "Besides, I'm not like that."

"Obviously," he said. "It's hard to imagine you walked

away with nothing."

"It had to happen, I suppose," she said.

"No, not at all. You're more than entitled to some money."

"How much though? My lawyer said I wouldn't even get twenty or thirty thousand, and was that worth fighting for when she would end up getting the bulk of that?"

He just stared at her.

She looked up at him and sighed. "I'm really an unsuspecting idiot, aren't I?"

"Let me talk to my brother. If your husband has the kind of money he seems to, chances are you are entitled to quite a nice chunk."

"What does that mean?" she asked, wrinkling her nose up at him. "Does that mean fifty thousand, one hundred thousand?"

"How about a couple million?" he asked, watching her astonished expression. "You were married fourteen years, and he built his business from the ground up with you at that time."

"He was an up-and-coming hotshot and had money from the beginning," she said, "but nothing like now."

"Exactly." Mack pulled out his phone and sent his brother a text. "Okay, I told him that you would give me the contact information he needs, and he is to go ahead and do what he can for free. He won't charge for any work without checking with us."

She warmed at the sound of the "us" part. "If he's willing to do something for free," she said quietly, "he definitely has my deepest thanks. But I don't have any expectation of him successfully changing my situation."

Mack tilted his head and grinned at her. "If nothing else,

you might want to consider that Nick will cost your ex some money and your lawyer some aggravation."

At that, she laughed. "In that case, go for it."

"Good," he said. "I hate hearing you're still willing for him to have everything his way. Sometimes you need to stand up and fight."

"I fight sometimes," she said with a smirk. "When reporters approach me, I get quite feisty." Her phone rang just then. She glanced down and answered, "Hi, Nan."

"Hi. How are you?" she said.

"I'm fine. What's up?"

"Nothing. I just wondered if you were doing anything today."

There was something crafty in her grandmother's voice. Doreen narrowed her eyes and said, "What are you up to, Nan?"

"Nothing."

Doreen groaned, settled back into her chair, crossed her arms over her chest, and said, "I'm not so sure about that. You sound like you're up to something."

Nan gasped. "I just wondered if you've gotten any information from that nice detective."

"You mean Mack?"

"Yes, yes, that's who I mean, dear. It's so nice to know you're spending time with him."

She got up and looked out the window, glancing over her shoulder at Mack. She mouthed, *Did you tell her?*

Mack shook his head, his eyes wide.

"Is he there now?" Nan asked.

"Why would you ask me that?" Doreen asked, puzzled walking back to the table, laying the phone down on the table so Mack could hear Nan's voice. "Have you got a betting pool going on?"

"Well, of course we do, dear. Your love life is very important to us."

At that, Mack howled with laughter.

Nan's delighted voice perked up. "Oh my, he is there. I do love to be right."

"Nan, stop," Doreen cried out in embarrassment. "He just got here."

"Did he now?" she said slyly. "It is a Monday morning. For all I know, you two had a lovely Sunday night together."

Doreen tossed up both hands, her face bloodred. "Stop."

Nan chuckled. "I can see it wasn't that good a night. I'll talk to you later." She hung up.

Doreen tossed the phone onto the counter, mortified. "I'm so sorry. My grandmother …"

Mack still howled with laughter.

She glared at him. "You're just lucky she hasn't gotten her claws in you yet."

"She's not going to either," he said cheerfully.

"She will if I tell her that you're interested in me," she said. "Then she'll start digging into your life, placing bets on everything *you* do."

He glared at her. "You know what? As a threat," he said with a nod, "that's not bad."

She gave him a fat smile. "I thought so too."

Chapter 20

Monday mid-morning...

MACK SOON LEFT, leaving behind the money for the gardening she'd completed the day before. She cleaned up the kitchen, bundled up the reusable grocery bags she needed, and headed to the grocery store.

First on the list was dog food, cat food, and birdseed. With that picked out, and the cost carefully calculated, she realized she only had twenty dollars left. She groaned and walked around to see what she could possibly get for twenty dollars.

She'd forgotten to get some of the money out of the bowl. That was foolish of her. She had her debit card but was really trying to avoid using that. At least that way she'd keep track of it.

As she wandered around, she picked up bread, more peanut butter, realizing she should branch out with more choices soon. Cheese would be good.

Mack had left the rest of the ingredients for tomorrow's omelets, but she didn't dare get into that later today. Emboldened by what she had learned, she grabbed a dozen eggs, thinking she could at least make something for herself with them, even if a plain cheese omelet.

With her purchases paid for and packed up, she headed to the parking lot, placing her bags in the passenger side. As she straightened, she turned to look at a flatbed truck parked right beside her car. The driver glared at her. She glared right back, until she realized who it was, and then she gasped.

He rolled down his window. "What's the matter? Surprised to see me?"

"If you harass me," she said, "I'll get a court order to keep you away from me."

"You've caused enough trouble, bitch."

"You're a thief. You broke into my house, so you're an intruder. You're also the one calling me. What were you doing? Trying to scare me into leaving? For all I know, you're also a Peeping Tom. I think you're probably to blame for all the thefts at Nan's retirement home too." The shock on his face was something to see.

"You can't prove I made those calls. Leave me alone," he snarled. "And I'll leave you alone. You're nothing but trouble, not even I want to go down that road." He turned on the engine, shut the window, and took off, spitting out gravel from under his tires.

"Like a bat out of hell. Good riddance." She chuckled at the phrase. "How many times would anybody ever use that line? It really dates you, Doreen. I think that came from a Meatloaf song. You're not supposed to like any rock songs, remember?" She changed her voice to imitate her husband's voice. "It has to be classical because that's the only real music."

With that idiot intruder loose, regardless of what he had said, she knew she would have nightmares about him returning to her place. But she remembered the security

Mack had put in and grinned. "Yeah, let's see what he does when he comes around the next time." She had been sleeping with the fireplace poker, just in case. It wasn't the best weapon, but it had worked well the time before.

She drove home, let herself into the house, then put away the groceries before sitting down at the kitchen table, realizing how bored she was. She needed more puzzle pieces to start putting some of this mystery together. She hadn't heard back from Nathan yet.

As if on cue, her phone rang. It was Nathan Trusswell. "Hi," she said with excitement. "Did you learn anything?"

"A couple buddies are going down and taking a look on Tuesday," he said. "Just wondered if you wanted to come enjoy the fun."

"Oh, my goodness, I would so love to," she said. "What time?"

"The guys can all make it that afternoon so about two o'clock or so. They'll go down for a bit, then take a break, change tanks, go back down again. It'll be kind of off-and-on throughout the day."

"Will they start from your place?"

"They'll take my boat out a little way, to where we figured the best chances of finding the truck would be. I explained what we think might have happened, and they were definitely on board to check it out. One of them has some experience with search and rescue and has pulled a vehicle out of the river before, so he has a good idea of what to look for."

She was brimming with excitement. By the time she got off the phone, she was dancing around. She just couldn't believe how well this had worked out.

"Tuesday," she cried out to Mugs. "Tomorrow afternoon!" Now all she had to do was get through the rest of today and tomorrow morning. Wouldn't it be wonderful to settle that problem? She felt bad because, once a negative suspicion, like being a pedophile or a murderer, was raised, it never went away. Unfortunately for Henry and his family ...

Chapter 21

Monday late morning...

D OREEN SETTLED DOWN at her laptop to do more research on Josh Huberts and both Cecily and Celeste Bingham. She didn't know how far along Mack was getting with his particular investigations, but, if Doreen could solve something, it just added fuel to her fire to solve something else. She checked her research notes and realized something had to be going on with the sisters.

She picked up the phone, and, as soon as Nan answered, Doreen asked, "Hey, you know the dead woman I found outside the Family Planning Center?"

"Yes. *Celeste*," Nan said. "Cecily is the one who runs the center."

"Did you ever hear rumors of anything going on with Celeste and Josh? Or maybe Cecily and Josh?" she added hesitantly.

Nan took a moment to figure out what Doreen was talking about. "Nothing at all about Cecily and Josh. As for Celeste and Josh, ... if you mean their fighting, that's just the type of relationship they had. Those two have been fighting since forever."

"About what?"

"Celeste didn't want a family. And her sister, Cecily, was totally on board with her. They were all about women's rights."

"I happen to agree with them," Doreen said drily. "At least to the point that women have the right to a choice. But what's that got to do with this now?"

"If the cops ever come here, they should talk to those of us in the know," Nan said. "They'd find out that Josh probably did kill himself. He loved her. He loved her dearly." On that note, she hung up.

Doreen sat at the kitchen table and stared at her phone. "But love can turn to hate. And to shoot somebody twice usually means there's a lot of anger, up close and personal too. So what would make him turn on her like that?"

And then she got it. Doreen picked up the phone and called Mack. "Did you ever get the autopsy results on Celeste Bingham, the woman who was murdered?"

"No autopsy has been done," he said. "Or will be done as it's been declared a murder-suicide."

"Don't you care about the whys behind a murder?"

"In this case, it's a murder-suicide," he repeated. "Really, there's no mystery behind it."

"I still think the reason why he might have done something like that matters."

"A falling out among lovers," he said. "It's very common."

"It might be," she said, "but that's why I was asking about an autopsy."

"No autopsy." In exasperation, he asked, "Why?"

"Have you talked to Cecily?"

"No," he said. "She wasn't around at the time."

"No, of course not," she said. "You said the center was closed, right?"

"Yes. Josh Huberts was actively working to shut it down."

"And that's understandable. I guess one could consider that great passion can turn to great rage. And great rage causes actions that are hard to reverse. So it would make sense why he went home and was unable to live with himself, and he killed himself. But ... only if you found more bullets. I did hear four shots."

"Yes," Mack said with patience. "But why are you still questioning the case?"

"I think she was pregnant, and she aborted it. Without telling him."

There was silence on the phone. And then Mack said, his voice sad and gentle, "Yes, that would probably cause it. But we can't just guess here, you know?"

"I know," she said in a low voice. "You might ask the coroner if she'd had an abortion recently, or maybe you can ask her sister. She might tell you."

"You think she knew about it?" he asked curiously.

"Who else would?" she asked. "And it would make sense, if he'd been so desperate to have his own child, and then she turned around and aborted it, well ..."

"Yes, that could send a man over the edge," he said, "particularly if he really wanted the baby."

"Exactly," she said. "So unfortunately there are no answers on this mystery for me in this case, but I do have a line on another one." And then, laughing, she hung up the phone.

When it rang again, she ignored it, snatched her cup of tea, and walked out into the backyard. Tomorrow couldn't come fast enough for her. She would love to solve that missing-child case.

As far as the dead couple, she worried about Josh's motivation. It was none of her business again, but ... would Cecily talk to Doreen about her dead sister? Then, why would she? Not to mention this had to be a painful time for her. Dredging up her sister's death wouldn't be a popular idea. Doreen frowned, thinking about it, wondering if Mack would follow through on their recent conversation and ask more questions.

Yet, he probably wouldn't—couldn't—proceed further, his hands tied by the murder-suicide decision made by some clueless higher-up. She guessed he had to live with those nonsensical decisions that probably happened all too often in his job. She was the one who couldn't let it go. Still, she could hardly broach the topic with the dead woman's sister.

Could she?

Finally unable to help herself, she loaded Mugs in her car and drove back to where she had found the body. Everything was cleaned up, more or less. The carnations were flattened, which just reminded her how she'd missed the government application deadline. She'd been so caught up in all the day-to-day stuff that she'd forgotten all about it.

She wandered around the garden, studying the area, when a woman called out from behind her.

"Hey, what are you doing here?"

Doreen turned and smiled at the approaching woman. She looked vaguely familiar, and then she realized this had to be Cecily, the dead woman's sister. She reached out a hand and said, "Hi, I'm Doreen."

The woman frowned at her and didn't shake her hand.

Doreen's hand fell to her waist. "I'm sorry. I'm the one

who found the woman's body." She rushed forward. "I just wondered if there was anything I could do to help memorialize the location where she died."

"It's a huge garden, for Christ's sake. Isn't that enough?"

Doreen's back stiffened. This was not the kind of reception she'd expected. Nor the tone of voice she'd have predicted. She nodded slowly and said, "Often we see on the media how wreaths, cards, teddy bears, things like that are left for those who were lost."

"She wouldn't have wanted anything childish," she said, her tone cold, bordering on waspish. "She didn't like children, never intended on being a mother." She waved a hand at the garden. "And obviously enough damage has been done to the garden already."

"I'm so sorry. Apparently you have strong feelings about the issue."

Cecily looked at her and snorted. "Ya think?"

"I heard her boyfriend who shot her then committed suicide," she offered. "I don't know if that'll help your family find closure or not."

"Not likely," the woman said. "She was my sister. She was headstrong and willful. I told her to leave Josh a long time ago. He wasn't like us."

Doreen studied the woman in front of her. It was on the tip of her tongue to ask what that meant but was afraid she wouldn't like the answer.

Cecily's anger simmered under the surface. Fine lines spread outward from the corner of her eyes, and her mouth was pinched too tight.

Something was going on here that Doreen couldn't quite pinpoint. And now she wanted to assess everything. Another puzzle had reared its head, and she was desperate to sort it out. "I'm sorry for your loss. It's hard to lose a sister."

The woman crossed her arms over her chest. "I think it's time you left."

Crestfallen, Doreen backed up. "I wanted to find closure myself. It's not often you come across a dead woman," she whispered. She was probably putting the act on a little too heavily, but she was being honest. Finding Celeste had been rough. That young woman was in her prime, not old buried bones. The feelings were very different but both required time to process.

The woman made a brushing motion, as if to wave her away.

Doreen hesitated, not sure how to crack through that tough facade. "Well, I guess I'll go then," She looked at the building behind her. "Is the center really closed?"

The woman glared at her.

"A friend of mine may be in a position to need its services."

At that, the other woman hesitated. "It's closed for the moment," she said. "Our funding has been cut, partly due to my sister's boyfriend, the bastard."

"Ouch. That hurts, particularly when he was almost part of the family."

"Yes," she said with a sniff. "He knew what we were trying to do, and yet, he went behind her back, telling everybody how wrong it was."

"It's a fairly difficult decision for a lot of people," she said. "It's a subject that causes strife all over the world."

"A woman's body is a woman's body," Cecily said. "It's her right to do what she wants."

Doreen had no intention of getting into an argument about that one. She didn't think anybody would win it.

Besides, to a certain extent, she agreed. "Why was he so against it?"

"Who knows?" she said. "I think an old girlfriend was pregnant with his child and aborted it. Apparently he was really traumatized by that. So, when my sister got pregnant, he just about lost it."

"In joy or in anger?" she asked, almost gratified to hear she'd been right about Celeste.

At that, the woman laughed. "Isn't that the dilemma? *Child support or raising a baby?*"

"Well, for many it would be the baby," Doreen said sympathetically.

"That's what he wanted. He was desperate to have his own child. Particularly after losing the other one."

"I can kind of see that," Doreen said.

"My sister got what she wanted. And, in this case, she didn't want him or the baby," Cecily said with a sneer. "And he got her for it too."

"Oh my, so they broke up, and he turned around and killed her?" She winced at that, thinking about how angry and heartbroken he must have felt. But could Doreen trust Cecily? Or was she spouting off lies that suited her? "He must have really cared for her then."

"That's the theory," Cecily said, turning to walk back up the steps. "Most likely he was just concerned about losing something he wasn't ready to lose. Men need to be in control at all times, and they want to be the ones who do the breaking up," she said.

Doreen wasn't sure that was always true either. Something was so adamant and defiant about Cecily, as if she was right and the world was wrong, with no room for a middle ground.

The woman sneered at Doreen.

"I guess you didn't get along with him."

Cecily shook her head. "Nothing to get along with. He was an asshole."

"Ouch. Most people don't say such strong things about the dead."

"Most people won't tell the truth. Why shouldn't I tell the world how I feel?"

"It sounds like you hated him so much that you're happy he's dead."

"Absolutely I am," she said with a laugh. "And, the way she was acting at the end, the same goes for my sister."

"What do you mean by that?"

"She took his side," she said. "That would never go down well with me." She glared at Doreen from the top step. "I've already said too much. Take a hike." And she walked in and closed the door.

As Doreen stood with her hands on her hips, almost openmouthed, she could see the curtains closing Cecily off from the outside. "Now that is one angry woman," she muttered to Mugs.

Mugs strained at the leash. She walked him to the side of the building, so he could take a bathroom break. She figured the woman would be even more pissed if Doreen let Mugs poop in the garden. But she did have doggie bags to clean up the mess if he had done that. She always cleaned up after him. It was just the polite thing to do. Not everybody was like that, but she was.

She waited until he'd done his business, then scooped it up and looked for a garbage can. But there wasn't a public one. There were, however, the garbage cans from the center. She walked over and put the bag in.

Inside she saw a whole pile of bloody notes and crumpled cloths below. She glanced up at the center, but the curtains were firmly closed. On instinct alone, she gloved her hands with the doggie bags before she snatched the notes, bagging them up, then took the dog back to the car, and drove away.

She didn't know what was going on, but she'd seen one thing—bloodstains. And a lot of them. As if someone had used the papers, possibly the cloths, to clean up. But to clean up what?

Had Cecily seen her sister in the garden and came out to try to save her, then gone inside when she couldn't? Because maybe Doreen had come? That didn't make any sense.

Back home again, she pulled on a pair of gloves, covered her kitchen table with a big plastic garbage bag, and carefully looked at the papers. Crumpled up, they were heavily bloodstained. But whose blood and why? She frowned. Should she contact Mack or not bother him? It was always hard to know what to do with him. If there were fingerprints, or the blood belonged to Celeste, how did it get onto the papers and into the garbage?

She knew Mack would probably either get angry or frustrated, but she had to do something about this. She called him. "I know it's your Monday, and you really don't want to hear from me again," she said hurriedly.

"What is it?"

"I went back to where the dead woman was found," she said. "I know you don't want me interfering, and I didn't want to, but I felt compelled to return to the spot and maybe find a way to memorialize the poor woman's death." She sighed. "But then the sister came out of the center. She was *not* friendly."

"She's a bit abrasive. She's a very strong-willed, stiff-necked feminist. And she's not shy about letting you know where she stands on issues," he said.

"Exactly. We were talking, but, at the very end, she said that, A, she was quite delighted her sister's boyfriend was dead, and, B, she was also happy her sister was dead because her sister was converting more toward her boyfriend's beliefs."

"What? So now you think her sister might have murdered her?" he scoffed.

"No, no. That's not what I'm saying ... exactly." She stopped and frowned. "Look. I don't know what I'm saying, but Mugs went to the bathroom. So I cleaned it up, and I took the bag to the garbage. When I put it inside, I saw a bunch of crumpled papers and rags. They were soaked in blood. Cecily had gone into the center and closed the curtains, so I snatched some of the papers out of the garbage and brought them home."

She ended in such a big rush it took him a moment to respond. "You did what?"

She groaned out loud. "I don't know why I did that," she said, "but there was a lot of blood, and I mean, *a lot of blood*, ... as if somebody had cleaned up after murdering Celeste."

He sighed quietly. "And I suppose you have those bloodied papers with you now?"

"Yeah," she said sadly. "They're sitting on my table."

"And you want me to come and get them to see if they have anything to do with the case, right?"

She winced because he didn't sound very happy with her. And with good reason. It was his day off, and he worked enough long hours, and she kept sending him on these wild goose chases.

"If you wouldn't mind," she said in a small voice. "If you figure out they have nothing to do with Celeste's death, then I apologize. In the meantime, there is a *lot* of blood."

"Oh, for crying out loud." He went quiet and then said, "Look. I'm not even at home. I'll swing by in about twenty minutes on my way to Mom's. I'll pick it up then. Or at least I'll take a look."

She jumped to her feet. "Thank you very much." She hung up the phone. As she stared at the papers, she found a weird list of random scribbled thoughts.

It would be nice to have a child.

It would be a pain in the ass to have a child.

I would love to know what motherhood feels like.

I would hate motherhood.

She shook her head. "Obviously somebody had a very confused mind-set when it came to parenthood."

She wanted to read through the rest of the pages but also knew that, whenever Mack arrived, she'd lose all of them, so she grabbed her phone and took pictures of each page. She didn't figure there would be any real mystery to the notes themselves. If these were Celeste's, that would make sense. She was obviously confused as to what was happening with her body and what she really wanted. Maybe she'd had an abortion, then regretted it terribly. But no answers were to be had on that subject, since the woman was no longer available to ask any questions of her. And neither was an autopsy done to get further details.

But Mack could at least confirm whose blood this was.

When Doreen finished taking her pictures, she put the notes on top of each other again, stuffing them once more into the doggie bag, and moved her phone off to the side, so

Mack wouldn't get suspicious.

She heard his vehicle pulling into her driveway. He came up the porch steps and pounded on her door. Mugs barked like a crazy dog at the front door. She opened it up and glared at Mack. "If you knocked like a normal human being, Mugs wouldn't have a heart attack. He knows who you are by now. But, when you're angry like this, he's not real happy."

Mack stood with his arms crossed over his massive chest. And to make matters worse, Thaddeus looked at him and said, "Damn thing. Damn thing."

Mack shoved his face toward Thaddeus and said, "You're a damn thing, Thaddeus. Damn bird."

"Mack! Don't speak to Thaddeus like that. You'll scare him too."

Thaddeus leaned forward, touching Mack's nose with his beak and said, "You're a damn thing."

Astonished, Mack just looked at the bird giving him the gimlet beady eye, and then he laughed. Tears ran down his cheeks before he finally stopped. He collapsed onto the mega-expensive couch and stared at the menagerie around him. Goliath, not to be outdone, jumped on his lap, making himself at home on his knees.

He looked at Doreen helplessly. "What on earth am I going to do with you guys?"

"Patience, tolerance, and goodwill would be helpful," she said with a tentative smile. "I know I'm a challenge, and I know you don't want anything to do with me when I get my head into these things, but they're really hard for me to get out of."

"Let me see what you've got." He scooped up Goliath and held him in his arms as he walked into the kitchen.

When he saw the papers, he froze. "You're right. That is a lot of blood."

She looked at him. "Right, and even more was inside the garbage can."

He shook his head. "Did you see anything else?"

"Rags," she said, "either cleaning rags or maybe clothing. I don't know what they were."

He sighed.

She nodded and handed the bagged-up bloodied notes to him.

"I'll go over there to go through the garbage," he said. "But stop doing this, please."

"I will." But she held back from promising. She watched as he turned around and left without saying another word.

Chapter 22

Monday noonish...

DOREEN HOPED THE garbage hadn't been picked up yet so Mack could retrieve the rest of the items she'd seen. Considering it was a weekend, chances were good it hadn't been. But, if Cecily had seen Doreen taking the notes out of the trash can, then she was pretty sure someone would empty it and fast.

When Mack phoned her twenty minutes later, he confirmed her fears. "The can is empty," he said, swearing softly.

"Of course it is," she said. "She probably saw me and decided to empty it herself."

"We still don't know that it has anything to do with the case," he said.

"No. But, like you said, it was a lot of blood. So short of somebody cutting an artery, taking off a leg or something, the chances are it's related to her dead sister—a sister she was no longer happy with, who had a boyfriend, who is also dead."

"You could be right," he grumbled. "But, without a warrant, I can't go in and check the premises."

"Would she take the contents inside? I mean, if you

think about it, wouldn't she expect a warrant next?"

"The only other thing she'd likely have done is put it in her car to dispose of elsewhere," he said.

"I didn't see a car when I was there," she said. "Maybe the parking is around back."

"There is a parking lot," he said. "But I haven't checked to see if any vehicles are back there."

"Why don't you make a casual drive-by?" she urged. "See what vehicles there are, take the license plates down, confirm that one is hers, and then maybe I'll take a look to see where she goes."

"And do what?" he scoffed. "You're back to playing amateur sleuth again. Remember how this is supposed to be left for the professionals?"

"Yeah, well, the professionals didn't check the garbage can that was there when you found the body."

"I'm not sure the can was out here," he said thoughtfully. "I won't know until I go back and scan the crime-scene photos."

"Oh, now that's an interesting twist too. What if somebody else put the cans out for pick up? And why then?"

"It's hard to say. Maybe she put it out earlier, thinking it was safe."

"But, if it's empty now, somebody emptied it."

"True. I'm seeing movement inside," he said. "Bye." And he hung up.

She chewed on her fingernails, worrying about it. And then she couldn't stand it anymore. She looked over at the animals. "Who wants to go for a car ride?"

Thaddeus squawked, "Me, me, me."

Mugs barked, and even Goliath jumped into her lap.

She sighed. "I didn't really mean all of you." But she'd

mentioned it, had even offered, so now she felt obliged to follow through. She didn't know when the animals became as important to her as people, or when her promises to animals became as important as her promises to people, but somehow they had.

She walked out to the vehicle with her cell phone in her hand in case Mack called back and loaded up her critters. As always Goliath took the front passenger seat, almost daring Mugs to fight him for it, and, with Thaddeus on her shoulder, Doreen drove past where she had found the body at the Family Planning Center.

Interestingly enough she couldn't see any sign of Mack's car. The garbage can was still where she'd seen it before. She drove around the building and headed into the back parking lot. It was empty also. But a small red car had just pulled out through the opposite exit. With a female driver.

Doreen hadn't noticed the car until then, but, as she watched, it drove to the end of the block.

On a hunch, she took a right turn and followed it. She had no way to know who was behind the wheel, and, of course, once again, her hunches were just blind guesses.

Except that Thaddeus urged her on from her shoulder.

"Thaddeus, we don't know that it's Cecily."

He gave Doreen a look and tried to hop up on her steering wheel. She brushed him back off. "No, no, no." Even Goliath sat up and put his front paws on the dash. She glanced at him. "What's gotten into you two?" She looked in the rearview mirror to see Mugs looking out the side window behind her. "At least you're being normal," she joked.

But then he turned to look out the front windshield and jumped onto the armrest between the two front seats and barked.

"Oh, boy. That's enough of that. I can't think, let alone drive safely and deal with all of you," she muttered. She tried to get Mugs to calm down, but he wasn't having any of it. She pulled off to the side of the road. "If you guys don't stop, I'm not driving."

The ruckus became three times louder. She hit the gas and followed the car again. It still trundled along at the normal speed limit, suspiciously so. Doreen was always five miles over the allowed speed limit. She couldn't imagine anybody driving spot-on. But this red car seemed to be maintaining the perfect driving speed. If Doreen were driving a car filled with bloody evidence, and she didn't want to get pulled over by the cops, then that's what she'd do too.

As she thought about this, a vehicle pulled up behind her, too closely behind her. Thaddeus turned, squawked once, and then faced forward again. She looked in the rearview mirror. "Oh, shit. Now I'm in trouble, you guys."

Then she giggled. Because, if Mack should have expected one thing, it was that Doreen would be in trouble—if not now, soon. She continued following the red vehicle, but she did lift a hand and give him a three-finger wave through the rear window. She knew that would just piss him off a little more, but that was okay too. It appeared to be one of the regular things she did without even having to think about it. Besides, it made her smile—so it couldn't be all bad.

Then Mack honked a few times.

The driver of the red car realized she was being followed. Whether she recognized Doreen's vehicle or Mack's, the driver put the gas pedal to the floor and whipped to the right at the next corner.

Startled, Doreen almost missed the corner but caught it on a wide turn. Mack was right on her tail. But now it looked like the woman in front was desperate to get away.

She drove hell-bent, taking multiple corners in succession as if trying to shake her tail, and it was all Doreen could do to keep up with her, wondering what this woman was up to exactly. For sure the woman was acting more than slightly suspicious. Finally she pulled into a massive parking lot, dashed out of the car, and ran into the mall.

And Doreen caught a glimpse of her. *Cecily.* Doreen had been right. She pulled up beside Cecily's car and parked. Only then did Doreen realize her hands were trembling.

She knew Mack would rip into her for this. But, at the same time, she needed to know what the hell the woman was hiding. Or maybe she was just terrified. Doreen hadn't even considered that. Maybe just the look of a crazy Doreen driving with a parrot on her shoulder was enough to scare Cecily into fleeing into the most public place she could find.

And, sure enough, a hard pounding came on her window. She rolled it down and went to speak, but Mugs and Thaddeus and even Goliath hollered at Mack as he glared down at her.

The force of the din set him back in surprise. But not for long.

He leaned forward again and asked, "Can you keep the menagerie quiet?"

She snorted. "Not likely." But they calmed in spite of her words. "Besides, shouldn't you be chasing after her instead of talking to me?"

"Other cops are on that. I wanted to make sure I had a talk with you first." He bit the words off as if he were seriously pissed. "If we weren't in a public place, I could choke you for what you just did."

"What did I do?" she asked innocently.

"You spooked her," he said. "I was trying to keep back and see where she went."

"Oh. Well, I was too," she said. "But then I figured Thaddeus must have spooked her. But more likely it was you honking at me. Hardly being subtle, were you?"

Mack shot her a hard look. "Thaddeus?"

She shrugged. "He looks kind of freaky when he's leaning forward like that. Every time I tried to pull over or to stop following her, the animals went crazy."

This time his expression looked like she was pulling his leg.

"Honest. You saw me pull off on the side of the road once, right?"

He nodded.

"The animals went crazy, absolutely ape-shit crazy," she snapped. "It's not my fault that right now they look like sweet and innocent critters." And they did. They were all just sitting, watching the exchange between the two of them.

And then Thaddeus hopped onto the open driver's side window, looked up at Mack, and said, "Hi, Mack."

Mack stared down at him. "Wow. Hi, Thaddeus. Since when did you learn to say, 'Hi'?"

"Hi. Hi. Hi."

Doreen groaned. "Don't encourage him, please."

But Mack wasn't looking at her. "So, Thaddeus, if ..."

And then Thaddeus walked up Mack's arm to his shoulder. Just when she thought he would stop there, he hopped over to the roof of the woman's car and slid down to the trunk.

Doreen opened her car door. "Thaddeus, get off of there." She was petrified his talons would scratch the paint job, and she'd be sued for damages.

But Thaddeus just walked around in a circle on top of the trunk. And then he chanted, "Body in the trunk. Body in the trunk."

Mack groaned.

Doreen gasped. Several people in route to their vehicles stopped and stared. She held her hands, palms up. "He's just a crazy bird."

But a crowd had collected.

"Mack, I don't know what to do."

"Well, you started this," he groaned. He reached over toward the bird. "Come on, Thaddeus. Let's get back in the car, buddy. Let's get you home."

But Thaddeus evaded his grasp. "Open trunk. Open trunk. Open trunk," he cried out.

And, when she wasn't looking, Goliath jumped out of the window and landed on the roof of the red car, right beside Thaddeus. Now two of her animals were loose that she had to contend with. But Goliath stood on the trunk, his tail twitching hard. Mugs, not to be left out, pushed open the door she hadn't quite clicked shut and raced around the vehicle, barking like crazy.

Suddenly two more cop cars pulled up beside them.

Doreen covered her face with her hands.

One of the officers got out and said, "Ma'am, are these your animals?"

She nodded. "Yes. I'm so sorry. They're very much out of control right now."

And then Mack stepped up. "Hey, Stanley."

"Mack?"

With a long sigh, Mack said, "Yep, that's me."

They looked at the animals, looked over at her, and a big grin cracked Stanley's face as he asked Doreen, "So what did you do? Catch another dead body?"

Again Thaddeus chanted, "Body in the trunk. Body in the trunk. Body in the trunk."

Silence settled over the crowd.

Stanley said, "Is that what we're thinking is going on here?"

Mack shook his head. "Honestly, I have no clue. There's just something about this bird. Actually, the cat and the dog too. Obviously something's attracting them. Maybe a scent."

"Well now, do we know who owns the vehicle?"

"Cecily does," somebody in the crowd said. "She runs the Family Planning Center."

From the background were all kinds of suggestions on what could be in the trunk.

"Maybe she's in there dead."

"Maybe there's a dead child in there."

Somebody else said, "Hey, maybe it's a cat. Maybe it's just something else that's been left close to the vehicle, and that's what they're smelling. Just because the bird talks doesn't mean he makes sense."

She snorted at that. "You've got that right," she said.

Chapter 23

Monday early afternoon...

THE COPS HELPED Mack disperse the crowd. One of the guys headed into the mall to join the search for Cecily. They announced her name over the PA system, asking her to return to her vehicle, but, after an hour, there was still no sign of her.

Mack looked at Doreen. Doreen looked at Mack, and they both shrugged.

"What's really going on here?" Stanley asked Mack.

In a low voice Mack told them as much as he could.

The two officers looked at Doreen.

She shrugged. "I called Mack when I found it," she said.

"You should have called him while you were there," Stanley admonished. "Now evidence has likely been lost."

"Which is why I followed the car," she said. "To see if she tried to dispose of the rest of the garbage."

Stanley's partner, Roberts, said, "I'll phone the chief. See if we can get some idea what to do about this."

"You do that," Mack said with a heavy sigh. "Nothing is ever easy about Doreen. The case was already closed as a murder-suicide, until she got involved."

Stanley nodded with a half grin. "And what's this I hear?" he said, turning to look at Doreen. "You've got some scuba-diving enthusiasts going out on Tuesday?"

Her gaze went to Mack, then down at her feet and the aging sandals she wore.

Mack turned slowly to face her. "Doreen?" His voice turned ominous.

She wrinkled her nose at him. "They just wanted to go scuba diving."

"I don't know about that," Stanley said, a grin widening on his face. "They were pretty fired up about it. Looking for something in particular, from what I heard."

With a groan, she let her shoulders slump. Somehow she figured she'd get to Tuesday without having to explain it all to Mack. She should have known better. "You know Mack will never let me leave the house again, don't you?" she told Stanley.

"From what I hear," Stanley said, "you can get into a heck of a lot of trouble without ever leaving that house of yours."

"Isn't that the truth?" she said, but she then confessed to Mack. He hadn't been pleased, but, when she had explained her theory, he had been quietly stunned.

"That's very good thinking," he said. "I doubt they'll find anything, but I appreciate what you've done for the family's sake. Nobody even considered that all the times we discussed the cold case."

"There was absolutely no reason for Henry Huberts, a man with no criminal past, to take the little boy for nefarious purposes. I know there are secret pedophiles, but something about this didn't feel right. When I realized his grandson, Josh Huberts, had been accused of Celeste's murder, then believed to have committed suicide, I felt like that was another whammy for the family. If I could help solve one of those problems, then maybe it would be easier on them."

Mack nodded.

Roberts turned to look at her. "By the way, aren't you the one we put in the security for?"

She smiled. "Yes, and thank you for that because honestly I can at least sleep at night now."

"Nothing has triggered it?"

"No, although I don't hold any hopes that'll continue after seeing the intruder at the grocery store earlier today. I can't believe he's free to run around and break into my house again," she snapped.

"I'm surprised you left the place long enough to follow this woman."

"But if she had anything to do with those two deaths …"

"So are you working for the police now?" Stanley said with a big grin. "You know, like part of the new volunteer amateur sleuths society?"

"Oh, God. Don't even get her started on something like that," Mack said instantly. "Roberts, did you get a hold of the chief?"

"He's talking to the prosecutor to see what we can get."

"Great," Mack said, turning to glare at Doreen. "You know that I'll never live this down."

"You know what else? I'll never live this down either," she mimicked, shooting him a matching glare. "You didn't have to follow me, you know?"

"That's about the only right thing I did do," he cried out.

At that, Stanley howled with laughter. "You two are

great together," he said with amusement. "You sound like an old married couple."

Both Doreen and Mack turned to glare at him. Stanley raised both hands in mock surrender and, still chuckling, moved to where Roberts was once again on the phone.

She turned to Mack. "I don't know what marriages he's familiar with, but this is nothing like what my marriage was like."

"You weren't married," Mack snapped back. "You were in bondage."

She looked at him and, after a long moment, said, "I really was, wasn't I?" Her tone was very low and sad.

All his aggression fell away. "Hey, I didn't mean that."

"No," she said. "But you should have meant it because it is the truth. Sad but true."

"Don't take it too bad," he said. "You're free now."

She nodded and turned, leaning against the car. Thaddeus, realizing she wouldn't take him away, hopped onto her shoulder and gently brushed his beak against hers.

"Bondage," he said just once and in a low tone.

She stroked his head. "That's why you don't live in a cage. That's why, like Nan, I can't have you confined in any way. I spent fourteen years in a gilded cage—but a cage nonetheless." She gently brushed and hugged the bird.

Goliath was on her other side. He rubbed his head against that side of her face too. She stroked both of them, loving that, at this moment, when she was feeling the pain of all she'd gone through, they were here for her.

She looked up at the sound of a camera snap, expecting to see paparazzi; instead it was Mack. She looked at him in surprise. He turned the camera around so she could see the picture, and she stared in delight as both Thaddeus and

Goliath had their heads turned against her. She had closed her eyes, and a gentle smile was on her face.

"Wow," she said. "That's a very special picture."

"I'll send it to you." He nodded and paused. "So you might have been in a gilded cage," he said, "but you've given special lives to these two." Then he looked down at Mugs who, in his typical fashion, was lying on her feet. He smiled. "You may have turned this town upside down, but the animals sure appreciate their new lives."

Roberts came back over and said, "We're to try one more time to find her. If there's no sign of her in an hour, we're to open the trunk."

Mack nodded. "You guys head in and help find her."

"She's already gone," somebody said from among the officers a couple rows over. "I saw her running out the back of the mall. She didn't look to be coming back anytime soon."

On that note, Roberts nodded. Mack walked to his car, picked up a pry bar, and came back over.

Before he opened the trunk, Doreen looked at him and said, "You don't want to just unlock it from the inside?"

The three closest cops looked at her, looked at each other, walked over to the front door, and sure enough the damn driver's door was unlocked. Swearing, Roberts hit the Trunk button, and the trunk popped open.

"We'd really appreciate it," Stanley said, "if you don't mention that to anybody."

She gave him a breezy smile and a wave of her hand. "I won't mention it. Believe me. I'd appreciate it if you didn't tell anyone about a few things either."

He chuckled, and then his gaze fell to what was inside the trunk. He stopped laughing. "That is a hell of a lot of blood."

Not only were the bloody cloths here that Doreen had seen in the garbage can but the carpet inside the trunk was completely soaked with blood too. She sighed. "That's why I was following her."

Mack nodded. "And that's why I was following her too. The difference between us is, I'm the cop, and you're not."

She stuck out her tongue at him. "In that case, I get to go home now, don't I? And you get to stay and work." She gave them all a big wave, bundled up her animals, and headed home.

Later that evening Doreen got through another ten hangers full of Nan's clothes, but her heart wasn't in it. She still burned with a sense of satisfaction from her day's adventures. But she hadn't had any follow-up from Mack. Now she half-expected to never hear from him again.

But, with any luck, they would trace that blood back to Celeste. And then they would take a serious look at the case again. Doreen grabbed a book, sat on her bed, then felt just too tired for that. She went back downstairs—did another walk through the rooms, checking that everything was still fine, made sure the alarms were set—then went back upstairs, and crashed.

Chapter 24

Tuesday morning...

S HE AWOKE THE next morning—Tuesday, her day to make an omelet. If Mack was coming over, she better shower and get dressed. It was already eight o'clock. He might be here very soon.

But then again, if he'd been working on that case yesterday into all hours of the night, he might have gone to bed very, very late. Still, she wouldn't take a chance, and, after a quick shower, she dressed and walked downstairs.

Once in the kitchen she frowned, wondering whether she was supposed to call him about getting breakfast started or not. She really didn't want to.

She brought out the video she'd made of Mack making the omelet and watched it again. Carefully. It hadn't taken him long, and he'd certainly done it nice and smoothly. She wondered if she could get on the prep work. She needed to learn to do this. Did that include having him here while she did it? There really wasn't a right or wrong decision here, but it felt like she was cheating without having him here for her to show off. Besides, she wasn't in too much of a hurry. She just didn't want to mess it up.

She didn't understand her relationship with Mack, but, considering the comments from the other cops, she figured there was already a lot of talk about them. It was hard not to wonder if that bothered Mack.

For herself, she didn't care. He was a friend, and one she was proud to call a friend. Especially considering the craziness in her life.

She disarmed the security on the front and back doors, snagged a cup of coffee, and called to the animals. "Come on. Let's go outside for a little bit, you guys. Get some fresh air and all that."

With the back door propped open this beautiful morning, all the animals barreled out of the house with her. She chuckled at their antics because it was just too sweet. It was also chaotic, but, hey, she'd take that.

She walked down the steps to the backyard and wandered through the garden, looking to see what would come up. This was a mystery garden. Nan remembered a lot of the plants and where she had planted them. Doreen herself recognized a lot of the plants already coming up. But a lot of the annuals themselves were still just flowering and leafing out. The black-eyed Susans had yet to come up. There was echinacea, as far as she could tell from the foliage, but, until the purple flowers bloomed, she wasn't too sure. She hadn't seen very much of it before, but it looked to be something she would thoroughly enjoy.

She walked back into the house almost an hour later. She checked her watch again as she walked over to the coffeepot and poured herself a second cup. "I can finish this pot myself," she said, "then put on another one when he comes, or I can leave him something from this pot. But, if he doesn't come until ten o'clock, then it'll be pretty nasty."

"Do you always talk to yourself?" came a strange voice from behind her.

A strange voice, and yet ... a not-too-strange voice. She turned ever-so-slowly to see Cecily, holding a snub-nosed revolver in her hand. Doreen took a deep breath. "Is that the gun you used to kill your sister and her boyfriend?"

"You mean, *my* boyfriend," she said. "At least some of the time."

Doreen sagged against the counter. "Oh, crap." So she had been right. Wow. Poor Celeste.

"Ha, see you don't know jack shit," Cecily said.

"And I don't understand that phrase. Why does anybody care about Jack's shit? That makes no sense. Is he some kind of monster pooper or something?" she asked in a droll tone. Her gaze was on the gun as her mind tried to spin a way out of this nightmare.

"What the hell are you talking about?" Cecily asked. "Are you seriously mental?"

"What does that mean? Seriously mental versus not being seriously mental?" she asked. "I'm confused. I really don't understand the question."

The woman's face turned from being congenial to confused to pissed. "That's enough messing around. I don't need that kind of crap from you."

"What do you need?" Doreen asked. "You break into my house, point a weapon at me. I don't have anything to do with you or your life. Why are you after me?"

"Because you're the idiot screwing up my life. You and those animals of yours," she said. "You ruined me."

"Why is it, whenever somebody is in the wrong, and they get found out, they turn around and blame everybody else? I didn't do anything to you," she said. "None of this is my fault, and you're not dumping the blame on me."

"It *is* your fault," she said, "and I will dump it on you because you had no business at the center. So it is your fault. If you weren't sticking your nose where it doesn't belong …"

"Considering I found your sister's body there, I would say I did have some business there," Doreen snapped. "At least someone cared about what happened to your poor sister. What were you going to do? Just let her rot out there?"

"I planned to call it in. But I didn't get a chance. I cared about her. But you didn't. You never even met her."

"Do I have to meet every woman who's been murdered to feel like she mattered?" Doreen asked in astonishment. "That makes no sense to me. But I guess for somebody who murdered her own sister, maybe that makes a twisted kind of sense to you?"

"She wasn't your problem, and you didn't need to get involved."

"She wasn't a problem," Doreen snapped. "She was a young woman with her whole life ahead of her. And she was obviously very vibrant, very passionate. You took all that away from her."

"Oh, she was passionate all right. Always about the god-damn wrong things. Somebody had to have a calm, collected, organized head," she snarled.

"I'm confused," Doreen said. "What could you possibly have against your sister that was worth killing her for?"

"How about the fact she was helping her boyfriend shut down my center?"

"So Josh was her boyfriend after all, not your boy-friend?" Doreen asked in confusion. She needed to keep Cecily talking, but it was kind of hard because Doreen was still figuring out how to get this woman to put down the gun.

"He was playing both of us," Cecily said with a sneer. "I figured, if my sister could see him for what he really was, she'd ditch him."

"So you seduced him to ruin their relationship? What kind of woman, much less a sister, are you?" She couldn't imagine such a thing.

Cecily said, "What kind of woman are you? You don't even have to work. You just laze around, get in everybody's face, cause trouble and chaos everywhere you go. And this? This is what happens. You get into other people's business because you're bored. You need a man of your own," she sneered. "If you would know what to do with one."

"I was married for fourteen years," Doreen said coolly. "So you'd think I'd know."

"Yeah, but you see the operative word there," Cecily said. "*Was.* So if you knew how to do your job, you would still be married."

"Oh, okay. That's interesting," Doreen said, "because, for you, marriage is a job. I never considered it that way. So, when you quit a job, that's what a divorce is to you then?" She chuckled. "That's an interesting take on marriage. I'm not sure it's all that complimentary to men, unless a divorce is them quitting their jobs too? Although I don't think you're really too bothered about the male point of view, are you?"

"This is a stupid conversation," Cecily said. "I came here to tie up loose ends, and you're one of them."

"You don't have to tie up anything with me," Doreen said softly. "You messed up, and the law is all over you. There's no statute of limitations on murder. They'll find you, whether you believe it or not, even if you leave town right now. They'll come after you, and they'll get you. It might take ten years, might take twenty. You might even have fifty years on the run, if you're really lucky. But the fact of the matter is, you will spend all that time looking over your shoulder, and they'll still get you."

"So then it doesn't matter," she said.

"You've already killed two people," Doreen said with certainty. "It's not like your sister's boyfriend killed her. *You* did. You killed her. Then you killed Josh and made it look like it was a murder-suicide."

The woman just stared at her. "How is it that you even figured that out? It's not like anybody was around as a witness."

"Nope," she said. "But somebody *heard*."

"What are you talking about?"

"You see? I heard four shots. Two, a little break, and then two more. And, with that fact in mind," Doreen said, "it's unlikely to be a murder-suicide. And that decrepit house? Why were they there? It hardly fit them."

"What are you talking about? Of course it was a murder-suicide. Two shots and two shots. As for the location, Josh had just bought the dump. He would flip it, he said. Likely story. And so not my sister's style. She never belonged in that place—not even for a minute," she said. "Two bullets apiece. What's wrong about that? He didn't have to kill himself at the time. He probably fired two warning shots, then fired two more that killed her. Who knows what was going through his mind at the time?"

"Except forensics didn't find any other bullet holes." At least she hadn't heard from Mack that they had. She knew Cecily had killed them both, but getting her to admit it would be hard ... or maybe not. Smoothly Doreen slipped the conversation back to Cecily's actions. "If you had left them where they had dropped, then no one would have been the wiser. But, for whatever reason, after killing them both, you felt the need to move your sister's body."

Cecily glared at Doreen for a long moment, then gave a nonchalant shrug. "I had to bring her back to where it all started," she said slowly. "It's also what Josh would have done if he'd killed her. To make a point. And to bring her home. Two motives blended together. And I had to make it look like she'd died by his hand."

"Sure." Doreen nodded slowly, grateful Cecily had admitted her actions but worried that she had because she obviously didn't see Doreen as a threat. And planned to make sure she wasn't alive to tell any tales.

She heard the front door open quietly. As long as Cecily didn't, it was all good. Doreen could hope it was Mack, but she didn't know if Cecily worked alone. "That's why so much blood was on the papers and the material. The material was your clothes, right? I guess your sister wasn't easy to move."

"No, she wasn't. I've always been strong and way bigger than she was, so I figured I could do it a whole lot easier than I did. I almost dropped her and ended up grabbing her by the neck at the garden," she said. "Afterward I didn't even think about it. I just changed and put the bloody clothes in the garbage."

"But you forgot there wasn't a weekend pickup," Doreen said.

"I missed Friday's pickup," she said.

"And, therefore, the bloody clothes were still in the garbage."

"Do you always go snooping in other people's garbage?"

Cecily asked in outrage.

"I was being a good citizen," Doreen said with a wave of her hand.

The gun lifted again.

"Easy. I'm just explaining what I did. I went there to pay my respects to your sister, and Mugs had to take a poop. When Mugs takes a poop, Mugs takes a royal poop. I had doggie bags with me. I cleaned it up, but I didn't want to take the doggie bag to my car, so I took it to the garbage can. As soon as I opened the lid, all I could see were the bloody papers. And if you know anything about blood," she said quietly, "you know that was a lot of blood. That was way more than a bloody nose could have made. It was way more than a small cut would produce. That was some serious blood. As in that was blood likely from your sister, who died in the derelict house. ... Did you even say good-bye to her? Or did you let your sister just lie in that house and bleed out while you laughed?"

"I said good-bye," Cecily said. "Do you think I wanted to do it? Of course I didn't want to. She's the only relative I had."

"Oh, I'm really glad to hear that," Doreen said.

The woman stared at her in surprise. "What? That my sister is my only relative?"

"Yes, because, if you still had a mother around, she'd already be suffering because of the loss of one of her daughters. And then she'd get another blow when she found out her second daughter had killed the first, and now she'll lose the second one as well."

"I'm the older one," Cecily snapped. "I'm the first daughter."

Doreen gave a slow nod. "Okay, whatever works for

you."

"And I'm not going to prison," she said.

"If you had just come in and shot me dead, then left, I would have more faith in that statement."

"Why?" she said. "I had to know how you figured it out."

"It wasn't all that hard. Think about it. You messed up on the garbage can." Doreen snorted, not sure why she was pricking the woman's temper. "Besides, now that you do know, you still haven't pulled the trigger."

"I'm getting ready to," Cecily growled. "But I need any cash you have."

"Cash?" Doreen laughed. "I don't have any. None at all."

"But you have to. You don't have a job. You live in this house all by yourself. And, according to the rumors, you have antiques. So stop with the games and give me all the cash you have."

Doreen leaned forward. "You heard about the antiques?"

Cecily waved the gun. "What are you, an idiot? The minute you do anything in this town, of course everyone finds out."

Doreen watched the gun. Time was running out. And Cecily would be even more pissed when Doreen didn't give up any cash. She thought she'd heard the door, thought she'd heard Mack enter but saw no sign of him.

Just then Thaddeus, who'd been on the kitchen counter, hopped onto the table and preened.

Cecily looked at the bird in disgust. "How can you live with that thing? It just shits everywhere."

"He's pretty decently trained," Doreen said cheerfully. "He has a couple places he uses for bathroom breaks, but, other than that, he just shits on selective people."

"He shits on people?" She stepped back.

"He does have a bit of an attitude. And he likes to shit on people with shitty attitudes too," Doreen said, giggling. She didn't know how long she could keep this up. Her gaze was ever watchful, looking for her chance. But Cecily was just too far away. If Doreen tried to kick the gun out of her hand, she'd likely get shot in the process.

But just then Thaddeus hopped up onto Cecily's shoulder. She shrieked. "Get it off of me. Get it off of me."

"I wouldn't worry about it," Doreen said. "He hasn't had a dump this morning. He's probably looking for the perfect spot."

She shrieked all the louder and hit the bird hard with her hand.

Thaddeus let out a cry as he tumbled off her shoulder onto the floor. Because he couldn't fly well, it was much harder for him to break his fall. But, as soon as he hit the floor, Goliath climbed up Cecily's thigh, howling in outrage. Mugs barked, twisting between her legs. She was in high heels, which just completely blew Doreen away because high heels were one of those torture instruments that she tolerated for a few hours in the evening. But during the day? Hell no. At least not now that her soon-to-be ex-husband wasn't here, forcing her to wear them.

She watched in fascination as Mugs tripped up Cecily at feet level, and Goliath tried to claw up her legs to her waist, digging in his claws for gripping purposes—and he was no lightweight. Cecily shrieked as if under attack.

When Mack snagged the gun from her hand, Cecily didn't even notice. She screeched and hit out at Goliath, kicking poor Mugs. But Goliath had a beautiful response. As a hand came toward him, he reached up and clamped down tight on her finger. Her shrieks turned to sobs of pain, and Mugs gave her one hard swat of his butt, then jumped up, placing both thick paws on the back of her knees. She went down, falling forward, collapsing hard on the floor, crying out in pain.

With Mack holding the gun on Cecily, Doreen tried to calm down Goliath. "Hey, Goliath. It's okay, honey. Take it easy. She didn't hurt Thaddeus." She glanced over at Thaddeus, hoping that was true.

Thaddeus ruffled his feathers, sitting on top of the table, looking down at the woman who had sent him flying, as if she deserved everything his friends had inflicted on her.

Finally, with a lot of pressure on his jaw, Doreen forced Goliath to release his grip on Cecily's finger. Cecily held her hand against her chest, crying as if her heart was broken—or maybe her finger.

Doreen figured probably both were possible. At some point it would hit Cecily that she'd killed her own sister. It was one thing to do that in a rage, but it was another thing to do it out of spite. Eventually the reality had to set in that Cecily was now alone in the world. And her future was not looking too bright.

Doreen reached up to high five Mack.

When their hands clapped and disengaged, he said, "You know what? My instincts told me not to knock. Figures you'd get into trouble, even early on a Tuesday. Apparently no day is safe with you."

She beamed up at him. "See? That's all due to the animals. They were probably sending you ESP messages."

He glared at her.

She chuckled. "Just kidding. I figured you were hungry."

He pointed down at Cecily. "I can't believe she killed them both."

"Were you listening that long?" she asked.

He held up his phone. "And I learned from you. I recorded the entire thing."

At that, Cecily burst into more tears and curled up on the floor in a fetal position.

"You better call a cruiser to come and get your prisoner," Doreen said. "I think we just cuffed a double murderer."

He looked at her and smiled. "Thanks for that."

"Thanks for coming to the rescue," she said. "I'm happy to solve your cases as long as you keep saving my poor sad ass in the process."

At that, he burst out laughing. "It's a deal."

Chapter 25

Tuesday late morning...

MACK WALKED BACK into the kitchen at eleven thirty, took off his jacket, placed it around the back of the chair, and said, "Now I'm hungry. Where is the omelet?"

She laughed. "I've replayed that video three different times. I'm still not sure I know how to do this."

"Come on. Get up there," he said. "It's not hard."

Under his watchful eye, she carefully sliced the bacon, taking five times longer than he had the day before. Every time she tried to apologize, he brushed it away.

"Forget about it. Do it right the first time, and you won't have to endure the learning curve again. You'll get faster eventually."

With onions and bacon simmering—and wasn't that something to turn on the burner and have it heat up—she thought this was the best thing since peanut butter. She added the mushrooms; then he showed her how to scramble the eggs, which she did. She removed all the ingredients from the pan when they were done, cracked in the eggs, stirring vigorously, and, when that was ready, she laid the rest of the ingredients on top, along with some grated cheese, and looked at him.

"Now take the flipper and gently fold it in half."

Knowing this was kind of an initial test of her cooking skills, she gently eased the flipper under one side, totally amazed when it lifted without a sticking problem, and carefully folded it over. And sure enough, it was beautifully golden on the surface.

He picked up the lid, handing it to her.

She plunked it down and grinned up at him. "I did it!" she cried out.

"Almost," he said. "It's easy to get cocky right now and burn it."

Her gaze locked back down at the pan. "How long do I leave it like this?" She chewed on her bottom lip. "Because I sure don't want to mess it up now."

"Not to worry," he said. "Maybe give it another thirty seconds. I'll get the plates." He took plates, knives, and forks to the table.

When she reached her count to thirty, she lifted the lid and sighed happily. "Somehow you got it onto the board without breaking it."

"You could cut it in the pan too," he said, "if that's easier. Just take the spatula, find your middle, and push down, separating it gently."

Deciding that was probably easier, she followed his suggestion and soon enough had two large pieces of omelet. It took a bit to get them out of the pan and onto the plates, but, when she was done, she'd never been prouder. She turned, sighed, and handed him a plate. "Brunch is served."

He laughed and gave her a kiss on her forehead. "I'll be very happy to eat it too."

They sat down and enjoyed their meal. She couldn't

believe it. "It tastes like an omelet." She almost got teary-eyed over this. Instead she took a dozen pictures. "I'm sending these to Nan. She'll be absolutely thrilled for me."

As soon as she did, Mack looked over and said, "You realize you sent pictures of both of our plates, right?"

She looked up at him and said, "Yes, of course. I made them both." She looked confused. "Why? What does that mean?"

His gaze lightened. "Nothing. Except for her penchant for betting on our love lives. Now she'll know I was here this morning too."

She sagged in place. "Oh, no. What did I do?"

He just chuckled. "Don't worry about it. This was cooking lesson one, and you did very, very well."

She rubbed her hands together with a smile. "You did it much faster and had extras to go with yours. But I made something on the stove." She hopped up to double-check that the stove was off, patted it with her hand. "Well done, Doreen."

Chapter 26

Tuesday mid-afternoon...

IT WAS NOW two o'clock. After Mack had taken away the gun-toting Cecily, the reporters had somehow found out she had been threatened at gunpoint in her home by the same person who had murdered the two recent victims in town.

The media had arrived in an irritating avalanche.

In defiance, Doreen had grabbed four lawn chairs, putting them on the sidewalk in front of her house. "If you'll wait here, you might as well be comfortable."

When it came time to oversee the scuba diving, she snuck out the back. Reaching the site, she stared at the beach, realizing how many people were here. She walked over to Nathan. "I'm so sorry," she said. "Somehow word got out."

He patted her hand. "Not to worry. I probably put the word out. I mean, it's a long shot that we'll find anything, but it's a darn good idea. We should have done this a long time ago. The fact that you're the one who thought of it has just cemented your reputation in town."

She sighed. "I didn't try to get a reputation, you know?"

He chuckled. "And you realize that's what reputations are all about. It's not something you try to get. It's something you earn. I'm glad to see you're also not injured from today's attack."

"Honestly, I think Cecily was attacked more by my animals than I was attacked by her," she confessed. "Goliath bit her hand. Mugs tripped her because she hit poor Thaddeus."

Nathan reached out and touched Thaddeus's wings. "Is he okay?" he asked with concern.

Thaddeus opened his beak. "Thaddeus is fine. Thaddeus is fine."

Nathan chuckled. "How he must enrich your life," he said in envy. "It's truly a remarkable relationship you have with them."

"It is," she said. "And you're right. They have enriched my life. It seemed so lonely before, and the three of them now are just so much a part of what I do every day."

Just then Mugs barked. They looked out across the water to see scuba divers coming up.

"You think they found anything?"

"We'll get a signal. Green means they found something, and blue means they didn't."

"They're far enough away," she said, "that the green and blue are likely to look the same."

"Oh, I don't think so," he said. "We should be able to see in a minute."

And there it was, a huge green board held up from the boat.

Around her the crowd cheered.

Her hand went over her mouth, and she gasped. "Oh my," she said. "I just never thought I could possibly be right."

"Well, my dear, it looks like not only were you right but you have just saved two families more heartache. Thank you. Thank you for coming to Kelowna. I'd really love to be involved in any other mysteries you get your hands into," he said with a chuckle. "How vastly entertaining you are to have as a friend." He tucked her hand into his, and they walked closer to the beach.

The crowd surged around them, and, sure enough, on the beach were cops and Mack himself. He turned to look at her, reached out a hand. She grasped his, and he tugged her ever-so-slightly toward him. She wondered if that had something to do with Nathan on the other side of her, but Nathan stepped up with her so the three of them were abreast.

"You did a very good thing today," she said to Mack, tears in her eyes and a smile on her face.

Mack said, "For that, we have to thank Nathan."

"My diving friends went down with a few additions Mack enlisted," Nathan said. "They used my boat. But you, Doreen, are the one who found them. You figured out where they were. And why."

She looked up at Mack. "Can the divers bring them up?"

"Two of the divers out there are cops. They're search and rescue and retrieval specialists," he said. "If there's any way to bring them up, they will." He turned to look out across the water. "I don't know about the truck though."

And, sure enough, by the time the afternoon wore on, and the boat finally came back in again, there were two body bags on board. She couldn't imagine what condition the bones were in now. Still, those small and thin bags carried the precious remains lost for decades. The cops hopped out and walked over to Mack. They shook hands.

One said, "We're not coroners but looks like a child and an adult male."

"Did you get any identification off the vehicle?" Doreen asked anxiously.

"Better than that," he said. "The license and insurance were in the glove box in a plastic bag. There's also a plastic backpack here with Paul's name on the inside. We brought that up too. You were right. It's Paul and Henry, missing for over twenty-nine years."

She stepped back, overcome with emotion. So maybe her reputation here had been solidified. But this time she was proud enough to not care about the publicity. Somehow she'd cleared the names of two different generations of Huberts. Henry was now clear of kidnapping Paul, and Josh was cleared of Celeste's murder. More than that, she'd brought two people home. And home was where they belonged.

She sniffled. Mack turned to look at her. She shrugged and smiled. "I feel like I need to go home, just like I brought them home. I'm feeling a little lost myself."

His gaze narrowed. "Are you okay?"

"I'm fine," she said with a smile. "I'm really fine. In fact, I'm the best I've been in a very long time." With a wave to the crowd, she called the animals to her and headed home.

Was there ever a sweeter word in the entire dictionary?

USA TODAY BESTSELLING AUTHOR
DALE MAYER

Dagger in the Dahlias

Lovely Lethal Gardens 4

Chapter 1

In the Mission, Kelowna, BC
Wednesday Morning, One Day After Solving Her Last Case...

DOREEN MONTGOMERY OPENED the front door to her home, pulling away the madly barking Mugs from the entrance. Since arriving in Kelowna to live in her Nan's house, she'd been adapting from her old life as a wife to a mega rich man to being a single woman living on her own – in poverty. She and her pedigreed basset hound had been saved from a bad marriage, where neither of them had been loved, to her new life with Goliath, an oversized Maine Coon cat and a talkative – sometimes too talkative – African Gray Parrot named Thaddeus. The moment there was a knock on her door, complete chaos ensued. Like now...

She stared at the stranger in surprise. He didn't look like media but the vans outside, the crowd with tripods and cameras said he most likely was. Mugs calmed slightly but he switched to sniffing the stranger's pant legs.

Suspiciously, she asked, "Yes, may I help you?"

The man in a three-piece suit, looking extremely elegant and way too perfect for the small town of Kelowna, particularly for her neglected house, smiled and held out his hand. "I'm Scott Rosten, an appraiser from Christie's, the auction house."

"Oh my," she said in excitement. She shook his hand with a little too much enthusiasm. "I wasn't expecting you until this afternoon." At her tone, Mugs started to get excited. She shushed him and moved Mugs back so Mr. Rosten could come inside away from the media watching avidly from the edge of her property. With a satisfied shove she slammed the door to the flashing bulbs outside. She turned with a bright smile to Mr. Rosten. "Sorry about them." She waved at the media outside. "Things have been crazy here."

"No problem. My flight got in early," Mr. Rosten explained, his gaze locked on Thaddeus, her African gray parrot on her shoulder. "There didn't seem to be any reason to wait, so, if I'm not putting you out, is it possible to talk to you now?"

He motioned at Thaddeus. "Wow. Is he friendly?"

"Absolutely. This is Thaddeus."

"Welcome. Welcome," Thaddeus squawked.

"Thank you," Mr. Rosten said chuckling. "He's quite a character."

"That he is, and I'm glad you're here. The earlier the better as far as I'm concerned." She motioned to the mess around her. "Take a look around, Mr. Rosten."

"Call me Scott." He stepped further into the living room, his gaze locked on the closest piece of furniture. "Wow."

She gazed at him anxiously. "*Wow*? Is that a good wow or a bad wow?"

"It could be a very good wow." Without hesitation he

went to the first little chair, picked it up, checking the maker's mark. "You see items like these in pictures, but they aren't quite the same as seeing them in real life."

"Not to mention there's just something about the feel of real wood in your hands," she replied bending down to tug Mugs back slightly, so he wasn't in the way.

"If you're an antiques lover, there's also a reverence for the history behind each piece," he said, his fingers gently caressing the carved feet, then the edges where the cushions met. "These are absolutely stupendous."

"Do you think they're real?" She hated to ask so bluntly but didn't know any other way to say it.

The antiques appraiser looked at her in surprise. "Oh, they are definitely real."

"Right. Okay. So I know they're real wood, and I know they're real furniture, but are they real antiques?" She scrunched up her face. *Doreen, get a hold of yourself. You're acting like a fool, a greedy fool.* "I'm not explaining myself very well," she said.

He held up a hand. "You're doing just fine. What you're really asking is, are these the same rare pieces we were hoping they were. And I can tell you, for this one in my hand, the answer is yes."

"And there's that one," she said, pointing at the second one across the room. Immediately Thaddeus walked down her arm and sat on her wrist. She chuckled and walked over to place him on the mantel.

Scott walked to the matching chair, picked it up, studied it, placed it beside the first chair, then fell to his knees in front of the coffee table. "Wow. Just look at the work that went into this."

"Wow, just wow," Thaddeus cried out as he hopped

from the mantel to the back of the chair they'd been looking at.

"Don't mind him," Doreen said as Scott stared at Thaddeus in surprise. "He loves to repeat our words."

"He's amazing." Scott reached out a finger smiling as Thaddeus stroked his finger with his beak. "He's lovely."

"And he'll take all your attention if you let him," she warned.

"Good point." Scott turned his attention back to the furniture. "Can you give me a hand?"

It took the two of them to gently flip the coffee table so he could see the maker's mark and the numbers on the underside.

He nodded. "These are three pieces of the same matched set. I was so hoping the photographs didn't lie. But until I came and checked it for myself ..."

"And the couch?" she asked, her voice doubtful. "It's really big." At her words, Mugs jumped up on the couch and immediately stretched out. Horrified, Doreen quickly moved him off. "Mugs get off," she cried. "Sorry, Scott."

"Don't be. The couch has been well loved. It's part of life. And the size of the couch is what makes it part of that very unique set. Montague only did two like this. It was intended for a large bedroom sitting area. He wanted it to match the bed."

Together they slowly flipped the couch, which was at least big enough to seat six. He checked it for scratches, smiled when he saw a couple, then crowed in delight when he looked at the maker's mark and said, "This is all the same set."

"Does that mean you think you can auction them off for a decent price?"

"Absolutely." He looked at her. "Are you ready to let them go?"

"Interesting that you should ask that. Before I realized this furniture belonged to my great-great-grandmother, I had zero attachment. Now that I know they've been in my family for a century, it's a little harder, but yes," she said looking around at her living room. "I can't even sit on them anymore now that I'm so petrified of damaging them."

"They have been sat on by your family for generations," Scott said. "I know you say they were in your family, and your grandmother is still alive. It's on her word that these pieces were in her grandmother's possession. Do you have any paperwork that proves provenance?"

"That's a new word I've just learned," Doreen said with a smile. "Fen Gunderson is the one who first introduced me to how important that is. My grandmother says a folder is in the house somewhere, but I'm not sure where it is. I was hoping we could move out some of these pieces, and then potentially I could find it."

"Right," he said. "I understand you have the matching bed too, correct?"

Doreen nodded, heading to the hallway. Mugs raced ahead of them.

"A bed and two night tables," she said, walking to the staircase.

Scott looked over the moon at her words.

She led him upstairs, apologizing every step, saying, "I'm sorry. I wasn't expecting you until this afternoon, so I didn't clean up yet."

"Doesn't matter. Doesn't matter at all." He chuckled as Goliath ran up the inside curve of the stairs, his movements fast and lithe.

Goliath was a huge golden Maine coon cat and had come with Nan's house as part of Doreen's gift from her grandmother. He was the size of a bobcat, but that didn't scare Scott, so the appraiser must really like animals. She knew she'd like him. And not just because he was here for her antiques.

"The animals are curious too," Scott noted.

On the heel of his words, Thaddeus cried out pathetically from the upstairs hallway, "Curious animals. Curious animals."

Scott laughed. "And a talking parrot."

"He is indeed and they are all curious." Doreen said as she scooped up Thaddeus. The large beautiful blue-gray parrot with long red tail feathers also came with Nan's house. Doreen was getting used to his constant repetitions. And definitely enjoyed his affectionate nature.

When they walked into the master bedroom, Scott stopped, delighted. Whereas she frowned. Both Goliath and Mugs had stretched out on top of the bedding. She groaned. Thankfully Scott didn't seem to care. He was standing enthralled.

"We sent pictures of the furniture in this room to Christie's," she said, placing Thaddeus on the window ledge. "I guess you've seen them already."

"And again the pictures don't do this set justice," he said with a smile. He lovingly stroked one of the large posts. "Absolutely beautiful."

"If you think so," she said. "Honestly, it's been my bed. So it doesn't seem out of the ordinary. I've been sleeping in it."

"Montague always designed a couple small drawers into the headboard. May I look?"

"Absolutely," she said, watching in surprise. "Why would he do that?"

"Because he wanted a place to put his glasses and for the pills he had to take at night. Montague built these little drawers to suit his needs. As I said, he built two complete sets. It was his way of covering his costs. One set for himself and one set for sale."

Scott sat down on the side of the bed and gently checked out the headboard. And, sure enough, it didn't take but a few minutes before she heard a light clicking noise, and a drawer popped out. Scott turned to look at her. "It's here," he said. "And now I know for sure this is his piece."

Doreen looked in the drawer, but it was empty. She hated the sense of letdown she felt when she hadn't even realized a drawer was here to begin with.

Goliath shifted on the bed beside them and rolled over, his tail flicking as he watched Scott carefully. Thaddeus hopped down to the mattress and walked closer to Scott. "Welcome, Scott. Welcome, Scott."

Scott chuckled. "He's quite something, isn't he?"

"You have no idea," Doreen muttered. Even as she watched, Thaddeus walked closer to Scott. He seemed very interested in their visitor. He didn't usually care who was here.

He got up and walked to the other side, asking, "Do you want to see how they open?"

Doreen nodded and leaned over his shoulder as he pressed a tiny little button. Sure enough, the second little secret drawer popped open. "Nan said her grandmother used to hide treats for her in a lot of the furniture, so Nan ran around and searched for stuff all the time."

"Well ..." He lifted a gold-foiled chocolate. Thaddeus

waddled closer the shiny foil attracting his attention. "That's what this is then. Maybe you should deliver it to Nan. Although it's likely decades late." Scott gently brushed Thaddeus back as he held the treat out to Doreen. "This isn't for you, big guy."

Thaddeus' crown lifted high and his head bobbed. "Treat for the big guy. Treat for the big guy."

Scott chuckled. "You'd better take this before he decides it's his."

Doreen held out her hand, completely enchanted at the thought of her grandmother as a little girl, running around the house, searching for chocolates. "This is a very special moment," she whispered. "Would you mind if we placed it back in the drawer? I want to take a picture to show her."

"If you're still willing to sell," Scott said, "I do have to arrange for proper shipping. And that'll take a couple days. Every piece has to be wrapped properly before moving them."

"Understood," she said. But she really hadn't considered what the process would be. In the back of her mind she was thinking an hour and they'd be all done. But ... somehow she doubted it.

He looked at her. "But that means you don't have a bed."

She smiled up at him. "I'm also starving. I don't have a job, and I'm trying to keep the roof over my head. I can find another bed to sleep in."

He nodded in understanding. "That's good." He looked at the night tables. "To find both the sitting room set and the bedroom set is absolutely wonderful. The second set is no longer together."

"Are there other pieces that go with the set, other than

what we've found so far?"

He nodded. "Three dressers—a tallboy, a short boy, and a vanity." He looked around the room, his eyes lighting on the vanity.

She'd never seen a grown man cry. But he stood trembling in front of it, as if it was the best thing he'd ever seen in his life. She got up and asked, "Is this the vanity piece?"

He just nodded. Completely unable to talk.

"I guess that's one of the pieces then." She opened the drawers. "I haven't had a chance to go through this vanity yet."

"We should do that now," he said, "because I should check the label underneath, confirming it's part of the same set. And that mirror looks like it's very delicate."

She was afraid to move it, but they dragged it forward, with Mugs getting in the way at every step and Thaddeus insisting on riding on her shoulder. Finally Scott could slip behind and check for the mark he sought, one on the mirror and one on the vanity itself.

When he stood, such a sense of peace appeared on his face. He kept stroking the edge of the mirror. "It's definitely one of the pieces. Two hidden drawers should also be in this piece."

She looked at him in surprise. "Where?"

He chuckled. "How about I give you a few minutes to see if you can figure them out yourself?"

She didn't see any drawers like the headboard had. As Thaddeus hopped then walked the surface of the dresser, her fingers slid over the top and then the side. She shrugged and looked at him. "I haven't a clue."

"That's one of the reasons to empty the drawers. Because one of the secret drawers is behind one of the big drawers."

She grabbed empty boxes and an empty laundry hamper nearby and then opened the drawers, gently sliding the contents into the boxes. Everything from papers, notebooks, perfume, and some jewelry had been stored in the vanity. It was going to take time to sort through and this was obviously not the time.

There were seven drawers—three on each side and a big drawer across the center. With all the drawers out, sitting on the vanity stool, Scott pushed a small depression on the panel inside where the drawers sat, and a drawer popped out at the very back. He removed the drawer. Inside was a little padded velvet envelope. He picked it up and handed it to her. Thaddeus made an odd cawing sound.

"It's not yours either," Doreen said affectionately. "Regardless of what you think."

She released the catch and poured into her hand what appeared to be a locket. She opened it, and her breath caught in the back of her throat. "Oh my." Inside was an image of a woman who was maybe fifty and on the other side was a baby.

"Do you know those people?"

"I think this is my Nan," she said, tapping the woman's face. "And I'll say that's me."

"Well, there you go. Family is family." He replaced the drawer. "Is it your mother or your father who is Nan's child?"

"My father," she said, "and he died, after a wild and reckless life, of a drug overdose many, many years ago. My mom stayed friends with Nan for my sake and because Nan helped us a lot when I was growing up." Doreen carefully closed the locket and put it back in the velvet pouch. Not wanting to lose it, she slipped it into her pocket. "I'll ask

Nan about it."

"You do that. Now let's find the other drawer." It was on the right side. He popped open the other secret drawer and found yet again another gold-foiled chocolate in it. Doreen laughed in delight and took another photograph, picked up the chocolate, and put it beside the first one she had set on the windowsill. Thaddeus immediately flew to the window ledge.

"Thaddeus," she warned, "don't you dare ..." With an odd snorting sound Thaddeus ruffled his feathers and shot her an injured look. She kept a wary eye on him as she turned her attention back to Scott.

He admired the vanity. "You are truly blessed."

"And I didn't even know what I had," Doreen said with a smile.

"You don't appear to have the two other dressers."

"A dresser is in the back of the closet," she said. "I can't reach it."

Scott eyed the closet, almost rubbing his hands together, and said, "It would be really good if we could see it."

She pulled open the closet doors so he could see what a nightmare it was inside. Even as the doors opened it was the push of the stuffed clothing inside being released that slammed the doors wide open. All they could see was the hangers full of garments.

Scott gasped, then chuckled. "Your grandmother is a clothes horse."

"Obviously." Doreen pushed back some of the hanging items so he could see in the back of the closet. "There's the dresser. It's short though."

He burrowed in with her. "We need to pull it out," he said in excitement.

It was very hard to do, but inch by inch, they cleared a path and moved the dresser forward. When it was finally standing free of the clutter of the closet, Doreen realized it looked to be part of the same set.

"That tells you how these pieces have been treated," she said with a shake of her head. "Instead of being prized possessions, this one was shoved in the closet for extra storage."

Scott busily examined it.

"Do we know for sure this dresser is part of the set?" she asked, waiting with bated breath to hear his answer.

He gave her a shout of joy and said, "Come look for yourself."

She bent behind him to see him gently stroking his fingers over the mark. "It really is, isn't it?"

"It is the short boy, indeed." He smiled. "This has been one of the best days of my life. Now are you sure you're ready to let all these pieces go?"

"Absolutely."

"Can we take another look around and see if you have the missing tallboy?"

"What exactly is a tallboy?" Doreen asked, when he straightened again.

He pointed to his chest. "It's about this high and is a narrow, tall chest, usually for the man."

"So this would be the woman's dresser?" She pointed at the dresser that had been pulled from the back of the closet. A dresser Thaddeus had now claimed as he paced the top. At least he was leaving the chocolates alone.

He nodded. "Yes. And it makes sense that it would be with the vanity and the bed. But I don't see any sign of the tallboy. If you did have it, it would be a huge asset. And, if you are truly ready to sell these, I will arrange for shipment."

"You'll give me receipts for them all, right?" she asked hesitantly.

He chuckled. "Absolutely. There'll be *lots* of paperwork to document this transaction."

Feeling relieved, she grabbed a couple empty boxes from the spare room and emptied the drawers of the short boy dresser from the closet.

"You don't even want to check what's in there?" he asked from behind her.

"I will go through it all," she said, "but obviously we don't have time right now." The whole top drawer looked to be scarves and accessories. The second drawer appeared to be stockings. She held up a pair.

"Those are silk," the appraiser said, "a quite beautiful silk."

She shook her head. "My grandmother had very expensive tastes apparently." She picked up several more items, placed them all in a box, and, by the time she got to the bottom drawer, out came a huge accordion file full of paperwork. At that, she got excited. "Maybe *this* is it."

Scott was at her side. "Maybe it's what?"

"The folder with the provenance," she said. "It'll take a while to go through it all. It's bursting at its seams." She motioned to the dresser. "Can you take a look and make sure absolutely nothing else is in there?"

"Let's take out every drawer," he said, "because, yes, two secret drawers should be in this dresser as well."

With all four drawers out, they could see several items had been caught in the back. With those collected, Scott pressed similar buttons as on the vanity, opening the two secret dresser drawers. One had a pair of cuff links inside.

Thaddeus stretched his neck to see them. The other two animals were stretched out on the bed ignoring the two of them.

She looked at them in amazement.

"They look valuable," he said. "I'm not an expert on gems though."

She admired the red stones. "Garnets or rubies?"

"Definitely rubies," he said with a smile.

She shook her head and put them inside the same little velvet envelope the locket was in.

In the other secret drawer was a picture. She flipped it over and back again. "Now this is Nan as a little girl." She looked at it and smiled, holding it out to him. "On the back is Nan's real name, Willa Montgomery. I am loving these little secret drawers," she said.

Scott looked around the bedroom and asked, "Is there any chance you can sleep somewhere else tonight? We've made a hell of a mess in your room."

"I can sleep in the spare bedroom," she said.

He looked at the big closet. "I'm sorry, but do you mind if I dig around to make sure more isn't there?"

"Be my guest," she said. "I do know there are shelves in the back too. I don't know why Nan would put the hanging clothes in front of the shelves."

"I think, once you get this cleared out, you'll find a space in between the two hanging portions to walk through. It's an adaptation of a walk-in closet."

"It's chaos," Doreen said, chuckling.

His grin flashed. "It is, at that."

Just then she heard the postal worker open the mail slot in her front door. Mugs barked like a madman and tore out of the room. Goliath followed and on his heels, Thaddeus flew off the dresser and soared through the hallway to land out of sight. She sighed. "I have to go downstairs and salvage the mail. My dog has decided it's something he should defend me from."

"Oh, dear," he said. "Go, go, go."

She dashed downstairs to the front door, and there was Mugs with a letter in his mouth. As he went past Goliath, the cat swatted him on the face. Mugs growled and dropped the letter. Thaddeus raced between the two, snagged the letter, and ran into the kitchen.

Doreen raised both hands in frustration. "What's gotten into you guys? Stop it." She cornered Thaddeus, who was still dragging the envelope along as he hopped onto the kitchen table. She took it from his beak and held it up high. "Stop! It's my letter, not yours."

At the commotion the appraiser had come down to see if she was okay. He entered the kitchen and smiled. "It is truly amazing that you live in this wonderfully chaotic house-hold."

"Just not so good for the antiques," she said with an eye roll.

He chuckled.

She opened the letter-size envelope. "Interesting. There's no return address, and there's no stamp."

"Somebody dropped it into your mail slot directly then," he said.

She nodded and opened it, finding a single sheet of pa-per. "*Dear Bone Lady*. Uh-oh," she whispered.

I see that you're very interested in cold cases, and you have such great talent in solving them. Even ones from twenty-nine years ago. That's why I'm contacting you. I wondered if you could help me with my personal cold case. My brother-in-law disappeared twenty-nine years ago in August and has never been heard from since. I know I don't have any right to ask, but, if you're interested in a mystery, please call me. I do have some evidence, a dagger of Johnny's that I found buried at the spot where he was last seen. I found it some time ago when I went to plant a new bed of dahlias, but I don't know if it's enough to even start your investigation. I'm hopeful. Please call me.

After that plea was a phone number; the letter was signed by Penny Jordan.

Doreen stared at it in surprise. "Well, how about this? It looks like we have our next mystery to solve. Dagger in the dahlias!"

That sounded perfect.

Chapter 2

Wednesday Late Morning ...

DOREEN WALKED SCOTT Rosten to her front door. As soon as she opened the door and Scott stepped out, Mugs took the opportunity to slip outside too. He headed for the grassy front lawn and started to roll. She smiled at his antics but turned her attention back to Scott.

"Don't forget now," he said. "I'll bring in the crew early next week so they can pack this up properly. I'll update you with a better time frame when I know."

She nodded but couldn't help thinking how it was a little too late to be concerned about packing up this furniture properly, when all of these pieces had been so well used for decades. "The sooner, the better. I'm afraid to use anything now," she confessed.

He smiled at her. "Obviously we don't want anything destroyed or broken in the meantime, but we also have to consider these have been gently used over the years. There will be some wear. Yes, that'll depreciate the value, but they're special pieces, and you've been very blessed to have them, so enjoy spending time with them while you can." He stopped hesitated, his gaze searching the living room. "Did you have any luck finding the tallboy?"

"Not yet, sorry," she said regretfully. "But I'll keep looking. I assume the packing will take a little time."

"Yes, possibly, but these men are professionals." He gave a shrug, almost philosophically, and a gentle laugh. "Just don't damage them in the meantime, okay?"

She gave him a bright smile. "I'll cover them in Bubble Wrap from now until then."

"It's the end of an era," he said. "And the good thing is, as an era ends with you, it opens for somebody else, so don't feel bad. The antique world will be absolutely delighted with your decision to part with these."

As soon as he left her driveway, easily maneuvering through the press, which thankfully had reduced to just one camera crew, she called Mugs back into the house and closed the door. Her fingers instinctively went to her pocket to the strange letter she'd received. She'd been so busy that she hadn't read it a second time, and it worried away in the back of her mind.

Her life had gone off the rails but in a good way. All yesterday afternoon and today, she had been smiling a happy smile. She'd survived an ugly attack from Cecily, found the little boy who had been missing for almost three decades. And Doreen had cleared the handyman's name of all kinds of accusations that must have hurt everybody who had loved him. However, his wife had passed away before that mystery had been solved, but at least the rest of his family now knew that he hadn't been trying to hurt the little boy nor had he attempted to start a whole new life with him. Instead they'd both drowned due to the record flooding that particular year. Definitely an unfortunate and sad event, but an accident nonetheless.

Yesterday, as Doreen had walked home, the Kelowna Detachment Police Commander had seen her on the streets. He'd pulled over, hopped out, and came to shake her hand. She'd been touched.

"We need people like you," he'd said with an expansive smile.

She'd chuckled. "I'm not sure Mack agrees with you."

The commander's eyes had twinkled like Christmas bells in the sunlight; then his voice had deepened as he said, "Oh, I'm pretty sure Mack is happy with the scenario too."

All in all, it had been a very special event and apparently had touched a nerve for someone else, if the letter in her pocket was anything to go by. No return address was on the envelope, no stamp on it, just a plea for help inside. Doreen wanted to help. She would absolutely love to help, but beginner's luck wouldn't hold her in good stead all the time.

She took out the letter once again to reread the details. They were sketchy, but that plea for help tore at her heart. And the woman said she'd found a dagger at the root of the dahlias in the same garden where she'd last seen her brother-in-law.

The problem was, the dagger had been out in the weather for so long before being found. Doreen highly doubted any forensic evidence remained on it at this point. Yet, as she already knew, DNA *could* last forever, and maybe some would be in the joints where the knife handle met the steel? But that didn't mean she could convince anybody to test the dagger. Particularly Mack.

She had to admit she was getting cold-case fever. How sad was that? But the puzzles fascinated her.

Who would have known Kelowna was such a den of evildoings? It almost made her smile, but, of course, there was nothing funny about that. Still, she *was* closing cases rapidly. She loved what she was doing. But how long could her winning streak go?

"This has turned into a full-time hobby," she muttered.

She folded the letter again and shoved it deep into her pocket. She wandered into the kitchen, where Goliath was stretched out on top of the kitchen table.

"Goliath, what are you doing?" she asked. "Get off the table. We've had this discussion before."

He looked at her, flicked his tail, and slid, as if boneless, to the nearest chair at this table, where he curled up. But he made it so slow and so of his own prerogative that she knew it was a case of *I'm doing this because I want to and not because you told me to.*

"Who knew looking after a cat would be so much trouble?" she asked out loud. "Who knew looking after a cat …" She stopped, smiled, and added, "… would be such a heartwarming experience?" She leaned over and scratched Goliath behind his ears, loving the soft silkiness to his fur.

As soon as she pulled away her hand, he swatted her, his claws lightly digging in to pull her hand back down.

She chuckled, squatted in front of him, and said, "You're totally okay with your new life, aren't you, buddy?"

He didn't have to answer. As he rolled onto his back, giving her his belly, and then stretched forward and backward, making him look even more monstrous in size, it was obvious he was a happy cat. If she'd done nothing else, she'd given him and Thaddeus a good life.

And speaking of Thaddeus, where was he? Because, wherever he was, trouble was sure to follow. There was just something about that bird.

She walked back into the living room. "Thaddeus?

Where are you, buddy?"

But she got no answer.

She walked through the lower part of the house, then headed up the stairs.

"I know you were here earlier because, when the auction house guy was here, you were all over him. Now where are you? ... Oh, that's right. I last saw Thaddeus stealing off with the letter ..."

When she saw no sign of him here in her bedroom, she went back down the stairs and, on a hunch, opened the front door. *Maybe he followed Scott outside.* "Thaddeus," she yelled. "Thaddeus?"

And, sure enough, he hopped out from underneath the bushes and looked up at her.

"What are you doing out there?" she said, walking to him and bending down to scoop him into her arms. "You have to stay close."

"Stay close. Stay close."

"Yes, Thaddeus, stay close. Now repeat after me, *Thaddeus, stay close. Stay close.*"

He stared up at her and never said a word.

She groaned. "I don't get it. You say what you want, when you want, but you won't be trained to say what I want you to say."

"Stay close. Stay close," he muttered. He reached up as tall as he could and brushed his head against her cheek.

Her heart melted yet again. "Okay. You guys have so enriched my family," she muttered, closing her eyes and cuddling him close. She walked back into the kitchen, carrying Thaddeus. "But honestly, it's time for a cup of tea."

"Thaddeus likes tea. Thaddeus likes tea."

"I know," Doreen said. Sadly she did know because he

had a habit of drinking from her teacup. "Maybe I'll make you a little bit in a bowl. How's that?" Although she should probably look up on the internet if tea was good for him. And then she laughed. "Of course it's not good for him. He already flies around the place like he's loopy. It'll probably just make him fly faster. Or crash into things more often."

Then Thaddeus didn't fly well to begin with.

She sat him on the kitchen table, only to have Goliath shoot her a dirty look. Right. Different rules for different animals. "Look, Goliath. You're too big for the table. Thaddeus is just the right size."

Just then Mugs reached up with his front paws, looked at Goliath on the chair, and she realized Mugs wasn't allowed on the chairs.

"See?" she told Goliath, pointing at Mugs. "Everybody has their own rules," she confirmed, hoping that would end the discussion.

Instead Thaddeus looked at her and said, "Thaddeus is hungry. Thaddeus is hungry."

She groaned, picked up a bowl she kept with a lid on it, like a sugar bowl, pulled out a pinch of sesame seeds and put them down in front of the bird. He went to work.

Goliath jumped up, stuck his nose into the seeds, and sniffed, sending seeds flying, then backed away, shooting Doreen another look, followed by a plaintive meow.

She groaned, picked up the cat treat bag, and gave him two. "Remember how you're on a diet?"

Mugs woofed at her feet.

With no other option but to make it fair, she picked up the dog treats and gave him some. "You're on a diet too," she admonished.

With all three of her animals happy with their midmorning snack, she plugged in the teakettle and waited for it to boil. In the meantime, she looked at the letter again. "You know what? To go down this path, Doreen, you're likely to end up a failure. If the police haven't solved it in all this time ... But then that doesn't really mean anything either, does it?" she said, immediately countering her argument. "Because they do their best. But they have a lot of active cases, and they're short on man-hours. They don't get to sit here with a cup of tea and meander through the cold-case files, one at a time."

With that thought, she took a chair beside Goliath and opened her laptop. The name on the bottom of the letter was Penny Jordan. She typed in *Penny Jordan in Kelowna*, and several articles about a church's Christmas bazaars came up. Penny was apparently some major volunteer. But the dates of those articles were from at least eight years ago. Doreen continued to read through articles that mentioned the Jordan family name, but they were few and far between.

Doreen groaned, closed the laptop, got up, and made her tea as she thought about that tidbit of information. "The only way to learn more is to contact her directly and ask. The letter did have a phone number. But nothing else." *Hmm.* "So are we doing this?" she asked her trio.

They all stared back at her.

Then Thaddeus bobbed his head; Mugs, probably because of Thaddeus's head-bobbing, woofed. Goliath swung a paw and smacked Mugs on the head.

She'd take all that as a joint yes.

"Okay, good enough," she said. "We'll give Penny a call and see what it's all about. But no guarantees. Just because we've had a run of good luck doesn't mean this case will end the same way," she warned.

Chapter 3

Wednesday Noon …

"HI. THIS IS Doreen," she started the phone conversation, a notepad and pen in front of her. The animals relaxed, surrounding her. "I'm looking for Penny Jordan."

"This is Penny," a woman said. *"Doreen? Doreen.* Oh, my goodness. You're the bone lady."

"Well, that's what some people call me," she said. "I certainly appear to have made the reputation for myself since I arrived."

"Everybody also knows you as Nan's granddaughter," Penny said with a chuckle. "Not sure what you prefer."

"How about just Doreen?" Doreen said with a smile. "Although my grandmother is definitely a sweetheart and has a reputation all her own."

"That she does," Penny said smoothly. "You got my letter then?"

"Yes. Yes, I did. But you didn't give me a lot of information. So your brother-in-law went missing?"

"Yes, my husband's younger brother. He was twenty-one at the time. The thing is, the police thought he chose to leave without telling us. Heading west, doing what all young men do. I will admit, you know, that he had some bad friends who were into drugs, but I think it involved the lighter stuff, like marijuana," Penny said anxiously. "I don't want you to get the idea Johnny was some cokehead and became homeless."

"Which happens," Doreen said quietly.

"I know," Penny said. "And honestly, for years, my husband drove around this and neighboring towns, looking to see if Johnny was just sitting on the streets, homeless, but we never heard any more from him."

"Is your husband okay with you contacting me?"

There was silence over the phone, and then Penny said sadly, "He died of a heart attack last year, and his dying wish was that I find answers before I passed away too. I keep his urn on the mantel as a reminder of his last wish."

"I'm sorry," Doreen said, wincing. "How old did you say his brother was when he went missing?"

"Twenty-one," she repeated. "We have accepted the fact he's probably dead because he and his brother were very, very close, and no way he wouldn't have called him all this time. So I have absolutely no doubt something bad happened to him. But it would be nice to have a body that I could bury and to have a memorial for my husband's sake. It mattered to him."

Doreen nodded, even though Penny couldn't see her doing that. "Your brother-in-law's name was Johnny?"

"Yes. There were just the two brothers, Johnny and George Jordan," she said. "Johnny went missing twenty-nine years ago, about the same time frame you've been dealing with. That's why I contacted you."

"Interesting," Doreen said, considering the time lines of

the other cold cases she had helped solve. "Are you thinking this had anything to do with the other missing person cases from back then?"

"No, no, no, no," Penny said. "I don't think so at all. I think Johnny got in with a bad crowd, and a lot of those people have since passed. So it's a really onerous job I've asked you to look into, but, for my husband's sake and for the sake of closure, it would be lovely to get to the bottom of this."

"And what's this about a dagger?" Doreen laid down her pen and picked up her tea, taking a sip.

Penny sighed. "The last time we saw Johnny, he was sitting on an alcove bench in the backyard. I was looking out the window, talking to my husband, and we were laughing and smiling at Johnny. He had a beer in his hand and a big grin. He lifted it up, as in a cheer, took a big swig. I went to the kitchen to clean it up a bit before I made dinner. My husband went back to the home office. We never saw Johnny again. We searched. The police came. They searched. About ten years later we decided to move that bench because, every time we saw it, it caused us pain. So we moved it to a far corner of the yard. I decided to plant dahlias where the bench had been, to change the atmosphere of the spot."

"Right," Doreen said. "Well, dahlias are beautiful, and they would certainly give you a lovely memorial for him."

"Exactly," Penny said. "We brought up this dagger when we dug up that area. The ground there wasn't very good, having been under the bench the whole time. We added soil, enriched slightly with some of the topsoil we brought in to top-dress the front yard."

"Okay, so the dagger wasn't in the dahlia tubers," Doreen said, switching her cell phone from one ear to the other. "It was buried in the dahlia bed or what became a dahlia bed afterward. Is that correct?"

"Yes, and, up until then, it was nothing but an empty space under the bench because obviously nothing would grow there."

"No, it's hard to grow anything without sunshine. I bet you had plenty of moss though."

"Oh, yes." Penny laughed. "The moss really liked that corner."

"So what did you do with the dagger?"

"I called the police and told them. They were sympathetic but said, chances were, nothing would come of it. But I couldn't let it go. I bagged up the dagger and took it to them. I asked them if they could test it, and they said the budget was so tight that they were only testing items with a viable chance for finding DNA. Of course, a knife found many years after my brother-in-law went missing, with no blood evidence to say it was from the scene of the crime, made no sense to them."

"Ah," Doreen said. "That is the exact issue right there. It made no sense because absolutely no forensic evidence was found at the spot where he went missing. So you haven't had the knife tested, correct?"

"No, and I have it still, sitting here."

Doreen added that tidbit to her notepad. "Had you ever seen that dagger before?"

"That's one of the funny things. It's Johnny's," Penny said. "That's another reason the police weren't too bothered because I told them how Johnny used to sit on that bench and have a beer, and he would flip it back and forth between his hands, like a lot of young men did back then. It was just this cool movement they were trying to do, and, at times, he would stab it into the ground, almost like he was playing darts, but with imaginary targets on the lawn."

"So the police assumed Johnny had stabbed it into the ground beside him one time when he was having a couple beers and forgot about it. Then, over time, it just worked itself into the ground. Or somebody unknowingly stepped on it, didn't recognize it, leaves piled in, the mulch, etc." She made another notation regarding this.

"It's of zero help, but, at the same time, it's a connection I can't mentally let go of."

"I don't mind taking a look at the dagger, unless you have photos of it."

"If you would take the dagger, I would be very happy," Penny said. "I know it probably has absolutely nothing to do with the case, but, every time I see it, it sends chills down my back."

"Okay, will do," Doreen said. "Where do you live?"

"I'm about a mile away from you. Up the creek."

"That's not a lot of help though," Doreen said with a laugh. "I haven't had a chance to explore much around town."

"Look. I'm planning to go shopping later," Penny said. "Do you want me to stop by and drop it off?"

"That would lovely," Doreen said. "If you wouldn't mind. And drop off any information you have—any police reports you might have a copy of, any interviews, anybody who was a witness. Just anything you have would be helpful."

"I have a folder of information we've collected over the years, but it's mighty thin."

"That's fine," Doreen said. "It'll help me get my mind wrapped around what happened."

"I'll make a copy for myself and bring you the originals. How about in a couple hours or so, about three o'clock? Is that okay?"

Doreen checked her watch. "About three o'clock then. That's fine." She hung up the phone and stared at the animals, though not really seeing them. Her mind was locked on a twenty-one-year-old, strong, young, healthy male going missing from one moment to the next.

"How awful, Mugs. You see a family member sitting on a bench outside in your backyard, and then you never see him again."

She was glad the young man, Johnny, had lifted his beer in a half salute of "Hey, it's a good moment" because at least it was a good memory of the last time Penny and her husband had communicated with Johnny. So many people had a fight before going off to work and getting killed in a car accident. The survivor's last memory for the loved one was of the fight. Not the way anybody wanted to be remembered.

Pondering, she went around the house, dusting off the furniture Scott would be collecting shortly. She was so afraid something would happen to these pieces. She'd joked about protecting it all with Bubble Wrap, but, then again, she was half serious. She just needed nothing to happen to these pricey antiques over the next few days.

She went upstairs to her bedroom, reminded of the ton of clothing she still had to go through. Plus that her bed would be moved next week. She hadn't asked Scott about the mattress. Maybe the mattress could stay, and she could sleep on it on the floor. That would be an easy solution as to where she would sleep tonight. Maybe not as regal an answer to her dilemma but definitely a workable one.

She had Scott's contact information and texted him as to the mattresses. His response came back quickly. As they were newer mattresses, they were hers. So that was good, but there wasn't much room to put the mattresses on the floor beside the big four-poster bed frame. There could be though, if she managed to clean out that corner. If she rearranged some things in here and then moved a lot of stuff into the spare bedroom, she could make it work. Or she could move into the spare bedroom until the bed was gone; then she could decide what to do with the mattress and box spring.

On that note, she walked into the spare room for a look. Mugs followed walking around the room, sniffing the old floor. The room had just a single bed but an old one that squeaked like crazy, even more noisily than the big bed in the master bedroom. She knew trying to sleep on this spare room bed would drive her nuts. Every time one of the animals rolled or shifted she'd wake up too. So what was the answer? She had to clear a spot on the floor in her bedroom. Before bedtime tonight.

She stepped back into her bedroom. Doreen had a lot of Nan's clothing due at Wendy's shop. With that thought in mind, Doreen bagged up the stacks designated for Wendy's consignment store and took them downstairs to the entry hallway. The next time Doreen went to town, she could drop them off and see what Wendy would like to keep.

Doreen had decided to keep an awful lot of Nan's clothing. She picked up an armful of those, still on their hangers, and walked them into the spare room, hanging them in that closet. At least it helped her to separate the old from the new, the keep from the don't keep, what she'd sorted from what she hadn't.

It took several trips to hang up all the clothes to keep.

But it felt like a bit of space had opened up in her bedroom. Considering the bed frame wouldn't be taken for a few days, she figured there was really no point in taking the mattresses off right now. Yet part of her said she should tear it all apart and inspect the pieces before she lost the opportunity. What if something else had been hidden in the bed? Besides, she also needed to change the bedding.

Except ... all the animals had given up on her, passing out on the bedding. And yes, they'd twisted and woven into weird contortions around the mess of stuff they'd placed on the bed earlier. Gently rousing them one at a time, she stripped off the duvet, tossed it to the side, and then went after the sheets. A big thick mattress cover was under the sheets as well. She took that off to be washed too, something she hadn't done since she had moved in. And she could see that the mattress, although older, was still in excellent shape. It had a big cushion top with no rips or stains or tears. All of which was good.

She went to the other side of the bed, lifted up the mattress awkwardly. She stood on the box spring so she could scoot the mattress completely off the box spring, ensuring nothing was underneath it.

Then she lifted the box spring from the big wooden bed frame and checked underneath it. Satisfied no envelopes were taped underneath and no hauls of cash were otherwise stuffed under the bed, she stepped inside the bed frame and slid the box spring over the side of the bed onto the floor. Now she was really making a mess.

It was her first chance to take a look at the four-poster bed without the mattresses. It was amazing. Absolutely amazing. The box spring was at an awkward angle, leaning against one of the four-poster corners, teetering, but it gave her a chance to check with her hands under the bed frame itself, all around the sides, though she couldn't see the back of the headboard.

She'd torn everything apart, so she might as well keep going. And she still had that accordion file to go through. She winced. Scott had specifically asked her to do that, and she'd promised she'd get to it. And here she was, off in a whole different direction.

She'd go through that paperwork as soon as she could because it might make a huge difference in terms of the value of the pieces. She slid her hands under and around the bed frame, checking, but absolutely nothing was here. The newel posts didn't even come off the four posts.

She slid the whole bed toward her enough so she could see nothing was behind the headboard either. "Good enough," she said. She pushed the four-poster toward the door, and the box spring collapsed onto the floor. She looked at it, frowned, and then shrugged. "Well, you were ending up there anyway," she said. "So, what the hell. Might as well stay there."

She quickly rearranged this corner of the room and, with a little effort, moved the big heavy mattress and box spring into place beside the big bed frame.

Mugs immediately jumped inside the slats of the big bed and barked, sniffing, his nose going steadily underneath. When he wouldn't stop, Doreen looked at him. "Seriously, Mugs?"

He barked again, his nose touching the center slat. She hadn't checked under all the slats, so she reached down to do so now. As she got to the slat where Mugs was, she could feel something taped to the underside. Excited, she didn't want to just rip it off—she didn't dare rip up whatever was here.

Someone had to have a reason for doing this, but how could she lift up the massive bed frame?

When her doorbell rang, she groaned and said, "Well, this will have to wait a moment, Mugs."

Only Mugs was already downstairs barking himself hoarse.

Chapter 4

Wednesday Afternoon ...

DOREEN RAN DOWN the stairs lightly, making her way past all the bags of clothing. She pulled open the door to see a lovely older woman standing outside, nervously holding a big brown 9"x12" envelope in her hand. Mugs dashed out and circled around their visitor. At least he was quiet now.

The woman looked up at her and smiled. "It is you! You've been all over the media." She smiled down at Mugs. "And of course, your trio of animals."

At that Mugs barked once as if to say, '*of course.*'

Doreen just rolled her eyes. "And you must be Penny. Come on inside. Let's see what you've got." As the woman stepped in, Doreen said, "Sorry. Please excuse the mess. I'm sorting through all of Nan's stuff and getting a lot of this cleaned out."

"I wouldn't doubt it," Penny said. "Nan has always been a collector of antiques. My husband was too."

That stopped Doreen right in the middle of the living room. "Really?"

Penny nodded. "He and Nan had all kinds of discussions. He loved this set, but Nan would never sell it. She said it was her retirement fund."

"And now that she's retired," Doreen said, "she doesn't need it."

"That's the best thing ever," Penny said with a smile, making a Vanna White arm sweep to the room. "Think about it. Nan doesn't need the money she set aside. I think that's a success in itself."

Doreen laughed. "May I see your file?"

"Oh. I'm sorry." Penny handed over the envelope. "The knife is in there too. And I did keep a digital copy of everything. I should have done that a long time ago. Then I could have just emailed them to you."

"If you could do that too, that would be great," Doreen said, "because I might do more searching that way."

"Sure. It's already digital anyway. Need your email address," she said, "and I can send it to you when I get home."

Doreen gave her the email address. "Now you understand that ... I can't guarantee this will go anywhere, right?"

"I know," Penny said, inputting Doreen's contact info into her phone. "I feel almost guilty asking you. It's just the police don't have anything to go on. Nobody I've talked to over the years has any idea what happened to Johnny. It's so very frustrating. I guess I'm hoping another pair of eyes will turn up something different." She grinned at Doreen. "You do appear to have a very different pair of eyes."

Doreen smiled. "Apparently I have a different perspective that's shaking things up a little. You're still in the same house you lived in when Johnny went missing?"

Penny nodded. "Yes, but not for much longer. I guess that's another reason why I'm feeling the time pressure to solve this. I'm listing the house for sale soon and hoping to move into a condo closer to my older daughter's as soon as I get my house sold."

"So that could be within two weeks, or it could be two months," Doreen said.

"Or two years. Depending on the market. But it's a lovely family home."

"Okay," Doreen said. "Would you mind if I come and take a look myself, to see the backyard and to get a feel for the location he disappeared from?"

"Sure," Penny said. "I'll give you my address when I send you the digital file."

"I'm sorry," Doreen said. "Would you like to sit down?"

"No, but thank you anyway. I don't want to bother you any more than I have, and I should be going. Whenever you're out that way, just pop on by. The thing to remember is, I don't know where the crime scene is, if there was one—whether he went for a walk or met his buddies over the back fence because a park abuts our property there or where he might have gone from our home."

"The park is behind your property?"

"Yes, and, to make matters worse, he used that gate all the time. I think he came and went most of the time that way."

"So, if somebody called to him from the park or sent him a text, he would have gone to meet him, using that gate, correct?"

"Except for the fact we couldn't afford to buy a cell phone back then, and texting didn't exist," Penny said with a smile.

"Right, of course not," Doreen said with a shake of her head. "But that doesn't mean he didn't have somebody who stuck his head over the gate and called out to him."

"We saw his friends do that often. At one point we had to stop him from buying drugs that way."

At that, Doreen's eyebrows shot up.

Penny nodded. "But what can you do? He had just George in his life. Their parents had died a couple years earlier. Johnny had been a teenager then, and George had given him a home, helping him to grow up. But Johnny was fighting that. He had a job at the hardware store. He had a girlfriend, but that relationship wasn't stable. As a matter of fact, the girlfriend said, at that time, they hadn't had anything to do with each other for a couple months before he went missing. She didn't mention any reason behind their breakup. Just that she'd found somebody else soon afterward."

"Is her name and other pertinent personal information in the file?"

Penny frowned. "I think so. Her name was Susan Robinson. She died of breast cancer about a year ago."

"Oh, wow," Doreen said. "So is everybody from his circle no longer around?"

"Yes. Johnny's two buddies and his girlfriend. They were together all the time. They didn't really hang out with any others to the same extent. At least not that I knew of. And, yes, they are all dead now. All you have are the witness statements in most cases. And I don't have copies of all those." She hesitated, then looked sideways at Doreen. "I know this is very inappropriate and pushy," she said, "but I was hoping you would have connections with Mack, and maybe you could get the other information I don't have."

"I'm not sure he can do that," Doreen said. Just then Mugs slumped to the floor half on and half off her foot. Squatting to scratch Mugs behind the ear. "I don't know what their rules and regulations are, but I can ask him."

"Right. I'm sure all kinds of red tape stop him from giving you too much information," Penny said with a sigh. "And how frustrating is that? All I want to know is what happened to Johnny."

"You've had no contact since, and he was a healthy young man?"

Penny nodded. "He was healthy. He was footloose and fancy-free. He was a young man, but he didn't have a whole lot of purpose. He didn't really know what he wanted to do. He didn't like working at the hardware store. He had visions of a much bigger, more grandiose lifestyle, but honestly he hadn't reached the point where he wanted to put in the work to make it happen."

"Oh. So a typical young man," Doreen said with a smirk.

"Exactly," Penny agreed. "George got really frustrated with him, and that was hard because I always heard about it. But, at the same time, I couldn't do or say anything to make it any better."

"No. Young men have to be young men, and they grow up in their own time frame," Doreen said.

"Do you have any children?" Penny asked.

"No," Doreen said. "Not yet. At my age, probably not likely to happen."

"We have two daughters," Penny said. "And I have to admit that it was much easier to have daughters than to always look at a son and wonder if the same thing would happen to him. We kept a very close eye on the girls growing up, but I think they understood just how devastating losing their uncle had been for us. Yet, of course, young people know it all and have all the answers." Penny laughed a little.

"Only as they get older do they realize they never had any wisdom to begin with." She gave a wry smile.

Doreen nodded. "Okay, I'll go through this. Please don't have any expectations that I will find anything."

"No," Penny said. "Of course not." She reached out a hand and squeezed Doreen's. "I'm just happy to know somebody will look into it and that Johnny won't be forgotten forever."

"I can understand that," Doreen said slowly. "I think that's one of the reasons why I pursue these cases. Because families are waiting for answers. People need closure. Some folks' whole lives are lost in worrying and wondering what happened. I can't imagine anything worse."

Mugs got up and walked over to sniff Penny's leg. He rubbed his head against her calf.

She bent to pet him. "Well, he's a new addition."

"He is, indeed," Doreen said. "Mugs came with me. Goliath is still here. So is Thaddeus."

Penny nodded, as if the names didn't mean anything to her, and it occurred to Doreen that she didn't know how long Nan had had Thaddeus and Goliath, a name Doreen had given the cat. So there was a good chance Penny hadn't met either of them.

Penny turned and walked back to the front door, smiling at the bags of clothing. "You have a lot of stuff to go to Goodwill."

"I do," Doreen said. "Honestly I'll probably take a bunch of this to the consignment store. Nan had some very good-quality clothing."

"Oh, that's a lovely idea," Penny said. "I shop there quite a bit. Wendy has a lovely store."

Interestingly she didn't look ashamed or in any way put

out by telling somebody she shopped at a secondhand store. "I'll have to check it out," Doreen said. "I dropped off some clothes already, but I've been so busy that I haven't had a chance to look for anything for myself."

"Wendy has a great selection," Penny said. "Check it out while you're there." With a wave of her hand, she walked onto the front porch and down the steps.

Once again Doreen stood on the front porch, waiting for somebody to drive away. She didn't know why she needed to make sure people left. It probably had to do with the fact she was still hoarding all these expensive antiques in the house.

As soon as Penny had driven down the cul-de-sac, Doreen stepped back inside, bringing Mugs with her, set the alarm again because now it was almost four o'clock, and headed into the kitchen. "Now to check the back alarm, then go upstairs to check that bed out," she said.

Her phone rang then. She groaned as she looked down at Mack's identification. "How do you always know when I'm getting ready to get into something?"

"What are you up to?" he asked as soon as she answered.

She rolled her eyes. "I'm trying to figure out what is taped underneath the bed frame in my bedroom," she said. "The packers will come early next week. Hopefully on Monday. I need to know about anything hidden in the furniture before they take it. And we found something, but I can't lift the massive bed frame."

"With your mind-set," he said, "I can certainly understand that. What's underneath it?"

"I don't know, that's what I'm trying to figure out. I've moved the box spring and the mattress to the floor, because the movers are not taking those. But the bed frame itself is very heavy. Mugs won't leave it alone. He kept barking at one of the slats, so I checked, and, sure enough, something is taped under it."

"Mugs, huh?"

"Right. That's why I'm trying to figure it out. For all I know, it's nothing. But the bed is heavy. How do I lift it and check out the slat?" She paused. "Are you on your way home?"

"Yeah. I'm leaving the office in five. Why?"

"Well, you could swing by," she said in a cheerful voice, adding, "and you could lift the bed, and I could look underneath."

"*Umm ...*"

She could almost see him give a mental shrug.

"Yeah, I can. I'll be there soon." And he hung up.

"Now that is perfect," she said to Mugs.

He just stared at her. She chuckled and headed the way back to her bedroom.

As soon as Mugs returned to the bedroom, he'd hopped inside the slats, which she found amazing because he was pretty rotund. He'd parked right where that piece of paper, or whatever it may be, was. It felt more like plastic than paper. She didn't know what that meant.

She continued to move stuff out of the master bedroom into the spare bedroom closet. She rearranged some of the furniture in her room so the movers could easily dismantle the bed when they arrived. Then she put new bedding on the mattress. By the time she'd fluffed up the pillows and put them on her makeshift bed, it looked mostly normal on the floor. Then she heard Mack drive up.

Mugs barked and turned around with his belly flat on the floor. He crawled underneath the edge of the bed frame and headed down the stairs. He knew it was Mack. How could he not?

She followed him to shut off the alarm at the front door and got it just in time.

Chapter 5

Wednesday Late Afternoon ...

MACK EYED HER as she opened the door. "Why are you so flustered?" He bent to pet Mugs and Goliath at his feet.

"I had the alarms on," she said. "I had to run downstairs and shut it off before you opened the door."

His eyebrows shot up. "Are you keeping them on, even when you're home?" He seemed a bit worried.

"I will until the antiques are picked up," she said. "I can't take the chance of something happening to those pieces."

He nodded. "I guess I can understand that."

She led the way back up to the bedrooms, the animals dashing ahead of them.

When he stepped into the master bedroom, he whistled. "Wow. That bed is even bigger than I remembered it."

"Right? I moved the mattresses to the floor and now it looks even more crowded. Look at the size of that bed frame."

"It's huge." He shook his head. "I'm not even sure how they'll take it apart."

"Well, someone got it in here somehow," she said. "Although I may have to ask Nan about that."

"I'd say so. She might have a trick or two," he said. "What is it you want lifted?"

She pointed to the bed. Just then Mugs wiggled underneath the frame again to the same slat, sat, and growled. Goliath hopped on top and swatted him. Thaddeus was on top of the bedpost staring down at them.

Doreen pointed. "Something is underneath the bed right there by Mugs."

Mack groaned, reached down with one hand, then bent his knees, lifting the bed frame.

Doreen dove underneath beside Mugs who shoved his snout right at her. She checked all the other slats first. "Nothing else is here, but, whatever this is, I don't know if I'll get it off."

He lifted the frame a bit higher. "Why don't you come out and grab those two chairs or the boxes you've got here, and we'll put the edge of this frame on them. The ceiling and the four posters to this bed won't allow me to lift this any higher."

Following his instructions, she propped up the frame on the boxes she was collecting for Goodwill and the consignment shop.

He tested the weight. "It's not supremely safe, but it'll be fine for a few minutes." Then he crouched under the bed and took a look. "It looks like a letter's been taped to the slat inside some plastic. Likely to protect the paper over the years."

He pulled out a pocketknife from his pants pocket and very carefully slid it in the top layer of plastic, just enough so he could pull out the letter. Once it was free, he handed it to her. At that point Mugs laid down under the propped up bed, Goliath had dug his claws into wood and had slid until he was stretched out fully.

She opened it and gasped. "It's from my great-great-grandmother. It's a letter to Nan's mother. I think. Nan was named after her mom, so they both share the name Willa. Another thing I'll have to clarify with Nan."

"*My dearest granddaughter Willa,*" Doreen read aloud. "*I'm hoping you'll have my passion for antiques. I'm not sure why so many have absolutely no love of things old and well-loved. This entire set is for you. I know what it's worth, and so do you. I also know it doesn't matter to you. Enjoy it in the spirit it was intended and know that it's listed in my will. But, should there ever be any contention, keep this letter with the bed so all will know it's yours. With all my love and the hope that you have an absolutely wonderful and fulfilling life, Nan.*"

Tears were in Doreen's eyes when she stopped reading. She held her hand over her mouth and looked up at Mack.

"So does that mean you don't want to sell it now?" he asked drily.

She gave a shake of her head. "No, that's not what I mean. Obviously I'm not in a position to argue about the need for the sale, and the furniture is really not my style. But to think a piece of my own personal history is here, that's so important."

He pointed to the date. "And look at that."

"Wow, 1909," she read. "Nan wasn't even alive then," she said.

He shrugged. "Makes sense to me."

"Wow," she repeated. "And she passed it on to my Nan. Just wow." She shook her head. "I want photos of this letter."

"Take photographs, and, if you can scan it, then do that too."

Doreen went downstairs to her printer and scanned the letter, then took a photograph of it with her phone too. She walked back upstairs smiling.

"This is really great. It's also huge for proving provenance," Mack said.

"Yes," Doreen said with a smile. "Nan is seventy-five-ish, and her mother would have been at least twenty or thirty years older."

"I don't know if you've had a chance to find the paperwork for any of this, but this gives you a specific date to go by." Mack turned to look at the bed frame. "Are you ready for me to put the letter back in?"

She nodded.

He carefully reinserted it into the plastic sleeve, where it had been kept safe all these years. "Now you can tell your auction house guy that you have that letter. Maybe send him a copy by email."

She nodded and immediately sent a text. Then, through her email function on her phone, she attached a copy of the letter and sent it off. She sniffled back her tears. "I can't wait to show this to Nan."

"Sounds like *Nan* has always been used as the name for the grandmothers in your family, hasn't it?"

Doreen nodded.

With his help, she removed the boxes tilting up the bed frame and helped him lower the massive bed frame to the floor. She moved the boxes back to where they had been.

Mack looked at her. "What are in all those boxes?"

She motioned toward the closet, both of its doors open, revealing the mess inside. "I'm slowly sorting through all of

Nan's clothes. The boxed-up stuff here will go to Goodwill. I have all the bags of clothing downstairs that will go to the consignment store. Items I'm keeping currently are in the spare bedroom closet."

He nodded. "That sounds like a good system with all the sorting to do here. And I'm glad to hear you're keeping some of Nan's clothing too. You might as well wear them, since it's expensive to replace it all." He motioned at the overstuffed closet. "Still a ton is in this closet alone."

"Speaking of which," she said, suddenly remembering what else she'd caught sight of in the back of the closet. "An old bookshelf is in the closet. It's jammed in the back. Who knew a closet could be this deep?"

He looked at her in surprise.

She pushed all the hangers to one side and pointed it out to him.

He shook his head. "Do you want me to pull that out for you?"

She looked at him in delight. "Absolutely I do."

"You should send pictures to your appraiser. Didn't you show him this piece?"

"No, it's not one of the pieces he was looking for." She removed more hanging clothes to give him access. Then stepped in and quickly dumped the contents of the shelf onto the floor under the hangers. A temporary solution at best. "I will send Scott photos though. And he can check it out when he returns to pack up this stuff."

It took a bit of maneuvering, but finally Mack dragged the bookshelf along the carpeted floor out to where Doreen could access to it. It didn't resemble the other pieces in any way. It was also scratched and beaten-up some.

"Can you imagine," she said, "that it's been in there for

probably fifty years?"

"Probably since Nan moved in." He nodded. "And with the passage of time and too many possessions, it got buried in the back. Still, it's quite useable, lots of life in it yet."

"It's pretty amazing," she said. "Nan seems to think nothing of leaving all this stuff behind."

"I think she left it behind for a very specific reason, and she was more than happy to share this with you," he said.

She smiled. "Maybe. I just hadn't expected it."

"No," he said, "but it's all good. I think you're doing the right thing."

She appreciated that. "I have to admit that it does wake me up in the night. I feel like I'm letting my family down."

"Not at all," he said. "I think the worst thing you can do is hang on to things out of guilt or because you think it's the right thing to do. I think it's time for you to do what's right for you."

She beamed at him. "You know what? Honestly it's been a pretty good week so far."

"No kidding," he said. "Yesterday certainly made it a great week. That was a very good thing you did."

"But it wasn't necessarily what I did." She hated to feel guilty about it. "I mean, really anybody could have sorted that out."

"The difference is," he said, "at the time, we didn't have most of the technology we do now. And that cold case hadn't been reopened because nothing new had been added in the way of facts or evidence or witness statements. We would have eventually reviewed it before boxing it up and putting it aside, but that's just the facts of life. You came at it from a very different angle, and you solved it."

"It was the license plate," she said.

He nodded. "That makes sense. And that's when we got that needed pop on the case. However, we didn't have time to take another look because you'd solved the case already."

She beamed at him. "Praise from you is high praise, indeed."

"Have you made another omelet yet?"

She shook her head. "I haven't had time," she confessed. "And I'm scared to. I figured that was beginner's luck."

He chuckled. "I haven't had dinner. If you haven't touched the ingredients, there's probably enough for another one. I suggest you try again, and we'll split it again."

She looked at him in surprise, then the nearby clock. It really was dinnertime. "I haven't touched anything. Do you think it's all still good?" She looked at him anxiously. "That's another thing I don't know anything about. How long does food keep?"

"Four to five days for sure," he said. "Come on. Let's take a look."

Downstairs again, they walked into the kitchen, and Mack opened the fridge. He pulled out the bacon first. "See here? A Best Before Date is printed on the packaging, and that's still another four days away. And the spinach, it's okay. It's wilting a little, but it'd make a good spinach omelet. And the eggs ..." He brought out the carton, checking the Best Before Date on the end of it, nodding, putting everything on the counter. Then he leaned against the counter and crossed his arms over his chest. "Go for it."

She looked at him nervously. "I haven't prepped."

"No prep required. No videos to watch. Just go by memory."

She wrinkled her nose at him as she stepped forward. "Are you trying to put me on the spot?"

"No," he said. "I'm trying to get food. It's been a very long day."

She laughed and got started. Since he had stopped by to lift her bed frame—and ended up moving that bookshelf as well—it was the least she could do.

Chapter 6

Wednesday Dinnertime ...

AS THEY SAT down to eat—and, boy, was she proud of the fact that her second attempt was damn near as perfect as the first—Mack looked at the big business-size envelope beside their plates.

"Johnny Jordan?" He frowned. "Why does that name sound familiar?"

Shoot. "I don't know," she mumbled. "Do you know that name?"

He glanced at her sideways as he took a bite of the omelet. "First, the omelet is divine. You did a great job."

She beamed at him. "It's not as hard as I thought."

"Nothing is," he said. "You just have to learn how."

She hoped so. But she didn't have the confidence yet to make that discernment.

Then he said, "And, second, you're up to something."

She sat back with a sigh. "How do you know?"

He snickered. "Because you get this weird little glare in your eyes and a wrinkle in your forehead as you bring your brows together. And it's almost always directed at me, as if to say, *I don't know what you're talking about.*"

She glared at him but could feel the wrinkles forming between her eyebrows. She reached up and eased them back.

His grin just widened.

She glared at him once more. "I'm not up to anything."

"Well, you just admitted you were," he said.

"Not really," she said. "But I do have an odd request." She patted her pocket and pulled out the letter and handed it to him.

As he popped another bite into his mouth, he picked it up and read it. His eyebrows rose toward his hairline. "Wow. Now they're bypassing the police and coming straight to you?" He shook his head. "What the hell will you do with this? Do you realize how dangerous this could be for you?" He looked at the letter again, then at the envelope. "Did she mail you that too?"

She groaned and sat back. "No, I didn't know what to do," she said, "so I called her. The end result is, she was here this afternoon and dropped off that envelope. I did warn her that I could probably tell her nothing because not only was it a long time ago but no crime scene was found. And no further word came from the young man in all these years. ... For all we know, it was possible he drowned, but he went missing *after* the heavy flooding that year. So it was doubtful he ended up in the lake." She let Mack ponder that for a moment, then added, "The dagger Penny was concerned about is in the bigger envelope she left with me earlier today." She tapped the big business envelope on the kitchen table.

"Yeah, for a while there," he said, "they were doing these 'stabbing it into the ground as hard as they could' kinds of things. Like darts, but downward with knives. It was a cool move but wasn't very good for the blades." He looked at the envelope. "You haven't opened it yet?"

She shook her head. "Mugs had just found whatever was under the bed when she arrived. I had to run downstairs, and, after she left, I set the alarm and came back upstairs. Then you came."

"You know what? For somebody who has nothing going on," he said, slightly sarcastically, "you're sure busy."

She nodded. "Almost too busy," she admitted. "But that's all right because it's pretty hard to not love life right now. The trick is, is there any way to figure out what happened to this poor Johnny guy?"

"I didn't know the family well. I can't recall much about the cold case. I remember opening it at some point, but there was nothing new to move forward with."

"No," she said, "and I'm not sure there is now either. It's a hard case. I'm also not sure what clues might be found in the witness statements either. So many witnesses have died." She hesitated. "I can't read the statements in the police file, can I?"

He shook his head.

She nodded. "That's what I expected. His girlfriend from around that time died of breast cancer last year. And his brother is gone now too."

"That is sad because then his brother never got closure, and even the girlfriend must have always wondered right up to the end."

"She certainly didn't leave any confession saying she'd murdered him," Doreen said drily.

"To date, we have no reason or no evidence to think Johnny was murdered," Mack said. "That was an excellent omelet." He slid the last bite in his mouth, put down his fork, and pushed back his plate. "The young man could have just gotten up and walked away."

"I get that," Doreen said. "But what would make a young man do that? What makes somebody, who is close to his brother—and we only have his brother's wife's word on that—but supposedly close to his brother and his sister-in-law, yet who gets up and walks away forever?"

"I think at the time they leave, they plan on returning, riding high on some future big successful wave. When that doesn't happen, they don't want the family to know they are a failure. A lot of people, after too much time has gone by, don't know what to say anymore, so they never say anything. Meaning they don't return either."

"That's very sad," Doreen said. "Somebody has to know what happened to Johnny."

"There's always another option," he said quietly. "You have to consider that, even though we have much higher statistics today, still an awful lot of suicides of young men happened back then."

"Wouldn't his body have shown up though?"

Mack frowned. Thinking about that, he pushed back his chair and looked at her. "Do you mind if I put on a pot of coffee?"

"Please," she said. She collected the dishes and walked to the sink. "I mean, surely if he'd shot himself, jumped off the bridge, or I don't know—I guess one of the favorite ways is a drug overdose or even driving into a semi coming down the highway or something—there would be a body. Obviously I don't know anything about committing suicide, but there's always a body left behind."

"There's *almost* always a body," Mack corrected. "But we don't always find everybody who is lost at sea, like we don't always find everybody who's been lost in the lake."

"Right," she said.

"And, if you think about all the country backroads we have here, all kinds of places exist where Johnny may have gone for a joyride and driven off into a ravine."

She stopped what she was doing, turned around, and looked at him. "Do you think, even after twenty-nine years, that would still hold true?"

"Of course it would," he said. "Think about the miles and miles of roads around here. And what would have been seen back then wouldn't necessarily be seen now, considering all the natural growth since then. Maturing trees and bushes can hide a lot."

"But we have satellite now," she argued. "People have drones traveling all over the place."

"Sure. That doesn't necessarily mean they know what they're looking at because a piece of shiny metal doesn't mean a vehicle is stuck underneath there. Besides, did Johnny have his own vehicle?"

"I forgot to ask Penny," she said. "She's sending all the digital files to my email too."

"Forward them to me as well," he said. "I'll take a look at what's in the police files again. I'm not promising anything, but, if something pops, maybe it's due to a communication error. Unfortunately we've seen that happen with cold cases too."

"What do you mean by *communication error?*"

"Different departments don't share info. Particularly back then. What if Johnny headed to Vancouver and got absorbed into the big-city life? He could be homeless. He could have been a John Doe in the morgue. We didn't have any automatic way to check across multiple jurisdictions. It had to be done manually."

"What if we got something of George's? Could we run DNA and check through some database to see if his brother has shown up elsewhere?"

"We could, except there's no budget money for things like that," Mack said. "In a perfect world we'd have lots of money, and we could run DNA for every missing family member. And, even if something still exists of the brother's DNA to check, sometimes it's not a close-enough match to ID a sibling."

Doreen sighed. "I know Penny is hoping to put her house on the market, but she hasn't done a heavy clean out yet. Maybe, if she kept a locket with strands of her husband's hair, we should ask her to preserve it, just in case."

"Back then DNA had to be directly collected from the missing person. So some evidence of Johnny's DNA might be hanging around related to his missing person file."

"That would be evidence, wouldn't it?"

"Obviously," he said. "But unfortunately stuff goes missing. So, when I return to the office tomorrow, I'll take a look and see if we have anything on file. And you might want to send Penny an email, asking her if she has anything of her husband's. A hairbrush would be ideal."

"Right. How much do you need?"

"Not too much," he said. "But we do need something. Hair, nails, skin, blood, tissue, bone. Things like that."

She wrinkled her nose at him. "What if he was cremated? I doubt there'd be much left in that case."

"Possibly not," he said. "It depends if she kept the ashes."

"She did. The urn is on her mantel. Can you get DNA from the ashes?"

He shrugged. "I'm not sure. I hear bone fragments remain, even with cremations at high heat. Bones retain DNA. However, in most cases, those remaining fragments are ground to ash before being handed over. I don't know that the ashes can be tested for DNA. It seems like DNA testing is moving forward in leaps and bounds, and nobody knows what we can get from whatever until the test is done. Now they're doing ancestry DNA, and that's making huge changes in cold cases."

"But, in this case, we don't have any foul play suspected. So we have no suspects to go after, like a killer."

"If you mean that we don't have any DNA of a killer at a crime scene, you're quite right. We don't even have a crime scene. All we have is that this young man got up one day and walked away."

"Supposedly. What about the dagger?"

"Same problem," he said. "Found years later, buried in the ground. When we opened the missing person's case, no DNA testing was really done back then. Great advances have been made, so who knows what it'll tell us now? It's a knife that Johnny owned, that he played with all the time. Of course he cut himself on it. Everybody would have at least once."

She sighed. "I get that, but it just seems like, if somebody had murdered him with the dagger, there would be skin cells of whoever killed him."

"Maybe," he said. "But I doubt it after all that time."

"Right, but can they test for other tissue?"

"Lab tests can certainly separate different people's DNA, plus what kind of tissue was found for each person," he said, "as in semen versus epithelial versus hair, for example."

She nodded. "I just don't know enough about it, but at least I have the knife, and, no, I know it won't be of much

315

value. I think what Penny is really hoping for is that her brother-in-law won't be forgotten."

"That's the hardest thing for any cold-case file. It's a cold case to the public. But it's never cold to the family. It just sits there forever."

"That's why she hung on to the dagger. It's a reminder. Not just of Johnny but of his life and probably his death. Of all that's hanging over her life all this time."

He stared at her. "And seriously? A dagger in the dahlias?"

"They had a bench in the backyard, where Johnny was last seen. It became something they found very difficult to look at. So they moved it and were digging a new bed and putting in dahlias when they found his dagger."

"Which makes sense, if he always sat there."

"I agree," she said with a shrug. "I don't have any angle to go on. And there was another thing," Doreen said with a sigh. "Penny was hoping that because of my association with you—and how the heck does everybody know about that?—she was hoping I might have access to Johnny's cold-case file. But ..."

"Which you know I can't give you," he said firmly.

"I told her that. I did explain that I couldn't do much," she said. "She seems to think I can do more than I can."

"But knowing you," he said, "you'll do your best anyway."

Chapter 7

Thursday Early Morning...

A S SOON AS Doreen had breakfast the next morning, she cleared off the kitchen table, except for her coffee cup, took out the large envelope from Penny, opened it up, and carefully spread out everything from inside. The dagger was small but had a lethal-looking blade with a very fine tip to it. She laid that off to the side.

She then read the collection of papers. There wasn't much—a couple newspaper articles about Johnny having gone missing, a poster asking for anybody to come forward who knew anything about Johnny's whereabouts, and a couple statements with a time line the family had given to the police. They all offered nothing new.

She frowned. "There isn't anything to go on. I'm sorry, Penny, but I have no clue what I'm supposed to do with this."

As she sat here pondering, an email came through from the appraiser about the letter she'd found under Nan's bed.

This is lovely, he wrote, *and definitely proof of provenance.*

She smiled at that. As she read further, she realized he still wanted her to go through the accordion folder of documents for any more paperwork related to the antiques. She didn't know why she was hesitating, but she needed to sort through it.

Putting everything back into the envelope Penny had given her, Doreen worried that she could do nothing for Penny. All Doreen could hope for was that Mack would send her something of interest from the police file when he had time.

After a trip to her bedroom, she walked into the living room with the accordion folder she'd found in the bottom dresser drawer. She sat on the couch and pulled out the envelopes stuffed inside, each with a handwritten generic label of its contents. Everything was in here from Last Wills and Testaments and personal certifications to medical records. They were important documents, but nothing to do with the antiques.

The very last envelope she brought out was only half the size of the others. She slowly set out its contents on the coffee table. The receipts were old; some were handwritten and hard to read. She could not make out very much of any of it. Maybe it would make sense to the appraiser, but she had no reason to believe these receipts had anything to do with what she and Scott were particularly looking for.

She put everything back in that envelope, then decided the only way through this was to ignore the envelope designation and sort out all the contents themselves. She took everything out of the accordion folder and laid it all one at a time on the coffee table.

She didn't find what she'd hoped for—provenance confirming a gold mine of million-dollar antiques—but still Doreen unearthed a gold mine of family information.

She pulled out the medical file and opened it, found a

copy of her own birth certificate, which was not surprising, until she saw a DNA certificate and froze. Nan had had Doreen's DNA tested against her son's to make sure Doreen was Nan's blood granddaughter. Doreen winced at that. But she couldn't really blame her grandmother because her mother had been much less than a one-man kind of woman.

Doreen laid that down along with her birth certificate and slowly went through everything she had from the first envelope. It was a hodgepodge file of everything her mom had sent over time to Nan. It brought back memories, but it was also sad.

Doreen put everything back in the appropriate envelope, reminiscing about a childhood she barely remembered. Obviously Nan had kept mementos of it all. And at least the DNA had confirmed she was truly Nan's granddaughter. She wasn't sure what Nan would have done if she'd found out that Doreen wasn't her blood relative. That would have been hard too. Particularly with her father gone, it would have been devastating for Nan to learn otherwise. And to think that Nan had some reason to get Doreen tested was just sad.

She went back through the other stuff, only to find nothing of the further provenance she searched for. A copy of Nan's Last Will was here, but it was sealed. Then the paperwork on the house, which was great because now Doreen had a place to file the new deeds when they came. Nan had saved copies of receipts for work done on the house years ago, like how the roof was fifteen years old. Also good to know that she'd at least get another five or ten years out of it hopefully.

Other receipts went even farther back but nothing regarding the antiques in questions. Another envelope was full of correspondence. Doreen pulled it out and looked at all the cards and letters; some of them were on very thin tissue paper. She went through them carefully, smiling at some that appeared to be from lovers who Nan had walked away from. Nan had led a wild and colorful life.

Doreen picked up a piece of paper, recognizing the handwriting. Checking the signature on the bottom, she saw it was to Penny from Nan. Doreen read it quickly—Nan sending condolences on the missing state of Johnny and hoping for a quick resolution to the problem. *How very like Nan*, Doreen thought. The letter was dated twenty-nine years ago. So then why was it in Nan's possession and not Penny's? Maybe Nan had written it but hadn't sent it? Doreen would ask Nan about it. She set it off to one side to deal with later, but ... she needed to know *now*.

She phoned Nan. When her grandmother answered, she said, "Hi, Nan. How are you doing today?"

"I'd be doing much better," Nan said in a testy voice, "if you came down and gave me all the facts clearly."

It was unusual for Nan to be in a difficult mood. Doreen wasn't sure what was going on. "What facts?"

"The bodies you found in the lake," she said.

"Oh," Doreen said, frowning. "You mean about finding Paul Shore?"

"We know what the news reported and how you're the one who put it all together." Her voice warmed as she added, "And of course it was you. You're the biggest sweetheart."

"And yet, you sound kind of cranky," Doreen said humorously.

"Well, everybody here was mad at me because I didn't have all the information from you."

"Oh my," Doreen said. "I never even thought to fill you in on the rest. Yesterday was fairly trying and very emotional.

I came home, and I didn't want to deal with people. Although Mack did come over for dinner." Then she remembered what she'd found earlier. "Oddly enough, I just found a letter from you to Penny Jordan, but it doesn't look like you ever sent it."

"*Hmm*," Nan said thoughtfully. "That doesn't make sense."

"It's about Johnny, her brother-in-law who went missing."

"Oh, yes, yes, yes," Nan said. "I was writing the letter, giving her my condolences, then realized it sounded like Johnny was dead. I didn't want her to think Johnny was dead. We all hoped the young man had just gone away to make his fortune and would come riding back into town as the 'big I am' he thought he was."

A tone in her voice made it sound like she knew Johnny better than Doreen had suspected. "Did you know Johnny?"

"He used to rake my yard every once in a while, but, like so many kids, he thought he should get paid way more for the little bit of work he did," Nan said with a sniff. "But he was pleasant enough. He was running around town with the wrong gang, and that made things difficult when he went missing."

"When you say, *the wrong gang*? Who?"

"Well, Freddy Black was bad news at the time. And Thomas Burgess. I can't remember who else. But they were always getting into trouble with the law. You know, like throwing rocks at cars and just generally being a nuisance. Vandalism. Then they got into the drug scene. But I don't think it was all that bad. At least I didn't hear too much about it."

"So you knew Johnny fairly well then?"

"Enough that, when he went missing, I felt sorry for the family. To think of it being almost thirty years ago now, that's so sad."

"It is, isn't it?" Doreen said sympathetically. "Penny asked me if I'd look into the case."

At first nothing but silence came over the phone; then Nan laughed. "Oh my," she said. "That is fantastic."

"No, it's not," Doreen grumbled. "I have absolutely nothing to go on. All of the cases I've worked on so far have had connections and trails, things I could follow up on. What am I supposed to do with a young man who walked away from his family's backyard twenty-nine years ago, for heaven's sake?"

"Well, you can't speak to the two people I mentioned because they're both dead. They were killed in a car accident not long after Johnny disappeared."

"Oh." Doreen walked into the kitchen and wrote that down on a notepad. "I wonder if it had anything to do with Johnny going missing?"

"Meaning, they might have committed suicide because of what they did to Johnny?" Nan's voice dropped. "You know what? I never even thought of that. You have a different perspective than most people. I'm glad you're looking into this. Now it's a big mystery I really want you to solve."

"I will try to solve it for Penny's sake," Doreen said, "but there isn't anything here for me to work with. Otherwise I'm sure the police would have done something with it."

"Cold cases from before the widespread usage of the internet and cell phones and DNA," Nan said, "just weren't the same types of investigations. We have so many more tools available now."

"Sure, but there was no body, no crime scene," she said. "We don't even know if he is dead or not. There were so many runaway kids back then that no one even tracked them. I swear it's in the thousands every year now."

"I think it's probably more than that," Nan said. "But, back then, we didn't have any way to maintain communication or to share databases between provinces. For all we know, Johnny went to Ontario and built a life for himself there."

"Did he have a vehicle, do you know?" Doreen asked.

"Yes," Nan said. "It was an old car. I don't know what kind it was, but I do remember it was the car the two guys killed themselves in."

Doreen straightened. "His friends were driving *his* car?"

"Yeah. We were all wondering what that was about, but the police didn't seem to think anything of it. When Johnny first disappeared his car did too, so we just thought he'd drive home any time. Only he didn't and the boys died while driving it."

"I suspect they did think *something* of it," she said, "but, if the car didn't reveal any evidence, then I'm not sure they had anything to go on."

"True," Nan said. "But you might want to cross-reference their case to Johnny's."

"Sure. What were their names again?"

"Burgess and Black."

"Okay. Got it." She wrote them down, then said, "I'll send Mack an email, asking if they're mentioned in the case files."

"Ha! He's a great source of information for you."

"I don't know about that," Doreen said with a smile. "He's not allowed to tell me much. But, in an unusual twist, the police commander stopped me yesterday on my way home after we found the two bodies in the lake. He shook my hand and thanked me."

"Oh, my goodness. Isn't that lovely? Peter Cochran is a nice guy," Nan said. "He was a little young for me, but, for a weekend or so, he was great fun."

Doreen's eyes popped wide open. "Are you saying you had an affair with the commander?"

"A very long time ago," Nan said with a delightful laugh. "He wanted more, but I wasn't the right person for him. He needed a wife, three kids, two dogs, one cat, and that perfect house with a white picket fence." She chuckled. "But that doesn't change the fact he is good at his job, and I'm very happy he did well by you."

Doreen was still struck by the admission that Nan had had an affair with a police commander. "If you know anybody at the old folks' home who has any information on Johnny's disappearance, let me know, will you?"

"Why don't you come down and have tea?" Nan said. "I'll get more details from you on yesterday too."

Just then Doreen remembered the letter she'd found underneath the bed. "Nan, that's an excellent idea. I have something to show you anyway."

"I'll put on the teakettle. You get the animals and come on down." Nan sighed. "I have to admit, I could use a hug today." And she hung up.

Chapter 8

Thursday Late Morning ...

IT TOOK A few minutes to round up the animals. Mugs was well-mannered, until he heard the leash rattle; then he barked all over the place, chasing Goliath, who appeared to take deep offense and cornered Mugs in the kitchen, swatting at him twice. Trying to separate the two was not fun.

Finally she got them all calmed down with a treat or two and had another pocketful of treats handy. With Thaddeus on her shoulder, she opened the kitchen door, and all four of them headed out to Nan's place, via the creek. There was just no other path for her. Any chance she had, she chose to walk by the water. Besides, she wanted to avoid her front yard and anybody wanting to talk to her.

So many things had changed since she had moved here. The animals were just one part of it. She used to deal well with people, mostly because she had a polished glossy tone, not giving offense, not taking offense, kinda like being dead inside. And now here she did everything she could to avoid people, at least certain people.

She was happy to see the sun shining. She loved the way

the long shadows of the sun's arms touched on the green leaves as they gently waved in the wind. This was a nice thing about her house being on the creek; it was in a bit of a valley, and the wind whistled down with such gentleness that it always made her smile. Listening to the water, listening to the wind and the birds, it was incredibly peaceful.

She wasn't sure when, if ever in all of her marriage, she'd had an opportunity to enjoy Mother Nature as much as she did here. And who knew it was something she would fall in love with, without actual gardening involved. Here she could listen to the birds for hours, just sitting beside the creek, dipping her toes in the icy water, even though she knew what had come out of it in the last couple weeks. The creek remained special. It made her feel connected.

She was thoroughly jealous of all those people who lived in the countryside. Not that she wanted to milk cows or to raise chickens for their eggs or anything, but she yearned to have some real space to wander without being hemmed in by houses or people. Yet what she had here was a great first step in that direction. She loved to dip her fingers in the creek, to feel that connection, that sense of peace, that oneness. How fanciful of her. Still, if she had learned one thing with all the recent chaos, it was that life was short, too short. What she really needed to do was find a way to make the most of what time she did have. She'd lost so much with her pending divorce, and yet, she'd already gained so much more. If she'd had any idea a life like this existed for her outside of her marriage, she'd have left a long time ago.

Of course she hadn't really left of her own choice. She'd been replaced. She'd fought it kicking and screaming; that had been because of fear—fear of what was happening, fear of what would happen to her afterward, fear of where she'd live, fear of the future. Those thoughts were so bad, so detrimental to her. Because of how absolutely stunningly wonderful her future was, even this early version of it.

Smiling, she opened her arms wide and did a jig, dancing and twirling on the path. "I know, Mugs. I'm acting crazy," she stated gaily. "But life is good. How can anybody not appreciate this?"

Mugs barked, jumping around with her. She chuckled and resumed walking, her footsteps light, her heart even lighter. "Let's go visit Nan," she said. "Unlike us, she hasn't had a good day."

In fact, her grandmother worried Doreen. Nan alternated between being "all there" in mind and in body and not even close. Now that Doreen finally had Nan back in her life again, Doreen didn't want to lose her grandmother. She'd do anything to give that special woman another twenty years on earth with her.

As it was, it was hard to know how to help her. Nan had friends and a busy life. She seemed to enjoy her current lifestyle too.

Doreen had the photocopy of the letter she had taken from underneath the bed. She wasn't sure if that would add to Nan's despondency or if it would make her feel better. Doreen wanted it to make her grandmother feel better obviously.

She was bringing back a lot of powerful memories. She didn't want to upset Nan any more than she had to. She was the sweetest old lady. Okay, so she had this gambling habit. But it really wasn't so much *her* gambling right now; it was Nan getting other people to gamble.

At that, she laughed out loud. "Nan, you keep Mack hopping. That can't be a bad thing."

She went around the corner, watching the traffic as they crossed the road. They weren't very far from the old folks' home. As she approached, she saw the gardener standing out front, talking to somebody. As soon as he saw her, he put his hands on his hips and pointed his finger at her. She stopped and asked, "And what is it you want me to do? I can't take the animals in the building. So, if I don't cut across the lawn, how do I get to Nan's place?"

"You come without the animals." His voice was gruff. "It's bad enough you walk on the grass, but now you get all the animals on it too." He crossed his arms, not budging an inch.

Not to be deterred, Doreen walked around the corner to where Nan sat with her teapot on a little bistro set. When she looked up and caught sight of Doreen, Nan waved gaily.

"Oh, there you are," she said.

Doreen nodded, pointing at the gardener. "He won't let me cross the lawn."

"Of course he will," Nan said. And then she held up her finger. "Oh, right. I forgot all about those."

Curious as to what she was up to, Doreen watched as Nan bent, then stood, holding something heavy in her hand. At least it looked heavy because her grandmother's arms were straining. She watched her grandmother study the patio, then the grass leading to the sidewalk, then very carefully placed one stepping stone on the grass. Then she repeated this until five were in the grass, leading from the sidewalk to her patio.

The gardener roared and raced toward her. But it was too late. Doreen skipped easily from one to the other until she was in Nan's little garden. Mugs and Goliath walked on the grass. The cat stopped short of the patio, lay down, and twitched his tail.

"That's perfect." Doreen leaned down to give Nan a hug.

"That's perfect. That's perfect," Thaddeus said.

But the gardener was having nothing to do with it, picking up one of the stepping stones.

Nan stopped him, crying out, "Leave those there. You won't let her cross that lawn because it'll hurt your grass. So now we fixed it. Put that back."

"I can't," he roared.

Thaddeus squawked loudly.

"The lawnmower will get caught on them every time."

"So dig them into the lawn," Doreen said. "Just take a cutting knife, draw into the sod all the way around each of the stones, lift up the sod, and place the stones down." She gave him a shrug. "That's hardly a big deal for a *gardener*."

He glared at her. "We'll see about that," he snapped. He picked up the first stepping stone and carried it inside the old folks' home.

Nan sighed and sat down, reaching out to calm Thaddeus, whose feathers were ruffled from the raised voices. "Now he'll complain to the manager."

"And what's the manager likely to do?" Doreen asked curiously.

"It depends if it's a good day or a bad day," Nan said with a smirk. "If he had fun with his girlfriend the night before, I'd probably get away with it. But, if they're fighting, as they usually are, then he'll get mad."

Doreen shook her head, sat down on the bistro chair, and smiled at her grandmother. "You look like you've had a tough day today, Nan."

Nan nodded. "I did. I had a bit of a tiff with an old

friend." She gave Doreen a wide smile. "We'll get over it. We always do. But it's a reminder that life is short, and, for those of us who have been around for a long time, we should know better, but we're still human," she said sadly.

"I'm so sorry." Doreen reached across the table and squeezed her grandmother's hand gently. Her translucent skin worried Doreen. "Are you eating enough?" she asked. "Have you had lunch?"

Nan gave her a lusty laugh. "I definitely am eating and had lunch. More to the point, are you eating? Did you have lunch already?"

"I am, and I'm not hungry yet, but thanks," Doreen reassured her.

"Just let me know when you are ready for a sandwich. I have some wonderful ham and homemade sourdough bread."

Doreen nodded, her smile grim. "I'm sorry about your friend. It's difficult when you are on the outs."

"And you know all about that too, don't you?" Nan said. "I'm so sorry your friends walked away from you when you left your husband."

"Just meant that they weren't friends, at least not mine," Doreen said with a smile. "And that's really what I have to remember. Just because I wanted them to be friends and thought that's what they were, you don't really understand what a friend is until you hit the rocks and need somebody to be there for you. And that's just called life." She shrugged. "I wouldn't give up what I currently have for anything in the world." She gently stroked the back of Nan's hand. "I'm so sorry I missed all those years with you."

"Not to worry," Nan said. "Just think about how good everything is now for us. Sometimes you have to wait for what you can really appreciate. If I can have all my remaining years with you close by, I'll be absolutely in heaven."

Doreen chuckled. "On that note, let me tell you what I found underneath the big bed." She reached into her pocket, pulled out and unfolded the photocopy of the letter. She handed it to Nan.

When Nan read it, tears came to her eyes.

Doreen immediately regretted bringing it to her, but Nan smiled through her tears.

"I'd forgotten this was there," she said. "A few times in your life you will find real turning points, and, with the death of *my* Nan, my life definitely changed too."

"Are you still okay if I sell that bed though?" Doreen asked. "I'm afraid you'll hate me for it."

"Of course I don't mind," Nan said, lifting her head from the letter. "I know the house is full of things, but honestly *things* are not what I care about. And the older I get, the more I realize it. For a long time I valued my independence. Now I value family, and that's you. The bed has a lifetime of memories for me, but it only represents them—it isn't the memory itself. And, when you sell the bed and move it out of there, it doesn't take the memories with it."

Doreen was delighted to hear that. "Well, I did separate the mattresses from the frame today. I'm waiting for a phone call as to when they'll pack up everything. I found some paperwork in a folder thing in the bottom dresser drawer."

Nan frowned, then poured their tea into the two cups. "I think that's all of the paperwork," she said, puzzled. "You didn't find anything about the pieces?"

"No. Oh, wait, we did find something…" She pulled out the two foil-wrapped chocolates and held out her palm. "Do you remember these? We found them in the secret drawers."

Nan's face lit up with joy. "Oh my," she whispered, staring at the chocolates. "I remember those. My nan used to hide them all the time for me to find." She looked up at Doreen. "I'm so delighted you brought these. Such wonderful memories are stored in that furniture."

Guilt seared through Doreen.

And it must have shown on her face as Nan reached a thin arm across the table and squeezed Doreen's wrist. "And, no, that doesn't mean you shouldn't sell it. Those are my memories, not yours," she said in such a firm voice that Doreen relaxed.

"If I hadn't found that letter," Doreen said quietly, "there wouldn't be any proof of how long we've had it." She then brought out the locket and cuffs. "We found these too."

"Oh my," Nan held it carefully, then clicked it open. A warm smile blossomed on her face. "Lovely to find this again."

"It is indeed." Doreen accepted it from her grandmother and pocketed it. "I still haven't found the paperwork on the antiques though."

Nan tapped her fingers on the table. "*Hmm*, I'm pretty sure more paperwork is somewhere. As you clear out the place, you'll find more and more pieces."

Doreen frowned. "Are you talking about the antiques or the paperwork?"

Nan blinked. "Both?"

"I know you inherited the bedroom suite, but did you invest in all the other pieces with your money?" Doreen asked half in delight and half in outrage. "Why would you do that?" She was generally curious because, if *things* didn't matter to Nan, why bother putting money into valuable antiques?

"It's not that the things mattered," she said. "It was the history of a piece that mattered. Once I realized who might have been the previous owners and why they had it, that's what I was fascinated by. But it was at the time when I was lonely. And what are you supposed to do when you're lonely? Well, you find things to fill your time with. You find things to be happy with. I was always very taken by everybody else's stories. And that's what antiques are. They are wood that has absorbed the stories of all the people who have owned them. So you'll find an eclectic mix of pieces in the house. And, no, I don't mind if you sell all of them."

"I worry you don't have enough money," Doreen said quietly. "It would bother me to think you had invested all your money in all these things. Then I sell them, and I get the money, and yet, you're suffering."

Nan's gaze opened wide. She patted her granddaughter's hand. "You really are a sweetheart, but I am *not* suffering," she said firmly. "I have lots of money in my accounts. I'm hoping you'll do something with the antiques, so you have some income, and so you won't be starving."

"And speaking of starving," Doreen said, straightening in the chair, "I made omelets the other day."

Nan clapped her hands together and chuckled. "Wow! I am so happy to hear that. Is that what you and Mack were eating?"

Doreen frowned at her. "As a matter of fact, it was, but I don't want you to make too much out of it."

"Not at all," Nan said. "And, if Mack is teaching you how to cook, then I am doubly delighted. If I was still there, I'd be helping you myself." She leaned forward and in a loaded whisper said, "But this gives Mack a really good reason to stop by all the time, doesn't it?"

"I don't think he needs any reason right now," Doreen admitted. "We have so much going on in our lives that keep intersecting. I don't think it's much of an issue."

"I'm glad you came over today," Nan said. "You've really put a sparkle back into my mood."

Doreen chuckled. "Ditto. I do love that it's just a short walk to visit you." She lifted her teacup, took a sip, and, when she put it down, she said, "Do you have any of your favorite recipes written down?"

Nan nodded. "They're still at the house. I don't do much cooking now. If I do, it's nothing I don't already know by heart."

"That would be lovely," Doreen said. "I can't wait until I can do things without recipes."

"You do lots of things," Nan said. "What you did for Paul's family was tremendous. Not to mention for the poor handyman who was accused of stealing that poor little boy."

"I guess everybody is talking about that now too, aren't they?" Doreen asked.

"Of course they are," Nan said. "Just think about it. Look at how much you've done for the families."

Doreen nodded. "Much less so for the Family Planning Center though."

"That Cecily was a problem to begin with," Nan said. "I warned my neighbors about her a long time ago. She was just trouble. Very strict, very opinionated, that woman," Nan said with an admonishing finger. "I'm sorry the other two were killed, but I really could see her life ending in a bad way."

"Well, she'll be in jail for a long time," Doreen said.

"So tell me more. I need all the details on how you

found Paul and the handyman. Don't leave anything out. The residents here are immensely curious." Nan smiled and waited.

Doreen sighed. She couldn't talk Nan out of this. For all Doreen knew, Nan was acting as bookie for many related bets among the old folks here on this particular cold case. Sighing again, Doreen began her tale. Nan had many questions. Doreen figured each one had to do with Nan's particular gambling matters. Shaking her head, Doreen answered each one. An hour later, Doreen was hungry. "You know what? That ham sandwich sounds pretty good right now. I'll make one, unless you want to share one with me?"

Nan shook her head, jumping up. "I've got this. You sit here and rest." Nan returned shortly with a sandwich and some baby carrots. "So what are you working on now?" Nan asked, easily sliding in that question.

Doreen caught herself from telling her grandmother everything she knew and settled on the basic truth. "Just the case of Johnny Jordan, who went missing."

"I think it's fascinating that Penny contacted you. And I do love that you came here to talk to me about it. It's like we're coconspirators or something," Nan said with a chuckle.

"Potentially we are," Doreen said, laughing. "Because everybody here is such a huge source of information that it would be absolutely amazing if I could find out more stuff on what Johnny was like, what his friends were like. Just think about it. I mean, there's a whole world I can't access because I didn't live here back then, but those of you who did, that's massive. You all have huge memory banks I can't even imagine."

"That's true enough," Nan said. "And we definitely have an awful lot of people here who would have been around back then." She pursed her lips as she thought. "I'll have to talk to some people here. I know Penny's neighbor. I think her name is Ginger. She lived there at the same time Johnny went missing. She might remember something about it."

"It would help if it wasn't a family member," Doreen said, "because family members always tend to remember the deceased with a kind eye but not necessarily an honest eye. Nobody wants to think of their family members as being anything other than delightful. But the truth is, as you and I both know, not everyone is always as delightful as the family members want to remember them."

Nan chuckled. "Well, Ginger is here, and she wasn't family, so I'll talk to her. If I can pin her down that is. She's gone lots."

"If you could, that would be awesome. I really have absolutely nothing to go on. A big strapping young man gets up one day and walks away. The end."

"Not necessarily," Nan said. "We know his vehicle was involved in an accident not long after he went missing that killed two of his buddies. We always wondered if they'd had something to do with Johnny's disappearance. Plus, how did they end up with his vehicle?"

"I'll ask Penny about that," Doreen said. "I plan to walk around her property to get an idea on the last-known location for Johnny and where his dagger was found."

"If you walk home on the other side of the creek," Nan said, "you'll get there in half the time. It's probably only a ten- or fifteen-minute walk." She glanced at her watch. "You could probably walk by her place after our tea."

Doreen loved that idea. She finished her tea and the last baby carrot, and said, "In that case, maybe I'll go now." Giving Nan a big hug and leaving her the copy of the letter, she turned and headed back out with the animals.

She stopped for a moment to orient herself, and, using the stepping stones, though of course one was missing, skipped across to the sidewalk, went down and around, then behind the old folks' home. She could cross the creek on this side and walk over and probably hit Penny's within a few minutes. At least according to Nan.

As Doreen rounded the corner, Mugs sniffed all over the grass, as if it was a common walkway for dogs. She was forced to tug him forward quite a bit because the last thing she wanted was the gardener to think that Mugs would pee on his perfect grass. She couldn't even imagine if Mugs left a turd somewhere close by. The gardener would probably have a heart attack. Smirking, she led her menagerie toward the sidewalk.

Chapter 9

Thursday Late Afternoon ...

DOREEN CROSSED THE bridge and walked happily, enjoying the late afternoon sun. She hadn't been very long at Nan's, although the hours had disappeared quickly. Still, she had time to check out Penny's home and to figure out where the missing young man had possibly gone to from there.

It wasn't long before she came to the row of houses described by Nan. Doreen wanted to check out the park behind them.

She took the access path to the large open green space. Goliath alternated from being distracted to running ahead. Mugs, well, he just moseyed along, sniffing with his big nose, and Thaddeus hummed at her shoulder. She noted a couple goalposts, as if for casual games of football. A pitcher's mound sat on the other side of the park. The nearby houses were all fenced with gates to the park—all chain-link construction per the park's guidelines for a consistent and symmetrical look. So, if Johnny had wanted to, he could certainly have opened the gate and stepped into the park, where anything could have happened.

Thaddeus flew to the ground and walked along the fence.

She wandered up and down it with him, considering what the growth of the trees and the shrubs would have been like some twenty-nine years ago. Many of the bordering properties had cedar hedges; some were very thick. Back then they would have been smaller, and anybody on the other side of the fence would be visible.

Somebody might have called out to Johnny. He would have willingly gone to them. It wasn't likely that somebody would have gone into the backyard, knocked him over the head, tossed him over their shoulder, and carried maybe a 180-pound male through the park without being seen. It was late afternoon on a sunny day at the time of his disappearance. Surely someone would have seen such an altercation.

His friends could also have asked him to pick up booze or to go to a party. The fact was, she didn't know what happened to him or, for that matter, to his car from the time Johnny went missing twenty-nine years ago to his friends dying in it just a few weeks after Johnny's disappearance. Anything was supposition at this point. And she knew what Mack thought of those …

As she stood, she heard her name called. She turned to see Penny peering over the gate.

"It *is* you," Penny stated happily.

Doreen walked toward her. "I wanted to see what the area was like," she confessed.

Penny opened the gate. "I'm so glad you're taking this seriously. I know George is smiling in heaven right now."

Doreen hoped so. It was kind of creepy though to think of all those faces up there, smiling down at the other poor sods who lived their life on earth. She walked around the backyard, studying where the kitchen window was and what the view would be like. "Well, I doubt someone would have come onto your property and knocked him out, picked him up, and carried him away," she said, "particularly with you watching."

"Although we weren't necessarily watching the whole time," Penny admitted. "We often wondered what we missed."

"Makes more sense to call him into the park, although any number of people could have seen him there too."

"Sure, but no one reported having seen him at that time on that day."

"What happened to his vehicle? I understand he had a car?"

"Yes. He had George's old car. The two worked on it constantly."

With Penny's assistance, they went through the motions of where the bench had been and where the knife was found. With her cell phone, Doreen took several photographs, including one of the gated entrance into the park.

She also noted that, if Johnny had wanted to, he could have gone around either side of the house into the front yard. "Do you know how his friends got the keys?"

She shook her head. "I assumed they stole them. Johnny may very well have had the keys on him, or he may have just left the vehicle unlocked. For all I know they were out for a joyride, they killed him and then took off in his car. I don't know. I understood that, for a while, they were all laughing at being able to hot-wire cars. They might very well have thought to pull that prank with his vehicle. But Johnny and George had done a lot to soup it up. Johnny was pretty happy with the aftermarket stuff they were doing to it. He really wanted to get himself a muscle car. But George cautioned Johnny about getting rid of this car too early. Though Johnny wanted to sell it, George didn't want him to."

"It's quite possible that one of his friends decided he should sell it regardless, and, if he didn't sell it, he should just give it to them, whether he liked it or not. So, when he went missing, they might have taken it as their due."

"That's a possibility," Penny said. "I know we tossed around an awful lot of theories back then. I don't know if that one in particular was ever brought up, but, in a way, it does make sense. I know he wouldn't have sold it cheap though. The aftermarket upgrades cost thousands even back them."

They talked a bit longer. When she felt she could learn nothing else, she started to leave but turned back. "Do you remember anything about the vehicle? License plate, model?"

Penny shook her head. "No, but I'm sure Mack can get it from the files."

Doreen nodded. "I'm sure he can. It doesn't mean he will share it with me though." She gave a slight wave, and, with the animals, headed back the way she'd come.

Penny called behind her. "If you go along the creek, you'll come up on the north side of your place."

Doreen looked at her in surprise, then tried to reorient herself from where she was. "Thanks. I'll try that." She headed off to the right.

The sun was setting and getting to that half-dusky light outside. That was a bit of a concern. It was also getting cooler. It was spring, but a breeze had picked up. Trusting in Penny, Doreen kept marching forward until she came to the creek.

She stopped, studying it, then realized Penny was right. Doreen was farther up from where her property was. Now if she could find a way to get to her familiar path on the creek, she could walk across the little bridge to her home.

Mugs barked and kept up a snuffling sound as he went through the bushes toward the path. Thaddeus took several steps closer to her, and she wasn't sure if that meant he was nervous or if he thought they were going into the water. Goliath appeared to have absolutely no issues either way as he raced ahead of Mugs, who wanted to run after the cat.

Pulled along by the basset hound, Doreen ran onto the path and took a right. "Well, this is definitely a different way to go home." She looked back but saw no sign of Thaddeus, so she tugged on Mugs's leash to slow him down while calling for the bird. Thaddeus came around the corner, then flew up, missing her shoulder and smacking into her head. She cried out and caught him before he fell. "Okay, you're staying with me, big guy. So no more freak-outs. Okay?"

"Okay, okay," Thaddeus shrieked, then snuggled in against her chest.

She continued homeward, marveling at the shadows lengthening around her. The moon was rising, but still enough sunlight remained to see. She wasn't scared in the dark, but it was hard to see the path. Definitely rockier than she was used to on her side—as if not many people ever walked here, which also made sense because she'd not seen many people come down the creek past her place either.

Finally she came to her little bridge, maybe twenty feet long, and her house was easily visible on the other side. She had left lights on inside, and something about it was almost fairy-tale-ish. "No, maybe more gingerbread-house-y," she said, chuckling.

And then she froze, sure she saw a shadow cross the window. *Inside.*

Her heart raced as she had forgotten to set the alarms before she'd come out with the animals.

With her companions in tow, she ran across the bridge, sneaked up the side of her fence, around to the front, and froze again. Mack's car was in her driveway. She groaned, picked up the phone, and called him.

His voice was irate when he answered. "Where are you?" he snapped.

"Maybe the question should be, where are you?" she said drily as she opened the front door. She could see him in the kitchen. Mugs barked, racing ahead to greet him.

He spun and put away his phone, bending to pet Mugs. "I was trying to get you on the phone for the last hour, and you wouldn't answer. I came over here to make sure you were okay and found the place empty and the alarms *not* set," he said accusingly. "You didn't even lock the front *or* the back doors."

She transferred Thaddeus to the kitchen table. He squawked in protest, then tilted his head and said, "Mack is here. Mack is here."

"Yes, he is," she said. She checked her phone, and, sure enough, the ringer was turned off.

She groaned. "I came down the creek and saw a shadow inside. I thought you were somebody after my antiques." She waggled her phone. "And the sound was off."

"I could have been an intruder," he said in a stern tone. "What's the point of setting up a security system if you don't use it?"

She raised both hands in frustration. "Okay, okay, okay. It was a foolish thing to do. Nan sounded pretty lonely, so I grabbed the animals and went to visit her."

He frowned. "So then why did you come from the far end of the creek?"

She wrinkled her nose at him. "You saw me, did you?"

"No," he said, but then he shrugged. "Well, I might have caught you coming around the corner."

She glared at him. "You saw me coming into the backyard anyway, and you still had to ask where I was, huh?"

He gave her a sheepish grin. "I wondered if you'd tell me the truth."

She rolled her eyes at him. "Of course I told you the truth. What's the point in lying?"

"I'll give you that." He chuckled. "In your case, you're not a great liar anyway."

"No, I'm not. But I'm not a terrible one either," she snapped. She walked in and checked the clock. "I didn't realize it was so late. I was hoping for a cup of tea before bed, but the caffeine might keep me up."

"So have something herbal," he suggested. "Particularly if you have something to help you fall asleep."

"Such as?" She walked to the drawer of teas. "Look at them all here. I have no clue what any of them do."

"If it says *Sleepytime*," he said drily, "I'm pretty sure it's not meant to give you energy during the day."

"Ha, ha." She picked up several more. "Chamomile, yarrow root, and dandelion. Are we seriously thinking dandelion leaves are crushed up in these packets?" She opened one of the little yellow boxes that had a picture of dandelions all over it, pulling out the little tea bags.

"Yes," he said. "I wouldn't be at all surprised."

She shook her head. "The only one I would count on as safe to drink in the evening is *Sleepytime*."

"Which wouldn't be a bad idea," he suggested. "You will be sleeping on the floor tonight, and that'll feel very different. You might need something extra to help you."

"That's a good idea," she admitted. She walked to the sink, filled the teakettle, and turned it on. Then she leaned against the counter. "Do you want a cup?"

"No," he said. "Now that I know you're safe, I'll go home." He walked toward the front door.

"Wait." She stopped him. "What were you calling me about earlier?"

He hesitated a moment. "It's really nothing." He continued to walk toward the front door.

"Well, if it was enough to call me," she said, trailing behind him, "it's enough to tell me now."

"It's the cold case you're working on," he said. "Two friends of his were killed in a car accident driving his car."

"Yes," she said. "I know that. What we don't know is how they got his car."

He looked at her. "According to one of the kids' fathers, his son bought it off of Johnny."

"Did that make sense at the time?" she asked. "Did he have money to do something like that twenty-nine years ago?"

"The dad said he paid a couple hundred bucks. He'd been saving up for it."

She shook her head. "Well, he might have been saving up for it, but no way Johnny would have accepted that money."

At the doorway Mack turned to her. "How do you know that?"

"Because Penny was just saying how George and Johnny spent hours working on that thing. Sure Johnny wanted another rig. He wanted a muscle car, whatever the hell that is," she said with a wave of her hand. "But the thing is, the two brothers souped up that car, and it was worth a lot more."

"This was twenty-nine years ago," Mack reminded her. "A couple hundred dollars bought a lot more back then."

"But they had put serious money into it," she argued. "According to Penny, they did an awful lot of aftermarket upgrades. I mean, like a hot rod for the kid."

Mack crossed his arms over his chest and leaned against the door. "And that can cost a bundle," he admitted. "How badly did Johnny want another vehicle?"

"Pretty badly. But what he wanted was out of his price range," she said, "and I doubt that a couple hundred bucks for his car would have done the job. Plus it didn't begin to pay George back for the money he put into the car either. Plus he didn't want Johnny to sell the car. Feel free to contact Penny and ask her yourself."

"No," he said. "But, if you want to ask her what the vehicle might have been worth back then, it wouldn't hurt to find out. Although I doubt its value had a financial aspect for the two men who worked on it so much."

"Good point." She looked up at the clock. "I'll think about asking her but I'm too tired to do that now though. She did say thousands of dollars in those upgrades so a couple hundred bucks doesn't make sense. I'll feed the animals, then maybe have a hot bath before I settle in for an early night."

He nodded. "Exactly. Get to bed and get some rest."

"Right. Tomorrow is a whole new day," she said with yet another heavy groan.

"What's wrong with tomorrow?" he asked.

"Tomorrow is Friday," she said. "I'm still waiting for that phone call from Christie's, but I will head to your mother's and spend a few hours weeding, as planned."

"Right, a phone call about the antiques. I keep forgetting." He looked around the living room, shook his head, and said, "I can't imagine what this place will look like when those huge pieces are gone."

"I know," she said. "But I'm still looking for paperwork that Nan says she had. Apparently what I found wasn't it."

"I'm not sure what you're looking for," he said, "but it's hard to find anything in here."

"I know," she said with a sigh. "And one of these days I'll venture into the garage. I did open the inside door to the laundry room finally, but then I had a hell of a time closing it. The garage is stuffed." She just shook her head. "I don't know what Nan was thinking."

"I would guess that, like a lot of older people," he said quietly, "she found it hard to let go of things."

Doreen smiled. "That could very well be. It was really nice to see her today. I would hate to lose her anytime soon."

"I'd hate that too," Mack said. He opened the door and stepped out on the front step. "And what are you doing as soon as I leave?"

She frowned at him. "Taking a cup of tea upstairs."

He banged his head lightly on the doorframe. "No. You'll lock this door and set the alarms."

"Well, I meant that too." She shooed him away. "Go, go, go, go. The sooner you leave, the sooner I can go to bed."

He snorted. "Now, if you had somebody you were going with, that would make sense. Otherwise, I don't know." With that cryptic remark, he turned and walked to his car.

She closed the door lightly behind him, reset the alarm,

and checked the back door. She fed the animals, while snacking on cheese and crackers. With the animals in tow, she picked up her tea, shut off all the lights, and walked up the stairs.

She could only hope everything went well with this antique stuff. She wanted it all gone, safe and sound, as soon as possible.

She walked into her bedroom and turned on the light. Everything looked the same, except for her bed on the floor. That was just a shame. She set down her tea and walked into the bathroom. It still amazed her that such a lovely bathroom was the only thing Nan had renovated in the house. She'd yet to mention it. Every time Doreen was with Nan, Doreen also forgot to bring it up. She needed a list for all the things she wanted to ask her grandmother.

Deciding a hot shower would be better than a bath, she got in under the spray. While stepping out, drying herself, she heard a commotion in the bedroom. She grabbed her robe, threw it on, and stepped out of the bathroom. And glared. "What are you doing, Mugs?"

Mugs was at the closet doors, barking like a crazy man. She frowned and thought about it. Mack had been here, but who was to say somebody hadn't come inside ahead of Mack?

Both doors to the closet were closed, but she tested them just the same, then tied the doorknobs together with a pair of nylon stockings, and stepped back into her bathroom. She pulled out her phone and called Mack. As soon as he answered, she said, "Was anybody in the house when you arrived?"

"Of course not," he said. "You were out."

"Would you mind coming back then?" she asked in the hushed whisper. "And fast."

Chapter 10

Thursday Evening ...

DOREEN QUICKLY REDRESSED in the same clothes she'd worn earlier, pulled her hair into a ponytail, making sure it was out of the way. She had no weapons, nothing that would do the job against a possible intruder. And since Mugs had entered the bedroom, he hadn't stopped barking. She knew she would have to make her way downstairs in order to let Mack in and to disengage the security system, but she didn't want to do it too soon. She had no idea if anybody was in the closet, but no way would she open it without Mack here to take a look with her.

She waited ten minutes. When she heard a vehicle, she crept to the hallway. Mugs still barked away at the closet. She ran down the stairs, entered her security code, and unlocked the front door. "Upstairs. I need you upstairs." And she bolted up the staircase, Mack behind her.

He grabbed her by the shoulders. "What's the matter?" he whispered.

She tried to explain, but it was garbled, as she was afraid the scenario had changed while she'd been gone. Thankfully Mugs still stood at the closet doors, barking like a crazy dog.

Goliath sat right beside him. Not to be outdone, Thaddeus perched on a newel post of the bed, overseeing the pair on the floor.

Mack strode toward the closet door, raised an eyebrow at her over the nylons.

She shrugged. "I didn't know what else to do."

He untied the nylons and opened both doors. He saw nothing at first. But Mugs dove under the clothes and growled.

Yelps sounded from inside, and somebody yelled, "Get him off me. Get him off me."

Mack dove into the closet, bringing out her intruder and tossing him to the floor, where Mack pinned him down.

"Well, well, well," she said, recognizing the intruder she had caught in her house just last week, taking her fireplace poker after him until Mack arrived and took him to jail, only to run into the same damn intruder on the loose again in the grocery store parking lot soon afterward. Sometimes the judicial system sucked. "So you *are* a Peeping Tom, just like I told you before, stealing into women's bedrooms at night too."

The man turned away, his astonished expression taking over his face. "No way," he argued. "You're not putting that on me. I'm only here because"—he waved at Mack—"he was coming inside, so I ran up here to hide. I'm not a Peeping Tom. No way."

"His name is Darth McLeod. And he's supposed to be locked up. I'll have fun finding out why you are loose once more." Mack pulled him to his feet. "You won't be getting out on bail this time. No matter how good a lawyer you have." He proceeded to march her intruder down the stairs.

Darth McLeod. Well, that was a name to commit to

memory. Hopefully she'd seen the last of him now. She followed them down and blocked the front door. "Check his pockets first," she said. "For all I know, while you and I weren't here, he made five trips out of the house with my stuff."

Darth sneered. "You don't even know what you've got here," he snapped. "There's a bloody fortune for the taking."

"No, there isn't. It's mine. You're not taking anything. And I might not know everything yet," she said, "but I'm learning."

Mack searched his pockets and pulled out a list. He held it up to her and said, "Does this make any sense to you?"

She frowned. "Snow globe, blue china vase, silver tea set." There were a few other items. She pulled out her phone and took a picture of the list, then returned it to Mack. "Thanks very much for letting me know what might be worth something," she told Darth.

He just glared at her. Nothing else was in the other pocket, so Mack led him outside. She shut the door keeping the animals inside.

"Should you drive him to the station on your own?" she asked.

Mack shook his head. "I sent a text for backup."

And, sure enough, an RCMP vehicle came around the cul-de-sac and up to her driveway. Two men got out.

"Hi, Chester," she said, recognizing one of the men.

Chester gave her a sheepish grin. "I see you can't stay out of trouble, can you?"

"Not my fault you guys let this jerk out of jail. You should add Peeping Tom and stealing underwear to his list of crimes."

"I didn't steal any underwear from you," the intruder

bellowed. "That's gross."

"You were in my closet and looking in my underwear drawer," she said, pointing to the open dresser drawer. "So, as far as I'm concerned, you're after women's lingerie too." She gave him a fat smile. "Let's see what the other prisoners think of that."

The two uniformed men roughly grabbed her intruder and forced him into the back of their car. With a wave to her and Mack, they took off with the prisoner.

She smirked at Darth as she waved goodbye; then she turned to Mack. "Now please don't let him out again."

"No," Mack said. "I'll talk to the prosecutor about him staying in jail until his court date."

"Good idea," she said. "We also need to figure out where his vehicle is and make sure he hasn't been hauling stuff out of my house."

Mack pulled out his phone. "I'll get a run on his vehicle in the meantime." He looked around the cul-de-sac. "Do you recognize all these vehicles?"

She looked around. "All but that truck down there."

Together they walked in the dark to the truck. It was an older model. Mack took a picture of the license plate. Then he bent down, brushed off some of the mud on the plate, took more pictures, and called it in. "Looks like it's his," he said, after ending his call.

"Can we search his vehicle?"

"He was caught in the act of a felony," Mack said, "so, yes, I can." With his phone flashlight turned on, he found several bags in the back of the truck bed as well as a box. He opened the box and pulled out a large snow globe.

"Wow! That's beautiful." The bottom of the snow globe had Nan's name written on it. "That dirty, rotten little thief," she said, stamping her foot. "Can I take this back up to the house?"

"No, I'm afraid not yet," he said. "We'll have to keep all this as evidence."

"How will I know what's mine?" she asked.

They went through the rest of the box and found a blue china vase with a lot of Bubble Wrap around it.

"That was on the front room mantel," Doreen said in a daze. "I have the pictures at home to prove it."

He nodded. "I can see that too. We'll have to move these to my car. But I want the entire vehicle gone over. Apparently Darth has a good eye for what he can pawn. The trouble is, I don't know what else he might have taken, and we'll need to give this truck a good once-over."

She hopped into the bed of the truck with her cell phone out. There was one more box. She opened it up and frowned. "I don't recognize this," she said. It was a carving of a dolphin's head.

"No," he said, "but I do. It's from another reported break-in."

"Well, now you know who your burglar is," she said with a snort of disgust. "Geez, as if we don't work hard enough to get where we are, and then to have somebody like him stealing all this stuff."

"Sure," he said. "But remember where you came from, and remember how you got your stuff."

At his dry tone, she stopped, considered his words, and winced. "I'm sorry. That was incredibly arrogant of me. I came from money, lost it all, and am eternally grateful to now have all Nan's stuff."

"Yes, it was arrogant," he said cheerfully. "But one thing I like about you is how you always admit to your mistakes."

She hopped out of the vehicle and opened the front passenger door. "Looks like a notebook's in here."

He opened the driver's side and reached across to get it. He laughed. "You see? The smartest thieves often have the dumbest systems."

"Are you telling me that he wrote down everything he stole?" she asked in amazement.

"Looks like it," Mack said. "So we'll definitely impound this truck and everything in it. We'll move the valuables in the back of the truck into my vehicle, and I'll get Darth's towed to the police lot."

"Good. I hope he never gets it back."

The bulk of the inside of the truck, outside of fast-food packages and a travel mug, appeared to be stolen goods. She searched behind the seat; it was empty but for more garbage, as best as she could see. She opened the glove box and whistled.

Immediately Mack was at her side. He moved her out of the way and took a look. "Now that's an interesting item to find in his glove box." He removed a handkerchief from his pocket and using it, he pulled out the small handgun and said, "I wonder if he has a license for this thing."

"Even if he does, he still must have a special one to keep it in the vehicle, and isn't that only good for a couple days?"

Mack shot her a look. "Interesting you would know that."

"My husband had guns," she said. "When we moved from one house to the next, he had to get a permit to move them."

"I'm surprised he cared enough to get a permit to move them," Mack said.

"He got the permit for the weapons the cops knew

about. And then just did what he wanted with the ones the cops didn't know about."

Mack stared at her.

She shrugged. "Come on. You know how many people have guns around here."

"A lot more than I would like," he admitted. He went through the rest of the glove box while she watched but couldn't find anything else of significance. He made a few phone calls, then, with the gun in his pocket, moved everything from the truck bed to his car.

"Are you leaving now?" she asked.

"Not until the truck is picked up," he said. "We have to consider Darth McLeod might be working with someone."

"That's a good point." She looked back at her house, the door wide open. The animals were milling around them at the intruder's truck, getting in their way. "Maybe I should go back inside. I hate to think somebody else has gone in there—or is still in there," she said with a wince.

"Come on," he said. "Let's get you back inside. I'll make sure everything's good. Then you set the alarms again."

"Yes, yes, yes," she said. "It was a little distressing to realize the intruder was *inside* the house. Not much good having an alarm system—"

"—if you don't set it," he snapped.

They walked into the living room to Mugs barking in excitement. Mack shut the front door and checked every room in the house, including closets and underneath the bed in the spare bedroom. Mugs followed his every step sniffing into every corner too.

Doreen laughed, "We'll make a watchdog out of you yet."

Finally he walked back downstairs. "Looks like you're

good to go."

Just then they saw the lights of a tow truck. "Perfect timing," Mack said. "If I can get that thing moved, then maybe I can go home to bed."

"Yeah, and you'll probably sleep," Doreen said without hesitation. "I'm not sure I will."

He looked at her in understanding. "It's been a trying time for you, hasn't it?"

"Particularly since I found out something valuable was in the house," she said sadly. "It's like a loss of innocence that I hadn't really expected to feel personally."

"Finding you had expensive possessions? Or the intruder?"

"Both," she said. "Realizing my husband had taken everything I owned before, I was feeling extremely possessive about everything here. One intruder was one thing, but to know he came back after more and was pilfering stuff from my house made me really angry. But now I'm just sad. It's an ugly world we live in."

"It might be an ugly world, but you don't have to let that ugliness touch you. Remember that. This is all about you. Your perspective. How you want to live your life."

"What am I supposed to do about people like Darth?"

"You learn a lesson," he said. "Some people are thieves, and all you can do is guard against them. But you can't judge the rest of the world by the actions of a few."

She smiled, knowing he was talking about more than just intruders. More likely he was talking about her husband. "I don't judge all men the same as my husband. I'm working on forgiving him. But he didn't have to be so mean as to take everything from me."

"Right. I need to check in with my brother about that."

And, with a honk from the tow truck driver, Mack raised a hand and said, "Now remember to lock that door again and to set the alarms."

And then he was gone.

Chapter 11

Friday Morning ...

SURPRISINGLY, THE NEXT morning Doreen woke up feeling rested. She rolled over and stared at the massive bed frame beside her. She wanted to laugh out loud, but, at the same time, she was also sad because she was letting go of part of her heritage. She knew it was important in order to make her future easier, but something was just so very comforting about the thought of all the nights her grandmother had slept in that bed. Not to mention all the nights her great- and great-great-grandmothers had slept in the same bed.

Doreen's past was part of that piece of furniture, and she didn't want to minimize the effect selling it had on her. She closed her eyes and sent out a moment of thanks to the women who had gone before her. They were strong; they had been through so much, and yet, they had survived. Not only survived, they had thrived. Doreen wanted to do the same. She wanted to do well for herself. She knew the challenges she faced were different from what the women in her family before her had faced, but that didn't make it any less important that Doreen also do her best at every turn.

She got up slowly to find Mugs had approved of their new mattress-on-the-floor situation. He slept at her feet. Goliath lay on the pillow beside her head. Thaddeus had retained his spot atop the closest newel post on the four-poster bed.

She'd forgotten to put newspaper under him, so she found one bird dropping. She walked into the bathroom, grabbed some toilet paper, cleaned it up, and used a spray bottle she kept close by to wipe up the last little bit.

With that done, she dressed. Casting another look at the antique bedroom set, she meandered downstairs, looking at the bright early morning sunshine outside. "One thing about being here in Kelowna," she said to herself, "the weather is divine." Unlike Vancouver, as a coastal city, which had constant rain. While living there with her soon-to-be ex-husband, Doreen had had lots of places outside where she could walk under cover. Yet it wasn't the same as seeing and feeling the sunshine. Kelowna did get winter here, but it was mild. At least she hoped it was.

She put on coffee and looked out at the yard, remembering last night's events—the intruder and the items he'd stolen from her. The outrage …

She walked from the back door to the front door, releasing the alarms at each entryway. That done, she poured herself a cup of coffee. With the animals in tow, she stepped onto the rear veranda and down the few steps to walk along the backyard, just wearing a pair of pink flip-flops on her feet as she meandered through the garden. It was a lovely sunny morning. The backyard looked so much bigger with the rear fence down, but she still had a lot of work to do on the garden beds. And yet, she didn't want to just dive in. She needed to make a plan and to see what all was here first. By now she should know, but so much of it was overgrown. And she'd been a little busy …

And, since today was Friday, that meant she needed to return to Mack's mother's house and do some more gardening there, which also meant more money tomorrow. She grinned at that. It hadn't been quite a week since she'd last been there, but there was no end of work to do on Millicent's lawn.

Doreen chuckled. "Hey, thanks, Mack. You're doing a good job keeping me in food," she said out loud. She also needed to pack up more of those clothes she'd set aside to take to Wendy's. Not to mention all the Goodwill boxes. She'd left it all sitting around the house to move out to her car, but she had yet to do so. And that was foolish. It was a relatively easy job, and it would relieve some of the household clutter. That would certainly make it easier when the men came to pack up the furniture.

With that thought uppermost in her mind, she checked her watch and found she had overslept. She went back inside, poured herself a second cup, then moved all the bags for Wendy's store out to her car. She had hoped to take a load to Goodwill at the same time, but it didn't look like that was possible. She'd have to make a second trip. She could do Wendy's first, as Wendy opened early.

With Mugs at her side, locking the other two animals in the house, she soon drove to Wendy's store. The proprietor of the consignment store, Second Time Round, was just unlocking the door when Doreen arrived.

"Aren't you out bright and early?" Wendy said with a smile. She motioned at the bags. "Are those for me?"

"They are, if you think you can sell them," Doreen said hopefully.

"Come on in. Let's take the bags right to the back room, and we'll start sorting."

"Sounds good."

Mugs stayed close on her heels as Doreen grabbed the bags one at a time, parking them on the sidewalk. By the time she had all the bags out, Wendy had come back out for two more, carrying them to the back room.

Inside the store, she turned on the lights and escorted Doreen to the rear section where she had large tables set up. "Do you want to wait or check in with me later?" she asked. "I do have to open the store before I begin. I can give you a call later, and you can come back and pick up what I don't think I can sell."

Doreen hesitated. "If you don't mind, I will come back when you give me a call. I have a busy morning planned."

"No problem." Wendy waved her off. "I might not get through it all today though. You brought me a lot."

Doreen chuckled. "And there's still more to come."

Wendy's eyebrows popped up. "Wow! Who knew Nan had so many clothes?"

"Right. And some of these are pretty stylish. I've kept quite a few for myself."

Wendy chuckled. "Why not? All the styles in fashion way back when are coming around. There's really nothing new in life. It's just patterns and cycles."

"I agree." Doreen gave a wave and walked with Mugs out to her car.

Back home, not giving herself a chance to slow down, she loaded up all the stuff for Goodwill and drove in the opposite direction. They were also just opening, but they had a drive-through section, and employees unloaded the stuff from her car. Doreen liked that system.

When the car was empty, she gave a bright cheerful toot of the car horn and pulled away. "Mugs, now it's time for breakfast."

He woofed beside her. He hadn't eaten either.

Back home she fed the animals, then studied the stove and wondered if she dared. She was a little lacking in the ingredients she needed—only eggs and cheese remained in her fridge—but it would be lovely to have an omelet again.

Very carefully, using the stove on a low heat setting, she proceeded to do the same thing she'd done twice before, and, lo and behold, she ended up with a beautiful-looking cheese omelet.

She sat down and chuckled. Then she took a picture of it, cut it in half, arranged the pieces a little more picturesquely on the plate, and took a second picture. She sent it to Mack. He should be happy to know she did it on her own.

While she ate her omelet, she thought about everything else she had to do that day. Finishing up her breakfast, Doreen got a call from the antiques appraiser.

"The men will be there at noon on Monday," Scott Rosten announced.

Her heart sank. "Okay." She tried not to let anything show in her voice. "I was hoping you'd come today. I'm nervous about having all these pieces here. There's been several break-ins already."

"Oh dear. I'm so sorry to hear that. I'm coming as soon as I possibly can. Maybe ask the police for some assistance?" he said. "I'll be there Monday."

She smiled as the call ended, placed the phone beside her, and it rang yet again. She recognized Mack's number. She hated to admit it, but something lightened inside her. "Good morning, Mack," she said cheerfully.

"Well, you're awfully happy for a Friday morning," he said. "Is it because you slept well?"

"Sure," she said. "Why not? And I made my first omelet, all on my own."

"I saw the photo you sent. Good for you."

"And the antiques appraiser just called and said the guys are coming Monday at noon to pack up."

"Not until Monday then," he said. "That's too bad. I was hoping, for your sake, it would be today or tomorrow."

"Me too," she said. "But it is what it is. Please tell me that you haven't let that thief out of jail again."

"No, he shouldn't be getting out anytime soon. But I have yet to talk to the judge."

"Do you *have* to talk to the judge?"

"No, that was just a phrase. I have to talk to the prosecutors. They will ask the judge to make sure McLeod doesn't get bail."

"Well, he's obviously not had a change of ways," she said. "And he remains a danger to society still."

"Sure enough," Mack said. "We have tagged and photographed the pieces he stole from you, but we'll have to keep them for a while yet. I'll let you know when you can get them back."

"Okay," she said. "As much as I'd like those pieces sold and moved into somebody else's hands for safekeeping, at least if they're in your hands, if you break them, you get to replace them."

"Ouch," he said with a laugh. After a moment's hesitation he asked, "What are you up to today?"

"I just made two trips, one to the consignment store and one to Goodwill. I'll probably go back upstairs and do some more cleaning out of my bedroom before the movers arrive.

But it's also Friday, so I'll work on your mom's garden for a couple hours."

"Right," he said. "I'll stop by tomorrow with some cash for you."

"Good," she said. "Then I can buy more omelet ingredients."

That brought a startled chuckle from him. "So what do you want to learn to make next?"

She hesitated. "What do you mean?"

"What else do you like to eat?" he asked.

"Well, what I used to like to eat, and what I like to eat now, are very different things," she said with a chuckle. "But, the fact of the matter is, it doesn't really matter what I used to like because I can't afford it."

"True enough," he said. "So, along with your change in budget, you've had a change in taste. What do you like now?"

"I used to love pasta," she said. "I had it with scampi and all kinds of mussels and fresh seafood." She warmed to the subject. "But I was wondering if pasta itself, without all the expensive toppings, would be cheap and possible to cook."

"Absolutely," he said. "Pasta is very easy to cook."

She brightened. "Are you serious? Or are you teasing me again?"

"Look it up on YouTube," he urged. "It's very easy. Just boiling water, a little bit of salt, a little bit of oil, pop in the pasta, and you've got plain cooked noodles. It's what you do with those noodles afterward that makes a difference."

Images of all the lovely pasta dishes she used to eat filled her mind. "I wasn't allowed to eat very much," she said in a low tone. "My husband used to tell me how it would make me fat, so he would cut my portions."

"Your husband was an asshole," Mack said. "Remember? We've already determined that."

"True enough," she said. "So what do you put on the pasta?"

"If you're broke," he said, "you put butter on it. If you can afford a little more, you put cheese with it. If you can afford even more, you can do a spaghetti sauce. You can also add steamed vegetables. You can do chicken and a white sauce. That's a chicken Alfredo. You can do amazing things with different ingredients. You know what? I think that's a really good place to start."

He sounded like he was warming up to the subject. She wasn't sure if she should ask or not, and then she decided there was really no point in *not* asking. She knew that he didn't mind helping her because he'd taught her how to make the omelet.

"So does that mean you're up for teaching me how to make some pasta dishes?" she asked. When she heard the hesitation on the other end of the phone, she tried to backtrack. "But that's asking too much. Just forget it."

"Not only will I remember that you asked," he said, "but I was figuring out where to start."

"You said with a pot of water, salt, oil, and pasta," she said drily. "And I'm broke. So, if we have just butter with it, that sounds pretty good to me."

"Maybe," he said. "But I'm not that broke. Although I like plain buttered noodles, I can also make sauces."

"Can you?" she asked eagerly. "Like a tomato sauce with ground beef?"

"Only if it comes with mushrooms, green peppers, and red wine."

"That sounds divine," she said excitedly. "After you

bring by my gardening payment, I have to go out shopping tomorrow. Maybe I can pick up a few of those things." But she could hear the doubt in her own voice. "I honestly don't know what to buy, how much to buy, or how expensive everything will be."

"We'll do the same as last time," he said. "I'll pick up the items and come to your house, and we'll cook."

"Okay," she said slowly. "Repeating it on Sunday too?"

"I'm not sure it'll work that way with the spaghetti sauce," he said. "Let me think about it. And stay out of trouble today, will you?"

"Of course I will. Easy peasey," she said. She hung up the phone, made a cup of tea, and said to her animal family, "I think we should get the gardening done while we can."

She poured her tea into a travel mug. With all the animals, she set the alarms and walked to Mack's mom's place. There Doreen set to work, weeding and pruning, like she'd done last week. Millicent's yard really did need more than two hours of Doreen's time a week, but, as long as she could do that much, it would keep it all mostly under control.

She had just begun work when Mack's mom appeared on the back steps and called out to her. Doreen lifted her hand. "Good morning." All her animals took off to greet Millicent too.

"You're here early," Millicent said, chuckling as she scratched Mugs's ears. Then she stroked Goliath's back as he rubbed against her. Thaddeus squawked and hopped up to the top of the porch railing, looking for attention too. "I figured, with all the excitement this week, you might not come today."

"Oh, I'm here," Doreen said with a smile, resting on her heels. "How are you?"

"I'm fine," the old woman said. "And you must be doing much better too. Everybody is just buzzing with the news about little Paul."

"Did you know him?"

"I didn't know the little boy," she said, grinning as Thaddeus nudged her hand, "but the handyman was a family guy. We all knew him."

"Well," Doreen said, "somebody asked me to look into another cold case, but I don't have any feelers." She stared at Millicent, guessing this woman was probably in her eighties, would have been in her fifties back when Johnny disappeared. "Do you remember when a Johnny Jordan went missing?" She walked toward the woman on the porch.

"*Johnny Jordan.*" Millicent sat down on her rocking chair. "I don't think I remember that case. Can you tell me any more details about it? Jog this old memory of mine?"

"He was sitting in the backyard of his brother George's place," she said, stopping short of the porch steps. "Then they never saw him again. Nobody knows what happened." Doreen shared a few of the details about George and Penny.

"Oh, poor Penny," Millicent murmured. "I remember something about that now. Everybody thought Johnny had just run away. Then two of his friends were killed soon afterward. For a while rumors were flying that maybe he'd killed them and taken off."

"Wait ... what?" Doreen asked. "Why would anybody think Johnny had killed his two friends? I thought they died in a car accident not too long after Johnny's disappearance."

Millicent nodded, pointing her finger at Doreen. "They did, but they died in his car."

"According to the father of one of the young men who died," she said, "his son had bought the car off Johnny."

"Oh, I don't think so," Millicent said, shaking her head rapidly. "No, no, no. That car was his baby."

"So you *do* remember him?" Doreen asked to be certain.

"I knew George," she said. "If you had told me that Johnny was George's brother who had gone missing, I would have remembered. George used to talk all the time about how he and his kid brother were working on that car."

"But maybe George cared more about the car than his baby brother did."

Millicent gave Doreen an assessing look. "That's possible too. Often we do things, thinking the other person we're doing them with or for is enjoying it as much as we are. But maybe Johnny didn't."

"What I don't understand," Doreen said, "is, if Johnny *accidentally* hit his friends, running them off the road, why would he take off? It was an accident. Nobody was at fault, as far as I know."

"No, and I don't think the police found any evidence of that either," Millicent said, "because the car went over one of the cliffs. The fire finished the vehicle afterward. They had a hard time identifying the bodies."

Doreen straightened. "So how did they know it was Johnny's friends?"

"I don't know," Millicent said, shaking her head, watching Thaddeus strut up and down the porch railing, flapping his wings to some unnamed rhythm. "But it was definitely a sad day in town here. We didn't have the same size population back then." She lowered her tone, as if nobody was allowed to know that tidbit. "With a lot less people living here, we knew each other better. And honestly, if they said it was those two boys, I trust it was those two boys."

Doreen nodded, but, in the back of her head, she won-

371

dered. She returned to a nearby garden bed, bent down, reached for more chickweed, pulling up several strands. "Do you remember anything else from back then?"

Millicent pondered that question for a long moment.

Doreen went back to weeding, staying close to the porch so they could still talk.

"You know? I don't think so," Millicent said. "I know George was terribly devastated."

"And he passed away last year," Doreen said, "so he never did get answers to the mystery."

"No, and that's very sad too. I just wonder if it had something to do with the families of those two boys. There had definitely been talk about those boys being involved in something they shouldn't have been. Although that's almost a normal state for young men."

"In what way?" Doreen asked.

"I can't quite remember. I know there were definitely some ill feelings among the parents, as if blaming each other's child for having led their son down the wrong road."

Doreen snorted. "Now that sounds familiar too."

Millicent gave her a wise look. "Nothing's so perfect as your own child," she said with a smile. "Just ask me."

At that, Doreen laughed. "Mack is a lot of things," she said, still chuckling, "but *perfect* he is not."

"Of course he is," Millicent said with a teasing smile. "He's my son. Therefore, he's perfect. Although ..." she added, "he was too young to have worked the original missing person's case. But then he never wanted to talk to me about his investigations, even when I expressed an interest in them. Said the details would give me nightmares. Plus he thought what I knew was based purely on gossip."

"Well, that explains why he treats me the way he does

with his cold cases. But you know what? Sometimes a kernel of truth can be found in gossip. So both sets of parents would have thought their children were perfect too, right?"

"Yes," Millicent said. "They would have blamed the other child. In this case, there were three boys who hung out together."

"One disappeared, and two were killed."

"Yes. So interesting circumstances but nobody ever heard from Johnny again."

"At least I'm not tripping over any bodies this time," Doreen said with a chuckle.

"Ah, that's because you've been looking in the wrong place. Those three were forever hanging out at the old park."

"What old park? And does Mack know about it?" She pulled out her phone and quickly asked him in reference to Johnny's disappearance.

The response came back almost immediate in the affirmative. Sighing she put the phone back in her pocket and refocused on the conversation.

"Of course he does. I'm talking about the one by the downtown center. It was pretty rough down there. A lot of junkies hung out in that park. If Johnny was killed anywhere, I'd have said that was the most likely spot," Millicent said. "There used to be lots of ravines on that edge of town. I always wondered if Johnny didn't go down there, and somebody maybe pulled the bank over on top of him."

Doreen winced at that. "That doesn't sound good. By the way," she said, straightening up, "was it only the three boys who hung out together?"

"Those three boys were really tight. There was another guy, and I think a couple girls. That one girlfriend was a little dodgy."

"If you're talking about Susan, she died a year ago from breast cancer," Doreen said. "So it'll be hard to get answers from her."

"Oh, not her. Another girl hung around with them a lot. Although she went from one boy to the next. It seemed like she was just moving through the four of them."

"Most likely all the relationships shifted constantly. Males and females alike, particularly at that age," Doreen said. "Do you know who that fourth boy was?"

"I don't remember. ... I mean, after all, when one goes missing and two die, there's not really a gang left. So the fourth guy must have hung out with a new group." Millicent spoke once again in that wise tone.

"True enough," Doreen said. "Do you remember what his name was though?"

"Alan," she said suddenly. "I think. Ask Penny. She'll know."

"I can do that," Doreen said. "I wonder what happened to him."

"If he were smart, he moved away. It seemed like that whole gang had a black mark against them," she said. "And that would be a tough way to live in this town."

"But it wasn't really a black mark, right? They weren't charged with anything serious, were they?"

"No idea," Millicent said. "Maybe ask Mack. He might know."

"But, as you also know," she said gently, "your son won't tell me much."

"Not in so many words, but he could certainly let you know little bits and pieces, and, if those boys were charged with anything, that's public record. Alan was his first name. I can't remember his last name. I want to say Hornby, but my old memory box isn't quite what it was."

Doreen chuckled. "I think your memory is just fine." She kept working and talking to Millicent, losing track of time. Finally she sat back on her heels once more and said, "I think I'm done for this week."

"Good," Millicent said, standing up, giving each of the animals a goodbye cuddle. "Then I'm going in and taking a nap."

"That's a good idea," Doreen said. "And, if you don't mind, I'm heading home."

"Perfect. It's nice to see you like this." Then she stopped. "Oh my," she said. "I meant to give you some zucchini bread. Hang on." She went inside and came back a moment later with what looked like one-half of a loaf of zucchini bread, sliced and wrapped up. She handed it to Doreen, who met her on the porch, and said, "Thank you so much for coming, dear."

With a finger wave, Doreen and the animals started back. As soon as she was out of sight, she had her phone out, looking up Alan Hornby. It turned out the Hornby family used to live in the same cul-de-sac where Penny lived. Doreen frowned and said aloud, "How about we walk the long way around, guys?"

And, with that, she turned in the direction of Penny's house, fully intending to see where the Hornby house was. Maybe Penny had a few more answers to help tie up some of this mystery because, if four men were originally involved, Doreen needed to hear about the last guy still living. To learn that two girls and another guy were hanging around the three boys, she had a lot more questions she needed to ask. And one of the biggest was, who identified the two boys who died in the vehicle?

Chapter 12

Friday Afternoon ...

AS DOREEN WALKED toward Penny's house, she knew a phone call would be faster, yet she found she preferred to do hands-on sleuthing. Not to mention the animals loved the fieldwork.

She chuckled out loud. "Hey, Mugs, listen to me. *Sleuthing. Fieldwork.* Doesn't that sound all professional?"

For a fleeting moment she wondered if she could get a private eye license, but that would mean sleuthing full-time. Would she still enjoy it like now? This was fun. This was intriguing. This kept her mind occupied and let her dwell on somebody else's troubles. She figured, by the time she got a private eye license, it would become drudgery and *work.* She'd be stuck in people's divorces, a thought to make her cringe. And the police certainly weren't hiring any private eyes. As a matter of fact, they probably hated them. Of course she was basing all this on the TV shows she watched occasionally.

She nudged her trio along. They were more into meandering than walking today. Thaddeus, well, he seemed to be singing.

As they neared Penny's house, Doreen stopped and reoriented herself, looking for the Hornby house. It was across the cul-de-sac at the corner. So the kids really had lived close together. As she walked up to Penny's door, Penny opened it and stepped out.

"I could hope," she said, "that you have good news."

Doreen shook her head. "No, just more questions."

Penny leaned against the doorjamb, crossing her arms over her chest. "Well, let them fly. What do you want to know?"

"Alan Hornby," Doreen said.

Penny glared across the cul-de-sac. "Yes, another one of Johnny's friends. Five or six of them used to hang around in a group. Another very unpleasant man."

"I think we only discussed the three guys," Doreen said, worrying slightly at the number that continued to grow.

"Alan and his family lived over there," Penny said, motioning across the way. "They used to be a family. Then his father lived alone in the house. Then Alan returned—not even sure where he went to begin with—and now his father is in the retirement home." She turned to look at the other houses. "It's hard to keep track of everyone."

"What happened to Alan and his mother?"

"A divorce," Penny said simply. "Let's clarify that. An ugly divorce." She gave a half smile.

Doreen winced. "I understand about those." Penny's eyes lit with interest, but Doreen quickly moved past the topic. "Did you see much of Alan after Johnny went missing?"

Penny frowned. "You know what? I'm not sure. It was so long ago. But I should remember, shouldn't I? It's probably important."

"Anything to do with anybody back then," Doreen said, "is important. It could be the slightest thing that helps this case. Somebody lying even a little bit can unravel a whole pile of new information."

"I hear you. It's just really hard to go back to that time and to remember the details." Penny shook her head. "You know? I remember Alan's mother coming over in tears, telling me that she was so sorry. At the time I didn't think much of it because everybody was telling me that they might have seen Johnny or that he'd come home soon, how he was just a wayward boy and not to worry."

"I know," Doreen said. "Everybody gives you their condolences, but it's only afterward you wonder if they really meant it or not."

"So you do know what I mean," Penny said. "I hope you didn't lose somebody too."

Doreen shook her head. "No, thankfully not. But I became very distrustful and leery of people's behavior for a while."

"And Alan's mom was very emotional. It seemed over-the-top. I wasn't sure what was going on," she said. "And because I didn't have any answers, I was just trying to move people along."

"Where was this conversation?"

"It was here," Penny said. "I was talking to the pastor at the front door. He'd come to talk to me too. And then, after he left, Alan's mother came over."

"Do you think she misunderstood? Maybe if she saw you talking to the pastor, she thought Johnny was dead?"

Penny rolled her eyes. "Honestly, with her, it's hard to say. She was not the smartest book on the shelf."

Doreen almost chuckled at that. But it was totally inappropriate to laugh, especially when they were talking about a missing person. She smiled and nodded instead. "Another question. ... Who identified Johnny's friends' bodies?"

"George and one of the boys' fathers did," she said. "The other father wasn't capable of doing the job. And he had asked George to see if it was his son. The two men went in separately, but you have to understand the remains were in bad shape."

Doreen didn't push any further. "It was nice of George to do that."

"Honestly, I think he was secretly wondering if it was Johnny," Penny said. "And it would be so like George to step in and do something like that. Just to make sure."

"Of course. But it wasn't Johnny though, right?"

Penny shook her head. "No, it definitely wasn't. Unfortunately, no." Then she caught herself. "Oh, that sounds terrible. I didn't mean it that way. But, at least, if it had been Johnny, George would have known what had happened to him. He would have had a body. He would have had something to grieve over, and he would have had answers to the big questions."

"I think that's always the worst, isn't it?" Doreen said slowly. "Always wondering what happened and why."

"How true," Penny said. "George suffered terribly without the closure he needed so badly."

Doreen backed away. "That's the only thing on my mind."

"Is that all?" Penny asked. "You could have phoned."

Doreen nodded. "But I love to walk, and it's good for the animals." She looked around but saw no sign of Goliath. "The trouble is, Goliath has a mind of his own."

"You should get a leash for him," Penny said. "I see

more and more people walking their cats."

"I think Goliath would be walking me."

Penny chuckled. "Well, he is a cat." As if that explained everything.

"That would be an explanation for everything to do with Goliath." With Thaddeus snoozing gently on her shoulder, tucked up in the crook of her neck, Doreen waved goodbye and headed back down to the sidewalk. "Goliath," she called out. "Goliath." But she got no answer. Heard no meow. She stopped, turned around, and looked. "Goliath, come on." She was getting a little worried. "Where are you?"

Just then he popped his head out of a huge dahlia bush in the front yard.

"Oh, thank heavens," Penny said. "I was afraid you'd lost him."

"Yeah," Doreen said. "I couldn't imagine." She called him, but Goliath wouldn't come toward her. "Come on, buddy. Come on."

But the cat was digging. Mugs barked and chased Goliath out of the bush. And then Mugs started to dig.

"Uh-oh," Doreen said a sinking feeling in her stomach.

"Did he find something there?" Penny asked, a note of excitement entering her voice.

"I don't know. With these animals, you can never really tell. I swear to God, they think they're some kind of amateur sleuths." She unconsciously echoed what she had said about herself earlier.

She yanked on Mugs's leash, but he wasn't having any of it. Instead the basset hound leaned in his shoulders and put all his weight behind him to stop Doreen's efforts in dragging him back. Not wanting to hurt him, she walked closer and grabbed his harness, trying to lift him. He growled, and finally she let him go.

"What's gotten into you?" But inside she knew it was something important, and he wouldn't let her stop him from finding out whatever this was. When she looked up, Penny came toward her with a shovel. Doreen laughed. "It's almost like you think my dog's found something."

"I've heard stories about these animals of yours," she said.

Just then Thaddeus, waking up from his nap, flew off her shoulder, landing on the big dahlia bushes. The stalks were thick, promising to be big with huge blooms.

"These are beautiful bushes," Doreen said.

Penny nodded. "Dinner plate Dahlias. They are huge blooms. I moved some of the same plants from the back garden, where Johnny used to sit. They multiplied so much that I needed to divide them up."

"Oh, really?" Doreen looked at her, wondering how Mugs knew. "Do you mind if I grab that shovel then?"

A pall settled over the two women as Doreen deliberately stepped in front of Mugs to push him away. And then, switching out the zucchini bread with the shovel, she gently wiggled the dirt in and around the base of the dahlias. When she thought she heard a metallic clink, she went down on her hands and knees, using her hands to dig deeper into the soil. When her fingers closed around something small, she pulled it up, brushed off the dirt, and revealed a medallion. She held it up, and the color drained from Penny's face. "Do you know what it is?"

"It's a medallion Johnny got from their father," she said in a shocked whisper, reaching out to touch the object. "Johnny would never have left it behind."

"Meaning that, if he ran away or walked away from you

guys," she corrected quietly, "he would have taken it with him?"

"I mean, he *always* wore it. It was *always* around his neck."

"So then how did it get here?"

"It must have happened when I divided up the bulbs and transplanted this group here."

"But I want to know how it came off his neck." Doreen had a theory, but she didn't know if she should say it out loud. When Penny stared at her, dread in her eyes, Doreen nodded. "It likely came off in a struggle." She picked up the chain that hung from the medallion. She held it so Penny could see it. "It's broken."

Chapter 13

Friday Midafternoon ...

WITH THE MEDALLION and the chain wrapped up in newspaper from Penny's recycle bin and in a plastic ziplock bag, and with her zucchini bread, Doreen walked back home. Lost in her thoughts, when her phone buzzed in her pocket, it startled her. She pulled it out to see it was Mack. "Hey," she said.

"What's wrong?" he asked.

"I don't know if something is wrong or not," she said, "but it's definitely something that makes me think."

"Explain," he said, as if unsure what she was saying.

"I went to Penny's to ask a few more questions, but, instead of getting answers, we found more questions. Mugs and Goliath were both digging in her dahlia bushes. Dahlia bushes she had moved from the garden in the backyard years ago because the tubers had multiplied and became these massive plants."

"Stop," he said. "I don't need a gardening lesson. I need an explanation."

She sighed and checked that the road was empty before she crossed it, so she could hook back onto the path along the creek. "Well, when I dug around the plants, we found a medallion on a broken chain. Apparently Johnny's, and he never went anywhere without it around his neck. I think he died the same evening he went missing."

Silence followed before Mack finally spoke. "Well, we don't know that for sure," he said. "Because you didn't find a body … right?" His tone sharpened.

"Nope, no body—at least not yet," she said. "Just remnants of the life of a person who's gone missing."

"I guess I can see how that would be upsetting, but that doesn't mean Johnny is dead."

"No," she said, "but it doesn't mean he's alive either. However … your mother told me that Johnny and his friends used to hang out in the downtown city park, among the drug sellers and buyers. At first I thought that would be a viable lead, but, now, finding this medallion at his home, I don't think so anymore."

Mack gave a huge sigh, which carried clearly over the phone. "Have you got the medallion with you?"

"Yes," she said. "I figured he must have been involved in a struggle and lost it."

"That would indicate maybe somebody saw him in the backyard. And yet, you say George and Penny didn't see what happened to him."

"Apparently," she said. "And, yes, Johnny was in the backyard, but Penny was cooking dinner and was busy. She didn't see him leave."

"Right," Mack said. "So good timing on her part that she saw him when she did. That narrows down the timing somewhat."

"Which hasn't helped yet."

"I'll take a look at it when you get home," he said.

"I'm almost there. I'm walking along the creek, coming down the back again."

"I wish you wouldn't walk there alone," he said with an unhappy sigh.

"What difference does it make?" she asked. "It's still sunny out. Besides, I am not alone. I've got my dog and Thaddeus on my shoulder and Goliath walking beside us, quite put out that I wouldn't allow him to keep digging."

"Of course Goliath found it."

"Well, he did." She chuckled. "Then Mugs jumped him in the bush, chasing him away, and the dog started to dig. Then I took over." She shrugged. "I'm at my little bridge now." She walked across and headed to her house.

"Is the alarm still on?"

"I'll find out in a second," she said.

"I'm glad your antiques guy is coming soon," he said quietly. "I won't stop worrying until those pieces are gone."

"Me too," she said. "At least this case gives me something else to focus on."

"That's nice," he said. "I sure wish it wasn't another murder you're trying to sort out."

"I didn't say it was a murder," she objected. "I just said we found a medallion and its chain, and Johnny was adamant about keeping it close. It was from his father, who was dead."

"Ah," Mack said.

She walked up and hit the alarm code to undo the security and let herself in. Immediately she could feel herself settling, almost like a sigh.

Chapter 14

Friday Late Afternoon ...

ONCE INSIDE THE house, Doreen reset the alarms, put a tea bag in a cup, and put water on to boil in the electric teakettle. She still had Mack on the phone. "I'm inside, safe and sound. The alarm was set, and I've reset it."

"Good. You take care."

"Yeah, I will," she said. "When are you coming for the medallion?"

"I'm heading into the office right now." His voice was distracted. "Depends on how late it is when I'm done."

"Well, it's not late right now," she said, "although, with that cloudy sky moving in now, it seems like it is."

"If I'm only about an hour longer at work, I'll swing by afterward and grab it." He hung up without saying goodbye.

She wasn't sure what was on his docket that he would go by the office at this hour, but he juggled a lot of cases.

As she let her tea steep, she carefully laid the medallion on the kitchen table and studied it. Thaddeus immediately walked over for a closer look. Although it was dirty, the motif on the metal was clearly visible. She thought about a young man who had hung on to probably the only possession he had left of his father's, and she thought about what circumstances it would take for Johnny to let that memento go. She kept coming back to the fact that Johnny wouldn't have given up the medallion willingly. So potentially an argument at the bench where he'd been sitting.

"It's too darn bad," she said to Mugs. She got up, seeing all the animals sitting here, staring at her. "Okay, okay. I see you guys haven't been fed yet."

She puttered around the kitchen getting dinner for the three of them. It was past time for her to get some food too. But the fridge hadn't been restocked, and she desperately needed to go shopping yet again.

"How come shopping consumes so much of my time?" she asked. "It should be fast and easy." She knew those newfangled delivery services were available, where she could order online to get the groceries she wanted. She wasn't quite ready for that yet. Nor could she justify the delivery fee.

With the animals happily munching away, she made herself a simple sandwich, with raw veggies on the side, and sat at the kitchen table to eat. Her gaze kept returning to the medallion. And her mind kept revisiting where it had been found, then took her to the patch of bare ground under the original site for the bench.

Somebody could have buried the body on Penny's property, but anyone other than George and Penny digging up the yard would have been seen and considered suspicious, so that narrowed it down to Johnny's family. Penny wasn't strong enough to manhandle a body, although she might have helped George.

But then why would George keep up the pretenses of looking for his younger brother? He'd already know where his younger brother was. He could have just turned his back on the whole farce and ignored it. Although, if he'd killed his brother, he'd have tried to throw off suspicion by acting as the grieving brother.

Doreen knew in her heart that Johnny was probably dead, and she figured Penny knew it too.

When Doreen was done eating, she washed her few dirty dishes, then glanced around the house, ensuring everything was still where it belonged. After the same intruder had gotten inside her house twice—maybe that third time too?— she felt more than a little paranoid.

As she prepared to go upstairs and to start in on Nan's closet again, Mack pulled up. Mugs barked at the door but his tail wagged happily. She walked to the front door, undid the security, and held up the ziplock baggie for him.

He looked at it and frowned.

"It's a nice piece," she said. "Do you think it's real gold?"

He nodded. "Not only is it likely real gold, that could be a gem in the center. But I can't be sure."

"Which means, if somebody saw it they would have most likely stolen it."

"Yes." His frown deepened.

"Maybe take it and see if any bloodstains are on it?" she asked hopefully.

He just raised his eyebrows.

She shrugged. "You don't have anything else to go on. You might as well take a look at this. It was his possession. It was found at the place where he was last seen. Maybe he was injured there. There could be blood."

"I'll take it back to the office, but it was his, so his skin cells would have transferred to his medallion. So that's to be expected." He pocketed the bagged-up item and stepped back, looking around the living room. "I'll be glad when these expensive antiques are gone."

"Hopefully on Monday," she said with a nervous laugh. "Now it's like sleeping in a mausoleum. I'm so worried about anything getting damaged that I don't sit on it, and I don't use it. I just walk around and give each piece a wide berth."

"Sounds like the right thing to do." He turned and walked down the porch steps.

She watched him go, hating that sense of loss she often felt when he left.

He gave her a wave as he got into his vehicle, backed out of her driveway, and drove around the cul-de-sac, disappearing from sight.

With a heavy sigh she stepped back inside.

Her grandmother called just then. "How is Doreen?" Nan asked. "And how's that lovely Mack?"

"I'm sure Mack is fine," Doreen said, desperate to keep her voice neutral. "And I'm tired, but I'm good. I took the long way around, walking back from your place."

"My place?"

"Sorry, I'm more tired than I thought," she said with a heavy sigh. "I was over at Mack's mother's, doing the gardening, then ended up at Penny's."

"Oh," she said. "I was hoping to invite you for dinner."

"I just had a sandwich and veggies," Doreen said in frustration. She'd have loved to have had dinner with Nan.

"Well, how about cake then?"

"I can always go for some cake and a cup of tea. Do you have a reason for calling?"

"Do I need a reason?" Nan asked craftily.

"No. But something else seemed to be in your tone," Doreen said. "As if to say, you found out something."

"Of course I did," Nan said firmly. "Do you have any

idea how much information is tied up in all the crazy heads here?"

"Which is one of the reasons why I asked you to talk to the residents," Doreen responded in a dry tone.

"It is still fairly early," Nan said. "Why don't you come on down? Maybe, by the time you get here, you'll be hungry again."

Doreen chuckled. "I did work hard earlier today, so sure. Why not?" She gave in easily. "Hopefully you'll have some good information to give me."

With the animals fed, they all wanted to lie down and sleep. She was of two minds as to whether she should take them, but it felt odd to go to Nan's without them.

Forcing them out again, and carrying Thaddeus, she walked slowly toward her grandmother's place. When she got there, she found the remaining stepping stones were still in a row, leading from the sidewalk to Nan's patio. She crossed over them, in case the gardener came out and told her off again.

Nan was watching her. She chuckled with delight when she saw the whole crew cross the lawn.

Mugs raced toward Nan to give her a bark of welcome and a kiss. Nan didn't seem to mind the slobbery wet kisses Mugs delivered on a regular basis. Goliath, on the other hand, appeared to be jealous and hopped up into Nan's lap and completely overwhelmed the space. Thaddeus was more concerned with the cake on the table. Although he had just eaten, he was working away on a corner of the treat.

"I do love these animals," Nan said. "They truly are a delight."

"They are, indeed," Doreen said. She gave Nan a hug and sat down to see a pot of tea steeping.

"And I like having you close," Nan said with a big smile. She motioned at the teapot. "By the time I make it, you're almost here."

"Perfectly steeped," Doreen said. "It's a bit longer than that, but who's counting minutes?"

"Exactly." Nan leaned forward. "So what else have you found out?"

"You mean, what else have *you* found out? Right?" Doreen asked.

"Not a whole lot," Nan said. "But you went to see Penny, and you also talked to Mack's mom, so both of those ladies must have known something."

"Do you know anything about Alan Hornby?"

"No," Nan said, frowning. "He was another one of those young men in Johnny's friend group, right?"

"Yes, he was," Doreen said. "More of a fringe member though."

"*Hmm.*"

"Also found out that George helped identify the two boys killed in the car accident."

"Well, that's interesting," Nan said. "I wonder why he did that."

"I think to make sure it wasn't Johnny," Doreen said. "It was Johnny's car the boys were driving when they died."

"Is there any reason why George would misidentify the victims?" Nan pursed her lips and stared across the green lawn.

To Doreen it looked like Nan stared across the years. "I wondered that myself," Doreen said. "But there wouldn't be any reason to do so. He'd have to be hiding his own actions or trying to protect somebody else."

"Most of us would do a lot to protect those we love,"

Nan said with a beaming smile.

"True enough," Doreen said. "But that still doesn't explain why George would in this case. The boys were friends of his brother's. I don't imagine there was any great loyalty or attachment on George's part."

"But, if George wanted his brother out of his life, then that's a good way to do it," Nan said with surprising insight.

Doreen chuckled. "Sure. At least then George would know Johnny was gone, but nobody else would. However, according to Penny, George spent his life and a lot of money trying to track down his brother. So I can't imagine George would have put that much effort into keeping up the pretense. Not after the first few years."

"No," Nan said. "But then you never know."

A tiny birdlike voice called out to Nan from the inside of her apartment. "Nan. Nan."

Nan's face turned thunderous. She lowered her voice and said, "Don't answer."

Doreen raised an eyebrow and studied her grandmother's face. "Why not?" she asked in a whisper.

"She's always bugging me," Nan said. "Maisie is a pest."

"Maybe Maisie is lonely," Doreen corrected.

"*Humph*." Nan snorted as she settled back.

"Oh, there you are." A tiny woman with a shock of lavender hair stepped through Nan's living room onto the patio. She turned her bright face toward Doreen. "You must be the granddaughter."

"Yes," Doreen said with a smile. "I'm Doreen."

Maisie caught sight of Thaddeus eating the bread. "Oh my." Her smile fell away. "Isn't that dirty?"

"Isn't what dirty?" Nan snapped. She stroked Thaddeus's back and shoulders defensively. "Thaddeus is hungry.

Why should you care?"

Doreen was quite perturbed at her grandmother's manner. She'd never seen her like this.

"That may be," Maisie said with a sniff, "but that bird is walking all over your table."

"Well, honestly, Goliath would too," Doreen said with a laugh. "If we let him, that is."

Maisie looked horrified at the idea.

"I guess you don't have any pets?"

Maisie shook her head. "No. I could never handle the hair or the dirtiness. Animals carry disease, you know," she said in a conversational tone, as if thinking—and heaven only knew where she got that thought from—that the two women listening to her would share her point of view. "Animals are terrible that way."

Nan rolled her eyes toward Doreen, who was hardpressed to keep the smile off her face. "Maisie, what did you want?"

For a moment Maisie looked confused.

Nan pointed back at her living room. "There's a reason I didn't answer the door, dear. I have company."

Maisie gave her a finger pointing. "Hardly. Doreen is family. That's not the same thing at all."

Watching the play between the two women was fascinating. It gave Doreen a different insight into her grandmother's life here. Doreen didn't understand the relationship between the two women, but it looked obvious it wasn't all that easy or smooth.

"I'm pretty sure Joe is looking for you," Nan said.

"Oh, that's all right," Maisie said blithely. "He's in my room, resting." She batted her eyes at Nan. "He does need his rest afterward, doesn't he?" And then, with a sweet smile and a chuckle, she disappeared.

Doreen gave a horrified gasp. "Did she mean what I think she meant?"

Nan nodded. "The two of them are carrying on like they're eighteen," she said. "I don't mind in the least, but it would be nice if they kept it to themselves. But Maisie is one of those shrieking partners."

"Oh, dear," Doreen said, struggling to stifle the laughter threatening to pour outward. "Most people like that are attention-getters."

Nan nodded. "I couldn't have said it better."

"So is it just Maisie who pisses you off?"

Nan gave an irritable shrug of her shoulders. "Not really," she said, "but Joe used to be my friend." The emphasis was on the last word.

Fascinated, Doreen studied Nan's face. "Did Joe ditch you for Maisie?" she asked gently.

Nan shrugged. "No, I ditched him first. But he sure didn't take long to pick up with Maisie."

"I rather imagine it has a lot to do with the perception of time," Doreen said. "When you're here, I think mortality is a little more evident. Maybe you guys don't wait the usual length of time that goes along with a breakup."

"Some men never wait," Nan said with a sniff. "And Joe is one of them."

"That's good to know," Doreen said. "At least now you won't make the mistake of going out with him again."

"Not too many men in here are any good anymore," Nan said. "I do keep the blue pills in my drawer. But it's kind of depressing when you have to give them to the men yourself."

Doreen sat back, choking on the words threatening to

come out.

"Don't look so shocked, my dear," Nan said drily. "You'd be a lot better off if you and Mack would get over the courtship part of your relationship too. A good old romp in bed would suit you two just fine."

Doreen laughed out loud. "Thanks for the advice, Nan," she said cheerfully. "Not that I'm looking for any."

"Of course you aren't," Nan said. "Which is why it's so much easier to give it to you. If you were to ask my advice, that'd be a pain in the arse. But the fact that you're not means I get to comment as I see fit." Then she broke into bright laughter.

There wasn't a lot Doreen could say to that. At least Nan was laughing again. "Did Joe or Maisie know any of the kids in the gang back then?"

"I don't know why they would," she said with a curl of her lip. "They're both newcomers."

"What does *that* mean?" Doreen asked with a laugh. "Have they only been here for twenty years?"

Nan straightened her back and looked at her granddaughter. "I hear the laughter in your voice, but, until you've lived in Kelowna as long as I have, you don't understand how the newcomers are so very different from all of us oldies."

"Well, if they are newcomers after twenty years," Doreen said, "I must be in the toddler category."

"You're my family," Nan said. "And that changes things entirely."

"I'm sure Joe and Maisie have family too," she said gently.

"Whatever," Nan said. Then she giggled. "But I did take fifty bucks off Maisie earlier."

"You what?" Doreen was afraid to ask.

"I bet her about Joe and a blue pill."

"Oh, dear. Nan, I really don't want to hear about this."

"It's all right, but that's why Maisie came over. She was trying to tell me, in her way, that he didn't need the blue pill."

"So how did you earn fifty bucks off her?"

"I bet he wouldn't need it," Nan said, "because I had given him the blue pill earlier."

"You gave him a blue pill so he could have sex with Maisie?" Doreen asked in shock. "And then you bet Maisie he wouldn't need one when she went to bed with him?"

"Now you got it," Nan said.

"I think that's cheating, Nan." But a part of her wanted to giggle out loud.

"All is fair in love and war," Nan said complacently.

Chapter 15

Friday Later Afternoon …

"OKAY, DEFINITELY TIME for a change of conversation. Do you know anybody here who is an oldie?" Doreen asked with a smile. "If so, maybe you could ask them about Johnny."

"I have," Nan said. "But nobody appears to know anything."

"Well, it was a faint hope. But you did call me for something, didn't you?"

Nan looked at her in surprise, and then her face lit up. "Oh my, I completely forgot." She hopped up, walked into her living quarters, and came back out. "I asked Richie because I know he's been here since Kelowna was basically established," she said. "Lovely man."

Doreen desperately wanted to ask if he needed blue pills but needed to keep the conversation straight and not let her grandmother go sideways.

"He did say not all was well within the group."

"How does he know?"

"The girl in question who died a year ago was his niece. His great-niece. And he said she had a lot of trouble with the gang."

"Gang, meaning all of them?"

"Yes. Apparently she was a little too free and easy with her affections," Nan said. "And her great-uncle didn't like that one bit. But, when he questioned her about it, she said she stopped going out with Johnny because she found someone else."

"Any idea who that was?" Doreen asked, sinking back into her chair. "I don't know that it matters at this stage, but it would be interesting to know who."

"I'm not sure," Nan said. "But, if anybody could figure it out, it would be you."

"What's Richie's last name?"

"Smithson," Nan said. "He is a lovely chap."

"How old is he?"

"I think he's eighty-two, maybe eighty-three," Nan said. "It doesn't really matter though. His mind is as sharp as anything."

"Good," Doreen said. "Maybe you could ask him some questions about the accident."

Nan reached across the little bistro table, pulled up her phone, and sent a text.

"Did you just text him?"

Nan lifted her face to study her granddaughter. "Are you having some memory problems, dear? You just asked me to question him about the accident."

Oh, dear. Another rabbit-hole moment. Doreen shook her head. "No, I was wondering if you were though because—just moments ago—you told me nobody here knew anything."

"Sure, but that's not Richie. Richie is different," she said with a wave of her hand. "He's not anybody. He's special."

And again the questions were itching to flow from her lips, but she dared not. Then she couldn't help herself. "Special in what way?" she asked.

"Not that way," Nan said shortly. "No better way to ruin a friendship than having sex, my dear." She lifted her head again from her phone, holding it, as if waiting for Richie to get back to her immediately. "You should remember that with Mack."

Doreen stopped and stared. "You're the one who just told me that Mack and I would do well for having a romp together." She snorted. "How does it figure that now you are telling me not to?"

"Oh, my dear, I'm not telling you *not* to," she said. "Absolutely go and do it. But, if it's not for the right reasons, you'll find you're not friends at the end of it."

"Right," Doreen said, shaking her head. "Did you hear back from Richie yet?"

"No, not yet," Nan said, waving her phone. "You'd have heard a ring, dear. Maybe you should go home and rest. You do seem to be a little off today."

Doreen snapped her lips closed. *Somebody* was off, all right. But she didn't know if Nan was taking her down that weird and wonderful rabbit hole again or if she was just playing with her. Sometimes Doreen couldn't really tell.

Just then Nan's phone warbled in her hand. "Richie says the two men who died were in Johnny's car."

"But we know that," Doreen said patiently.

"So then why did you ask?" Nan asked in irritation.

"Nan ..."

Her grandmother sighed and settled back. "I do appear to be a little irritable today."

"I'm so sorry," Doreen said. "Maybe I'll go home now."

"No, no, no, no," Nan said with a smile, patting Doreen's hand. "I'm the one who's sorry. I guess Maisie upset me more than I expected."

"I'm sorry for that too." Obviously her grandmother felt jilted that her lover had quickly found someone else. "Maybe Richie will have some other information tomorrow." Doreen pushed back her chair and stood.

Nan's phone warbled again. "Ritchie says the accident was caused by another vehicle."

Doreen's butt thumped back down on the chair.

"Like a hit-and-run?"

Nan was still reading. "Something like that. Car went over a cliff, and the cops never found the other vehicle."

"Then how would they know somebody ran them off the road?"

"There was a witness," Nan said, looking at her in surprise. "Didn't I tell you that?"

Doreen pinched the bridge of her nose. "No, you didn't tell me that. Who was the witness?"

"The girlfriend of course."

"So she wasn't in the boys' car, but she saw another car run them off the road?"

Nan nodded. "That's what Richie says. She was adamant another vehicle was involved."

"Why would she be so adamant about it?"

Nan shrugged. "Who knows? It happened at that really bad corner on the outskirts of town. Big hairpin turn up in the Black Mountain area."

"Well then, maybe a vehicle didn't run them off the road," Doreen said, "if it's such a bad corner."

"Which is also why the police didn't necessarily believe her."

"Of course they didn't," Doreen said. "Because it sounds like she was making it up. And what was she doing there at that time? Because that makes even less sense."

"Apparently she was driving behind the guys," Nan said. "And she'd tried to get help for them, but the vehicle was already on fire."

"So she called the police and told them that another vehicle had run them off the road, correct?" Doreen wanted to make sure she understood what supposedly went on.

"Yes, exactly. And now she's dead, so we can't ask her anything."

Doreen felt like she was going in circles. Sometimes Nan's mind seemed to be even more circuitous than usual. "Unless ..." She leaned in and studied Nan's face. "Unless the girlfriend wasn't alone in the car."

Nan immediately picked up her phone and sent another text. They waited for a long moment; then Richie sent back an answer. "No, she wasn't alone."

Doreen groaned; getting information was like pulling teeth here. "Who was in the car with her?"

"According to Richie, Alan Hornby."

Chapter 16

Friday Evening …

AS DOREEN AND her animals strolled home, she pondered through the muddle of information from Nan. Doreen didn't know if Nan had been really tired today or just upset because of Maisie. But, either way, Nan's mind had been definitely irrational. Was Nan getting Alzheimer's? How she could possibly ask her grandmother to go to the doctor to get some testing done she didn't know, because she would be more than a little horrified and insulted to hear about Doreen's train of thought.

But really, with all this muddling of conversations, it was harder to sort out what was true and what was false. Maisie had obviously hurt Nan with the affair with Joe. At least that was Doreen's take on it. Still, her grandmother would get over it, like she'd gotten over many other breakups in her life. Maybe Nan was more upset that Joe had chosen Maisie as Nan's replacement and not somebody else. It was amazing how many times people were okay with a lover going off and dallying with somebody else, as long as the previous lover approved of the someone else.

Doreen wandered home, contemplating this Hornby

character. When she got to her house, she found an unfamiliar vehicle parked out front. She walked around the back of the vehicle and took a quick photo of the license plate. As she walked up to the front door to see where he might be sitting or waiting for her, she found nobody there. She walked around to the backyard with Mugs sniffing heavily at her feet and found a late-middle-aged man sitting on her back steps.

As she approached, he hopped up and gave her a big wide smile. "Hi," he said.

"Hi," she cautiously said in response. "What can I do for you?"

"For one, you can stop poking into things that don't have anything to do with you."

"Such as?" Her head tilted as she studied him. He had to be about fifty years old, maybe a little older.

"I'm Hornby, Alan Hornby," he said, "and you keep asking questions about me."

"Who would have told you that?"

"You gotta understand the old folks' home," he said. "Richie told my aunt Velma that you were asking questions."

"I am," she said, "because nobody has seen Johnny since he disappeared."

"What does that got to do with me?" he asked. "And Johnny disappeared decades ago."

"Maybe nothing," Doreen said. "I was trying to cross the Ts and dot the Is. Apparently you were in the car with Susan when you saw another vehicle swipe the two guys driving Johnny's car. Is that correct?"

He frowned, his head also tilting to the side as he studied her. "What business is it of yours? Where did you hear that?"

"I heard it," she said, "while I was visiting Nan. I think it came from Richie because that was his great-niece who was in the vehicle with you."

Hornby glared. "Man, I tell you. Those old folks, if they don't have something to gossip about, they make up something to gossip about," he said.

"Isn't that the truth?" she said. "But, so far, you haven't answered the question."

"You're right there," he said, "because, to be truthful, I can't remember anymore." He tapped his head. "It was a long time ago."

"You don't remember whether you saw two good friends die in a fiery crash of a stolen vehicle right in front of you? Talk about suspicious." Not that she had proof the vehicle had been stolen, but there was also no proof Johnny had sold it either.

She studied Hornby, looking for any signs of deceit. The trouble was, he had that big beaming smile that said he knew she had no proof and that, with the girl dead, nobody knew anything, so he could say whatever the hell he wanted.

"Nope, my memory is not very good anymore," he said. "Too much booze and drugs."

That was just possible enough for her to consider it. "It's a little hard to believe you don't remember *any* of it," she said.

"I remember Johnny's disappearance," Hornby said, "mostly because it was on all our minds for such a long time. We had absolutely no way of knowing what happened to him. And we all wanted to know."

"Did you though?" she asked. "Did you really?"

He glared at her. "What are you suggesting?"

"I don't know what I'm suggesting," she said honestly.

"But think about it. Johnny disappears. You have two good friends die in a fiery crash in front of you in Johnny's car. Followed by ... by what? Who was driving the vehicle that ran them off the road?"

"The police never found out," he said. "And I don't understand what difference it makes all these years later. They're still dead."

"Maybe it doesn't make any difference. Maybe it was an accident. Then again, maybe it wasn't," she said. "But it makes a difference since Penny still has no idea what happened to her brother-in-law."

The humor drained from his face. Hornby nodded. "I know George was completely cracked up about it. George and Johnny were close."

"They were close," she said, "according to Penny. But were they close according to Johnny?"

Hornby took a minute to process that; then he nodded. "Yeah, I think they were. Johnny hung on to George as the stalwart part of his world. Once their father passed away, it was just the two of them. He had a medallion he got from his father. He wore it all the time. Played with it sometimes around his neck. It was like a piece of his father that Johnny carried with him."

"We found that," Doreen said. "We found it broken in the yard where he was last seen."

Alan just stared at her.

She could see him withdrawing slightly inside. Was he looking down memory lane? "How much did he care about that medallion?" she asked.

"He'd never take it off," he said. "And I mean *never*."

She nodded. "So, considering we found the medallion— and we found his dagger too, by the way—we have to wonder what happened to Johnny."

"He was probably killed by a drug dealer," Hornby snapped. "He was always trying to score drugs for us."

"Maybe," she said. "But, in that case, there'd be a body."

"Not if the drug dealer was scared of what he'd done and decided to take the body and deep-six it somewhere."

"*Deep-six it,*" she said conversationally. "That sounds more like dropping it into the ocean."

"Considering we live by a lake," he said in a dry tone, "I hardly think the ocean would come into play."

"Point taken," she said with a big smile. "However, I think, after all this time, the body probably would have shown up again."

But then she remembered the vehicle she had just found with a little boy and the older man. "Unless he drowned in the lake inside a vehicle."

"In which case," Hornby said, "it should have been his own vehicle because then he'd have made a clean getaway, and nobody would ever know what happened to him."

"True." Stumped, she just stood here.

"If you're trying to find a killer," he said gently, "you're barking up the wrong tree. We were all messed up back then. Johnny was messed up back then. George was the mainstay in his life, but they fought all the time. Just like all brothers fight."

"Understood. Thanks for answering the questions."

He chuckled. "No problem. How about a cup of coffee?" He motioned his arm toward her kitchen.

She hesitated, not really sure why.

He saw the hesitation and chuckled. "I guess you're Mack's property then, huh?" He hopped up, gave her a mock salute, and walked away.

Chapter 17

Saturday Morning ...

THE NEXT MORNING Hornby's words still burned a hole in Doreen's head. *She belonged to Mack.* It wasn't that it was right or wrong, just that such a complete connotation of ownership was too much like her marriage. She didn't want any more of that in her life.

To think somebody was making those kinds of insinuations, making a mockery of her friendship with Mack ... well, it was just wrong.

She stared gloomily out the window, wondering why the clouds always seemed to match her moods. "Too bad I don't have the power to create sunshine everywhere," she muttered, feeling off since her conversation with Hornby last night.

She almost chuckled because plenty of self-help gurus out there would tell her, if she switched her mood, then everything around her would appear bright and sunny too.

"Too bad I'm not of that ilk." She poured her first cup of coffee and stepped out on the veranda. While she had outdoor furniture on both the veranda and the front porch—courtesy of Nan—Doreen wandered down the steps and across the backyard so she could look at the creek. Thaddeus wandered behind her, pecking away at various things on the ground. Goliath had raced ahead, dashing around like a crazy cat. Still, he was happy, so she could hardly begrudge him that moment. Mugs uncharacteristically moped alongside her.

"What's the matter, buddy? Didn't you get enough sleep last night?"

He didn't bark or even woof. He didn't pick up his pace. He just dragged his feet beside her.

"Yeah, I kind of feel the same way today."

If anybody else heard her talking to all the animals like she did, they'd think something was wrong with Doreen. *Maybe so.* But the truth was, she preferred having her animal family around more than a lot of other people. Particularly that guy, Alan Hornby, from last night. She shouldn't let his words get to her, but it was hard not to.

She was still outside at the creek when she heard her phone ring. She'd left it on the kitchen table. She shrugged and said, "Tough. Whoever it is, they'll have to call back." It was probably Mack. And, for a perverse reason based entirely on Hornby's conversation last night, she figured she would just let Mack wait. She wasn't here to jump when he said jump.

Immediately she felt terrible because it wasn't his fault. "Come on, guys. Let's go in and see what Mack wants."

She sipped her coffee as she walked back. The animals were all uncharacteristically silent now. In the kitchen, she picked up her phone. Sure enough, Mack had called. She called him back.

When he answered, she said, "I was out in the garden."

"Good," he said. "It's Saturday. You should be enjoying

yourself."

"When you don't work Monday to Friday," she said, "Saturday has as little meaning as Monday does."

"Well, that's a good thing," he said with a laugh.

"Did you do anything with that medallion?"

"I sent it to forensics," he said. "Don't forget. Just because the case has never been solved doesn't mean it's been forgotten."

"No, but you don't have man-hours to keep putting work into these cases," she said, "and that seems very sad and wrong too."

"We can't take our efforts away from current crimes either," he said.

"I know. Budget, budget, budget."

"Exactly. You're in an odd mood this morning."

She groaned. "Yeah, I had a visitor last night."

"What?" he cried out. "Are you okay?"

"Oh, sorry," she said. "It wasn't an intruder. When I came home from Nan's place, a car was in the drive, and nobody was on the front porch, so I went to the backyard to find a visitor sitting on my back steps."

"Were you expecting this person?"

"No," she said. "It was Alan Hornby. He wanted me to stop asking questions about Johnny's disappearance."

The silence lasted on the phone for all of ten seconds, then Mack exploded. "What? Did he threaten you?"

"I think he was almost flattering me. Maybe flirting a little. I'm kind of out of the game, so I'm not sure. But he did suggest we go into my house and have a cup of coffee together, which I not-so-politely declined," she said with a note of humor. "Maybe he got the better part of that deal because it is still *my* coffee."

"Your coffee is great," he said. "What else did he say?"

"He doesn't really know anything. He was in a vehicle with Susan, when a car sideswiped Johnny's car ahead of them, and their buddies were run off the road."

"They saw a vehicle run the two guys off the road?"

"That's what the girlfriend told her uncle. But she's dead, and her uncle Richie told Nan. Richie also told Velma, who is Hornby's aunt, that I was asking questions. Then Hornby came over here to tell me to stop. He also said he can't remember anything about the accident, but, if he said they were run off the road back then, then that must have been what happened. Now he's saying too much drugs and alcohol over the years have caused his memory to dim."

"Is that right?" Mack said in a dry tone. "I don't doubt the drugs and alcohol have certainly had an impact on his memory, but, when you see your two good friends burn out in front of you, I highly doubt you forget that."

"Can you check the file and see if anything was mentioned about the car being run off the road?" She sighed. "Richie just told Nan about it, but that should have been something the cops were all over back then at the time of Susan's statement."

"Sure, they would have been," he said. "I can check and see what's in the file. I don't remember offhand. I'm not sure I saw anything about it actually."

"That's what I'm afraid of," she said. "It's been a long time, and memories slip. Maybe they didn't see or say anything. Or it's just a convenient excuse."

"That's certainly possible."

"What are you doing today?" she asked.

"Not sure yet," he said. "I'm hoping to spend some time doing yard work, and I'll visit my mom for a bit. I'll drop by with the cash I owe you today."

"That would be good," she said. "I need to go shopping again."

"Right. We were supposed to do pasta, weren't we?" he asked in surprise. "Was that today?"

"Maybe," she said, "if that's okay with you."

"Sure," he said. "I'll go shopping and pick up what I need. It slipped my mind. I'm really sorry about that," he said, his tone apologetic and surprised at the same time.

She understood how he felt. Normally he was very good at remembering things like that. "It's no biggie," she said. "What time do you want to eat?" She checked the clock. "It's early, not even nine o'clock yet."

"We'll plan on pasta for dinner tonight. If you want to come with me, we can go shopping now. I could drop the stuff and you back off, then go about my day, whatever that'll be, and come back later this afternoon. We can cook then."

She brightened. "That might not be a bad idea because then I can see what you buy too."

"Right. I tend to forget shopping is something you're not used to either."

"Unless it's for one-thousand-dollar shoes," she said in a dry tone.

"Seriously?"

"Yeah, I've had a few of those." She groaned. "I wish right now I had all that money back in my pocket."

"I'm sorry," he said. "I'm sorry you've had to reassess how you live."

"I hear you, but I'm much better off where I am," she said. "Much happier."

"Good," he said. "I'll swing by in about twenty

minutes."

Just enough time for another cup of coffee. She poured herself a second cup and put on a piece of toast. "Getting a little low on peanut butter here, guys." She wandered around, making a short list of a few necessities, like toilet paper. She raised her eyebrows at the single roll left. "That ain't happening."

She could use treats for Mugs. And, after all the omelets, she needed more eggs. But thankfully Mack had bought the last ones anyway. She didn't have much in her fridge, so she could definitely use more cheese and sliced meat. Sandwiches were a standard she thankfully loved.

As soon as she was done, she grabbed her purse and walked to the front door. "Mugs, I have to leave you behind, buddy."

He woofed several times. He hated being left behind. Maybe because he thought Goliath would pick on him; she didn't know. She reset the alarm and stepped out the front door, locking it.

She walked down to the end of the driveway just as Mack pulled in. She hopped into the front of his truck and said, "Mugs is not happy."

He chuckled. "I don't think it's a bad thing for him to get used to being alone for a little while."

"Maybe not," she said, "but I worry he'll turn the fancy furniture into toothpicks."

At that, Mack laughed. "That image is a good way to start the day."

"Good for you," she said. "I woke up feeling like the world was against me, and no sunshine was left anywhere."

"Do you think it was because of Hornby's visit last night?"

"I don't know," she said. "I feel like people are lying to me, lying to everyone else. I really think Johnny is dead, and people know more than they're letting on."

"Who is it you think is lying?"

"Hornby, for one," she said. "But I'm not sure which part he's lying about."

Mack drove straight to the grocery store and hopped out. Doreen got out on her side, once again remembering Hornby's words about her being Mack's possession.

When he grabbed a cart and waited for her, she realized they were acting like any normal couple, and anybody outside their circle would assume they were dating. A part of her really liked that, but another part worried she and Mack were giving the wrong impression. Still, it wasn't her fault that others just assumed something.

As they wandered through the grocery store, she stopped in front of the fresh vegetables, looking for her salad and sandwich stuff. She picked up a head of lettuce, some radishes, green onions, cucumbers, and tomatoes. Happy with that, she turned to watch Mack in surprise as he grabbed carrots, celery, lots of tomatoes, and something dark and leafy.

"What's that?" she asked.

He looked at the big leaves in his hand. "This is kale."

She nodded. "I've heard of kale shakes and kale chips, but I didn't think it would look like that."

"This is what it looks like," he said. "This is the black kind, but it's always nice to have a bit of green veggies."

"You mean, *black* veggies," she said with a smirk.

He nodded.

She put her groceries in the top little basket, and he filled the base. She wasn't even sure what to do with half of the vegetables he put into his part of the cart. She found herself wondering if she should get her own. "Am I taking up too much of your space?" she asked hesitantly.

He looked at her in surprise. "You mean, that little bit?" He shook his head. "No, that's nothing. Surely you're getting more than that, aren't you?"

She gazed back at him blandly. "I like my veggies and dip, and I have enough here for sandwiches too."

"It's barely enough to keep a hamster alive."

She shrugged, walked to the fruit section, found a few apples on sale, and picked up two bananas to add to her pile.

He chose a big bunch of bananas and bagged a dozen apples.

She stared at him. "That means you're eating like three to four pieces of fruit a day."

He counted the fruit and shrugged. "I might not get back to the store in the next week, you know?"

As they walked down the aisle, she saw a man smirking at them. She froze, and somebody behind her stepped into her. She yelped. Mack turned, and the person behind her apologized.

Flustered, Doreen motioned with her hand. "Sorry, it was my fault." She hurried forward past Mack.

"What was that all about?"

"Hornby," she snapped. "He's up ahead."

While Mack scanned the crowd around her, she deliberately kept her head down so she didn't have to look at Hornby. As she and Mack continued their shopping, she found mushrooms, but they had a hefty price tag. She really would like a few, if only for raw munching. She bagged four small ones, putting them with her items.

Mack leaned over and said, "Are you deliberately buying

420

a couple items because that's all you want or because they're expensive?"

"It's a combination," she said.

He didn't say another word, but he filled a bag with mushrooms and tossed it into the cart.

She looked at it and smiled. "Can you really use that much food?"

"Absolutely," he said. "Lots of this is going into the spaghetti sauce."

She scrunched up her face. "Which ones?"

He chuckled and separated out the celery, onions, tomatoes, and mushrooms. "I've got a bottle of red wine that I'll open and use with it too."

"Interesting," she said. "Red wine in bourguignon maybe."

"Do you know how to make a beef bourguignon?" he asked with interest.

She shook her head. "No, but I like eating it." She stared at all the vegetables he'd pointed out. "It will be interesting to see how you make all of that turn into something yummy. Personally I don't like celery."

"It doesn't matter if you do or not," he said with a grin. "It goes into the spaghetti sauce. And we need garlic too."

She watched him in fascination as he picked up some weird little clove things. "Don't you bake those whole and serve them with camembert?"

"Maybe *you* did," he said. "But the rest of world chops it up and sautés it with meat."

She followed him as he added eggs, bacon, hamburger, and milk in the cart, stacking up a grocery bill that her heart would have loved to afford. But, as it was, she couldn't justify that kind of money much less know how to cook most of it.

When they got to the bakery, she picked up several loaves of bread and several tubs of peanut butter to go with her milk for her tea and more eggs for a new omelet—and she added in some cheese.

Mack looked at her purchases. "Well, it's growing slightly, but it looks like I'm a pig and you're a bird."

"Not at all," she said. "I wouldn't know what to do with most of what you have."

"Good point." He motioned toward the cashier. "Let's go."

She pulled into the first nearly empty register. As she unloaded her groceries, she looked up to see Hornby two aisles over, staring at her. He had a big grin on his face.

"Don't look now," she said in a low tone that only Mack could hear, "but Hornby is at eleven o'clock."

Mack looked up and checked out the guy who had been hassling her. "What's that smirk mean?"

"I think it has to do with one of the comments he made to me."

"What was that?"

She shook her head. "I don't want to talk about it."

Mack shot her an odd look.

She shrugged. "I think it's safe to say, Hornby is one of those troublemaking kinds of people."

"Yeah? Is that a new talent, or did he make trouble back then too?"

"I rather imagine he made a ton of trouble back then," she said. "He's probably gotten better at being subtler about it now."

"Interesting insight," he said.

She shrugged. "Not really. It's just a fact of life. People

get more experienced and become sneakier at causing pain. And they learn how to maximize the pain inflicted. It's manipulation at its best." Sensing his odd look, she refused to look at him.

After a moment Mack said, "Do you think Hornby had something to manipulate?"

"I didn't believe anything that came out of his mouth," she said, "so I assume he had an awful lot to do with either Johnny's disappearance or his buddies who died in the vehicle."

At that, Mack sucked in his breath, and his gaze turned lethal as he studied her face. "You think Hornby had something to do with their deaths?"

She tossed him a look. "It was one of the first things I thought when he said he couldn't remember anything about the accident."

"But that would also imply Susan knew all about it."

"According to her uncle, she kept telling everybody who would listen that a vehicle had run the guys off the road."

"And?" he prompted.

"Maybe a vehicle did," she said drily. "Maybe she was trying to tell the cops without implicating herself. Maybe the vehicle that ran their friends off the road was the one they were driving."

Mack nodded thoughtfully. "I didn't see anything in the files, but I haven't had a chance to get through the whole thing."

"I'm sure not much is in there," she said. "Johnny sat down on the bench, was having a beer, and the next thing his family knew, he was gone. Nobody supposedly knows anything about him. Yet the medallion he would never part with, the vehicle he adored, and his favorite dagger were all left behind."

"When you put it that way," Mack said, "it does sound like something very suspicious happened, doesn't it?"

"Absolutely," she said. "I'm pretty damn sure Hornby was a big part of it."

"We're back to that assumption thing."

"Absolutely no way to prove anything," she said. "Everybody involved is dead except him."

"Convenient, isn't it?"

"Except Susan died of breast cancer," she said. "Last year as I heard it."

"Huh," he said. "Maybe we should take a closer look at that death."

Doreen froze, slowly turned to him, and in a low voice asked, "Do you think he could have killed her?"

"I don't know," Mack said. "Depends if she got ill and had a change of heart, wanted to cleanse her soul of some wrongdoing."

"And how would we ever know that?" she asked with a chuckle.

"Maybe you should talk to Richie," he said.

"That's a great idea."

Chapter 18

Saturday Midmorning ...

MACK WAS GONE; the groceries were put away, and she once again sat on the front stoop with a cup of coffee. She looked at her coffee and said, "I need a job, so I can keep drinking you at the same pace I have been. Talk about addictive."

Still, a full-time job wouldn't give her many free hours for her hobby. Something she was loving more and more every day—of course, she was still riding the wave of success, which reminded her of her current case. And right at the top of the things for her to do was talk to Richie.

She wondered how to get a hold of him. Was it fair to go through Nan? And would it bring up sad memories if she asked him questions about his great-niece? It seemed hardly fair when they'd only lost her a year ago. Would he have dealt with the loss mostly by now?

She pulled out her phone and sent Nan a text, asking about Richie's great-niece's health.

Nan called her. "What have you found out?"

"Nothing really," Doreen said feebly. "I just wondered what her state of mind was before she died."

"Richie is sitting here, playing poker with me," she said. "I'll put you on Speakerphone."

Doreen heard cards slapping on the table.

"I'm here," said a man with a rough masculine voice. "What's this about my great-niece?"

"I'm sorry to disturb you," Doreen said. "I was wondering about her state of mind before she died."

"What kind of a question is that?" he asked, snorting. "She was pretty darn sad. Knew she was dying of cancer. She was also in a lot of pain."

"Did she give any signs that she wanted to, you know, go to confession or had trauma she wanted to … ask forgiveness for?" She winced. "I know that's a really rough way to say it. I wanted to figure out if she wished she hadn't done something in her life or had done something better."

What an idiot she was. But this was better than her actual question. What she really wanted to know was did his great-niece confess to any murders before she died. And who could answer that question?

"She was very melancholy at the end," Richie said gruffly. "Sad for all the things she wouldn't get to do."

"I'm sorry for her," Doreen said. "She was young still."

"Yes," he said, "but she also knew she was paying the price for a life lived hard."

"Drugs and alcohol, you mean?"

"That too," he said. "She was also a thief for a while, due to her drug habit."

"Ah, so maybe she was sorry about that?"

"Definitely," he said. "But, if you're asking if she had anything to do with the deaths of those two boys or Johnny, you're barking up the wrong tree. She was a very gentle soul."

Doreen held back her gasp when he acknowledged what she'd been hinting at. She hadn't known the right way to say it. "Do you think there's any chance she was in the vehicle that ran those two boys off the road?" she asked quietly. "If she was a passenger, and Hornby had been the one driving?"

"I don't know," he said, his voice thickening. "I have to admit though that the thought did cross my mind a time or two. According to her, the vehicle that hit Johnny's car was patched with lots of pieces from other vehicles," he said with a chuckle. "It was a very noticeable vehicle out there."

"That's what I mean. If there had been yet another vehicle on that road, surely the cops would have found it."

"Well, you would have thought so," he said. "But the truth of the matter was, they never did. Susan said she gave them the description over and over again, but, without a license plate, they could do little. They did put out an alert, but the vehicle was never seen again."

Just like Johnny. But she kept that thought to herself. "Do you remember her description of the vehicle?"

"She said it was a small car with lots of different colored panels. But I think the real issue you should be looking at is, why would somebody run them off the road?"

"Right," she said. "We're back to lack of motive."

"Except they were all into drugs," Richie said with a hardness that surprised her. "I did everything I could to get that girl off those, but, once they got into her system, she was lost."

"I'm sorry," Doreen said. "I won't bother you any longer. If you think of anything else Susan might have said, or if she might have kept journals or notebooks or a diary or something," Doreen said hopefully, "keep me in mind."

"You're really looking into Johnny's disappearance,

huh?"

"Penny is still looking for answers," Doreen said without hesitation. "I'd like to see her get that before her time runs out."

"Like George," he said with a *harrumph*. "That was a sad day."

"Also the day that George helped ID the two boys," she said. "I'm sure, in the back of his mind, he was afraid one of those bodies was Johnny's."

"I think we all thought that," he said. "It was his car. So who else would be driving that sucker?"

"Good point," she said and hung up.

Immediately she called Mack. "Hey," she said as soon as she heard his voice. "Can you check in the cold case file if anybody did a forensic check on the vehicle the two men died in?"

"I've got the file here," he said, "but I haven't gone through it all. Obviously the forensic team went over the vehicle. What aspect is bothering you?"

She grinned, happy he wasn't asking her to butt out. "We know for sure it was Johnny's car. But do we know for sure that, A, Johnny wasn't in the trunk, dead already or dying from the vehicle crash, and, B, did any forensic evidence show something like a ton of blood to say that maybe Johnny had been there?"

"After a bad fire like that, blood wouldn't have been traceable, but a body in the trunk would have been found," he said. "Notes in here state Johnny had no reason to disappear and made no further contact with his family, but nobody could prove one way or another that he was deceased. He's still a missing person's case."

"Did Penny or George ever try to declare him legally

dead?" she asked.

"No notes are in the file about it," he said, "and it's not something necessarily that would have been followed up on here. That would be a question to ask Penny."

"Maybe," Doreen said. "I'm not sure how much tolerance Penny will have for these questions though."

"She's the one who asked you to look into it, right? So, therefore, she shouldn't have a problem with you asking for clarification."

"So far, she has been decent," Doreen said, "but you never really want to push it."

He chuckled. "I don't think you understand what that point is. You're forever pushing everything."

"I'm not that bad. I can see how *you* might feel that way," she admitted. "But I just find this case makes no sense. I mean, when you have a family who you love, why would you walk away?"

He said, "Let me ask you this. You had Nan, and you loved her very much, but still how much contact did you have with her in previous years?"

She could feel his words almost as a visceral blow. "That's not fair."

"No," he said, "it isn't, but extenuating circumstances in your life stopped you from having a closer relationship with Nan. You have to consider maybe something similar happened in this young man's life."

"Like a wife?" she asked cynically. "More likely he was protecting George and Penny."

After a moment of silence, Mack finally said, "That's one angle the police had to look at. Was the family threatened? Was Johnny made to do something to keep his family out of danger? We don't know what went on back then."

"I still think it connects to the group of kids," she said.

"Maybe it does, considering only one person is left alive from that group."

"I think another girl was involved too," Doreen said. "Somebody a little bit on the outside, kind of like Hornby was a little bit on the outside. I don't know her name yet."

"Well track her down," he said humorously. "You seem to have taken over this case completely."

"Can you tell me if any police man-hours are available for this cold case?"

"Depends what comes back from the testing on the medallion," he said seriously. "I expect it to be only Johnny's DNA. Who else's would it be?"

"No clue but it would be nice if someone else's DNA were on it. We'd at least have a suspect to look at."

"At that point the case would become very active, and it wouldn't be a case of *us* doing anything," Mack reminded her in that tone of his that said she would be butting out, whether she liked it or not.

She groaned. "So I bring you all the information to help you move things forward, and then you force me to step back?"

"Remember the 'It's dangerous' part?"

"It's not my fault I always get to the root of the matter, and, by the time I get there, people are a little pissed that I found them out."

"Just like Cecily," he said. "You got into trouble at the end."

"Okay, so *you* can get into trouble this time," she said in exasperation, getting up in a huff and returning to the kitchen for more coffee. "I don't have a death wish, you know? It's not like I'm trying to cause trouble. I'm trying to bring peace and closure for Penny."

"I get that. Penny gets that, and maybe half the world would get that, but whoever might be involved in this case won't give a crap."

"Like Hornby?"

"He really bothered you, didn't he?"

"Not only did he come to my home," she said, "but he also threatened me, and then he was flirting with me."

"Which one bothered you the most?"

She pulled her cell away to stare at it, frowning. "What kind of a question is that?"

"Just wondered how terrified you are of getting back into a relationship. You never seem uncomfortable around me," he said, "but Hornby was directly in your face, pushing the issue."

She hated the direction he was going. "Whatever," she said, dismissing it.

He chuckled. "I'll be over there in a few hours. Try to stay out of trouble."

She tossed her phone on the kitchen table, looked at her animals, and said, "Let's go outside and do some work in the garden. Maybe that'll make me feel better."

Normally gardening was a soothing activity for her, a balm to her troubled soul, not to mention giving her some exercise and helping her to wear off some pent-up energy.

With her gardening gloves, a bottle of water, and her proverbial cup of tea, she headed out to the back corner, where they had pulled up the dilapidated fence and the posts. She figured, if she did the worst part of the weeding at the far back corner first, maybe it would be easier as she got closer to the house.

Setting down her water and tea, she pulled on her gloves.

The corner was filled with what looked like huge pockets of daisies, black-eyed Susans, and maybe some echinacea. It was hard to be sure as most of the plants were just showing the early foliage.

She studied the leaves to confirm this plant was truly echinacea when she heard a soft noise. She spun around but couldn't see anything. Then she heard Mugs chuffing—this weird sound he made that wasn't a bark, wasn't a growl, but like a heavy sniff upon a sniff, with some added background noise. He chuffed his way to the corner of the fence, but it wasn't her fence; it was her neighbor's fence. Mugs stood there, intently investigating everything around him. Goliath, not to be outdone, walked along at his leisure. And then he took off like a golden orange streak.

She followed the cat as she walked closer to the creek. "Goliath! Goliath, stay here please."

Instead of answering her, Goliath remained silent. And the continuous *chuff-chuff-chuff* came from Mugs. Then, in a startling move, Thaddeus hopped on Mugs's back. At this point Mugs was so focused on the trail he was following that he didn't seem to notice the bird.

She studied the two cautiously. "Thaddeus, that might not be the best idea."

"Giddyup, Mugs. Giddyup, Mugs," Thaddeus squawked in a loud voice.

Doreen gasped as Thaddeus tried to ride her dog. Mugs took several hesitant steps forward, then stopped. Thaddeus dug his claws in and pecked at the dog's head. Mugs took off, barking like crazy, racing around in a circle, as if trying to bounce Thaddeus off—which didn't work—but finally Mugs slowed and returned to the same spot. Thaddeus, apparently happy with his ride, hopped off, and strutted at the dog's side.

She studied the area, trying to figure out what was upsetting them. The last time they'd behaved like this was when they found a license plate that led her to solve the previous cold case on Paul Shore. It had been an amazing and a very heartwarming, worthwhile exercise.

"Has this got something to do with my current case?" she asked Mugs.

Now Mugs couldn't take his eyes off whatever was bothering him on the far side of the creek. Thaddeus, however, shot her a look that said, *Boy, are you stupid.*

She glared back at the bird.

He ruffled his feathers and ignored her.

She should be used to that by now but wasn't.

Doreen walked closer to where Goliath had disappeared. Brush grew all alongside the creek. She didn't spot Goliath, but she thought she spied Goliath's tail twitching, flicking back and forth. She crept up behind him, not wanting to scare him into the water, but, at the same time, if he was hunting a bird or something equally lovely, she would tell him off right and royally.

And then suddenly Goliath exploded backward through the brush, wrapping himself through her legs, racing past Mugs.

She almost tripped and fell as she regained her balance. She stared at the streak as it veered toward the veranda. "Goliath, are you okay?" Unable to leave yet, she returned to where Goliath had been, and, holding on to the brush as an anchor, she crept down a couple feet toward the creek. Just two or so weeks ago, the water had been icy-cold. She hoped the creek water had warmed up by now, with all the sunshine and hopefully no more snowmelt. If she fell in, the water should be fairly warm at this time of year.

Standing just inches from the trickling stream, she inspected the area Goliath appeared to look at. But nothing was there. She crouched lower; then suddenly Mugs was at her side, chuffing away. Thaddeus, now at his side, hopped up onto her shoulder, and the three looked at the water.

Chapter 19

Saturday Afternoon ...

"OKAY, GUYS. YOU are really starting to freak me out," Doreen said. "We're not supposed to find any more bodies. Remember?"

Mugs shot her a look.

"The good news is, I don't see anything." She stared in the direction of Penny's house. It wasn't far from the creek either.

With a sinking feeling, Doreen wondered if Johnny had been knocked unconscious and put in the creek. "No, no, no," she said. "That's silly. No way that could have happened without finding a body in all this time."

Then again, the high floodwaters from decades past had sent a full-size truck down this very creek and even poor little Betty Miles's arm and hand, so who knew what else might have come past Doreen's house? But still, she wasn't going there. Not yet.

She reached out a hand to dip into the creek, and Mugs growled. She froze. "What's the matter with you?" she asked. "Have all the animals gone nuts right now?"

But his gaze was still on the spot in the creek in front of

her. She dug around but didn't see or feel anything. Nothing reflected the sunlight. Nothing appeared to not belong here.

She removed a few rocks in the creek, and water rushed in to fill those holes, lifting up some of the sand beneath and pulling it back. Unable to help herself, she kicked off her flip-flops and gingerly stepped into the creek. *Warm enough.* She proceeded to pull away some of the muddy creek bank, opening up a much larger area in the creek bed, allowing a bit of a run for the water to flow in and to flow out, taking a lot of the sand with it. Within minutes the area was down to just the rock layer. She loved how water worked that way.

She still couldn't see anything out of the ordinary. She worked her way farther up the creek in Penny's direction, with Mugs getting ever closer and closer. Finally she looked at him and asked, "You want to take over?"

He barked and then barked again.

She sighed and kept digging. "This better be worth it," she muttered and reached in again.

As she moved rocks around in the water, something small popped to the surface and started to float away. She snagged the small piece of wood. She was about to toss it aside when she saw *Johnny* scratched on one side. Upon closer inspection, it wasn't a single piece of wood but two pieces of wood nailed into a cross with his name filling the crosspiece. She sat down on the bank beside Mugs as he sniffed her new find.

"Okay, this is a little creepy," she said. She laid it on the path and took a picture with her phone, immediately sending it to Mack. Thaddeus waddled up and tilted his head to stare at it. For once he was quiet. Making the cross was something she could see the kids of their gang doing, as some kind of a memorial. But why here? Particularly if

Johnny's body had never been found. Meaning, his death had yet to be confirmed.

Her phone rang.

"What is that?" Mack asked.

"It looks like a little cross with Johnny's name on it," she said. "This thing is only like six inches long and maybe four inches across. Mugs found it in the creek. Actually maybe Goliath found it."

He groaned. "Seriously?"

"What do you want me to say?" she said. "I was working in the backyard, and Goliath came out here. Mugs started chuffing away ..."

"*Chuffing?*" Mack asked.

"Hey, Mugs. Could you chuff a little more again so Mack can hear you?"

But Mugs just yawned.

"Okay, so he's not doing it right now," she said. At Mack's barely smothered laugh, she snapped, "*But* he was doing it. ... And Mugs wouldn't leave this area alone either—at least once the scaredy-cat took off for home—so I dug up a section along the bank to widen the creek a bit, plus removed some rocks in the stream itself to get the water moving along better. Mugs barked the closer I got to where this was buried. Then he became completely unconcerned the minute this thing surfaced."

"Why is it you think it's a memorial thing?"

"You know how when someone dies on a trail, people put a cross there as a memorial? That's what this looks like. It's obviously old. It looks like it's been in the creek since who-knows-when, and it's got Johnny's name on it."

"So you think somebody threw it in the creek or had it standing up nearby as a memorial for him?"

"That's what this feels like," she said. "But you know what? Don't trust me. When you come by, I'll show you."

"You've already pulled it out and sent me a picture of it. How will I know where it was?"

"I'll grab a stick," she said, reaching for a broken branch, "and mark where I found it. How's that?"

"Good enough," he said. "It'll still be a few hours before I'm done at Mom's."

"Okay, I have lots to keep busy until then," she said. "Of course now ..."

"*Of course now* nothing," he said. "Finding somebody's way of saying goodbye to an old friend doesn't mean anything more sinister than that."

"Nope," she said. "But I'd love to know who threw it in here. ... And why they picked the creek as the memorial site." With that she hung up.

She sent the picture to Penny and then called her. "Hey, I just sent you a picture. I found something in the creek bed. I was thinking about how your place isn't far off the creek itself. Anyway, I found a little tiny cross with Johnny's name on it."

"I just looked at the picture," Penny told Doreen. "I have no idea what that is or who would have made it."

"There's not a ton of craftsmanship in it. It's pretty crude," Doreen said hesitantly, sitting nearby it and the creek. "It reminded me of how people will hang wreaths and crosses on the side of the road when there's been a fatality."

"Exactly," Penny said. "But to put that on the creek implies maybe he drowned?"

"The year he went missing was the year of the heavy flooding. Did Johnny swim?"

"Oh, absolutely he did but not well," Penny said. "That

was also the year Paul Shore went missing."

Doreen sat down with a hard *thump*. "Right. Didn't other children go missing back then?" she asked, her voice sounding a little bit the way she felt on the inside, dreading to hear her answer. "There were other missing boys, right? As I recall, two."

"There were," Penny said. "I can't remember how many. Or their names. Again you'll have to talk to Mack because that was a long time ago. But I think you're right. Two little boys went missing. It's one of the reasons I think the town turned on the handyman Henry Huberts so quickly because they suspected him in all three children's disappearances."

Doreen remained silent, considering these other unsolved cold cases, her cell phone at her ear.

Penny eventually said in a cautious tone, "But I don't know what that has to do with Johnny's disappearance."

"You said in your letter that he went missing in August of that year, right?"

"Correct."

"And now we're reminded of the horrible flooding that happened earlier that same year, and today I find a cross with Johnny's name on it in the creek bank. Maybe somebody accidentally killed him. Maybe they had a fight, and Johnny drowned, or maybe he got lost in the water, and they were afraid they would get blamed," Doreen said.

Penny was quiet, thoughtful, before she said anything. "We were always warning him about the dangers of the floods when he was younger. He wasn't big on being around water. He would never go to the lake, even though we live in one of the most gorgeous locations in the world."

"And people kayak down this creek a lot, don't they? Not yet, obviously, as there's only a little water, although," she looked around the area, "I guess it's been rising steadily."

"Oh, yes. Canoe, kayak, float on tubes all summer while there's enough water. It's quite the place." Penny smiled. "It's always low in the spring but with every month it rises until the snow melts up in the ski mountains and then ..."

"Right," Doreen said, nodding, yet of course, Penny couldn't see this over the phone. "But, in high-water times of the year, it would have been dangerous."

"Yes. I think Paul Shore went missing in May that same year, when we had the really big runoff. Johnny went missing later in the summer," Penny said. "The water would have dropped back to normal levels by then."

"Okay. That's good to know," Doreen said, relaxing a bit with relief. "I guess by August we are into much lower water levels, aren't we?"

"Yes, even though the floodwaters got superhigh that year and had caused chaos earlier. But, once that heavy rush of water passed, what with the melting snow coming from the tributaries into the main creek, the water levels kept dropping. ... I know Johnny did spend a fair bit of time with his buddies at the creek, but mostly drinking and hanging with his friends, not swimming or anything like that. I don't think we ever thought he might have drowned."

"That's because, if the water level was low, and he had drowned, his body would have been found already," Doreen said calmly, staring at the calm creek before her. "Which puts us back to somebody hiding the fact that Johnny had died. Any chance that one of the kids involved with him would have had something to do with those two missing little boys?"

"I have no clue," Penny said in surprise. "I don't remember any rumors to that effect. I just know the two little boys went missing that year, and I think it was early in the year, even before Paul went missing. But you found Paul. We never found the other two."

"Once Johnny went missing, that's where your focus went," Doreen said.

"Of course. George was a good boater. He was a really strong swimmer, and he was forever trying to get Johnny to practice swimming, but Johnny was very resistant to the idea."

"He could have been resisting just because his big brother was telling him that he should do it," Doreen said with a chuckle, picking up a small rock and tossing it into the creek.

"Quite possibly. But George was very insistent, because, to him, it was a safety issue. One of those life skills everybody should learn," Penny said in all seriousness. "Like learning to drive."

"I agree totally," Doreen said, nodding her head again. "Anyway I just wanted to let you know what I found." She stood, brushing off the seat of her pants.

"I can't believe everything you are finding," Penny said. "I mean, that's major progress. I found the dagger, but we just now found his medallion, and now you found that creepy cross."

Doreen had to agree with Penny on the description. After she hung up, Doreen picked up the cross and carried it past the deck to the veranda, where she laid it on the small table there. She studied it for a long moment. The small piece of wood had a fairly uniform shape, like the edges were shorter on the top of the crosspiece and wider on the bottom, as if maybe a deliberate design attempt. And the name had been carved in it with a knife, Doreen thought. Not very deep, but it wasn't burned in or etched in with some wood-burning tool. All in all, it wasn't as crudely made as she had first thought, but it was effective, especially when she considered the fact it had survived all those years in the water. Unless another Johnny had gone missing. She groaned at that idea.

"It *is* a common name," she muttered. "And it's all too possible that somebody else with that name might have died, and this referred to somebody else's Johnny."

On that note, she decided to take a look at deaths and other missing Johnnys in the area from around the same time that Johnny Jordan went missing.

Back inside, she made herself a sandwich for lunch, then sat in front of her laptop to research drownings of anybody with the name of Johnny. She found two in the last thirty years, one closer to Fintry, which was almost an hour up the lake on the opposite side. The lake currents operated in weird and wonderful ways, and bodies floated so they could have ended up all over the place.

The second Johnny was from Kelowna but had gone missing from a boat in the middle of the lake while out drinking. She winced at that thought. Apparently a large group of young men and women, nineteen in all, were on a big party boat. One of the guys had gone overboard. Nobody had noticed until he was almost underwater. Two men had jumped into the lake to rescue him but lost him in the murky depths below. His body was never found.

That sent chills down her back because of the similarities. But this particular Johnny had disappeared nineteen years ago, so it wasn't the Johnny that Doreen was looking for. But if large groups of young people were partying on the lake nineteen years ago, they definitely were twenty-nine years ago.

Then she searched for missing kids named Johnny. The only one who came up was Johnny Jordan. Then she searched for John, Johnny names with different spellings, Johan even, etc. The cross was very definitely for a Johnny with a *Y*. After that, she looked for car accident victims because, if someone had had a child who had been killed in a car accident, but his favorite place was the creek, his mother might very well have left a memorial at the creek closest to where he'd died.

Doreen was grasping at straws but didn't have a lot of other options right now.

She picked up her sandwich. Hearing a weird sound, she turned to see Thaddeus sitting on the kitchen table, watching her. His head tilted to the side and bobbed, as if willing her to understand. She pulled off a slice of cucumber from her sandwich and put it in front of him. Immediately he pecked at it.

Meow.

She glanced at Goliath, staring at a piece of ham hanging off the corner of her sandwich. She groaned but tore off that piece and put it in front of him. Mugs jumped up with his front paws on her chair, his most woebegone look on his face. She sighed and gave him a piece of cheese. "That's it, you guys. No more."

Of course they didn't listen. She shifted so she couldn't see them and quickly finished her sandwich, then put her plate in the sink. "What do you think? Back out to the garden?" But the animals had already raced ahead of her to the back door. She chuckled, grabbed a dry pair of gloves, and headed outside.

She stopped working at four. She was hot and sweaty, and what had started out as perfect working conditions had ended up getting really warm. She had maybe a six- by ten-foot stretch weeded and dug out nicely. The daisy patch looked absolutely wonderful. They needed water now that she'd disturbed their roots so much. She struggled to bring the hose all the way to the back of her property, ended up connecting several hoses to reach this bed, but finally she stood in the heat and soaked them down.

As she glanced at the next bed, the echinacea were overcrowded and heavily leafed, crying out for attention. "You guys are next." Then she sprayed Mugs with the hose. He ran around, jumping at the drops. Goliath was nowhere to be seen, likely off snooping in the bushes along the pathway. Thaddeus sat atop a rock, drinking the fresh water that had pooled on the ground. She laughed, turned the spray on above her to cool off a bit and then walked back up to the house to shut off the water.

With Mack coming over soon, it was time for a shower. She felt she had done enough work for the day. At this rate, it would take months to get her own garden back under control. And that was without planting, transplanting, or incorporating any new design elements. But it was her place, and it was her time and energy, so she would do what she wanted to do, when she wanted to do it. Depending on her finances of course.

Chapter 20

Saturday Dinnertime ...

B Y THE TIME Mack arrived, she was in the kitchen, fresh coffee dripping, counters and table all cleaned up and ready for whatever magic he was prepared to show her.

He walked in, placed more groceries on the counter, and smiled at her. "Are you ready?"

She motioned toward the bag. "I thought we had everything already. Isn't that what's in my fridge?"

"We had most of it, but I didn't buy any pasta. Remember?"

She frowned, then shrugged. "Honestly, I don't."

He withdrew a bottle of red wine from his bag and placed it on the table.

She studied the label. "I've never seen this before," she said, eyeing it. "I'm not a huge fan of reds, but I do love whites and rose. Especially the sparkly stuff." She grinned.

"Welcome to how real people eat," he said. "That's a cheap bottle of wine. It's good, and it's local. Plus it's absolutely perfect to have a glass while you're making pasta sauce with some of it too."

"Interesting." She watched as he unpacked a few more

mysterious items she didn't recognize.

He shooed her away and said, "You work on the pasta. I'll work on the sauce."

"If that meant anything to me," she said with a tilt of her lips, "then I would hop to it and get started."

"Get your largest pot." He stopped, frowning at her. "I hadn't thought about that. ... Do you have pots?"

She lifted her finger in the air. "I don't, but Nan does." She went to one of the pantry cupboards and opened it. "What size pot do you want?"

He joined her, rubbing his hands. "Now this is what I'm looking for." He reached inside and pulled out a decent-size pot with two small handles on opposite sides. "This Dutch oven will do."

She looked at it curiously. She'd never heard the term before and didn't know how it could possibly apply. It wasn't an oven, and what on earth made it Dutch? Or was that what the Dutch called a pot? Not wanting to ask and to appear even more foolish, she closed the cupboard door and watched as he took it to the sink.

"Give it a quick wash and a rinse and then fill it with water up to here," he said, drawing an imaginary line on the inside of the pot.

Obediently she stood at the sink and did as he asked. Cleaned and rinsed, she waited until the pan filled up. She shut off the water and looked back at him. "And?"

"Put it on the large burner at the back of the stove," he instructed.

He busily chopped onions and garlic, and she saw he had snagged another pot while she'd been filling hers. It was on the front burner. She sniffed the aroma coming from his pot as she lifted her pot to place on the back burner. With that done, she leaned in closer to sniff the pot in front of her. Mugs stretched up his front paws to the oven door and sniffed. Then, he'd missed out on a lot of good smells now too.

"What is this? Butter and garlic?"

"Butter with a little bit of garlic, yes, and a bunch of herbs. If you use dried herbs, warming them releases the flavors."

"I can definitely agree with that," she said. "I don't remember anything quite so aromatic."

He chuckled, stirred the contents, dumped in freshly chopped onions and then added ground beef. She watched as he calmly took a wooden spatula and stirred the mix.

"When do you know it's done?"

"When the meat turns brown and the onions turn translucent," he said. "The garlic you don't really have to worry about because it cooks so fast."

The combination was really getting her appetite going. "I don't know what else goes in there, but I want to snag a forkful right now."

"That's exactly how it should smell," he said.

She watched in fascination as he proceeded to add more ingredients. When she wondered what came next, he reached across and turned her pot of water on high.

"Grab the olive oil," he said.

She looked at him sideways.

He lifted an eyebrow. "Surely you've had olive oil served with your fancy meals?"

She nodded. "So, I'm looking for one of those little glass cruets that you pull a stopper from and pour?"

His eyebrows shot up. "Maybe in your world, but, in my world, we don't pour olive oil into a crystal jar just so we can pour it back out again." He chuckled. "Nobody has time for that." He pointed at the kitchen table. Beside the wine was another bottle.

She picked it up and read the label. *Olive oil.* "Isn't it supposed to say *extra virgin?*"

"It does," he said. "Read the fine print underneath."

She squinted. "I would have thought that fine print should be bigger." She handed him the bottle.

"It probably is on *your* bottles," he said in a dry tone. He took off the lid and poured some olive oil into the Dutch oven. "I count to three and figure that's good."

She looked at the amount swimming on the top of the water. "How am I supposed to learn if you don't measure?"

"Are you taking notes?" he asked, while he now chopped tomatoes and celery.

She gasped, grabbed her phone off the counter, and started videotaping everything. "I completely forgot." She hesitated, wondering if she should ask him to start again, but he must have caught a sense of what she would say because he held up a hand.

"Don't even bother. I am *not* starting over."

She sighed. "Okay, but, on the video, could you at least tell me what you did and how much?"

"One pound of ground beef, a couple smashed cloves of garlic, chop up a whole onion, and cooked until the meat is brown and the onion translucent. As for the herbs, well, that's a little hard to remember," he said. "I'm a cook who doesn't measure. I add a bit of this and a bit of that."

"A bit of what this time?"

"In the original group," he said, "oregano and thyme and marjoram, some paprika ..."

His voice trailed off as he dumped in his freshly chopped

tomatoes, celery, and she wasn't sure what the other thing was. She leaned in and asked, "What's that?"

"It's a bay leaf. Not to worry, I'll pull it out before it's served."

She'd never seen such a thing before. He'd taken a leaf, like one from her plants outside, and plunked it in his sauce. Instead of being bright green, it was dry-looking, brittle. He continued to add what looked like canned tomatoes. "Why fresh *and* canned?"

"Because it'll be too dry if I don't add some liquid," he said, "and I didn't have quite enough fresh tomatoes."

She nodded, as if that made sense, but, from her point of view, that was a ton of fresh tomatoes. Still, the aroma was kicking in beautifully.

He pointed to the pot with the water and olive oil. "Now get the salt and add it in that pot."

Obediently she walked to the table, picked up a salt shaker, and put in a couple shakes.

He looked at her and said, "More."

She shook again.

"More."

She shook again.

"More."

Finally she stared at him in exasperation. "How much salt do you want in there?"

He pulled the top off, poured some into his hand, and dumped it into the pot of water.

She gasped. "That much salt is seriously bad for you."

"It's going into the water," he said. "We're not drinking the water, and I'm not adding it to the sauce. We'll put pasta in the water. It will get just the right amount of flavor. Then we'll drain it, so we leave all that salt behind."

She frowned, not sure she believed him, muttering that too much salt was bad for their health.

He ignored her, which was probably a good thing. Then he picked up the lid and shoved it on top of the pot of water with a little more force than was necessary.

To get back at him, she picked up her cup and poured herself some coffee—but not him.

He put the spoon down, crossed his arms over his chest, and glared at her.

She shrugged. "Well, it's not like you were being nice."

"I'm making you dinner."

She wrinkled her nose. "That's not fair."

He stared at her in astonishment. "Why is that not fair? You should pour *me* a cup of coffee when I'm making *you* dinner."

"You asked to make me dinner a while ago. So now you're taking something from a few days ago and bringing it forward to today to get your way."

He stood there, confused, then shook his head. "Forget it. Nobody could work their way through that."

She decided she should probably be nice anyway. He was a guest, after all. She picked up a clean mug out of Nan's stack of mugs and poured coffee for him, placing it beside him and said, "Thank you."

Once again he looked at the cup and said, "You said *thank you.* Isn't it me who was supposed to say *thank you?*"

"You're welcome," she said, beaming a smile in his direction.

He snorted and returned to stirring his pot. "You and Nan have a lot in common."

She looked at him suspiciously. "I don't think you meant that in a nice way." She looked down at his cup and then back up at him. "Just take a sip before you say anything because I'm pretty sure that whatever comes out of your mouth won't be nice."

"Nan is a great woman," he said.

She started to feel better.

"But she's also as nutty as a hatter sometimes."

She slammed her cup down. "Are you saying I'm crazy too?"

"No," he said, "but crazy is as crazy does."

She stared at him, trying to understand.

He waved a hand. "Forget it. Now I'll let all this simmer."

She checked on the contents in his pot that had somehow turned from being a lot of different chunks of ingredients, separate and distinct, into this beautiful-looking sauce. "How did it go from one to the other so quickly?"

"Cooking," he said succinctly. "That's all it takes, leaving it alone to simmer. We'll add a bunch of peppers, and then we'll let it simmer some more while we have our coffee."

She nodded. "What about the pasta water?"

"The pot is pretty full, so it'll take another ten minutes to boil, maybe longer."

"Is this one of those dishes that's better the next day?" she asked, eyeing the pot of spaghetti sauce suspiciously. She'd never seen anything quite like it.

"In a way, yes," he said. "It's definitely something that gets better with lots of time to simmer."

"So we can't eat it today?" She stared at him in horror.

"I am," he said with a huge grin. "I'm starving."

"So am I," she admitted. "I had a sandwich earlier, but I also did a lot of work in my garden, so I'm tired too."

He looked out at the garden and pointed to the far back corner. "Right, and I almost forgot. Where's the cross?"

She walked toward the formal dining room table and pointed out the cross leaning against the little window. "There."

He stepped closer but didn't touch it for the longest moment. Then he picked it up and checked to see how the two pieces of wood stayed together. "They've used a pinner."

"And that means what?"

"It's not a nail," he said. "Anybody could have used a nail, but they've used a pinner, which means somebody had good equipment because this looks like an air-compressor pinner." He rotated it in his hand. "It's just as likely a father made it for their child to carve the name in and place where they wanted it. Help them deal with the loss of a friend.'

"Which means it could have been anyone." Doreen bent closer to see what he was talking about. "It looks like a staple."

"Almost," he said. "This isn't from a staple gun though. It's much finer. And there are two of them. That's why what you see looks to be a staple."

She didn't quite understand, but, as long as he did, she was good with it. "Does that mean anything to you?"

"No. But we see similar items at crash sites and often at crime scenes. It's human nature to want to honor a difficult death." He set it back up in the window.

"I figure it had been made specifically for this purpose," she said, "because you can see how evenly centered the crosspiece is and how the ends go down at an angle. It's not like this was just two jagged pieces of driftwood tied together."

"You're right," he said. "Plus *Johnny* is less scratched in as much as carved in."

"Exactly. But I don't understand why. I wondered about it and asked Penny if Johnny might have drowned, like Paul Shore did."

Mack turned to look at her. "Was that the same year?"

She nodded slowly. "Paul went missing in May, just as the high floodwaters hit," she added. "But Johnny didn't go missing until August, and the water should have dropped by then."

Mack looked out at the creek, as if thinking back. "High water can start anytime in May most years—there are always exceptions—depending on how much snow is up in the mountains and how quickly it comes down, which also depends on rainstorms and other types of weather. We can get heavy flash floods right through July. But you're right. By August the lake level has dropped, and the creek itself has slowed down to a narrow slow channel. By September it's completely calm."

"Also Johnny didn't swim well." Her words were quiet. "So what's the chance he drowned accidentally? Or maybe had a little help," she emphasized. "Then whoever was there didn't want to leave him to be found so moved him to a new location where nobody would ever find him."

"All plausible," he said, "but remember that part about needing evidence."

She pointed at the cross. "That seems to indicate somebody thought maybe Johnny died in the creek."

"Sure. But we found it down at your place again," he said.

"Not quite," she said. "It was up a bit. Maybe ten feet away from my place."

"Close enough," he said. "It's hardly worth arguing

over."

She shrugged. "Well, I'd argue about it," she said. "Otherwise you'd just pin that one on me too."

He groaned. "Even if Johnny did drown in August, there would be a body at that time of year. And, no, I wouldn't blame that on you."

"Unless there was another strange accident," she said. "You know? Like, did a bridge collapse? Did a truck hit a bank and crash down a bridge? I mean, all kinds of terrible things could have gone wrong. But, yes, I would say the likelihood of finding a body in the dry season would be in the 80 or 90 percent mark."

"Right," he said.

"So then we're back to maybe Johnny drowned and was moved," she said. "Or there was a fight, and maybe somebody held him underwater too long and killed him. You realize that a person can drown in just like two inches of water?"

"And again we're guessing," Mack said in a dry tone. "Have you ever considered writing novels? You have a vivid imagination."

"I know," she said. "But, once my mind gets locked on a problem, it won't let go."

"I noticed." He walked back to the stove and gave the sauce pot a stir.

Doreen joined him, watching over his shoulder, and could see these lighter-colored bubbles popping up through the center before Mack turned them under into the mixture. Then he lifted the lid on the pot of water and put it back down again.

"It's a nice little stove," he said.

She nodded. "It looks nice, fancy, modern. In a way it

almost doesn't fit the atmosphere of my kitchen for that reason alone."

"Sure, but you're learning," he said. "And you're a blend of old and new yourself."

"I certainly am while living here. I could go check up and down the creek for more evidence," she said thoughtfully. "The only thing is, it's been twenty-nine years."

"True," he said, "but you still found the cross."

"Goliath and Mugs did."

At that, Thaddeus squawked. "Thaddeus did. Thaddeus did."

She reached out her arm, and Thaddeus walked up it.

"Where have you been, big guy?" Mack asked, stroking his feathery back.

She could tell Thaddeus had just woken up. "He sleeps a lot," she said. "Is that normal?"

"No clue."

"But then we are doing lots of activities," she said thoughtfully. "So he likely needs his beauty rest when he can get it."

Thaddeus sat on her shoulder and pecked at her ear.

"He's hungry," she said in surprise. She looked around, and, sure enough, all the animals' food bowls were empty. She groaned. "I still can't seem to get in the habit of feeding them at a regular time."

"So does it mean he's hungry when he pecks you?" Mack asked, studying the bird. "Did he hurt you?"

She shook her head. "No, not at all."

Heading to the front closet, Doreen got Thaddeus's food and placed a little on the kitchen table. Immediately Thaddeus hopped off her shoulder and sat on the table, pecking away at his food. And then, out of the corner of his eye, his gaze fixed on the green piece of celery stalk, leftover from Mack's chopping tasks. Thaddeus hopped up to the countertop, walked over, and pecked at it.

Doreen glanced at Mack. "Do you mind?"

He shook his head. "It's going in the garbage anyway." He moved it over to the kitchen table, so Thaddeus could have better access. Between the bird seeds and the celery, Thaddeus appeared to be quite content.

She fed Goliath then, but he only made his appearance when she banged her spoon against his bowl and placed it on the floor. Then he was right here, winding between her legs.

"I already put it down for you, silly," she said affectionately, reaching down to rub his ears.

As soon as she did that, his nose came up high enough that the aroma of his food hit the right spot, and he launched himself forward and started to eat, crouched down on all fours.

Mack chuckled. "At least they enjoy their food."

"Yeah, they do," she said.

She fed Mugs, who seemed to be much less interested in his dog food than in the pot on the stove.

Mack noted Mugs's focus and shook his head. "Oh, no you don't, big guy."

Just then the front door bell rang. Mack looked at Doreen, his eyebrows raised.

She shrugged. "I don't have a clue." She picked up a towel, wiped her hands, and walked to the front door.

The alarms weren't set because she and Mack were inside. She opened the front door and found Hornby, grinning like a crazy man.

He pushed past her and said, "I thought I'd come by and have that cup of coffee."

"Don't bother," she snapped, pointing toward the front door. "Get out."

"Why should I?" he said. "It's obvious you live all alone and need somebody to keep you company," he said with a half leer, half sneer.

Insulted, she shook her head. "Get out, or I'll call the cops."

Mugs, who had followed her, obviously didn't like her tone of voice because he growled at Hornby.

Hornby looked down at Mugs. "God, he's ugly."

She gasped. "Don't say that." She stepped to the fireplace and picked up her poker. She marched up to him and held it out like she would hit him. "Get out of my house."

He laughed at her. "Oh my. Aren't you so cute. What's the matter? How come you're not friendly to a single guy like me? I just want some company too."

"I choose my own company, thanks, and you're not on the invitation list," Doreen snapped. "Now get out." Then she noticed his gaze roaming the living room, looking appraisingly at all the knickknacks and furniture. She took a few more steps toward him, threateningly. "Get out now."

He turned to sneer at her. "Or what?"

Chapter 21

Saturday Evening ...

"OR ELSE I'LL arrest you for trespassing and any other charges that apply," Mack said from the kitchen doorway, his arms across his chest. He looked at Doreen, the fireplace poker ready for her time at bat, and raised his eyebrows.

"He's assessing the contents of my living room," she said, "not to mention threatening me."

"I didn't threaten you," Hornby said, sauntering toward to the front door. He turned an eye on Mack. "What the hell do you want with this dried-up old prune anyway?"

She gasped and charged after him.

He laughed, stepped onto the front porch, and slammed the door in her face.

She opened the door and yelled, "I'm warning you. Get off my property and stay off." She slammed the door again as she stepped back into the living room. She watched through the window as he drove down the cul-de-sac. But something about his small car made her wonder. "Does that bumper belong on that vehicle? And, on this side, there's a panel of a different color."

Mack studied the vehicle and nodded. "Yeah, but it's not that uncommon. Particularly if people have accidents without insurance coverage, and they want to fix the damage cheap. They'll go for parts from a junkyard, and it doesn't matter what color it is."

"Do you think people's buying habits are the same everywhere?"

"What are you talking about?"

"Susan said the vehicle that ran the two boys off the road was put together with all different panels. As in, it was a mishmash of colors, like somebody had tried to build or repair a vehicle with other auto parts from, you know, destroyed vehicles."

"Yes, I do remember that."

"So could this be the same car from twenty-nine years ago?" she asked.

"Not sure, but I'd say it's newer than that. But … maybe all of Hornby's vehicles ended up looking like this. I'll have to check into that further." He withdrew a notepad and a pen from his pocket and jotted something down. "But Hornby was supposedly in the vehicle with Susan."

"Right." Doreen tried to put it together in her mind. "Do you think she gave a half-assed confession?"

"I don't know," he said. "I'd have to look into that file, see if her statement is even in there."

"*Something* should be there."

"I hope so as she's not around anymore for us to question."

"No," she said, "but her great-uncle is. Maybe other family members are still alive too."

He turned to look at her, his hands on his hips. It wasn't anger that she saw; it was worry. "Hornby is dangerous," he said bluntly. "You get that, right?"

"I do now," she said. "He forced his way into the house. Then he wouldn't leave as he was casing the joint."

"Only when he saw me standing in the kitchen doorway did he turn to leave."

"Hey," Doreen asked, "how come he didn't see your car in my driveway?"

"One of your neighbors must have visitors parking on the street, and one of them cut off part of your driveway. I didn't want to box you in, so I parked a couple doors down."

She nodded, but her frown remained.

"It's not like Hornby should recognize my personal vehicle."

"What do you think he would have done if you weren't here?" she asked slowly.

"Well, funny you're considering that now because you weren't thinking about your own personal danger earlier," he said. "You were thinking about him assessing the contents of your house. And where to hit him with that fire poker."

She winced. "Because he was staring at individual pieces, as if calculating its value. As if he already knew this house was full of valuables."

"So maybe we should check his association with your intruder," Mack said thoughtfully. "The last thing I want is yet another intruder in here, picking up what the first one missed. It would make it look like Darth McLeod was innocent, since he was locked up at the time of this proposed future break-in. That could give rise to enough reasonable doubt that his case would get thrown out."

She didn't quite follow all the legal parts, but she did understand the part about another intruder. "That is not what I want." She looked at Mugs. "And Mugs couldn't stand Hornby, which is also very indicative of him being dangerous."

"True enough," Mack said. "But I wish Mugs had barked when the intruder had initially forced his way in."

"Well, of course he didn't," she said, looking at Mack in surprise.

He frowned at her. "What are you talking about?"

She beamed up at him. "Mugs knew you were here. So, if anybody would get into the heavyweight-protector mode, Mugs would expect you to be it. If you weren't here, he would have been much more of a guard dog."

"I doubt it." He shook his head, looking at Mugs, who now lay on the floor with his ears puddling beside him. "He's not a watchdog."

"Don't insult him," she warned. "You two have a great relationship. Don't ruin that."

"Come on, let's eat," he said. "Dinner is ready."

She stared at him in surprise, her mind still trying to switch from Hornby's potential involvement in the accident that had killed the two men long ago back to tonight's dinner. "How can it be done? We didn't do anything with the pasta yet."

"I was putting it in the pot of boiling water when Hornby arrived. And that was a surprisingly longish encounter," he said. "Let's get the table set. By then it should be done."

And very quickly they sat down with two beautiful plates of spaghetti.

She sighed happily. "The only thing missing is garlic bread."

"I meant to pick up some French bread and make some," he admitted, "but I forgot. Sorry, I saw a few signs that my mother has been declining mentally. It's worrying me." He glanced over at her. "I've been distracted."

"Ugh that's tough," she said. "And I get that you're worried but I'm stuck on something else you said—you can make garlic bread?" Her eyes rounded. "I used to eat it as a snack when my husband wasn't looking," she said with a wince at the bad memories.

"Why didn't you want him to know?" he asked in an ominous tone.

She gave him that breezy smile. "Oh, you know. Back to that *I might get fat if I ate too many carbs* thing," she said.

Mack just shook his head and proceeded to twirl his fork into the spaghetti, getting a big mouthful.

She watched in amazement as the entire forkful went into his mouth. By contrast, she used a spoon and a fork. "I learned a long time ago to only take a few noodles at a time." Carefully she coiled up several noodles using her spoon, and then, with a nice tiny little bite, she popped it into her mouth and swooned. "Oh, my. That's absolutely fantastic."

Mack appeared mollified as he watched her thoroughly enjoy her dinner. "The thing about a sauce like this is," he said in a conversational tone, "we can make a large pot of it. Then you can eat it for several days, and you can freeze some."

She looked back at the pot. "So there are leftovers?"

He nodded. "Absolutely. And it's no trouble to put it in the fridge. We cooked too many noodles today, so you can warm up both them and the sauce in the microwave."

She stared at him in delight. And then she shook her head. "So that's what people do? They make enough meals for several days at a time?" As far as she was concerned, that was genius.

He smiled. "That's what I do. I'll make a stew and eat it

for two or three days. I'll make a chili and have it for two or three days."

She sighed rapturously. "Just the thought of having food for two or three days sounds wonderful." She dug into her pasta again. When she could feel his hard stare, she refused to look up. "I'm eating. I'm eating."

"Not enough," he said. "Just in the few weeks you've been here, you've lost at least ten pounds."

She considered that and shrugged. "I've been active," she said, "but it is what it is."

"That isn't something you can just brush off," he growled. "You have to take better care of yourself."

"With your help I'm doing that. But I'm a long way off from learning how to make that sauce."

"True. It was probably not a good one to start with." He pondered that a moment. "We could do something a lot simpler tomorrow," he said thoughtfully. "There's still leftover pasta. I can show you how to make a carbonara pasta. That's super, super simple. Or even just a scramble."

She listened to the terms roll off his tongue, like she was supposed to understand what language he spoke. But she was determined to learn, especially if it meant she would get food like this again. She stared at her plate. "Honestly, I've seen videos on YouTube where they have these fabulous dishes at the end, but I'm always suspicious a chef has arrived with a meal just before they're ready to sit down, so it looks like they actually made it."

He laughed. "You know what? Probably a lot of people out there do pull stunts like that, but I wouldn't count on it. It's not hard to cook. A few more dishes and you'll be fine."

"One dish," she said, "the chef used to make for me that I loved so much. It had feta cheese, fresh tomatoes, basil, and pasta. With some vinaigrette, served like a salad."

He nodded. "Pasta salad is good."

"It had artichokes in it." Suddenly her mouth watered at the remembered taste of pickled artichokes. "I have no clue what made me think of that right now. But I loved that dish."

"I'd have to pick up some artichokes, pickled of course. I presume that is what you want. But it would be easy enough to toss together. I could show you how to spin plain pasta into four or five different meals."

She wanted to cry, yet, at the same time, her laughter bubbled out. "You are a godsend," she said. "But I'll stop talking now, so I can focus on eating."

And that was what she did. With every bite, she closed her eyes and moaned in joy. When she was done, she looked up to see Mack watching her, leaning back in his chair, resting against the nearby wall, his arms across his chest, his plate empty too.

"What?" she asked suspiciously.

"I don't think I've ever seen anybody enjoy their food more," he said quietly. "It makes me think all kinds of things."

She narrowed her gaze at him. "Like what?" Was he flirting with her? It seemed to be a trend lately. She wasn't sure she liked it. She really liked Mack, but, at the moment, she liked his cooking more than the thought of getting into a troubled relationship.

He brushed a hand in the air as if washing away the conversation. "So probably two meals' worth are left in the pot of just spaghetti. What would you like to make tomorrow?"

"Something simple," she said.

"Well, there's probably nothing simpler than the salad

you were just talking about. So, when I come tomorrow at dinnertime," he said, "you can make that for me."

She frowned. "But I don't know how."

He chuckled. "Was there anything else in it, like black olives or chickpeas?"

She nodded slowly. "Both of those sometimes. But usually just black olives."

"Then I'll pick up a can and show you how easy it is."

"Perfect," she said.

He got to his feet. "Now let's get the dishes done." But then his phone rang. He pulled it out. "Damn. I have to leave. There's been an accident."

"Whereabouts?" she asked.

He frowned. "A few blocks from here."

"Oh, dear," she said. "Go. Duty calls. I'll do the dishes."

He hesitated and looked around the kitchen. "I don't usually leave the kitchen this dirty."

"It's not dirty," she said. "Go."

"If you don't mind," he said, still hesitating.

She patted him on the arm. "I mean it. Go. I had an absolutely fabulous dinner. I'll put it all away, and tomorrow we'll pick up the pieces and make something new."

He chuckled and snagged her into a big hug. "Thank you." As he stepped out the front door, he turned and came back into the kitchen. "Set the alarms. I don't want Hornby coming back inside."

She winced, followed him, closed the front door, and set the alarm. She didn't bother with the kitchen one yet because she was still working in there. Plus she might take a cup of tea out to the backyard shortly.

Clean up took longer than she'd expected, but finally she was done. With all the counters cleaned off, she made herself a cup of tea and sat outside to watch the sunset. When her phone rang, she was surprised to see Mack's number.

"Hey," he said.

"Hey," she said. "Dishes are done. I'm sitting out in the back, having a cup of tea."

"Sounds good to me. It was a car accident," he said. "It was Hornby."

"What?" she asked in surprise. "Was he the one hurt?"

"Yes," he said. "The trouble was, he had the accident because he'd been shot. He'll be okay, but I wanted you to know he's not a danger to you. At least not tonight."

"What?" her heart sank. "Will people think it was me?"

Mack went silent for too long.

"You're making me nervous. Say something."

"Why would they think it was you?" he asked curiously.

"Because he was at my house, and we had an ugly confrontation," she said slowly.

"I was there with you," he said. "I was a witness to that. And he left healthy and very unhappy."

"True," she said thoughtfully. "But this doesn't feel right."

"It doesn't feel wrong either," he corrected. "People like Hornby make enemies. A lot of enemies. So don't go thinking it was connected to your cold case."

She hesitated, her mind busily considering how it all fit together. "I get what you're saying," she said, "but you know it'll be hard not to."

"He's alive. He's in the hospital, likely heading for surgery. I can't speak with him until at least tomorrow."

"Check his vehicle over very carefully," she said. "Look for anything connected to Johnny's death."

"What would that be? It's not even the same vehicle

most likely," he said. "You think a confessional letter will be in his glove box?"

"For all you know, he's got something of Johnny's tucked away that he's been carrying around with him all this time. Too bad he didn't see the cross in my dining room," she said. "We might have learned something by seeing his reaction to it."

"You weren't too worried about what kind of reaction he might give you at that time," he said. "You were a crazy Amazonian woman with a poker in your hand."

"He was after my priceless antiques that I need to get packed up and shipped out of here as soon as possible," she cried. "I still have to wait until Monday."

"So two more nights," he said. "Anyway, you probably don't have to worry about Hornby tonight."

"And, for that, thank you," she said warmly. "I'll sleep much better now."

Chapter 22

Sunday Morning ...

WHEN SHE GOT up the next morning, Doreen couldn't resist pouring fresh coffee into a travel mug, and—with all the animals in tow, and the alarms set—she walked up the creek. It was her favorite place to stroll. Although she'd slept well last night, still something about Hornby made her uncomfortable. Also, she couldn't help but wonder who had shot him and why.

As she passed the turnoff to Penny's house, Doreen wondered if it was too early to call and to ask a question. Deciding there would never be a better time, she hopped across the creek on the rocks with Thaddeus on her shoulder. Mugs traipsed through the creek behind her, now dripping little dribbles of creek water. However, Goliath howled on the far side, where he'd been left behind. He wasn't into getting his paws wet at all.

She walked back over and scooped him up against her chest. Only Thaddeus didn't like that and tried to peck the top of his head. Finally she plunked Goliath down on the other side. "Sorry, buddy. Not quite enough dry rocks here for you, are there?"

She kept walking until she came to Penny's door. She knocked several times. No answer. Frowning, she wondered if Penny was still asleep. How rude Doreen was, knocking early enough to wake up Penny.

Doreen waited a little longer, then stepped out of the yard.

One of the neighbors came out of his house, looked at her, and said, "Penny isn't here."

She turned to face him. "Really?"

He nodded. "She left last night with a suitcase in her hand."

"Oh," she said. "I'm sorry to hear that." She wasn't sure what to do about it. "Any idea how long she'll be gone?"

The neighbor shook his head. "Not a clue."

"I don't see a For Sale sign," she said out loud.

He looked at her in surprise. "I don't think she's selling, is she?"

Doreen thought back to their earlier conversation and had to wonder if Penny had said she was selling or if she was *planning* on selling. "I thought it was her intention, but I can't remember if she said it was already for sale or not."

"Maybe," he said. "She didn't have a lot of savings after George's death so might need to sell the house. That way she can buy a condo and have money in the bank. But then again, maybe she wants to get away from the memories."

"I imagine," she said, "it could go either way."

She was a little perturbed as she headed back toward the creek. She pulled out her phone and called Penny's number. When there was no answer, she left a voicemail.

The foursome tripped their way back down the creek bed to her little bridge and walked across, having come full circle from home. "It's still early, guys. Do we want to do some garden work?"

They all looked at her like she was crazy. She had to admit that she probably was. Not to mention she was also hungry.

When she got back in her house, she gave them breakfast and made toast and cheese for herself before she sat down at her laptop. How much did she really know about Penny? Not a lot and still that niggling question remained as to why she might have left. She could have gone to a friend's house in town, staying overnight because they wanted a couple drinks, and she didn't want to drive home. Really no way to know. Besides, no need to be suspicious of Penny because she had asked Doreen to look into Johnny's death. If Penny had had something to do with his death, then she wouldn't expose herself to an investigation like that. Besides, Penny was pretty small. She couldn't have killed Johnny. Or rather, she could have killed him but not moved him afterward. At least not alone ...

It was also an interesting coincidence that Hornby arrived at Doreen's house, got shot shortly thereafter, and Penny disappeared, just like that.

Doreen's mind was trying to fit the pieces together. The trouble was, she didn't have enough pieces. What if Penny had shot Hornby? What if Penny thought Hornby had killed Johnny, and she'd shot Hornby, hoping he'd crash and kill himself?

"Guys, once again Mack would be shaking his head at me." In her mind she could hear him clearly. For fun she tried to imitate his voice in a comical way. "Doreen, we can't go around making assumptions or wild guesses. We need proof."

Mugs woofed several times.

She chuckled, got up from her laptop, and poured herself another cup of coffee. She sat back down and researched Hornby and then Penny. She was younger than her husband, younger than Hornby too. Penny might have been closer in age to Susan or that other girl in Johnny's group. Yet Penny said she didn't know about any girl but Susan. As Doreen's searches failed to give her any leads, one question she had been trying to answer resurfaced once more: who was that second girl in Johnny's group?

She called Nan. "Would you mind asking your friend Richie who his great-niece's girlfriend was during the time of Johnny's disappearance," she said. "I understand the three guys hung out with Susan, but I thought another girl did too."

"Good morning to you," Nan said in a delighted twitter. "I'll call you back in a few minutes." And, like Nan was prone to do, which was great, she hung up without needing any further explanation.

Doreen sipped her coffee and continued to research Penny but found nothing out of the ordinary. Penny and George had been married for a long time. And, outside of some volunteer work she was involved in at a church's Christmas bazaar or some fund-raiser, Penny's name didn't show up very often. Doreen thought about who else she could contact from back then, but there wasn't anyone. She sent Mack a text and asked if there was any reason for Penny to have up and left.

When the phone rang, she assumed it was Mack. But instead it was Nan.

"Her name was Julie," she said. "But we're not sure what her last name was. Her parents lived across from the Hornbys in the same cul-de-sac."

"That makes sense. The kids lived next door to each other," Doreen said. "But how am I supposed to find out what her last name is?"

"You can probably check the land title records," Nan said. "Or you could ask Mack." On that note, she went off on a peal of laughter and hung up.

"*Ask Mack*," Doreen repeated. "Well, that's not helpful."

She brought up a map of Kelowna, zoomed in on the cul-de-sac where Penny and Hornby had lived and came up with an address for the house across from Hornby's childhood home. Because they were both on the corner of the cul-de-sac, it was pretty easy to tell which house it was. At least she hoped.

Just then Goliath laid across her keyboard. She groaned and dragged him off to cuddle him. Finally she picked up her cell phone.

How would I find out who lived at this address 29 years ago? She typed into a text, adding the address, and fired it off to Mack.

After she sent it, she wondered if he would get fed up with her questions. She went to the internet and typed in that address to see who was on the current registry. But it wasn't online. That database was unavailable. She thought it should be available. Now if anybody wanted to check all of Doreen's private information, she might have something different to say. But it was frustrating to be close to answers but not able to get the real ones.

Whoever this Julie was, she was important to the case. If for no other reason that she might be the last one of the girls alive—or the last one alive period. With Hornby shot and in hospital, as much as Doreen didn't like the man, she didn't want to hear he had died from his wounds. This Julie person was the only other one with possibly any answers as to what had happened so long ago. If Julie was even still alive.

Mack's answer came back. **Willoughby.**

She grinned and typed in the name Julie Willoughby on her search window. And up popped all kinds of articles. Poor Julie had had a rough life. She was arrested in one article, apparently for breaking and entering when she turned eighteen. A group of kids had had a wild party, drank too much, and then somehow thought it was a good idea to break into one of the neighbors' homes. But no mention was made of the other kids in the group.

A few other articles mentioned Julie, but they didn't yield anything new. And, in the last few years, nothing was said about her.

Doreen sighed, then wondered if the Willoughbys were still living here. She sent Mack a question. **Is the same family still living there?**

She had to wait for more answers. Goliath slid to the floor, bored.

She got up and checked the fridge because, by now, she was starving again. She pulled out some cheese and crackers, knowing they would have pasta for dinner again. She figured she'd survive on this quite nicely.

He sent back a simple text. **Yes.**

She crowed. "Okay, guys. Road trip again."

She finished her cheese and crackers and grabbed Mugs's leash. Goliath joined them at the door. Thaddeus wanted a ride. She led the way out the backyard again and up the creek to the cul-de-sac. Penny's house was still dark. Hornby's house was dark also, but the house across from it, the Willoughbys' house, had lights on.

Doreen walked up to the front door, Thaddeus on her

shoulder, Goliath strolling behind her at his pace, and Mugs sat at her heels. When the door opened, a woman answered.

Doreen looked at her and smiled. "Don't suppose you're Julie Willoughby, are you?"

The woman looked at her in surprise. "Yes, I am. Who are you?"

"I'm Doreen. Nan is my grandmother," she said by way of explanation. It seemed to her all the townsfolk knew who Nan was.

Julie's face brightened. "How is Nan?" she asked affectionately.

"She's doing just fine," she said. "I have a few questions, if you've got a moment."

The woman opened the door. "Sure, come on in."

Doreen hesitated at the doorway. "What about my animals?"

Julie's gaze widened as she took in Thaddeus. Then she saw the cat and the dog, and she laughed. "Now I know who you are," she said. "You're the bone lady." She waved all the animals inside. "Come on in. I was just sitting down to a muffin. Would you like one?"

"Yes, I would," Doreen said. "Thank you." Seated at the kitchen table, she said, "I wanted to ask you a few questions about Johnny's death."

The woman looked at her in surprise. "Johnny?"

"Johnny," Doreen said. "Johnny Jordan. Your neighbor's younger brother."

Julie sat back, as if the shock was more than she expected. "Oh, that's definitely not a period of my life I talk about very much."

"Understood," Doreen said. "Do you know Penny very well?"

Julie nodded. "Well, not only are we neighbors but Johnny and I used to be good friends."

"Of course. Penny asked me to look into Johnny's disappearance. I came over here this morning to ask her a few questions again, but she's not home."

"I just saw her yesterday morning," Julie said.

"One of your neighbors said she took a suitcase and left last night," Doreen said. "I presume she's gone on an overnight trip somewhere."

Julie stared out the window at the house across the street. "I always wondered what went on in that house. George and Penny seemed to be so happy that it was almost sickening, but that was to hide the truth."

"What truth?" Doreen asked in confusion.

"Nobody is *that* happily married. I used to ask Johnny about it. He'd laugh and say that's who they were."

"A sickening-sweet, happy, loving couple?" Doreen asked. That had been her impression from what Penny had said.

"No. A fighting, backstabbing, very unhappily married couple," Julie corrected. "One of the reasons I spent as much time as I did with Johnny was so he could get away from the place."

That took Doreen a moment to digest. She didn't want to think Penny's marriage had been so bad that Johnny had just wanted to get away from it all …

"You have no idea where he disappeared to?" Doreen asked slowly, tilting her head to study the woman across from her. She was older than Doreen, younger than Nan, caught somewhere in a time loop. Her hair was in a bun at the back, but it oddly suited her. "Are you an artist?"

The woman laughed and nodded. "I am. How did I give

myself away?"

"You have a very creative look to you," Doreen said with a smile. "I don't suppose you have any paintings of Johnny from back then, do you?"

Julie shook her head. "No. I didn't start painting until later."

"What caused you to go in that direction?"

"Losing Johnny," Julie admitted. "I loved him dearly. But I wasn't part of the in crowd. Like Hornby, I was more or less in the outside circle."

"Hornby was in an accident last night." She watched Julie's reaction carefully. The color drained from her skin.

"He was what?" She switched her gaze to Hornby's house across the road from her.

"I gather you know him well too?"

"Of course," she said. "We're all tied to the events of so long ago. But we're hardly friends."

"And you have no idea what happened to Johnny?"

Julie shook her head. "No, of course not. If I had any idea, I'd have spoken up. For a long time I wondered if it was Hornby."

"You mean that Hornby might have killed him?"

"Well, no doubt Johnny is dead," she said, "because I know for a fact that he would have contacted me."

"Why is that?" Doreen asked.

"Because he loved me," she said simply. "We were going to run away together and start a whole new life, but he disappeared."

"Do you think he might have run away without you?" Doreen asked, hesitating to put the thought into words.

"Lots of people asked me that," she said with a sweet smile. "But, no, that's not what happened. I knew him too well. Besides, he could have just told me that he would go and come back for me. We were supposed to meet that evening and make plans, but he never showed up."

"How long was it from when you last talked to him and then when you were to meet him? What kind of time frame was that?"

"An hour," Julie said quietly. "An hour tops. If I had just walked across this yard and spoken to him at the back of Penny's place, there's a good chance nothing would have happened to him. But we were going to meet at the park in an hour. I got there a little early. But saw no sign of Johnny. I walked around to Penny's backyard and looked over the fence and called for him. But there was no sign of him. I never saw him again."

Chapter 23

Sunday Late Morning ...

DOREEN STOOD OUTSIDE Julie's house, studying the Hornby place, thinking about the triangle between Hornby, Johnny, and Julie. Definitely something had been going on here. Julie thought maybe Hornby was part of it.

As Doreen walked down the steps, the door opened again behind her. Julie leaned against the doorjamb and frowned at her. "Do you think Hornby had something to do with Johnny's disappearance?"

"I don't know," Doreen said. "I have my suspicions. But without a body ..." She shrugged. "I don't know that there's anything we can do about it. What would be the motive?"

"Me," she said bleakly. "Hornby wanted me, and I had made it very clear I wasn't interested. Johnny was the perfect person for me. We had a fantastic future all mapped out." She glared at Hornby's house. "I always wondered. But I never could figure out how or why."

"I had guessed somebody arranged to meet him in the park," Doreen said, "like you mentioned."

"I did arrange to meet him," Julie said. "But he wasn't there, and he never showed up."

Doreen knew she had no reason to believe Julie, but there was just something—that note of desperation to Julie's need to look for answers—that Doreen trusted. "So far the only suspicious character in all of this is Hornby, but he's just been shot and in a car accident. So if somebody really hated him …"

"Not just somebody," Julie said. "Everybody."

"Tell me more," Doreen said invitingly. They still stood on the front steps. "Did George and Penny know about your relationship with Johnny?"

"No," Julie said. "We kept it private. Johnny didn't think they'd approve, since he'd recently broken up with Susan. But we'd liked each other before that. He didn't want to hurt Susan, so their relationship limped along longer than it should have. As soon as they split, we hooked up."

"Thank you for sharing that. I'm looking for something important, and I can't quite figure out what it is." Mugs wandered into the garden beside her. Doreen immediately shoved her hand into her pocket and pulled out a poopie bag. "I hope you don't mind." She motioned at Mugs.

Julie looked into her garden bed and chuckled. "No. A dog has gotta do what a dog has gotta do."

Grateful for that attitude, Doreen walked behind Mugs, waited until he did his business, then carefully scooped it all up, making sure she got the pieces of bark mulch that had a little bit of the droppings with it. She turned to walk to the garbage cans. "May I put the bag in one of your cans?"

Julie waved her hand at them. "Go ahead."

"Thank you so much. I don't know when your garbage is picked up, but I'm hoping this won't stink too badly." She walked toward the cans.

"For the longest time, we didn't have to worry about

garbage collection. The garbage truck driver for this area lived across from me," she said with a laugh, pointing at the house across the cul-de-sac. "Sometimes he'd even make special trips just for us."

Doreen stared over at Hornby's house and then back at her. "Hornby?"

"No, not Alan," she said. "His dad. That's what I meant about *for the longest time* but not anymore as his dad is retired now."

"Wow though. That would have been helpful. I have all kinds of stuff I'll be getting rid of. How convenient to have a garbage truck accessible."

"Absolutely," Julie said. "My mother was forever putting out pieces of junk furniture, and he'd take them away for her. The rules have all changed now, and the city is stricter about that stuff."

"Did he ever take the garbage truck home?"

Julie chuckled. "He wasn't supposed to, but sure he did. Sometimes I think he did that to help out the neighborhood, so the residents could throw extra garbage in. He was very, very conscientious. Although the city wanted forty hours a week from him, I swear he gave them forty-eight every week." She smiled.

"Is he still around?"

"Oh, sure," she said. "He's down at one of the old folks' homes. He's getting on now. Not sure how old he is, but he's gotta be close to ninety. He's heading toward a hospice, last I heard." She frowned. "Honestly, he might have already passed away. I don't know. And that would be a sad day. He was a good man."

"Did you guys ever get to ride around with him?" Doreen asked.

"Well, his son often did," she said with a big grin. "And Mr. Hornby did take us around one Halloween. We were pretending to be garbage men." She chuckled. "I think we were only about ten or so. Then we thought our buddy Alan had the best dad in the world."

"I bet," Doreen said, chuckling. "I guess you don't remember if he ever brought the truck home the summer Johnny went missing, huh?"

"Johnny wouldn't have taken off in it, if that's what you're thinking. Johnny couldn't drive it. It was big and cranky. Alan used to operate the levers for his dad sometimes. But it was never a smooth, sleek model. In fact, Mr. Hornby protested getting one of the *newfangled* trucks," she said, grinning at the memories. "He much preferred the old ones. Said all that new computerized wizardry would break down."

"Right. Still how convenient for you," Doreen said with envy, thinking of her crowded house. "Did you guys ever run over and put extra garbage in?"

She nodded. "My mum did. You could fill the bin in the back, and then it would get mushed up the next time he'd put stuff in. Back then the trucks weren't very sophisticated."

"Right. Back then you had a different landfill system than we do now." Doreen had yet to go to the Glenmore Landfill that serviced all the Kelowna area, but she'd heard it had gotten much more high-tech in the last few years. The new landfill was at a totally different location too. The old landfill had been reclaimed, with a new subdivision built atop it. The new location was bigger and had space for recycling.

"Yes," Julie said. "Back then we barely had anything like we do now, which is probably really too bad because a lot of the stuff we tossed could have been recycled."

"So he'd drive the truck, collect garbage, take it to the dump, and drop it all in?"

"Usually," Julie said. "There was always heavy equipment to move the garbage around, and then some of garbage would get burned."

"That makes sense," Doreen said slowly. Then a horrible idea filled her mind. She gave a final wave. "Thanks very much. If you see Penny return, could you tell her to give me a ring please?"

Julie gave a wave and walked back into her house, closing the door.

Doreen wondered how Julie would feel about Doreen's current theory.

She headed to Hornby's house and knocked on the door. No answer. She brought out her phone and called Mack as she headed toward the creek.

"I have a working theory on what happened to Johnny," she said. "The trouble is, twenty-nine years later, it'll be damn-near impossible to confirm it."

"Oh?" he said in a lazy voice. "Can't wait to hear this one."

She snorted. "Well, I'm not telling you then. Can you tell me who is living in the Hornby house now?"

"Your grandmother can answer a part of that question or at least get the answer," he said. "Old Man Hornby was our local garbage collector forever, since eons ago, and he's a resident at Rosemoor now."

"Right. I just heard that, but also that he's headed to a hospice or might have passed on recently," Doreen said. "Was he married? Did he raise his son alone? Do you know?"

Mack gave a long-suffering sigh.

She could hear the *click* of his keyboard. "Oh, can you access your cop stuff from home?" Excitement lit up her voice.

"No," he snapped. "*Hornby, Alan* is the only son. Mother died when he was sixteen. Old Man Hornby never remarried."

"No other siblings?"

"No," he said. "Just Alan."

"Thanks." She picked up the pace as she headed toward the creek. "I'm coming home again."

"Where have you been?"

"Trying to talk to Penny," she said, "but there's no sign of her, and one of the neighbors said he saw her take off with a suitcase."

"If you think about it, that doesn't seem very sinister," he said, snickering. "She's probably had enough of all your questions."

She frowned into her phone. "That's not very nice."

"True," he said.

"I imagine she's still looking for answers, particularly for George."

"Maybe," he said. "But what if they weren't that happily married couple, as you initially thought? Or maybe George killed his younger brother in a fit of rage."

"I did consider the idea," she said, "but then tossed it. George spent way too many of the ensuing years trying to find the truth. ... I did consider Penny," she said after a moment. "But I don't think she could've done it alone. She could have killed him, you know, by hitting him over the head when he was sitting there, unsuspecting. But she certainly wasn't strong enough to move the body on her own."

"So what now? You have an imaginary lover helping her out? A man no one has seen or heard of? What motive could there possibly be?"

"I don't know," she said. "That's one of the reasons why I tossed away that idea."

"Huh. Well, I agree with that. It also doesn't make any sense for Penny to contact you after all these years, asking you to look into it if she's the guilty party."

"I know," Doreen said. "That just added to it."

"I'm glad to hear it," he said.

She skirted around the outside of the cul-de-sac and headed for the creek, all three animals in a single line behind her. "I do have another theory though. I'll hang up now and call Nan. Bye." She clicked off and dialed Nan's number as she headed down the creek toward her home. Nan didn't answer. "Come on, Nan. Pick up. Please pick up."

But there was no answer. She tucked away her phone and marched as fast as she could back home. Thankfully the critters approved of her pace.

As soon as she saw the creek again, she felt a huge sense of relief. She could barely contain a sudden nervousness. She dialed Mack as she realized part of her unease. "I know you said he was shot and in a car accident, but just how badly injured is Hornby?"

"I don't know," he said. "Do I need to check for you?"

"Yeah," she said, "you do." She hung up on him. Inside her heart warmed that he took her concerns seriously.

When she reached the back of her house, she was happy to see she had truly set the alarm. She disabled it, stepped inside, then checked the front door, also relieved to see its alarm was set. With all the animals inside, she shut the door and turned on the alarm system again.

She couldn't explain it, but, all of a sudden, she had this horrible sense of urgency. She looked around her house, wondering how safe it was. Just because the alarms were set, that didn't mean her house was impenetrable. But it was better than what she'd had before.

Taking off her shoes, she did a quick check of the lower level. Everything appeared to be normal. Mugs wasn't upset in any way.

She glanced at her watch. It was later than she'd expected. Still, her mind buzzed uneasily. She crept upstairs, trying to miss the squeaky stairs, still hoping it was safe up here. She slipped into the spare bedroom and listened. No way she could hide the animals' presence, and that was a problem. She waited a long moment, checking the spare room, finding nothing here. A bathroom was across the hallway, but Mugs had gone in there and came back out again, his tail wagging.

She eyed him suspiciously. The only person he'd wag his tail for would be Mack. Still Mugs headed toward her, so that was good too. She probably was going crazy, but the last thing she wanted to do was go into her damn bedroom.

Goliath, however, had no such qualms. With his tail twitching, he sauntered into the bedroom and disappeared from her sight. Mugs followed him. When she didn't hear anything, she sighed with relief. She stepped into the bedroom with all its chaos and found nobody there.

Just to be sure, she checked the en suite bathroom and then, with a deep breath, plunged into the big closet to make sure nobody was hiding in there. There wasn't anyone. Feeling foolish, she came out with her phone ringing. It was Mack.

"Why did you hang up on me?"

"Because I had this terrible feeling once I got inside the house," she said. "I just finished checking under the beds and in the closets, and nobody's here."

His voice turned grim. "I'm on my way over. Back your way out of that house for the moment."

She froze. "Why?"

"Because Hornby is no longer in the hospital."

Chapter 24

Sunday Late Afternoon …

SHE HADN'T KNOWN her legs could carry her that far or that fast. But spurred by her, the animals flew behind her. She quickly unlocked the front door and stepped outside, racing down the front porch steps to the end of the driveway. There she danced around, waiting for Mack to show up. She hated that Hornby was loose.

Why would Mack even assume that Hornby would come after her again? Well, maybe because he'd already come here twice, and the last time he'd threatened her. So what were the chances he would come a third time?

Probably pretty damn good.

She turned to stare out into the street, looking for Mack's vehicle. When she still didn't see it, she walked into her front yard and then around to the back of the house. Surely if somebody were here, Mugs would have picked up on it.

As she walked past the side door to the garage, it burst open, startling her. A man jumped out, snatched her in his arms, one going around her neck to choke her. She couldn't even cry out. She gargled, scratched him hard with her nails, tried to stomp on his toes, then kicked up backward, trying to hit him in the groin.

When Mugs realized she was in trouble, he jumped on her attacker. Thaddeus came squawking down, landing on her attacker too, digging in his claws and pecking at his forehead. The man roared behind her, his grip loosening, cursing. And, dammit, she recognized Hornby's voice.

She spun around, her fist out, and clocked him one in the jaw. He stumbled backward, took one look at her, his eyes full of hate. "You're all nuts," he roared, brushing Thaddeus off his head. He disappeared, running as fast as he could through the backyard.

Doreen snatched Thaddeus up, crooning to him, even as she tried to control Mugs.

Just then Mack's truck came flying up the driveway. Mack must have caught sight of them from the entrance to the cul-de-sac. He was out of the truck, racing toward her in a heartbeat. He wrapped her in his arms. "Are you hurt?"

She shook her head. "Go after him. It was Hornby."

Mack had his phone in his hand. He ran behind her house. She grabbed Mugs again, fighting to keep him at her side. There was no sign of Goliath.

"Go left," she yelled to Mack. "Go left."

He changed direction and headed to the creek.

She stood, looking at the outside garage door she couldn't open fully before. She slid a hand around the wall, checking for a light switch. When she found it, she flipped it on, groaning because the garage was completely full of old furniture and boxes. But, from what she could see, nobody else was in here. Nor was there any room for someone to maneuver through the mess.

The door had been forced open and appeared to be

planed off on the edge to make it easier to open and close. So he'd been hiding, right inside the door, waiting for her. Either waiting for her to go to sleep and would trigger the alarm or hoping to catch her outside, like he had. Because of Mack's warning, she'd gone straight outside and had fallen victim to the maniac waiting for her.

Shaking, she walked back inside the house and put on the teakettle. She couldn't see Mack and had no idea if he'd called for backup or not. Just the thought of him out there with that crazy man made her quake in her boots.

"What if Hornby has a gun?" she asked Mugs. "He could turn around and shoot Mack dead."

What she also had to consider was maybe the asshole was coming around again, back to her place. She made herself a cup of tea, and, as she turned, she heard a hiss. She spun around to see Hornby standing in the kitchen doorway. And, sure enough, he had a gun in his hand.

She looked at him, knowing, when she'd come into the house, she hadn't reset the alarm. "Damn it, Mack will be really pissed at me for this one," she said with a bad attempt at humor.

Hornby's gaze just glinted.

"What did I ever do to you?" she asked.

"Asked too many questions," he said. "I wondered how much trouble you would be. But when I saw you continuously talking to Penny, I realized you would be a bigger problem than I thought. Once I saw you coming out of Julie's house, I knew you would be a huge pain in the arse. One I had to get rid of."

"Interesting," she said, leaning against the counter behind her, her hot cup of tea in her hand. She judged the distance between them. Boiling water was a poor weapon against a gun, but it was what she had. "So what did you do? Break Johnny's neck?"

He just shrugged, not saying anything.

"Are you sure you don't want to tell somebody after all this time?" she asked. "Or do we have to bug your father for the real answers?"

"You leave my dad alone," Hornby snapped. "He's a good man."

"Yep, he sure is," she said. "Does he know what you did? Did he help you out with that?"

He glared at her. "You don't know anything."

"If that was the truth," she said, "if I really didn't know anything, then why would you be worried about me?"

He took two steps forward, and she switched her hold on the hot tea in her hand, readying herself.

And then she heard footsteps. Mugs woofed several times at her feet. "*You* could attack him," she said to Mugs.

Mugs woofed several more times. This time his neck bristled, as did the hair along his back.

She studied it in interest. "He really doesn't like you, does he?"

"That's okay," Hornby said. "After I shoot you dead, I'll make sure I kill all three of these friggin' animals." He put a hand to his head. When he pulled away his fingers, she could see blood on them.

"*Ooh*, yeah. That's Thaddeus. His beak is hard. And, when he's pissed off, you really don't want to get in his way," she said, chuckling.

"What the hell are you laughing about?" he roared. "You should be pleading for your life. You're one crazy-ass lady."

At that, Mugs raced toward him.

He lowered the gun to shoot the dog.

She stepped forward, crying out, "Don't!"

He raised the gun toward her, but it was too late. The hot tea flew in his face. She bent over and tackled him as his arm went up to wipe at his face. She hit him in the belly and down he went, his gun going off and firing into the ceiling.

She heard a roar behind her and saw Mack had arrived. But it was too chaotic to keep an eye on him. Mugs busily chewed on Hornby's arm. Hornby screamed for help, and Mack stomped on Hornby's gun arm, kicking away the weapon.

She, on the other hand, sat on Hornby's chest and plowed her fist into his face. "You were going to shoot my dog." Then the pain hit, and she cried out, staring at her throbbing hand.

Goliath, sitting on the fifth stair up, came through the railings and jumped on Hornby's face. Then he jumped off, leaving huge claw marks across it.

Hornby screamed as the claws ripped open his skin. And then he started to sob. "She's crazy. Somebody needs to lock her up, and somebody *needs* to shoot these animals."

She couldn't help herself. She smacked him across the face with her injured hand. "I am not crazy, and nobody is hurting my animals."

Mack reached down, grabbing her by the shoulder. "Easy," he said. "He's not going anywhere. I've got him. Can you please get off him and let me flip him over to put cuffs on him?"

She stared up at Mack, loving that worried expression on his face as he stared down at her. She smiled. "I'm okay, you know?"

He nodded. "I know you are, but you might want to take another look at yourself."

Frowning, she saw she was now covered in Hornby's blood from Goliath's claws. She reached up to pat her cheeks and sighed. "Now I'm really upset. The last thing I want is to get covered in this crazy man's blood."

"Who are you calling a crazy?" Hornby roared. "You're the crazy one."

"Really?" she snapped. "You're the one who broke your friend's neck and stuffed him in your dad's garbage truck and then used the truck to smash his body in with the trash, so nobody would see him. When your dad went out the next day to collect garbage, not knowing Johnny's body went along for the trip, Johnny was then taken to the landfill at the end of the day. That's how crazy you are. Why would you do that?"

"Because he was taking off with my girl," Hornby snapped back. "He had no right. Julie was mine."

"Julie and Johnny," Doreen said with heavy emphasis, "were an item. Julie didn't want anything to do with you. Even back then she saw what a crazy coot you were." Her fists balled up on their own, and she went to punch him again.

Mack grabbed her arm and stopped it just inches away from Hornby's face.

She glared at Mack. "Somebody needs to knock this guy out."

"Nobody will punch him, at least not again," Mack said with a sigh. He tugged her forward and off his captive. "Besides, you hurt your hand."

She glared at Hornby, her throbbing fist still held back by Mack. "What about those friends of yours who died in the car accident? Did you kill them too?"

"I had to kill them," he said simply. "They saw me."

She gasped. "So, not only did you kill Johnny but you did it in front of others?" She shook her head in disbelief. "How stupid are you?"

"You crazy bat," he roared. "I am not stupid. I didn't mean for them to see. I was in the back yard and knocked him out. He must have lost the medallion then. I got Johnny home by dragging him through the park. I decided to put him in the garbage truck right away, so nobody would know. And they happened to be coming by."

"What was the price of their silence?" she asked. And then she knew. "Johnny's car, wasn't it?"

He nodded glumly. "Yeah, it was. But I knew that wouldn't be enough, so, when I saw them on the road, I ran them off. At the time I knew it would look like an accident, or at least Susan would believe it was an accident because she'd been sleeping. She'd been out partying hard the previous night and was still stoned and drunk. She was the passenger in my car and had passed out. Only she woke up in the aftermath, and I gave her the explanation she ended up telling the cops. So she didn't know anything firsthand."

"What about her identifying the multicolor vehicle?"

He shrugged. "She glommed onto the image of a multi-colored vehicle because that's the one she was in. She was so stoned and still drunk that she didn't have a clue. As for the rest, well, she just mimicked what I said to try to hide her mental state. Afterward she didn't remember much at all. We were *witnesses* to our friends' death," he said sarcastically. "And no blood or scrapes were on my vehicle, not obvious ones, so the police couldn't do anything."

"Did you kill her," she asked abruptly.

"No." He chuckled. "I thought about it but she was useless all her life. The only good thing she did was die early."

Mack hauled Hornby to his feet, snapped his arms behind him, and cuffed him.

"Wait," she cried out. "Did you break into my house trying to steal antiques? Were you working with Darth?"

"No way would I work with him. I was getting in on the goldmine before he could." He snorted. "Or would have if you hadn't interrupted me."

Doreen looked toward the doorway to see two uniformed cops. She recognized both and shrugged. "Hi, guys."

Chester, the younger one, reached up and scratched his head. "Hi. So do you have access to our cold cases or something?"

"Or does Mack just give you access," Arnold said with a wide grin.

She pointed her finger at him, grimaced from the pain, then just frowned. "Neither. Penny Jordan, Johnny's sister-in-law, asked me to look into the case. What was I supposed to do, say no?" And then she understood another little piece. She turned to look at Alan Hornby. "You threatened her, didn't you?"

He glared at her. "Who the hell are you talking about now?"

"Penny. You threatened her. That's why she took off. My questioning her scared you. You realized it all came from her, so you threatened her."

"Hell, she was putting the property on the market anyway," he said. "I just made a hard suggestion that she should do it sooner rather than later, before she didn't have a chance to do it at all." He sported a big grin. "Besides, you know how everybody talks about their *great* marriage? They fought *all* the time."

"Did it ever occur to you," Doreen said quietly, "that

sometimes fighting is people's way of airing grievances. But afterward, things are good again."

"Whatever," he said. "Personally I think she probably had a hand in George's death."

"Why the hell would you say that?" Doreen asked.

The two cops stared at Hornby in avid fascination.

He shrugged. "Because the guy just upped and died. Everybody said he had a heart condition. But I saw him at the time, and white foam came from his mouth." He snorted then. "Besides why haven't you figured out who shot me? Like you give a damn about that."

"Maybe no one cares about you. But I'm sure somebody did an autopsy on George," Doreen said. "And foam doesn't necessarily mean he was murdered."

"No, but Penny having a lover at the time George died could." He sneered. "So your nice and perfect Penny was not so nice and perfect."

Doreen gave him a bland little smile. "People like you can't stand to see anyone happy. There's rot in your core. You can't resist spreading it all around you. Well, now you'll be with your own kind. The rotten kind. You should finally feel right at home."

With that, Mack marched Hornby out the front door to hand him off to the two cops following them.

They just shook their heads. "Man, oh, man," Chester said. "Since she arrived in town, all we do is work overtime."

"You're welcome," Doreen called out. "I've also made the streets much safer. And, when you get overtime, you get extra pay, and I don't get paid at all for my help. So quit your complaining."

The two men probably didn't even hear what she'd said though. They were down the steps and walking toward the cop car. She held her uninjured hand over her eyes for a long moment, her mind running endlessly as she thought about poor Johnny's end.

When she felt Mack's arms come around her and hold her close, she burrowed in deeper. He held her for several long moments. Finally she let out a heavy sigh and felt some of the tension rolling off her back. She looked up at him. "Thanks for the warning," she said. "I got out as soon as I could."

He nodded grimly. "You did and right into Hornby's arms."

"Yeah. That wasn't your fault," she said. "I'm the one who said nobody could get in or out of the garage via the outside door, and I was so wrong because he was hiding in there."

He tilted her head up. "You mean, there's room in there to hide?"

She wrinkled her nose. "Barely. But it looks like I need to get one of those big garbage bins and put ninety percent of what's in the garage in the bin. It's pretty bad. And I think Hornby must have done something to the door because it opens and closes now. Before, when I tried, it was all I could do to open it a little. And then it squeaked terribly too."

"Which means this was premeditated, his attack on you," Mack said. "Good to know." He gave her a slight shake. "Did you throw your tea at him?"

She leaned back, looked down at her tea-covered, blood-stained blouse. "Yes. And now I need another one." She stepped out of his arms, walked back into the kitchen, and put on the teakettle. She stared out at the garden, collecting her thoughts. But her mind was just such a mess. She turned to look at Mack. "You know what? If I had the money, I think I would sign up for one of those self-defense courses."

He crossed his arms and looked at her grimly. "It would be nice if you would stop getting into situations where you need self-defense."

She nodded. "But I don't try to get into trouble. Once I figured this out, I was going to tell you. But I wanted to check the maps on the old Kelowna landfill to see if there was any hope of finding Johnny's body."

Mack shook his head. "I highly doubt it. We can see if there are any records, but it's been twenty-nine years, and the old landfill has been completely covered over and reclaimed. No, there won't be much chance of finding his bones, especially with the new subdivision built on top of the old landfill."

She nodded. "So, in a way, it was the perfect crime."

"It was," he said. "Except for you."

She gave him a wide smile. "I didn't do anything really," she said. "I just asked a bunch of questions, poked a bunch of people, waited to see what would pop up. Secrets like that are really great big zits. When you poke hard enough, they explode with all kinds of nastiness coming out."

He shook his head. "That's one hell of an analogy. I'm not mentioning that one to the cops at the station."

The teakettle squealed. Doreen turned it off and made herself another cup of tea. "Do you want a cup?"

"Hell, I want something a whole lot stronger." He went to the front closet, reached up to the very top shelf, and pulled out a bottle of whiskey.

She stared at it. "I didn't know that was up there." Disgruntled, she added, "I'd have had half a dozen drinks myself over the last few weeks."

He poured two glasses with a shot in each.

She noted they were freehand shots and rather hefty.

He handed her one and said, "Drink up."

"I'm not in shock," she said.

"No, I am," he said in a hard tone. "And I don't drink alone. So drink up." He lifted his glass, clicked it with hers, and then tossed his back.

She shrugged, did the same, and coughed as the liquid fire poured down her throat. She choked and gasped, finding it hard to catch her breath. "Are you trying to kill me?" she croaked.

He gave her a glass of water, which helped.

Finally she sat at the table and relaxed. "Will this day ever be over?"

"It will," he said. "It definitely is now."

She looked up at him and smiled. "So how about spending a few hours at the end of this very long day with a friend? We'll take a cup of tea, sit in the garden, and forget about murders and murderers."

He smiled, made himself a cup of tea, and reached out a hand. "Come on. Let's go outside for a few minutes and relax. Then we'll create something from the leftover pasta and enjoy a meal. Afterward we can call it a day."

"Agreed," she said as together they walked out to her garden.

Epilogue

In the Mission, Kelowna, BC
Sunday afternoon ... on the same day she closed her last case

M ACK GOT A hold of Penny over the phone to give her the official account, and she returned home from visiting a friend in Vernon. As soon as she hit town, she walked to Doreen's place. When Doreen opened her front door, Penny threw her arms around her.

"Thank you so much," she cried out and hugged her again. After a moment, she stepped back and said, "I'm so sorry. I didn't mean to run out on you. But I didn't know what that horrible man meant to do. I couldn't stick around long enough to find out."

"It's okay," Doreen said. "He can't hurt you again."

Needing to walk and talk, both of them still too keyed up to just sit inside, they walked along Doreen's backyard as Doreen gave Penny all the details. When their questions and answers ran out, Penny noticed the large garden beds along the side fence. "This is going to be lovely," she said, motioning to a long stretch of Doreen's overgrown garden.

"I've got a long way to go to get it back to what it was,"

Doreen said. "It's a lot of work."

"Understood. It's the same at my place," Penny said. "And not sure I want to now. Before Johnny disappeared, I loved gardening. Then it became a way to wear off the worry and tension over the years, but after George's death …"

"I'd leave it as is," Doreen said. "You're selling, and your yard doesn't look too bad."

"And yet, selling the house feels like a betrayal to George."

Doreen looked at Penny. "Were you happy with George?"

Penny beamed. "Very happy with him. He was a good provider, a good man."

Doreen didn't know if she should ask about George's death. It was an uncomfortable topic. Just because Hornby had made some accusations, that didn't mean it wasn't true but also didn't mean Hornby wasn't just causing trouble. "How did George die again?"

"A heart attack," Penny said, her face stilling. She put a hand to her heart. "He went very quickly."

Penny walked toward the rear of the property, where a large bunch of echinacea stood tall. The blooms hadn't opened yet, but it looked to explode with flowers soon.

"I'm sorry for your loss," Doreen said. "That must have been very difficult."

"Oh, it was," she said. "It was, indeed."

Doreen looked at the low patch of echinacea in her garden and smiled. "I remember how your plants are much bigger than mine." She motioned at her poor echinacea, adding, "I have all kinds of other plants crowding mine, as well as more plants I need to move like foxglove, belladonna, nightshade…" She slid her glance sideways, checking

Penny's reaction to her list of poisonous plants, but saw absolutely nothing. Satisfied, Doreen linked her arm with Penny's and faced her new gardening friend. "I wanted to give you more of the news personally, before you heard it elsewhere."

"Thank you for that," Penny said. "I should get home now." She looked back at Doreen's gardens as they walked toward the creek. "You know what? Considering we found the dagger in the dahlias at my place and then that medallion out in my front yard too, I won't ever look at a big clump of plants like that without wondering if more evidence is hiding in it."

Doreen's mind kicked in, repeating *evidence in the echinacea, evidence in the echinacea.* But that was not today's story. That would have to wait for another day. With a smile she said, "Forget all about that for now," she said. "We can garden another day."

Penny chuckled. "Sounds good to me. At least we have something in common."

Doreen nodded. "We do, indeed. We plant things, all kinds of seeds, even ideas we weren't aware we were planting ..." Her tone was cryptic.

Penny looked at her sideways, but Doreen just smiled and suggested, "Maybe you should set up a memorial garden for Johnny now." At Penny's startled look, Doreen explained further. "I know that came out of the blue. But I was thinking, you know, as I looked at that echinacea, how you have lost both Johnny and George, and both of them loved your home."

"But I'm selling it," Penny said. "Remember that?"

Doreen nodded. "Maybe that's a nice way to leave it then, as the home you all shared together," she said. "Creating a memorial garden before you move out would be a very nice thing to do for them. If the new owners rip it out, well, all fair and good. You wouldn't have to do much. Just set up two rings of rocks and a little marker stone in the center of each ring and say some kind words over it. You'll get Johnny's medallion and his knife back at some point in time from the police. There is that little cross as well."

Penny looked thoughtful as she stared at the creek. "You're thinking about me getting closure, aren't you?"

"I am," Doreen said, but she was also thinking of something else that just wouldn't leave her alone. "For your own sake. Plus you don't know how long it'll take to sell your house." she said. "But, if you think about it, it could be a few months or even a year. You haven't put it on the market yet, have you?"

Penny shook her head. "I couldn't while you were investigating," she said starkly. "It seemed wrong to. Now that you're done, and we know what happened ..." She shook her head. "George spent most of his adult life searching for his brother, and to think that he never found out, ... but, in just a few days, look what you accomplished?"

"I'm really sorry about the long passage of time without answers," Doreen said, her voice compassionate. "I think one of the hardest things for people is to never find out the truth."

"And you did it so fast," Penny said in amazement. "That's what really blows me away. I only talked to you like, what, last Tuesday, Wednesday? And then, all of a sudden, it's Sunday, and here you are already, with it solved."

Doreen didn't know what to say. While she formulated an answer, Penny burst out, "Why couldn't the police have done that years ago?"

"Because years ago, people stayed mum for a lot of different reasons. Things were different back then. People kept secrets, likely out of fear," Doreen said slowly, thinking about what it had taken for the answers to come to the surface. "And I think Hornby stayed low and out of trouble, until he left town as soon as he could. Now so much time has passed, he thought he was safe."

Penny said, "It makes no sense. He killed all three of those boys, for nothing."

"Yes," Doreen said, speaking slowly. "It also helped Hornby keep his secret when Susan couldn't remember anything from the car accident. She was under the influence of the drugs and still hungover, so it's no wonder the cops didn't take her seriously. Yet she's the one who kept saying a multicolored vehicle was involved, whereas Alan said it happened so fast that he couldn't remember anything, other than a small car. Black, he thought, but he wasn't even sure of that. Could have been dark green or dark blue. Apparently he'd been fighting with Susan."

"And, of course, it was all make believe anyway," Penny whispered. "It's just too incredible."

"It is," Doreen said, "but, honestly, often the truth is the simplest answer of all."

"They had found no DNA back then that led to any suspects. They had no digital anything back then," Penny said, "like to see if Johnny showed up in another county or whatever."

Doreen nodded. "And, of course, Alan's father stuck up for him and gave him an alibi. Mr. Hornby believed his son was at home and didn't see the body in the trash truck's compactor. Julie's family wasn't any better. Nobody wanted to point the finger at Alan Hornby, even though nobody liked him. Even Julie had no way of knowing that an argument or picking one man over another would cause this kind of a reaction."

"But to think it was love triangle gone wrong," Penny said in bewilderment. "And for all of it to stay a secret over all these years ... We didn't even know about Julie."

"But Mother Earth gives up her secrets eventually," Doreen said. "Think about the dagger. Think about the medallion. Think about the cross."

"There's no chance of Johnny's body being found, is there?"

"No, I doubt it," Doreen said softly but firmly. "I'm afraid that idea has to be set aside. He was placed in the old landfill. Everything there was all mulched together and reclaimed, as the city does its job, and now a whole new subdivision has been built up there. I think the community of Wilden is there now."

Penny looked at her. "All those new fancy big houses in Glenmore?"

"I think so," Doreen said. "If not that area, another one nearby." She watched her friend, still trying to take it all in, to make peace with it. "Come on. You're a bit shaken up. I need a walk anyway. Let's get you home."

"It'll be dark soon. Are you sure?" Penny asked, but she looked grateful nonetheless. "I have to admit that I'm feeling pretty shaky. Knowing that it's over, that all this which haunted us—which haunted almost my entire marriage—is over. Now if only you had moved to Kelowna years ago," she joked, "then George would have known what happened before he died."

"The thing is, back then, I probably wouldn't have been doing what I'm doing now anyway."

"Why is that?"

"Because I'm a different person from who I was even a few years ago," Doreen said with half a smile. She called for Mugs. "Mugs, you want to go for a walk?"

Immediately her basset hound, who'd long lost his pedigree and his good manners, appeared, jumped up, and twirled around on his back legs. She giggled. "Now if only we could make money with a circus act," she said. She bent down, gave him a quick hug, then pulled his leash from her back pocket to hook it on.

"You don't normally put him on the leash, do you?" Penny asked.

"No," she said. "Not since I moved here, but he is leash trained. I just figured that, every once in a while, I should do it to keep him in the habit."

At that, they stepped out on the creek pathway, and a streak of orange bolted toward them. "Goliath, want to go for a walk?"

From the veranda at the back of her house, Doreen could hear Thaddeus calling out, "Wait for me, wait for me."

Doreen chuckled. "I guess Thaddeus wants to come too."

Penny was fascinated as Doreen squatted down, waiting for the bird to waddle to them. She stretched out her arm, and Thaddeus hopped onto the back of her hand and sidestepped all the way up to her shoulder. Once there, he brushed his beak against her cheek. She reached out and gently stroked his back. "I wouldn't go without you, big guy."

As if he understood, he nudged her a couple more times and then settled in. Just as she was about to take a step, he said, "Giddyup, giddyup."

Instantly she froze, turned her head to look at him, and said, "No way am I following your commands."

He twisted his head, looked at her, batted those huge eyes of his, and said, "Thaddeus, go."

"Yes," she said in exasperation. "You can tell that you'll be going somewhere," she said. "You're already on my shoulder, and we're already out of the house."

And then he seemed to settle without more arguments. As she glanced at Penny, her new friend tried to hold back her chuckles. She rolled her eyes at Penny. "It's pretty bad when the bird treats me like some sort of an old gray mare," she snapped. "Oh, wait." She returned to her house, reset the alarms on the front and back doors, and then rejoined her animals and Penny. "Now let's go for a walk."

"I heard the beeps." Penny glanced back at the house. "Do you always set an alarm when you go for a walk? You don't look like the type to me."

"Normally I wouldn't be," Doreen said cheerfully. "But I have an antiques dealer coming tomorrow to look at a few pieces," she said, carefully fudging the truth. "I would hate for anybody to go inside and help themselves."

Penny nodded. "Oh, my, no," she said. "When I think of all the hours George and Nan spent arguing about her antiques …"

"Why arguing?" Doreen asked.

"Because George thought she should sell them, and Nan said she had another plan in mind."

Doreen's heart warmed when she thought about Nan's *other* plan. "Yes, Nan was holding on to them for me," Doreen said with a wistful smile. "My grandmother is pretty special."

"Oh, she's special all right," Penny said, chuckling.

"George used to come home from one of his visits, and, although he'd be brighter and full of laughter, he'd say that Nan was especially crazy."

"A lot of people have told me that she fell somewhere in that realm," Doreen said. "I am afraid she's losing some of her memory now though."

"She's probably not taking all those supplements George told her to take. They worked like a charm for her."

"What kind of supplements?"

Penny shrugged. "I'll have to take a look," she said. "I have the notes at home somewhere. George always had a fascination for natural remedies. Nan was having trouble even back then."

"And they helped her?"

Penny nodded emphatically. "Oh, yes. George used to comment on it all the time."

"Well, if you could get me that list, that would be awesome," Doreen said. "I have absolutely no idea about supplements. And I really don't like doctors."

"No, once you deal with something like George's heart condition," Penny said, "you have to consider how much the medical profession actually knows. Obviously they're helpful a lot of the time, but some of the time it makes you wonder if they aren't just pushing drugs."

"Exactly," Doreen said. "But if you had supplements that worked instead, that would be huge."

"I think it's the same list he gave me, so I can certainly find out when I get a moment," Penny said. "Do you think Nan would take them?"

Doreen nodded. "Particularly if I say it was the same stuff that George used to give her."

"That might work too," Penny said. "Those two really

did get along like a house on fire. Nan was pretty upset at George's funeral."

"I'm sure she was," Doreen said. "I think one of the hardest things about getting old is watching all your friends die before you."

"Very true," Penny said. As they walked up to Penny's house a good half hour later, Penny motioned and said, "If you want to come in for a few minutes, I can look for that list."

Doreen brightened. She'd been looking for an excuse as it was to go inside and see how Penny lived. So far she'd only been invited into a few houses, Nan's, Julie's and Doreen's murderous neighbor, Ella. Doreen nodded and said, "Sure. Thank you very much." Together, the five of them trooped into Penny's home.

Inside Penny's house, Doreen looked around. It was stuffed with pretty floral-patterned couches, large floral paintings, and, yes, ... floral carpets. It was also pristine. "You haven't started packing, have you?"

"Well, it's not like I've sold my house yet," Penny said in a dry tone.

As Doreen looked at Penny's big living room, it wasn't really cluttered, but it was overstuffed with mementos. "If you got a staging crew or a Realtor in here," she said, "I'm pretty sure they'll insist on all the pictures coming off the walls, all the stuff being moved off the countertops, hauling out the big hutches you've got. Realtors can be quite brutal."

Penny's jaw dropped. "You know what? I was thinking about bringing in a stager to see what they'd charge me. But it sounds like you know a lot about it."

"Not necessarily," she said, "but I've watched lots of shows on TV. And my husband did a lot of buying and selling."

"Right," Penny said.

Doreen could almost see that, in Penny's mind, those disqualifiers just raised Doreen's status several notches. Doreen didn't understand how that worked because, of course, people should be doing their own investigation and research on this type of thing before deciding. Besides, in Doreen's mind, she should be demoted not promoted for her husband's activities. "Have you picked out a Realtor?"

"Absolutely. I was going to ask Simi Jeron," she said. "I've known that family for thirty years or more."

"Oh, good," she said, "that should make it easier. Ask her about staging and decluttering when she's here."

"Well, she's already been here once, but we haven't signed any paperwork yet."

"That's when the boom will get lowered," Doreen said, chuckling.

"I hope not," Penny said, walking into her kitchen, approaching a large cupboard, opened it up. She took out a small notebook sitting on top of the box of vitamin bottles and brought it to the kitchen table and sat down, flipping through the pages. "Ah, here it is," she said, "a page just for Nan." She held it up and then read from it. "Vitamin D, ginkgo, B12, and I'm not sure what this other one says."

"Do you mind if I take a look?" Doreen asked, holding out her hand. Penny handed it over. As Doreen looked at it, she said, "I'm not sure what that is either. May I get a copy of this?"

"We'll photocopy both sides."

Passing the book back, Penny made copies of both sides and then gave Doreen the two sheets.

"Thanks."

Penny nodded with a smile, and both women returned to the kitchen, where Penny tucked the book back into the vitamin corner.

"Must've been nice that George was so interested in health," she said.

"A lot of good it did him," Penny said bitterly, and she winced. "I'm sorry. I shouldn't have said that."

"I guess you're angry he died, huh?"

"Isn't that the stupidest thing?" Penny asked. "Even after a year, I still look around our house, and I get mad at him. We had all these plans for retirement, all these things we would do now that he wasn't working anymore, and here he ups and dies on me."

"Well, can't you do those things on your own?"

"I could," Penny said, "but I don't really want to. They were things we would do *together*. They were *our* plans."

"Versus *your* plans?"

Penny froze for a moment and slowly nodded. "Very insightful." She glanced at her watch and said, "Oh, my goodness. I have to run. I have to meet someone."

"Oh, absolutely no problem," Doreen said. "We'll go and let you get on then." She and her animals were ushered to the front door. Goliath had taken up a seat in the middle of George's big recliner. Doreen scooped him into her arms, with Thaddeus still on her shoulder, and Mugs trotted behind them. "It was a nice visit," she said, "and I'm glad I had good news for you."

As she stepped down the front steps, Penny said, "And once again, thank you," she said sincerely. "I will definitely sleep better now."

With a half wave, Doreen watched as Penny got into her vehicle and reversed out of her driveway and headed down the street. But Doreen had stopped on Penny's driveway. Doreen *really* shouldn't do what she was thinking of doing. But it was pretty damn hard to talk herself out of it. With a shrug, she decided it would worry away at her, so she might as well put her mind to rest.

She put Goliath down, Thaddeus taking the opportunity to get down as well, and quickly headed into Penny's backyard, where Johnny had his favorite place to sit. Doreen didn't even know why Penny's echinacea bed was bugging her, but she thought she'd read somewhere how echinacea was used in all kinds of medicine. It certainly wasn't—as far as she knew—a killer, but anything was a killer if you took too much of it.

Doreen made a quick trip through Penny's backyard, mentally jotting down what was here: marigolds, lilies, calla lilies, black-eyed Susans. None were flowering yet. Daisies were about to explode with blooms. ... This would be a lively garden when summer hit. She really appreciated the wide variety, even a few straggling tulips. She stopped and stared at them and shook her head. "What are you guys doing drooping over like that?"

She stopped to study stalks reaching for the sky. They wouldn't bloom for another month or two, and this bed was far too crowded for them to do well. Then there was the belladonna and foxglove mingling in the patch too. *Drat.* So was their presence that bad? She couldn't tell. But as the same poisonous plants lived in Nan's garden... Possibly Nan and George had shared a love of poisonous plants as well as antiques?

Glancing around, Doreen noted how little shade the echinacea plants would probably get during the daylight hours, backed up against the fence as they were, which wouldn't help their growth. As she dropped down in front of the massive green patch—at least three feet across, with dozens of plants in there—she frowned, realizing their roots would be completely twisted together. Echinacea plants loved company, particularly its own family, but, at one point in time, they would fight and hate each other—just like every other family.

Too-close confines caused too-much strife.

She checked the ground around the roots, unable to help herself, and realized that they were also very dry. The ground was poor here, with many rocks noticeable in the soil. Echinacea could survive in crappy soil. A lot of plants could survive. But the intention of a garden was not to have them survive; it was to have the flowers thrive. And again, as she glanced around the backyard, what had once been Penny's pride and joy at this point in time was probably just a constant source of work and bad memories. As Doreen walked past the echinacea, she thought she saw something else burrowed in the center of one of the plants. But just then, a man asked from the park side of the fence, "Hey, what are you doing back there?"

She popped out of Penny's backyard gate guiltily, leaving the gate open for her animals, and plastered a bright smile on her face. "I walked home with Penny," she said, "but she had to take off. I just wanted to take a quick look at her garden. She has done so well here," she said, injecting a bright warmth to her voice.

The man looked at her suspiciously.

She looked him over, from the top of his six-foot frame to his dirty sneakers and held out a hand. "I'm Doreen Montgomery, and who are you?"

Reluctantly he shook her hand. "I'm Steve."

"Steve?"

His frown deepened. "Just Steve."

She nodded and smiled and said, "Well, if you see Penny, and you want to tell her how I was in her backyard, that's fine," she said. "She knows that I'm a crazy gardener too. I was checking out her echinacea."

"Echinacea?" he asked doubtfully, looking at the green splotch against the fence.

"Echinacea," she said firmly. "We were talking about mine at my house earlier."

At that, his face seemed to settle, and his shoulders sagged, as if with relief.

"Not to worry," she said. "I'm not a thief. I'm the one who helped solved Johnny's disappearance."

At that, awareness came into Steve's eyes. Of course Mugs's slow approach, his head lowered and moving from side to side like a pissed-off bull drew more attention to Doreen. So did the orange streak that raced between Steve's legs, and he grinned. "Now I know who you are."

Thaddeus, not to be outdone, squawked, "No you don't. No you don't."

"Yeah, sorry about them," she said. She gave Steve a quick finger wave. "And now I'll head home before my critters decide that they like Penny's garden better than mine," she said in a joking manner.

Steve watched as she and her animals ambled toward the creek. "Why are you walking along the creek?" he asked, calling behind her.

"Because I love it," she said. "It's my favorite place to walk."

He shrugged and said, "Nothing but dirty water down there. It's full of ducks and all kinds of waterfowl."

"Hopefully I'll see some today."

"You won't catch me walking through the water, that's their toilet." And with that, he headed off.

She walked a few more steps and turned to look back. He strode away, not having explained his presence at Penny's property. Doreen frowned and thought about that, then sent Penny a quick text. **Stopped to take a quick look at your echinacea plants. A stranger named Steve came up and didn't seem terribly friendly. Wasn't sure what he was doing in the park behind your place. Just a heads-up.** And she left it at that.

"Come on, Goliath, Mugs ..." Thaddeus squawked as he waddled toward her, but then Mugs came racing forward with Goliath on his heels, and, in a surprisingly quick move, Thaddeus jumped on Mugs, screaming at the top of his lungs, "Giddyup, Mugs. Giddyup, Mugs."

By the time Doreen had crossed the bridge and headed up her backyard, Thaddeus had long giving up riding Mugs, subsequently walking. Now he was tucked into the crook of her neck, swaying with her every step. She crossed the bridge as her phone beeped with a return text. **He's a lovely neighbor, but he doesn't like strangers. That echinacea is doing terrible. As are some of my more specialized plants. Suggestions?**

Doreen grinned. Perfect entrance to find out more. **Absolutely. Maybe we'll have tea another day and check it out.**

Perfect.

This concludes Book 4 of Lovely Lethal Gardens: Daggers in the Dahlias.

Read about Evidence in the Echinacea: Lovely Lethal Gardens, Book 5

Lovely Lethal Gardens: Evidence in the Echinacea (Book #5)

A new cozy mystery series from *USA Today* best-selling author Dale Mayer. Follow gardener and amateur sleuth Doreen Montgomery—and her amusing and mostly lovable cat, dog, and parrot—as they catch murderers and solve crimes in lovely Kelowna, British Columbia.

Riches to rags. ... Controlling to chaos. ... But murder ... well maybe ...

Doreen's success at solving murders has hit the newswires across the country, but all Doreen wants is to be left alone. She has antiques to get to the auction house and a relationship with Corporal Mack Moreau to work out, not to mention a new friendship to nurture with Penny, Doreen's first friend in Kelowna, and Doreen doesn't want to ruin things.

But when a surprise accusation won't leave Doreen alone—about Penny's late husband George's death and made by one of the men Doreen helped put away—she thinks that maybe it can't hurt to just take a quick look into her new friend's past.

Before Doreen knows it, she's juggling a cold case, a closed case, and a possible mercy killing... along with cultivating her relationships with Penny, Mack, and Doreen's pets: Mugs, the basset hound; Goliath, the Maine coon cat, and Thaddeus, the far-too-talkative African gray parrot. And while Mack should be used to Doreen's antics by now, when she dives into yet another of his cases it's becoming increasingly hard to take ...

Book 5 is available now!
To find out more visit Dale Mayer's website.
https://geni.us/DMEvidenceUniversal

Get Your Free Book Now!

Have you met Charmin Marvin?

If you're ready for a new world to explore, and love ill-mannered cats, I have a series that might be your next binge read. It's called Broken Protocols, and it's a series that takes you through time-travel, mysteries, romance... and a talking cat named Charmin Marvin.

Go here and tell me where to send it!
https://dl.bookfunnel.com/s3ds5a0w8n

Author's Note

Thank you for reading Lovely Lethal Gardens, Books 3–4! If you enjoyed the book, please take a moment and leave a short review.

Dear reader,

I love to hear from readers, and you can contact me at my website: www.dalemayer.com or at my Facebook author page. To be informed of new releases and special offers, sign up for my newsletter or follow me on BookBub. And if you are interested in joining Dale Mayer's Reader Group, here is the Facebook sign up page.
http://geni.us/DaleMayerFBGroup

Cheers,
Dale Mayer

About the Author

Dale Mayer is a *USA Today* best-selling author, best known for her SEALs military romances, her Psychic Visions series, and her Lovely Lethal Garden cozy series. Her contemporary romances are raw and full of passion and emotion (Broken But ... Mending, Hathaway House series). Her thrillers will keep you guessing (Kate Morgan, By Death series), and her romantic comedies will keep you giggling (*It's a Dog's Life*, a stand-alone novella; and the Broken Protocols series, starring Charming Marvin, the cat).

Dale honors the stories that come to her—and some of them are crazy, break all the rules and cross multiple genres!

To go with her fiction, she also writes nonfiction in many different fields, with books available on résumé writing, companion gardening, and the US mortgage system. All her books are available in print and ebook format.

Connect with Dale Mayer Online

Dale's Website – www.dalemayer.com
Twitter – @DaleMayer
Facebook Page – geni.us/DaleMayerFBFanPage
Facebook Group – geni.us/DaleMayerFBGroup
BookBub – geni.us/DaleMayerBookbub
Instagram – geni.us/DaleMayerInstagram
Goodreads – geni.us/DaleMayerGoodreads
Newsletter – geni.us/DaleNews

Also by Dale Mayer

Published Adult Books:

Hathaway House
Aaron, Book 1
Brock, Book 2
Cole, Book 3
Denton, Book 4
Elliot, Book 5
Finn, Book 6
Gregory, Book 7
Heath, Book 8
Iain, Book 9
Jaden, Book 10
Keith, Book 11
Lance, Book 12
Melissa, Book 13

The K9 Files
Ethan, Book 1
Pierce, Book 2
Zane, Book 3
Blaze, Book 4
Lucas, Book 5
Parker, Book 6
Carter, Book 7
Weston, Book 8

Greyson, Book 9
Rowan, Book 10
Caleb, Book 11

Lovely Lethal Gardens
Arsenic in the Azaleas, Book 1
Bones in the Begonias, Book 2
Corpse in the Carnations, Book 3
Daggers in the Dahlias, Book 4
Evidence in the Echinacea, Book 5
Footprints in the Ferns, Book 6
Gun in the Gardenias, Book 7
Handcuffs in the Heather, Book 8
Ice Pick in the Ivy, Book 9
Jewels in the Juniper, Book 10
Killer in the Kiwis, Book 11
Lovely Lethal Gardens, Books 1–2
Lovely Lethal Gardens, Books 3–4
Lovely Lethal Gardens, Books 5–6

Psychic Vision Series
Tuesday's Child
Hide 'n Go Seek
Maddy's Floor
Garden of Sorrow
Knock Knock...
Rare Find
Eyes to the Soul
Now You See Her
Shattered
Into the Abyss
Seeds of Malice

Eye of the Falcon
Itsy-Bitsy Spider
Unmasked
Deep Beneath
From the Ashes
Stroke of Death
Ice Maiden
Psychic Visions Books 1–3
Psychic Visions Books 4–6
Psychic Visions Books 7–9

By Death Series
Touched by Death
Haunted by Death
Chilled by Death
By Death Books 1–3

Broken Protocols – Romantic Comedy Series
Cat's Meow
Cat's Pajamas
Cat's Cradle
Cat's Claus
Broken Protocols 1-4

Broken and... Mending
Skin
Scars
Scales (of Justice)
Broken but... Mending 1-3

Glory
Genesis
Tori

Celeste
Glory Trilogy

Biker Blues
Morgan: Biker Blues, Volume 1
Cash: Biker Blues, Volume 2

SEALs of Honor
Mason: SEALs of Honor, Book 1
Hawk: SEALs of Honor, Book 2
Dane: SEALs of Honor, Book 3
Swede: SEALs of Honor, Book 4
Shadow: SEALs of Honor, Book 5
Cooper: SEALs of Honor, Book 6
Markus: SEALs of Honor, Book 7
Evan: SEALs of Honor, Book 8
Mason's Wish: SEALs of Honor, Book 9
Chase: SEALs of Honor, Book 10
Brett: SEALs of Honor, Book 11
Devlin: SEALs of Honor, Book 12
Easton: SEALs of Honor, Book 13
Ryder: SEALs of Honor, Book 14
Macklin: SEALs of Honor, Book 15
Corey: SEALs of Honor, Book 16
Warrick: SEALs of Honor, Book 17
Tanner: SEALs of Honor, Book 18
Jackson: SEALs of Honor, Book 19
Kanen: SEALs of Honor, Book 20
Nelson: SEALs of Honor, Book 21
Taylor: SEALs of Honor, Book 22
Colton: SEALs of Honor, Book 23
Troy: SEALs of Honor, Book 24

Heroes for Hire

Gavin, Book 11
Shane, Book 12

Bullard's Battle Series
Ryland's Reach, Book 1
Cain's Cross, Book 2
Eton's Escape, Book 3
Garret's Gambit, Book 4
Kano's Keep, Book 5
Fallon's Flaw, Book 6
Quinn's Quest, Book 7
Bullard's Beauty, Book 8

Collections
Dare to Be You...
Dare to Love...
Dare to be Strong...
RomanceX3

Standalone Novellas
It's a Dog's Life
Riana's Revenge
Second Chances

Published Young Adult Books:

Family Blood Ties Series
Vampire in Denial
Vampire in Distress
Vampire in Design
Vampire in Deceit
Vampire in Defiance

Vampire in Conflict
Vampire in Chaos
Vampire in Crisis
Vampire in Control
Vampire in Charge
Family Blood Ties Set 1–3
Family Blood Ties Set 1–5
Family Blood Ties Set 4–6
Family Blood Ties Set 7–9
Sian's Solution, A Family Blood Ties Series Prequel
    Novelette

Design series
Dangerous Designs
Deadly Designs
Darkest Designs
Design Series Trilogy

Standalone
In Cassie's Corner
Gem Stone (a Gemma Stone Mystery)
Time Thieves

Published Non-Fiction Books:

Career Essentials
Career Essentials: The Résumé
Career Essentials: The Cover Letter
Career Essentials: The Interview
Career Essentials: 3 in 1